THROUGH A CANOPY OF STARS, THE LIGHTS OF MANHATTAN ROSE UP TO MEET THEM

Ben swooped the magic carpet low, coasting to the top of the building that had become his new home. After a gentle clap, Maddie was in his arms and he was carrying her down the hall of their apartment and into her bedroom. He had started to lay her on the covers when she surprised him and opened her eyes.

"Are we home?" she murmured sleepily.

Ben's heart turned as he gazed into her dark-lashed golden eyes. Against his aroused body's wishes, he set her on her feet. "Yes, Mas . . . Maddie. We are home."

She smiled as she stared up at him and gave a little yawn. "That was very nice, but you shouldn't have done it. I thought I told you, *no magic.* Aren't you supposed to obey me in all things?"

He almost raised a hand to touch her and thought better of it. If he touched her now, he might not be able to stop.

BOOK YOUR PLACE ON OUR WEBSITE AND MAKE THE READING CONNECTION!

We've created a customized website just for our very special readers, where you can get the inside scoop on everything that's going on with Zebra, Pinnacle and Kensington books.

When you come online, you'll have the exciting opportunity to:

- View covers of upcoming books

- Read sample chapters

- Learn about our future publishing schedule (listed by publication month *and author*)

- Find out when your favorite authors will be visiting a city near you

- Search for and order backlist books from our online catalog

- Check out author bios and background information

- Send e-mail to your favorite authors

- Meet the Kensington staff online

- Join us in weekly chats with authors, readers and other guests

- Get writing guidelines

- AND MUCH MORE!

Visit our website at
http://www.zebrabooks.com

I DREAM
OF YOU

Judi McCoy

ZEBRA BOOKS
Kensington Publishing Corp.
http://www.zebrabooks.com

ZEBRA BOOKS are published by

Kensington Publishing Corp.
850 Third Avenue
New York, NY 10022

First Printing: April, 2001
10 9 8 7 6 5 4 3 2 1

Printed in the United States of America

One

Madeline Winston pulled out a chair and plopped down with a thud. Holding her head in her hands, she began to cry—softly at first, then with heartbreaking intensity.

"I don't believe it!" She slammed her fist onto the latest copy of a popular New York gossip-cum-society magazine and ran her other hand through her short, spiky hair. "How could Trevor have had the nerve to break his promise and announce his marriage to the press before I could end our engagement? He swore he'd let *me* be the first one to report the split, but he just couldn't wait to tell the public he'd eloped. How could he do this to me?"

Sylvia Winston heaved a sigh, her heart aching in sympathy. It had been six long years—since the funeral of Maddie's parents, in fact—that she remembered seeing her granddaughter so distraught.

"There, there, dear," she patted Madeline's back as she had when Maddie had been a little girl. "Maybe it wasn't Trevor who gave the story to the press. Isn't it possible the magazine could have discovered it?"

Maddie raised her tear-dampened face. "Possible, but unlikely. He only dropped his bomb this morning. The magazine couldn't have had time to print this unless they were told about it earlier. Trevor knew how furious I'd be, so he lied. The way that blurb is worded makes me look like a jilted fool."

Judging by the way Madeline swiped angrily at her cheeks, Sylvia guessed her granddaughter was furious with Trevor Edwards III more for making her look like a fool than for breaking their engagement and running off with a petite, bubbleheaded French wine heiress. It had been all Sylvia could do to hold her tongue when she first met the jet-setting playboy. She had recognized instantly that his designs on Maddie were a front for his greed. She could only thank heaven his true colors had blossomed before he became her grandson-in-marriage.

"Well," Sylvia reminded her gently, "if you must use that unpleasant and old-fashioned term, you *were* jilted. And in the worst possible way, I might add."

Maddie sniffed her agreement. "I know, but Trevor said he was willing to let it appear I'd broken it off with him while we were on vacation if I promised not to embarrass Felice. Like an idiot, I agreed. I thought he was being honest with me. Swear to God, if I had a gun I'd hop the next plane back to New York and shoot him."

Sylvia smiled at the girl's fighting spirit. With her naturally sun-streaked hair and lovely sherry-brown eyes, Maddie looked exactly like her father, James, who'd been Sylvia's only child. And when Maddie's temper flared, it was just as if Sylvia had her dear, departed William back by her side.

"I have to tell you I'm relieved, dear. You know I never trusted Trevor. There was something about his eyes that gave me the willies. If you'll remember, I said he wasn't the man for you, but you wouldn't listen."

Madeline gave Sylvia's I-told-you-so a distasteful *tsk*. "I recall. You don't have to remind me of my stupidity."

Sylvia held her tongue. Now was not the time to point out her granddaughter's character flaws, although the words "stubborn" and "hot-tempered" immediately came to mind. The rest of Maddie's personality was unique. But being determined, driven to succeed, and generous to a fault, while not everyone's description of the ideal woman, made Sylvia very proud of the girl. Now if only Maddie could lose some of her more manly traits and become a little more feminine, maybe let her Uncle Lucius handle the inner workings of the company or—

"Gram? I asked if you thought I should call a press conference to counter Trevor's lies. Where were you a second ago?" Maddie queried, dabbing at her nose with a tissue.

Sylvia smiled. "Here . . . and there. Now what's this about calling in the press?"

"I guess talking to reporters is a dumb idea. I'd only put my size ten Nikes in my mouth, like I did the last time." She shook her head in dismay. "I can't believe I was so gullible. Why didn't I see the warning signs? Trevor insisting he needed to stay on the Riviera a few more weeks, his pitiful story about having to relax and unwind. He unwound, all right—straight into the arms of Felice LeBonne."

Sagely, Sylvia added a point in Maddie's favor. "Well, he is a man, and not nearly as honorable as your father or grandfather were. I'm so glad you didn't let him push you into making him a vice president of Winston Design. It was one of your smarter moves."

Madeline gave an unladylike snort. "It was plain common sense. I can see now Trevor has never worked at anything in his life more difficult than totaling a woman's assets. I should have been suspicious from the second I found out he spent most of his time on the ski slopes. If his business degree had meant anything to him, he would have taken the job his father offered last year. I should be thankful we only put him in charge of researching future clients."

She gave a little hiccup as she again slapped her hand on the magazine resting on the table. "I hope he drinks up all the profits and runs his new father-in-law's winery into the ground. I hope he turns purple like those precious grapes he covets so much. Better still, I hope he withers on the vine and turns into a little black raisin himself."

Sylvia stifled a giggle at the idea of the tall and officious Trevor Edwards decked out like one of the California Raisins. It would serve the young man right.

Madeline rose and walked to the refrigerator, a huge stainless steel behemoth that occupied nearly an entire wall of the kitchen. Opening one of its many doors, she pulled out a pitcher of iced tea and poured herself a glass, then leaned against the counter and took a long sip. "I have something else to tell you. Something I know you don't want to hear."

Sylvia raised her brow. When Maddie had first taken over the family company nearly five years ago, it had been doing well. But over the last two years Winston Design had barely broken even, a fact of which Sylvia's younger brother Lucius never failed to remind her. Sylvia, holding thirty percent of the stock, was continually being hounded by her brother to vote his way at the company meetings, but she steadfastly refused. She felt positive Maddie was too bright, too business-minded, and too loyal to let the company fall to ruin. The girl just needed to find her own style. As long as WD held its own, she would stand by her dutiful granddaughter and guide her as best she could.

Sylvia sat down slowly, wondering what had gone wrong this time. Accepting the glass of tea Maddie offered, she took a sip and prepared for the worst, smiling encouragement when Maddie sat across from her and began to shred a paper napkin onto the table.

"The day I left on vacation with Trevor, someone forged my name on a memo to the development department ordering them to stop production on our new computer chip. Max says he called me about it the second he received the note, but we were already on the plane. When I didn't respond, he assumed I *had* sent the memo. He didn't want to disturb the first vacation I'd taken in five years, so he simply followed the memo's orders. We now believe it was some kind of techno-sabotage. We're about three weeks behind schedule, and it will take us close to that long to catch up."

Sylvia took a drink of her tea, Maddie's words tasting about as sweet as the lemon wedge sitting at the bottom of the glass. Though she had retired to Key West ten years ago to run the bed and breakfast of her and William's dreams, she still kept up with the company's interests. The computer business her husband and son had so carefully nurtured to success now hung by a thread. Competition from the larger companies was fierce. If WD didn't meet its contractual agreements, its customers would simply turn to another supplier, and the firm would be ruined.

"How long do we have before deadline?"

"Three weeks. I can only stay the weekend. I want to get back to the office on Monday to talk with Uncle Lucius, while Max uses this weekend to regroup and come up with a miracle."

Sylvia smiled. The "plant" was still the same old warehouse in North Jersey she and William had founded over twenty-five years ago. Ten years later, they had diverted from making small electronic parts for radios and televisions to the development of specialty computer chips, knowing instinctively it was a wise decision. The corporate offices were in Manhattan, the pulse of the industry, but the heart of the company was still in a red brick building in Bergen County. The inside had been totally modernized, but on the outside it looked exactly as it had all those years ago.

"I see," Sylvia managed. "And do you have a plan, a way to make the deadlines?"

Maddie sighed, rubbing at the bridge of her nose. "I'm going to have Uncle Lucius call our customers to ask for an extension and handle the leaks, if there are any. He's so much better at public relations than I. And with my name in the papers about this broken engagement—well, I have a less than sterling reputation already. No use antagonizing Butler & Maggio or Comdisc or any of our other buyers."

Sylvia patted Maddie's clenched fingers. For all her usually logical thinking, the girl's current train of thought wasn't making much sense. "Nonsense. No one will blame you for the breakup. Those four little lines about Trevor leaving you to marry that wine heiress aren't worthy of a second notice from normally intelligent people. And what has it to do with your business sense? I say we use it to our advantage. Instead of acting irate, why don't you turn Trevor's betrayal from a negative into a positive? A little sympathy never hurt anyone."

Maddie's eyes brightened. "You mean use the blurb about my being dumped to buy us time? Let them think I'm so upset over the breakup I can't cope? I don't know . . . I have this reputation for being a kick-ass negotiator. I only met Mr. Butler once, but I hear he still complains to people about the way I brought him to his knees with our first contract. And Comdisc is only buying from us because they don't have enough volume to play in the big leagues. I can't imagine them thinking I couldn't handle the problem."

She sat a bit straighter, a frown marring her generous lips. "I'd have to grovel, maybe even put up with their pity. God, how I *hate* to be pitied."

Sylvia squeezed Maddie's hand a little harder. "If I remember correctly, as a child you were quite a little actress when you wanted something to go your way. Your father and grandfather could never resist your clever ploys. And you were captain of the debate team. That should count for something."

Maddie gave a wistful smile, and for just a few seconds Sylvia caught a glimmer of the same young girl she had applauded after winning her first debate as a freshman in high school, nearly fifteen years ago.

Furrowing her brow, Maddie gave Sylvia a look of determination. "I'd eat sand to buy us more time, Gram. Max swore to me the latest project he's working on will take the computer world by storm. If Uncle Lucius can get us an extension, we can put the production line on overtime, maybe ship the orders in halves. It just might keep our buyers happy."

"Max Hefner is a fine man. William and your father trusted him, and he's stuck by us through good times and bad. If he says he has something that will help, you believe him."

Maddie leaned back in her chair and gave her first real smile of the morning. "Do you realize Max is still carrying a torch for you? I see it burning in his eyes whenever he asks me how you are or what you've been doing. He'll be retiring soon and he says the Keys sound like the perfect spot. I'd be ready for him, if I were you."

Sylvia felt a long-forgotten heat rise to her cheeks. "Nonsense. I'm too set in my ways to bother with another man in my life. William was enough. Besides, Max is still grieving over losing Ruth. He and I are simply friends."

"Bull. You're only sixty-five, and you know you don't look it. You have plenty of time for another romance, even marriage, if you want it," Maddie teased.

Sylvia heard a car in the gravel drive and stood, grateful for the distraction. "Enough of this foolish talk. My new guests are here, and you have only a day or so to plan your strategy. Get out there on the beach, where you think best. Take a long walk or something, will you?"

With a loving pat, she placed both her hands on Maddie's back and pushed her toward the door. Though the girl towered over her, Sylvia had always admired Maddie's long legs and generous bosom, much more like her mother's than Sylvia's own petite frame. Catherine Jessup

Winston had been one of the finest women Sylvia had ever known. She and James would have been proud of their daughter—if they had lived to see her graduate with honors from Harvard. When Maddie reached her potential, and Sylvia knew it hovered just around the corner, the girl would bloom.

Maddie looked quite fetching this afternoon in a pair of tailored yellow shorts and a sleeveless red and yellow top that showed off her impressive figure. Now, if only she could be convinced to let her hair grow again and to stop wearing those utilitarian business suits and sturdy shoes.

"Go. But don't forget to put on sunscreen," Sylvia commanded. "And come up with something brilliant."

The balmy day was perfect Key West weather. Lower humidity and a cool ocean breeze relaxed Maddie as she ambled along the white sandy beach, turning abandoned shells over with her toes. Slowly, she followed the graceful shoreline in thoughtful concentration. This island had been her retreat all through adolescence, a haven after her parents' sudden deaths. Though it wasn't the home she'd grown up in, it was her favorite.

She turned to view the bed and breakfast from the beach. Three stories high, with a gabled roof, weathered white paint, and shiny green shutters, the house stood tall against the elements. Near one hundred years old, it had withstood season after season of angry squalls and raging hurricanes.

Though it looked the same as it always had on the outside, the interior of Winston's Walk had been completely remodeled ten years ago, when her grandparents had finally retired to the Keys. It boasted five guest bedrooms, all with lavish private baths, window seats, and magnificent ocean views. The top floor had been turned into a four-room apartment for her grandparents, with an elevator that ran directly to the kitchen from the third floor suite. The other levels were comfortable living quarters for visitors.

Written up in several tourist books, mainly because of Gram's superior cooking and the house's isolated location, Winston's Walk was almost always booked to capacity. Maddie could just make out a couple carrying luggage up the broad back porch and reasoned Gram had given them the downstairs suite, a room done in lavender and pink with a king-size bed and Jacuzzi tub. The guide books had dubbed the Lilac Room the most romantic room in the house.

"Romance!" Maddie spat out, turning away from the sight of the happy couple climbing the porch stairs. What a joke the word had become. All the while Trevor had been romancing her, telling her she was the woman he wanted to marry, he had been having a fling—a torrid affair with a tiny, brainless bimbo from the Loire Valley.

More than a broken heart, she felt the sting of humiliation. Who else was aware of the faithless bastard's betrayal? Did the entire world know Madeline Winston had been played for a fool?

She ran a hand through her hair and sighed. She sounded like a cuckolded man instead of a jilted woman, but there was no way she could face what had happened other than with a man's grim practicality. She had learned long ago she had to be tough to make it in a man's world. The glass ceiling for women in big business might be thinner, but it was still locked firmly in place.

In fact, Trevor had always told her how much he admired her masculine side. How was she to know small, kittenish women attracted him? She'd cut her hair when he had commented it might make her brown eyes look larger. She'd dieted down a full dress size when he had mentioned it would make her five-foot-nine-inch frame

more delicate. She'd changed herself just for him, and he
had thanked her by eloping with a petite French bonbon.

Hell! Any woman trying to balance a size fourteen body
on size ten feet while the rest of the world's women wore
size six dresses and shoes would be edgy.

Dropping to her knees, Maddie settled under the shade
of a cluster of palm trees and tried to put Trevor out of
her mind. Contemplating her next move, she sadly admitted her choices were few. Even if Uncle Lucius managed
to pull strings, there were no guarantees Winston Design
would be granted delivery extensions from their customers. In her quest to play with the big guys she had made
enemies along the way. She had even heard Harrison Butler call her a butch-macho-wanna-be behind her back after
their first round of contract negotiations. Since then, Mr.
Butler had retired and she hadn't yet had the opportunity
to deal personally with Mr. Maggio. Now, it seemed, he
would have the upper hand.

The morning breeze blew warm and steady, lulling
Maddie into a soothing slumber. When she woke several
hours later, the beach was awash in the rays of the blazing
noon sun. Stretching, she looked back toward Winston's
Walk and saw a man and woman holding hands and kissing at the shoreline. Since they were on the inn's private
grounds, she assumed they were Gram's newest guests.

Well, hell. There was no way she'd have breakfast with
the lovebirds tomorrow morning. And damn Trevor for
turning her into a cynic where love was concerned.

Somehow she would find true love, exactly as her parents and grandparents had, and she would do it honestly.
Never again would she cut her hair or starve herself for
a man. The guy she next chose to spend her life with
would love her exactly as she was—tall and full-figured,
stubborn and determined, character flaws and all.

And if she didn't find him . . . well, she would come
here and spend the rest of her days alone, helping Gram

run Winston's Walk. And she would be happy about it, too, damn it!

Brushing away a grain of sand that had somehow gotten into her eye and made it tear, she stared out into the ocean. Sitting straighter, she squinted, shading her sunglasses with her palms. There in the distance, bobbing madly, was a strangely shaped drab object.

She stood to get a better view, fairly certain it was only a piece of driftwood or useless debris. In all her years of snorkeling and treasure-hunting along the shore, she had never found anything of value. Why would she be lucky enough to discover something now?

The object disappeared under a wave and she shrugged. Quickly brushing off her legs, she picked up her sandals and headed back to the house, planning to rehearse a very humble and pathetic speech in front of her bedroom mirror for the rest of the day—or at least until she was positive Butler and Maggio and their other customers would agree to an extension.

Maddie woke at dawn, dressed, and tiptoed through the small-but-elegant upstairs apartment to the lift, riding it down in near darkness. Though it was the off season, the B&B was almost full, and she didn't want to take the chance of waking any of Sylvia's guests. The doors slid quietly open, and she blinked as bright kitchen light assaulted her. Gram, humming along to an oldies song on the radio, was bent at the waist as she peered into one of two ovens under the huge six-burner range.

Maddie sniffed at the delicious aroma of blueberry muffins and fresh coffee. "Mmm, it smells heavenly in here."

Sylvia jumped a foot. "Good Lord, Madeline. You scared me to death."

Maddie watched her grandmother lift a huge tin of muffins from the oven and set it on the burners to cool. "It's barely six. I didn't realize you still rose so early."

Sylvia turned and gave her a healthy *tsk.* "In case you've forgotten, Miss City Girl, this home is still a business. I have guests to feed and a house to clean and—"

"What about Marcy? I thought you said she was coming over early every morning to start the baking and coffee."

Heaving a sigh, Sylvia turned and began to break eggs, two at a time, into a large mixing bowl. "That young lady can barely keep herself awake these days. Seems the silly thing's gone and gotten herself pregnant. If I had anything to say about it, her father would be chasing Joe Turner up and down these islands with a shotgun until he married the girl."

Maddie almost swallowed her tongue. Marcy Jones—pregnant? And Joe Turner the father? "Are you sure, Gram? Marcy's not exactly—"

"The promiscuous type? You've got that right. But like my daddy used to say, 'There's an ass for every seat.' Apparently Marcy's found hers."

Maddie giggled at her grandmother's outrageous assessment of Joe Turner. She remembered him as being shy and quiet and kind of . . . dumb. Too dumb to use a responsible form of birth control, it seemed.

"Are they planning on getting married?" Walking to the monster refrigerator, she pulled out a mesh bag of oranges, took out a dozen, and began cutting them up for the juicer.

"Darned if I know." Footsteps sounded on the back porch, and Sylvia gave a snort. "There's Marcy now. Why don't you ask her?"

The back door opened and in walked a girl of about eighteen. Plain, with protruding teeth and lank black hair, Marcy Jones was the last woman Maddie would have thought capable of being promiscuous. In fact, Maddie had always had a hard time believing the unattractive girl would even find a fellow, isolated down here in the Keys. Suddenly Maddie wondered if her own fear of permanent spinsterhood had caused her to gravitate toward Trevor prematurely. For all her desires of corporate success, she truly wanted a loving husband and a family.

"Morning, Mrs. Winston. Sorry I'm late," Marcy said with a sleepy but satisfied smile. "Joey and I got married yesterday. Oh, hello, Madeline."

While Maddie could only stare in surprise at the girl's nonchalant attitude toward such a momentous occasion, Sylvia beamed at her approvingly. "Well, congratulations, Marcy. Or do I call you Mrs. Turner now? Glad you finally talked Joe into doing the right thing. Not thinking of quitting on me, are you?"

Marcy hung her sweater on a hook at the back door and put on one of the many colorful aprons Sylvia kept for the help. "No, ma'am. Joey and I are saving to get a place of our own, so until the baby's born I'd like to keep on here, if that's all right."

"Fine. Think your sister Laura could help out if things got to be more than the two of us can handle?"

Marcy nodded and emptied the fresh coffee from its glass carafe into a fancy insulated hot pot, after which she began a second round. "Sure thing, Mrs. Winston. School will be out in another week, and she'd appreciate the work."

Maddie had finally found her voice. "Marcy, are you happy about the baby . . . and marrying Joey? I mean, do you love him?"

Marcy gave a beatific smile which magically transformed her plain-as-pudding face. "Of course I do. Oh, Joey might not be able to give me a fancy ring like the rich fellow you're engaged to did, but he loves me and he's good to me, and that's all I think's important. Don't you agree?"

Maddie's lips stretched into a tight little smile, relieved the news of her breakup with Trevor had yet to find its way to the isolated tip of southern Florida. Marcy had nodded toward the flawless, three-carat round diamond Maddie still wore on her left hand. She and Trevor had argued over the return of the costly ring, and he had finally, grudgingly, agreed to let her keep it in atonement for his treachery.

"I do. And if it's what you want, I'm happy for you. Now, do the two of you need help here?"

Sylvia turned from her bowl of eggs. "Not a bit. And after the hectic day you had yesterday, I know you have plenty to think about. Why don't you take a muffin and a cup of coffee and walk along the beach for a while? Maybe things will look brighter with the sunrise."

So, armed with napkins, a muffin, and a large mug of black coffee, Madeline found her way to the beach, walking the same path she had taken the day before, straight to her cluster of palm trees. Settling into the sand, she chewed vigorously, finishing the fluffy, berry-filled treat in four bites. She hadn't eaten anything as tasty since she'd started her diet for Trevor—the rat.

Smiling smugly, Maddie twisted the ring on her finger. Trevor had threatened a court battle when she'd insisted upon keeping the solitaire, but she had been adamant. He'd given her the ring on her twenty-seventh birthday, so by law it was rightfully hers. Besides, if the company ever needed quick money, this would be the first thing she would sell to keep WD afloat.

With the sun rising at her back, Maddie drained her coffee cup as she gazed out onto the ocean. A sudden ripple in the sand caused her to blink. There, just as the tide pulled away from the shore, was something that looked like the debris she'd seen yesterday bobbing in the waves.

She stood and made her way to the water's edge. Stepping into the warm, caressing pull of the surf, she bent down and found about six inches of metal sticking up from the sand. Maddie tugged, working quickly to beat the next wave, until the object popped free into her hands. Feeling like a kid who'd found a jeweled Easter egg, she skipped back to her seat under the palm trees and set her find, a large gray bottle, on her lap.

The heavy, dark metal felt warm to the touch. Caked with bits of seaweed and sand, it was decorated with some strange form of writing, a mix of stick characters and unrecognizable lettering. Resting in the design, which ran the circumference of the bottle, were square pieces of red and green glass. In its own way, the bottle looked strangely attractive, though Maddie didn't think it had any monetary value.

She held onto the bottle top, shaped like the roof of a Byzantine mosque, and wrapped the napkin in which she had carried her muffin around her finger, rubbing until a spot the size of a half-dollar glowed like a mirror. Wrestling with the possibility that the bottle might be heavily tarnished silver, she gradually widened the area.

Maddie worked diligently, unaware of the change in the atmosphere around her. With the napkin in shreds and only a small bit of the bottle polished, she had just about decided to bring it back to Winston's Walk to finish the job properly when she raised her eyes to the still deserted beach.

Instead of brightening with the dawn light, the sky had become dark, with angry clouds swirling on the horizon.

A wind stronger than the normal morning breeze had whipped up from nowhere, furiously rustling the palm branches.

The ocean, usually crystal clear with a beautiful blue-green cast, had turned ominous.

She was about to run to the house to warn Gram to batten down the shutters against the rising squall when, without warning, the bottle quivered in her hands.

She watched in fascination as the top popped off, landing in the sand. Slowly, hypnotically, a thin stream of smoke drifted from the opening. Light gray and strangely aromatic, the smoke feathered skyward into the slowly brightening morning sun.

Two

Maddie scrambled to her feet and dropped the bottle like a burning coal. Her hand to her heart, she watched the thready smoke grow thicker, undulating slowly in the morning light. She blinked as the smoke quivered and rose, forming itself into a large, hazy shape. Quickly, she scanned the deserted beach, then looked back again at the rapidly building vision.

The smoke took on a more solid form and Maddie swallowed—hard. From the rolling mist, a large man appeared. He was barefoot and dressed in loose-fitting, red satin pants gathered at the ankle. Over his impressive torso, he wore a small black vest studded with colored stones.

Solemnly, the man put his palms together as though in prayer and bowed from the waist. Straightening, he kept his eyes trained on her feet as he spoke. "Master, your wish is my command."

Maddie took a deep breath. "Excuse me?" she managed through slack lips. "What did you say?"

At the sound of her voice, the man, now fully formed and quite good-looking, raised his blue eyes and inspected her thoroughly from head to toe.

"Your wish is my command."

Maddie felt herself warm from her hairline to her feet.

His eyes, an unusual and mesmerizing blue, caused her to stutter. "But . . . but that's so silly. Who are you?"

The man, at least six-foot-two inches, of polished muscle, raised a sinister-looking black brow. "I am Abban ben-Abdullah. I am yours to command."

Maddie stooped to pick up the bottle, then shook it upside down. Frowning when nothing fell out, she gave him a disbelieving stare, closed one eye, and peered back inside, positive she would find a video camera or holograph equipment. Instead, dark, swirling fog blocked her vision.

The man folded his arms across his chest and Maddie thought instantly of the old *Mr. Clean* television commercials. But this guy wasn't bald or genial, and he certainly didn't seem the type who would enjoy polishing her floors. Instead, he had a full head of softly curling black hair and an altogether too impertinent glint in his laughing eyes.

"Where did you come from?" she managed, looking up and down the beach again. There wasn't a soul in sight, she realized sadly. If she were going insane, there would be no one to attest to the reason why.

"From the bottle, of course," he replied calmly. "What is it you wish of me?"

"Wish? Of you?" She pointed the bottle at him as if it were a sword. "I don't want a darned thing. Now, just pop yourself back into this . . . this whatchamacallit and hightail it off this beach. You're trespassing on private property."

The man raised one corner of his well-sculpted lips in a mocking smile, nodded and bowed again. "Your wish is my command."

His voice, deep and dark and rich, reminded Maddie of hot, steaming chocolate on a cold winter morning. Before her eyes, his body shimmered like silver, dissipating into the same wispy smoke from which it had formed. As if dancing to a silent melody, the smoke drifted toward her hand. She let go of the bottle and watched it land in the sand at her feet, sucking up the whirling smoke in the blink of an eye. When all the wisps had cleared, the decorative stopper rolled over and popped itself on top.

Maddie stared down and raised a hand to her forehead. Feverish. She definitely felt feverish. Wiping the perspiration from her face, she paced, glancing at the bottle as if it were a ticking time bomb. Then again, it could be stress causing her to hallucinate. She inched closer and poked at the container with her bare foot, hopping back when it rolled in a semicircle on the sand.

"This is ridiculous," she muttered, scanning the shoreline again. Alone. She was absolutely, positively alone.

Bending low, she reached out and touched the tip of the bottle once, then twice, waiting for something to happen. She smiled when the bottle lay motionless like the inanimate object she knew it to be.

Dropping to her knees, she covered her face with her palms. If this wasn't a hallucination, there could be only one person nasty enough to want to see her go crazy. "I'm going to kill Trevor for doing this to me."

Peeking from between her fingers, she saw the bottle still on its side, the red and green bits of decorative glass twinkling in the morning sun. She reached out and touched it again. Cool on her palm, it gave off no suspicious vibes or strange movements. She stood and hefted it in her hand, then took a deep breath. Grabbing the stopper, she pulled hard—then harder.

Nothing happened. The stopper didn't budge, the bottle didn't quiver, and the earth didn't stop revolving on its axis.

Maddie frowned. Tucking the bottle under her left arm for leverage, she hugged it to her side and grasped the top with her right hand. Even pulling with all her might, she wasn't able to remove the stopper.

Frustrated, she tugged harder. Suddenly, from nowhere—or was it all around her—she heard an ominous chuckle. She stopped tugging and stared up and down the beach again, squinting through the sunlight. She was still alone, still here in the Keys, still breathing and alive.

She pulled at the stubborn stopper and heard it again, a booming sound that might have been a chortle—or was it a snicker? She couldn't be sure.

"This is stupid," she muttered aloud. Marching to the water, she hoisted the bottle high, ready to toss it back into the sea.

"Uh-uh-uh," came a dark, disapproving voice from no-where.

Maddie jumped and dropped the bottle into a rushing wave, then scampered backward until she was under the cluster of palms again. Sitting with a plop, she propped her elbows on her upraised knees, held her head in her hands, and squeezed her eyes tight. After several seconds, she stared out onto the water and scanned the shore.

Good. The bottle was gone. It had been a figment of her imagination after all.

Lowering her gaze, she stared at her feet and gave a shriek. There, resting between her ankles, sat the bottle, standing upright in the sand. Closing her eyes, Maddie began to mutter. "When I open my eyes it will be gone. I am not going crazy. I am not."

Heaving a sigh, she raised one eyelid, only to find the bottle still there, its red and green stones blinking like a cross-wired traffic light.

She squared her shoulders. Of all the names she had ever been called, "coward" had never made the list. This was an irrational dream brought about by stress and sun and sadness. She decided to recreate the scene, doing over again exactly what she'd been doing when the hallucina-tion began. This time, she assured herself, nothing strange would occur.

She reached for the bottle and held it in her hand. Pull-ing a fresh tissue from her pocket, she began to scrub madly. After a few seconds, a blustery wind rose up from nowhere and the stopper popped off. Maddie set the bottle in the sand and stood, watching as the hazy gray smoke did its thing, rising and undulating until it took solid form. The man appeared before her, his arms at his sides as he waited for her to speak. This time his startlingly blue eyes were not looking at her feet. Instead, they gazed at her chest, then her legs, and, finally, her face.

"What is it you wish, Master?" he asked, a faint smile playing about his lips.

Try as she might, Maddie could discern no trick or sleight of hand. She wrapped her arms across her breasts, disgruntled to find them throbbing, her nipples raised to hard points. "Listen, buster, if this is Trevor's sick idea of a joke, you can just tell him to stuff it. Now, I suggest you take yourself back to Miami or New York or wherever he found you and forget you ever saw me. Got that?"

The man smiled and folded his own arms, mimicking her *Mr. Clean* pose. "Who is Trevor?"

She raised a brow in disbelief. How stupid did he think she was? "You know very well who Trevor Edwards III is. Now get out of here."

"Do you wish me to go back in the bottle?"

Maddie began to pace. "Back in the bottle, back to Hohokus, back to hell for all I care, you big jerk. Just leave me alone."

The man nodded. "As you wish, Master, though it would be best if you gave only one direct command at a time. I am not sure where this Hohokus is and I am not allowed to enter the gates of Hades. Are you positive you want it to be the bottle?"

Maddie glared. Where had Trevor found this guy? "Look, out-of-work-actors and magicians are a dime a dozen, but you're pretty good. I have an old college buddy who's a theatrical agent. You tell Trevor you scared me good, and I'll set you up with an appointment. Do you dance?"

The man frowned. "Dance?"

She stepped back and appraised him slowly. Walking around to his back, her gaze took in his taut rear end and perfectly formed shoulders. "You know—strip. Like the Chippendale men. That's some physique you've got there."

He turned to her and smiled, his white teeth flashing. Instantly, his bronzed, exotic-looking face transformed into *GQ* material. "Strip? You mean remove one's clothing, as Salome did? I have never tried. That type of dancing is for women."

Maddie's heart skipped a beat. The guy was drop-dead gorgeous, but he sounded about as intelligent as a coconut. "What century do you come from? This is the new millennium, bud. Plenty of men strip for women these days."

Eyebrows raised in question marks, he gave her a puzzled look. "The new millennium? You mean it is no longer the year one thousand ninety-nine."

Maddie walked around to the palm trees and sat down. Resting her head back against the rough bark, she gave an exasperated sigh. "Brother, you are good. Ten-ninety-nine, huh? Look, why don't you just go away and leave me in peace? You and Trevor have had your fun."

Instead of picking up the bottle and walking away, he folded his arms again. Turning into gray wispy matter, he began to drift directly into the bottle. "Hey, hold on a second," Maddie called, still not believing her eyes.

The smoke reversed direction. Spiraling upward, it reformed back into the hunky *Mr. Clean.* "Yes, Master?"

Maddie rose to stand in front of him. "Just walk away from here the way you came in, you got that?"

Frowning, he pointed to the bottle. "But that *is* the way I arrived, Master."

She drummed her fingers on her sand-covered thigh, suddenly self-conscious of her shorts and clingy red and yellow top. "I want you to stop calling me that."

He stepped back and crinkled his forehead. "You do not wish to be called 'Master'?"

"Of course not. Who in their right mind would?"

The man raised a hand and began to tick off fingers. "Sulimen the Second, the Grand Vizier of Cadawal, Sulimen the Fourth, the Third Caliph of Baghdad, the—"

Maddie stood, picked up the bottle and shoved it in his upraised hands, disrupting his exacting recitation. "Here, take it and just get lost, would you?"

Turning, she marched toward the house without a backward glance.

Night breezes cooled the room while the sound of the surf filled her senses. Still ruminating over her problems, Maddie packed for her early morning return to New York City. After cleaning the kitchen and making the dough for fresh cinnamon buns, Gram had said her good-byes and bedded down hours ago. Sylvia had said she trusted Maddie's judgment and would agree to whatever decision she made to rescue the company, confident Maddie would handle the latest crisis in stride.

Maddie gave a wry chuckle. Sure she would. She was a regular crisis maven. She lived for turmoil and tragedy—thrived on it, in fact. Her life had been one crisis after another since the day her parents had been killed in an automobile accident on their way to her college graduation. Since that fateful day she had handled everything.

She had braved Uncle Lucius's contesting of her father's will and, with her grandmother's support, had taken on the tasks of a large portion of the company. Over the last four years, she had staved off attempted buyouts from competitors, retooled and remodeled their manufacturing rooms, and written a company mission statement more bold and innovative than Tom Cruise's in *Jerry McGuire*.

She had restructured Winston Design's marketing program and run it single-handedly until Uncle Lucius had bullied her into letting him take back control of that department. It hadn't been her fault she'd been misquoted by the press and lost two major contracts, had it?

And she had negotiated deals and made sales after every major advance WD had accomplished, keeping costs down and profits up—sort of.

Maddie sat on the bed in a heap, a pair of shorts knotted in her hands. Who was she kidding? She may have done all those things, but she hadn't done them very well. In fact, under her leadership, the company was barely getting by. If she didn't do something brilliant to forestall this latest calamity, Uncle Lucius would probably convince Gram he had grounds to take over permanently—and she knew what would happen then.

For the past two years, Lucius Fulbright had been lobbying to sell out to a major player in the business. Butler & Maggio had wanted to buy the WD patents and factory outright and manufacture on their own, but Maddie had always managed to hold them off. Now, with the possibility of failed delivery dates and bad PR, Butler & Maggio was just big enough and brazen enough to accomplish their goal and purchase the company.

And their offer, ten million dollars, was nothing to sneeze at. After paying outstanding debts and taking care of other fiscal responsibilities, she, Gram, and Uncle Lucius would clear a little over two million each, and Max Hefner close to a million with his ten percent ownership. A nice chunk of change for something she'd inherited and not earned.

She tossed the shorts into her suitcase and sighed. That was the problem. She had inherited Winston Design, not earned it. The company had been her father's. Her grandfather had started the electronics business, but it had been James Winston's vision and brilliance that had turned the little factory into a viable player in the computer industry. And he and her mother had died before they'd had the chance to see the company thrive.

Maddie rubbed at her temple, hoping to stop the ache she felt niggling in her head before it turned into a full-blown migraine. She needed to get a good night's sleep and still make it to the Miami airport early enough to catch a ten A.M. flight. She wanted to be in the downtown offices by three to tackle this latest catastrophe and come up with a plan to present to Uncle Lucius by nine on Monday morning.

She stood and hoisted her suitcase onto the floor, setting it in a corner under an open window. After brushing her teeth and changing into her nightgown, she crawled into bed and lay down, wide awake and aching. Raising her hand to the moonlight streaming into the room, she gazed at the flawless three-carat round diamond on her left hand. Another disaster to add to her list—this one more personal than the company.

She remembered the day Trevor had put the ring on her finger, whispering, "It's a big rock, Madeline, but you're a big girl. You can handle it." If she'd known then the insufferable snob was going to cheat on her, she would have thrown it in his face. She would have avoided another catastrophe.

Her first real romance, her first engagement, her first lover—gone. All of it gone forever.

How could she have been so stupid? She should have listened to her best friend, Mary Grace, who'd advised Maddie to think twice about marrying Trevor Edwards. He'd begun his pursuit when they were in college, and Maddie had never understood why a wealthy young man who had his pick of debutantes had decided on her. She had finally succumbed to Trevor's charms and begun dating him in earnest two years ago. She and Trevor had known one another long enough for her to have seen the signs, noticed the way he looked at other women when they were out together. Why hadn't she trusted her first instincts and admitted no man would be interested in a gawky, plain-Jane of a girl like herself?

Mary Grace had been right, as usual. Where men were concerned, Mary Grace had more common sense in her little finger than Maddie had in her entire hand. She had taken Maddie under her protective wing from the first day they had met at college. She had tried to warn her, had told her Trevor always checked financial statistics before he dated anyone. Why hadn't she listened?

Now, to top it all off, she was going crazy. The stress of WD's possible failure and sellout, coupled with the breakup, were causing hallucinations of mammoth proportion. Strange visions of a man who looked like he'd just stepped from the pages of *The Thousand and One Arabian Nights*, for God's sake.

Either she was going nuts or the big weasel had thought up a clever way to guarantee she'd leave him and Felice alone for a while. She'd be so busy trying to figure out who the guy from the beach was and how he did his act she'd have no time to retaliate.

Besides, if she started telling people she'd found a genie in a bottle, Trevor would look like a genius for dumping her in the nick of time, and Uncle Lucius would have her committed to a loony bin. No one in his right mind would do business with a nutcase who claimed to have found a magical bottle on the beach.

Sensing it was going to be a long night, Maddie tossed and turned, trying to get more comfortable. When she was still wide awake at two A.M., she decided to resort to emergency measures and dug through her bag until she found a bottle of over-the-counter sleeping pills. Downing two of the tablets, she decided her only recourse was to forget about Trevor, forget about the coconut-headed hunk from the beach, and get on with her life, pathetic though it might be.

No matter what, she had a duty to her father's memory. She wouldn't let him or the company down.

Maddie stomped into her apartment at six that evening, exhausted and furious. Never, in all the times she'd flown, had she been held up and interrogated as she had today. The sleeping pills had forced her into a drugged sleep, which caused her to doze through her alarm and arrive late to the airport. When she'd laid her little wheeled suitcase on the conveyor belt, the security guard had insisted she open it. She'd happily complied until the guard started digging like a hound on the scent.

After several minutes, during which time the man emptied her carry-on and laid its entire contents on the counter, Maddie had lost her temper. "Hey, what do you think you're doing?" she'd shouted, then felt foolish about causing a scene.

The guard had glared. "Protecting the people of this airport and the flight you're supposed to be on, miss. May I see your ticket and your handbag?"

Maddie had grudgingly handed him her ticket, then waited while the officious man searched her purse and inspected her paperwork and her carry-on a second time. Finally, he had called over his supervisor.

"Don't know if it's anything for sure, sir," the guard had stated. "I saw something strange on the scanner, something dark and shaped kind of funny, but there's nothing here now."

The supervisor had done his own cursory inspection, then turned to Maddie and apologized. It had taken her five minutes to stuff everything back inside. By the time she'd arrived at the gate, her plane had left.

Beyond annoyed, she'd gone to the ticket counter to book the next flight. Unfortunately, the only seating available was standby, and the plane was so full the ticket agent demanded she check her bag if she wanted to make the flight. After getting the last seat on the plane, she'd been forced to ride between two unhappy travelers from some foreign island on their way to visit relatives in the Bronx. Not an enjoyable trip.

Upon landing and wending her way to the baggage claim area, she'd been dismayed to find her suitcase missing. She flagged down a porter who directed her to the luggage information desk, where she had to wait for what seemed like hours before she found someone who could help. After checking her claim tag, the clerk explained that her suitcase had been red-tagged and reinspected, then inspected again once off the plane at Kennedy.

"Sorry, miss," the clerk had said cheerfully. "We can't be too careful nowadays. That little bag of yours set up a din when it went through the security scanner at this end."

By the time Maddie retrieved her bag, hailed a cab, and arrived at her apartment, she was ready to cry. It was too late to go to the office, her mind was fried, and she felt the beginnings of a major headache lurking in the background.

She listened to her message machine with a heavy heart. "Hey, kiddo," came Mary Grace's snappy New York accent, "it's me. I hope you're ready for some excitement, because Greta the Gossipmonger is chomping at the bit. Seems she heard about your and Turdhead's, I mean Trevor's, breakup and she wants an inside scoop. I stalled her, but if you're smart, you won't answer your phone until you come up with a believable story. Call me tomorrow and we'll do lunch."

Next came two messages from Greta Miller, freelance writer and one of the city's worst gossip hounds. Both messages sounded pleading and sympathetic, begging Maddie to give her the true story, at least her side of it, as soon as possible. She had a column planned for the middle of the week and wanted nothing more than to tell Maddie's view of the breakup.

The fourth message was from her grandmother, checking to see if Maddie had landed safely and instructing her to phone if she needed anything.

The last and most brazen call came from Trevor. "Madeline, it's me. I just wanted you to know I had absolutely nothing to do with that little piece in *Talk of the Town*. Both Felice and I are just sick over the idea of someone leaking the news to the press and we . . . umum . . . well, I just want to remind you of our agreement. You promised you wouldn't call attention to the fact that . . . I . . . um . . . married Felice while you and I were still engaged. It would really upset her father and Felice, too. She's very delicate, Madeline. And it would definitely ruin my relationship with her parents, so . . . anyway, I know you're a woman of your word. Thank you."

Fuming, she unhooked the answering machine, picked it up, and walked to her kitchen trash container. Raising the box high, she gave a half smile as she dropped it into the can. Leave it to Trevor to play on her good nature and remind her of her promise. First thing tomorrow, she would get an unlisted phone number and give it to Gram and Mary Grace and one or two people at WD, but no one else. Then she would order the computerized message system her phone company had been trying to sell her for the past three years and finish streamlining her life.

Maddie sighed, then unzipped her carry-on, pulled out her robe, and walked to the bathroom. After soaking in a tub of gardenia-scented bubbles for half an hour, she ate a low-calorie microwave supper. By nine, feeling just a tiny bit better, she was ready for a restful night's sleep and a fresh start.

Bone-tired, she entered her bedroom and did a double take. Stepping slowly, almost afraid to breathe, she stopped at the foot of the mattress, one hand on her heart.

There on the center of the bed sat the bottle from the beach, its colorful stones winking at her in the lamplight.

Three

Maddie laid a shaking hand over her eyes and gave herself time to gather her wits. She'd never had hallucinations before her betrayal by Trevor, so she only had him to blame for what she *thought* she saw on the bed. Taking a deep breath, she opened her eyes, without a clue as to what she would do if the bottle was still there.

It was.

Prickly sensations rippled through her. She had not packed the bottle—hadn't seen it since she'd left the beach yesterday morning, in fact. Her suitcase had been searched and triple-searched at two airports. She had thrown both dead bolts on her door the moment she'd set foot inside her foyer, so she was positive she was alone in her apartment.

How had it come to be here?

She rubbed her palms up and down her arms and took a step closer to the bed. Reaching out tentatively, she touched the bottle's metallic surface. It felt solid and slightly warm to her fingers. Definitely not a hallucination.

She sat on the edge of the bed and pulled the container closer. Holding it to the light, she inspected the outside more closely. The stick figures etched around the circumference vaguely resembled the cave drawings she'd studied in her art history classes, while the writing looked like nothing she had ever seen before. Running a finger over a glittering green stone, she narrowed her gaze. Could the stones possibly be real emeralds and rubies and not pieces of colored glass, as she'd first thought?

Get a grip, Maddie!

She tugged at the bottle top and found it as stubbornly stuck as before, only this time no dark laughter mocked her. Gripping the bottle in both hands, she shook it up and down, then held her ear to the side to see if it emitted any strange noises. It didn't.

Did she dare try polishing the bottle again? Would the coconut-headed *Mr. Clean* have the nerve to make another surprise appearance here in her apartment? She glanced down at her fuzzy bunny slippers and faded cotton sleep shirt—the one with a disgruntled Garfield eyeing a peacefully slumbering Odie on the front—and shook her head. Not with her in this outfit, he wouldn't.

Maddie racked her brain, telling herself there had to be a perfectly logical reason for the bottle to be here, but nothing made sense. Even her earlier thoughts on genies and magic lamps sounded stupid. She wouldn't be taken in by anything even remotely fairy-tale-like ever again. Fairy tales were for children and not-yet-grown-up adults who had good things to look forward to, not jilted women with ruined reputations and failing companies to run.

She stood and jerked on her bathrobe. Picking up the bottle, she marched down the hall and undid the double bolts on her door, then stomped into the hallway and directly to the elevator. Next to the elevator was the garbage chute that took her trash to the outside dumpster. With a flourish, she opened the metal door and dropped the bottle inside, listening to the metallic clatter it made on its way down four flights and into the alley below.

Maybe a homeless person would find the container and pawn it for a few dollars or, better yet, find the genie inside who would make all their dreams come true. Maddie gave a little snort at the impossible thought and headed back up the hall.

Dreams, she told herself firmly, would never come true for a girl like her.

Staggering slightly, Maddie walked past Letitia's empty desk and let herself into her office. If she was quizzed by her perceptive receptionist, she would fold like a pressed shirt. She had awakened two hours ago with a brain foggy from sleeping pills to the sound of rain drizzling down her windows. After a restless night, she'd let the shower's stinging spray wash the sleep from her brain as she fought to push her thoughts of the previous two days to the back of her mind. How had the bottle managed to find its way into her suitcase without her knowledge, despite the expert investigation of a dozen airport security agents?

And what had happened to the hunky magician who appeared and disappeared at will?

Maddie laid her briefcase on the desk next to her computer and sat down. What did it matter *how* the bottle had arrived in New York or come to be on her bed? It was gone and good riddance.

Her gaze settled on the messages lined up neatly on her blotter. Since she'd lost her last personal assistant and hadn't found the time to hire another, her messages were at the mercy of whoever was manning the main switchboard. To date, they had done an adequate job.

She crumpled two messages from Greta the Gossipmonger and tossed them in the trash, then tore the one from Trevor marked "urgent" into dozens of tiny pieces. Her uncle had left one confirming their meeting and Mary Grace had left another reminding her about lunch. The last three messages concerned minor problems she could let her assistant handle—if she had one.

Realizing the catastrophe facing Winston Design

wouldn't magically go away, she turned on her PC and called up the contracts waiting to be filled with the delayed computer chips. Her last assistant had been given the job of tracking and graphing the time frame for delivery, but the girl had lied when she'd stated she was familiar with the current programs that transferred facts and figures to graphics.

Maddie had been forced to fire three assistants in the past six months, all for the same reason—incompetence. How inane was that? She had never asked one of them to handle any task she wasn't capable of herself, so why did she keep having the same problem with her help?

She made a mental note to call the employment agency they regularly used and give them a piece of her mind—at least a very tiny part of it. She would demand the potential candidates be tested and the results sent over ahead of time. If she didn't find the prospects satisfactory, she wouldn't bother to interview them at all. She was sick and tired of having to do everything herself and—

God, but she hated whiners, and here she was sounding like one of the worst. She needed to forget about Trevor, forget about the darned bottle, and forget about hiring an assistant. She needed to confront Uncle Lucius and explain to him what had happened with the forged memo, then get a production update from Max, not necessarily in that order. Checking her watch, she decided she had fifteen minutes to prepare for her first meeting.

She set her shoulders and scrolled through the latest agreement with Butler & Maggio, determined to find a loophole, some small glitch that might buy them time. Seeing nothing immediate, she ran a hand through her hair. Unless she managed something miraculous, WD was in deep sneakers.

Her phone rang and Maddie started in her seat. Picking it up, she said hesitantly, "Hello?"

The echoing sound of a speaker phone greeted her.

"Madeline? Madeline Winston?" said a gruff-sounding voice.

Maddie sat upright. "Sorry, you caught me off guard. This is Madeline Winston. How may I help you?"

The speaker phone clicked over to a regular line and Maddie tensed, still not sure to whom she was speaking.

"This is Dominic Maggio, Ms. Winston. Of Butler & Maggio."

Maddie swallowed her surprise. In all the years she'd been in charge, Dominic Maggio had never once spoken with her directly, though he kept in contact with her uncle. When Butler & Maggio had presented their first decidedly stingy buyout offer last year, Mr. Maggio had made the proposal privately to Lucius, before laying it out in writing for her perusal. "Uh . . . good morning, Mr. Maggio. How can I help you?"

"I've heard a rumor, Ms. Winston, and I'm feeling very unsettled by it. I don't like feeling unsettled. It makes my ulcer act up."

"I'm sorry to hear that. Tell me what you heard."

He laughed, a growling bark that could have been interpreted as threatening. "I heard your company is going to stiff us, Ms. Winston. You're not going to come through with your order, causing us to delay the marketing of our latest system. Is that so?"

Resting her head against her palm, Maddie wondered how he had found out about their dilemma so quickly. Who else in the industry might already know the same? "It's just a small production problem, Mr. Maggio. I can assure you—"

"Hold it, Ms. Winston. Let *me* assure *you*. If you fail to meet your contractual obligations, if our order is late by so much as one hour, my attorneys will begin lawsuit proceedings immediately. Is that understood?"

Maddie sucked in a breath, surprised by his bullying tactics. "Mr. Maggio. Please be—"

His nasty chuckle sent a chill up her stiffened spine. "Good day, Miss Winston. See you in court."

Maddie heard the droning dial tone and slammed down the receiver. In a heartbeat, she felt her big-businesswoman persona begin to crumble. So far, she'd been able to bluff her way through hundreds of meetings and contract negotiations, never letting on to anyone of her insecurities at not measuring up to her father's expectations. Would this latest crisis finally be her undoing?

The jangling phone startled her again, and she quickly lifted the receiver. Max Hefner's cheery voice made her smile through her doubts.

"Maddie, my girl, how are you?" he asked, a bit too brightly.

She sighed. Even Max, who never read anything but the comics, sports, and *The Wall Street Journal,* must have heard about her and Trevor.

"I'm fine, Max. How about you?"

He paused half a beat too long. "I'm good. I just wondered . . . do you need anything? A shoulder to cry on or a chest to pound? I can have both available on short notice. Or I can contact a friend of mine in Bayonne and have him beat the crap out of Trevor Edwards III. What's it to be, my girl?"

Maddie imagined him, his brown eyes compassionate, his gray hair on end, standing in his cluttered office in New Jersey. Max had refused a bigger, more modern office when the building had been remodeled, insisting the company needn't waste its money on him. He'd reminded her he would be retiring in a few years and the next product development manager could be the one to redo the office. He was happy with things exactly the way they were. Max had been her grandfather's best friend and a great comfort when she had lost her parents. And here she was, still needing him, still seeking his advice.

"Thanks, Max, but I don't think so. I wouldn't want

ou to waste your hard-earned money on the creep." Maddie tried for a little chuckle, but it ended up sounding like sob. She fisted her hand and gave her blotter a small ump, hating the sound of weakness in her voice.

"Not a waste, if you ask me. The man's an idiot to not otice the treasure he held in his hands. He went for the ash of brass, Maddie, when he could have had pure platium."

She held back a tear and took a breath. "If I were thirty ears older, I swear I'd give Sylvia a run for her money. mentioned you to Gram over the weekend, and she had twinkle in her eye. It looks promising," she confided.

"You mean Sylvia is actually willing to allow me on he Keys when I retire? Hot damn!"

Maddie smiled at his enthusiasm. The man had it bad or her grandmother, but right now he was her only hope or saving the contract on her computer screen. If she told im about the call from Dominic Maggio, Maddie knew Max would go off like a bottle rocket. "We'll soften her p yet, don't you worry. But it'll have to wait until our igger problem is settled. Do you have anything promisng I can report to Uncle Lucius on the status of those hips? He's due here any minute and I can't hold off telling im another day."

Maddie felt her heart sink to her stomach as seconds assed. "I know you think I'm a miracle worker, Maddie, ut I'm only an old man fresh out of ideas. I've put the actory on double shifts, but it's costing us. At the rate ve're going, we won't make a dime on those contracts, ven if we manage to pull half the order in on time. I'm orry."

Maddie leaned back in her chair, hoping Max could elp her figure out who might be the source of the comany's leak to Butler & Maggio. "Does anyone else know? Vhat did you tell the operators?"

"I haven't told a soul. The assemblers think we've

speeded up production to make way for another order. The
memo appeared on my desk the same day you left with
Trevor. After I read it, I ran it through the shredder. If i
was a plant, as we suspect, we shouldn't even mention i
via e-mail. There's no telling who might be monitoring us.'

Maddie couldn't help but agree. In today's volatile
computer market, industrial espionage was big business
With most companies developing the same products a
almost the exact same time, the winner was whoever
could produce the goods first, no questions asked. Ever
if Winston Design could prove outside interference, they
would have a hard time in a court of law. And from the
sound of it, they wouldn't have the extra funds to pay
the legal fees, especially if their customers decided to
take them to court.

"OK, Max. No one but you, me, and Uncle Lucius will
know the whole story. I'll keep Sylvia informed from my
home phone. It's unlikely anyone would have an opportunity to plant a bug there. No one's been to visit for weeks
and, well, with what's happened between me and Trevor, I
certainly won't be doing any entertaining. Sound good?"

"Yep. Can you come out here tomorrow? I might have
better news once the boys have had the time to work today."

Maddie heard a knock at her office door and sat up
straight. "Just a second," she called out, then returned to
the phone call. "Tomorrow's fine. Got to run. Uncle Lucius is here."

She ran her fingers through her hair and found a small
spike standing up from the top of her head. Great. Looking
like Alfalfa would really impress her stuffy uncle, she
thought, and groaned. After fumbling through her bag,
she pulled out a brush and began to work on the wayward
lock of hair. A few seconds later, she tossed the brush
back into her purse and smoothed over the spike a final

time with her hand. Standing, she tugged at her boxy navy jacket. "Come in, Uncle Lucius."

The door opened on a rush of air. "Madeline." Her uncle nodded, striding directly to her desk. "You know I hate to be kept waiting. If you could hold on to a personal assistant for more than two days at a time, she could see to it you stayed on schedule."

Pulling a chair nearer her desk, he made a production of sitting down and aligning the razor-sharp pleats in his slacks. Lucius Fulbright looked perfect, as usual. Impeccably groomed and not an ounce overweight, this morning he wore a hand-knotted bow tie and an immaculate white shirt decorated with a pocket protector full of pens and pencils. At fifty-five, he could have been an ad for Nerds Incorporated.

Maddie gave him an apologetic smile, disappointed by her irreverent thoughts. Lucius Fulbright was one of her two closest relatives, all the family she had left in the world. She looked down at her own tailored suit and sensible shoes, then the staid leather briefcase on her desk top. Nerdidity ran in both branches of the Winston family, she being another perfect example. How could she be so nasty?

"Uncle Lucius. It's nice to see you. I was on a long distance call"—well, New Jersey *was* across the river— "and I wanted to finish up in private. I'm sorry."

Lucius slid to the very edge of the red tufted chair and pushed his glasses up his aristocratic nose. "Were you speaking to Trevor? Have you decided to reconcile? I think what you did was very foolish, Madeline, ignoring him until he was forced to turn to another woman. We could have used his father's influx of cash to bolster the company—maybe hired one of those sharpshooters from Silicon Valley to take over research and development or—"

Maddie clenched her fists against her rising anger. In typical Uncle Lucius style, he'd managed to blame her for what was going wrong with her love life and the company all at once. Uncaring that her personal life was in shambles, he'd made her feel small and stupid to boot.

"First of all," she began, positive she could feel her cowlick springing up like a two-foot weed on a newly mowed lawn, "Trevor is married. I have no intention of breaking up something he so obviously desired, even if I wanted to—which I don't. And just to set the record straight, I didn't ignore Trevor. I offered to stay with him in the south of France, but he told me he wanted to be alone to relax and think. It came as a total shock when he waltzed in here last Friday wearing a wedding band. Second, there never was any promise from Trevor's father to pour money into this company. Third, though you don't agree, we already have a top-notch research and development man in Max Hefner. It would be foolish to hire another."

Lucius folded his arms and leaned back in the chair, his clear gray eyes studying her as if she were a bug under his microscope. "Max Hefner is as old as my sister Sylvia, and more than ready to retire. And if you'd been brighter and more perceptive, you would have suspected something was wrong between you and Trevor. I'm sure Catherine would have known instantly."

Maddie turned at the mention of her mother's name and paced to the office windows. Staring down at the traffic on the street below, she fought to hold back the tears she'd kept at bay all morning. To be judged and found wanting—again—was almost too much to bear.

"Let's leave my mother out of this, Uncle Lucius. I'm well aware she was the perfect woman. God knows you've told me so often enough. I called this meeting because something much more serious than my being jilted has happened. The company is in jeopardy."

At her uncle's gasp, Maddie took a deep breath of her own. Walking briskly, she returned to her desk, sat, and folded her hands, willing herself to be calm and professional. Any show of weakness would only allow her uncle to point out how well she had proven him right—she wasn't cut out to run a business. "Before you start berating me, let me explain what's happened," she managed, giving him her best frown. "You can shout when I'm through."

Without telling him about her nasty conversation with Dominic Maggio, Maddie quickly brought her great-uncle up to speed on the forged memo, what she'd done to counter its damage, and her planned meeting the next day with Max. After explaining to him that any contact between the three of them about the problem should be done in person, she waited for the roof to cave in. In the past, Lucius Winston had never been kind, patient, or understanding.

Instead of blowing up, he surprised her by glaring through eyes turned as frigid as a glacial lake. He stood, rested his palms on her desk and slowly leaned forward, his gaze direct. "I tried to tell you, Madeline, but you wouldn't listen. I tried to tell Sylvia, but she championed you at every turn. Since you've been at Winston Design's helm, we've had nothing but problems. Maybe now you'll both heed my advice. I say we call an emergency board meeting and vote to sell out to Butler & Maggio before the news is all over the industry that this company is failing."

More surprised at his icy demeanor than his demand to sell or his criticism of her, Maddie sat back. Seen through his eyes, she knew the truth seemed damning. Seconds passed while she answered his chilly stare with one of her own. "We're going to wait, Uncle Lucius. Both Max and Sylvia think we should play for time. Max has hopes we'll be able to supply half orders by the contracted date. We have twenty-one days until we need to bail out, and I'd like us to take them one day at a time."

Slowly, Lucius straightened his shoulders. She watched as he clenched and unclenched his hands, positive he was imagining her neck in his bony fingers as he squeezed tight. Maddie could feel sweat gathering at strategic pulse points in her body, but she didn't blink or move a muscle. Her uncle would pounce on any flaw, no matter how small.

Only after his left eyebrow stopped twitching did Lucius answer her. "I'll give you fourteen days, not a day more, before I call Butler & Maggio myself. This company is as much mine as it is yours, Madeline, no matter the instructions in James's will. You'd best remember that.

"I assume I'll still be handling the company to company relationships and any leaks the press might pick up on, or am I to be ousted from the one job you and Sylvia still allow me?"

Maddie nodded. "Of course. Gram and I want you to continue your excellent handling of the press. And please see to it everyone in the company is made to feel secure while you squelch all rumors of instability. Thank you for your patience. I'll keep you informed."

Without another comment or backward glance, Lucius Fulbright marched from the room. The sweat pooling between Maddie's breasts turned cold and clammy. When the door slammed, she jumped, then slumped in her chair with relief. She'd done it again. She'd managed to keep control and hold her demanding, pessimistic uncle at bay. But for how long this time? And what about Dominic Maggio's phone call?

At best, she had fourteen days to save her company.

Unable to reach Mary Grace personally to cancel her lunch invitation, Maddie left word on her friend's answering machine that she might be able to meet her in a day or so. Then she called the phone company and put in an order for computerized voice mail and an unlisted number. She spent the rest of the morning studying the endangered contracts on her PC. At two o'clock, she placed a lunch order with the deli downstairs for a tuna on rye with light mayo, lettuce and tomato, and a diet soda. The sandwich arrived twenty minutes later and she stopped just long enough to pay the delivery boy and devour half the sandwich in three huge bites.

Leaning back, she stared out her office window. Rain still drizzled down the dirty panes, mirroring the emotions in her heart. The weather looked exactly like she felt—bleak, dejected, and miserable.

Rubbing her hands over her eyes, Maddie took a deep breath. She'd been staring at the computer screen so long she was seeing double. It was time to take the original contracts out of her briefcase and read them over again, word for word. With a new approach, she might find something she'd overlooked for the past four hours.

She opened her briefcase, but her hands stopped in mid reach. Suddenly cold all over, the icy sweat she'd experienced earlier rushed back to claim her.

She stared into the attaché, her mouth wide, then slammed the lid and quickly closed her eyes. If this kept up she would need to have Max, who seemed to have a friend for every personal crisis, recommend a psychiatrist. She was going crazy.

Furtively, she glanced around the room, relieved to find she was still alone. Lifting the lid just high enough to see inside, she peered into the case. Greeted by a little twinkle of green and red, she groaned. This could not be happening to her.

She sat upright, prepared herself, and fully raised the lid, then reached inside, took out the bottle—covered with bits of congealed tomato sauce and eggshell—and placed it on her desk blotter.

Thoroughly confused, Maddie caught her reflection in the small section she had already polished, surprised to see a lone tear, like a raindrop on her window, skim its way down her cheek. Brushing the tear aside, she stared at the bottle, then folded her arms and sat back in her desk chair.

If she were smart, she would drive to the Jersey shore and toss the darned thing right back into the Atlantic.

After ten minutes had passed, she took a deep breath and headed for her private bath. Refusing to allow herself to look like a runaway from some mental institution, she splashed cold water on her face, dried her eyes, brushed her hair and teeth, and smiled broadly at her reflection. If she was going to be carted to an asylum, at least she would look her best in the straitjacket.

She rinsed out a washcloth and walked calmly to her desk, where she promptly wiped down the bottle, then began polishing another small section. Her fury grew when nothing immediate happened. Rubbing harder, she began to mutter. "Come on, show yourself, you coward. I'm going to get to the bottom of this if it's the last thing I—"

The bottle quivered under her punishing attention, and she jumped back. With a little thunk, the stopper popped off and rolled to a corner of the desk. Smoke, light gray and aromatic, began to curl into the air, as it had every time she scrubbed the metallic surface. Raising her gaze to follow the wispy trail, Maddie watched a figure form in the air. Tall and formidable, the man—magician or actor or whoever he was—appeared before her.

Dressed as he'd been on the beach, in full gathered pants and a small, gem-studded vest, he bowed at the waist. "Master, your wish is my command."

Maddie plopped into her chair. Before she could utter a word, the man unfolded to his full height and smiled through dazzling white teeth. "What is it you wish of me?"

She shuddered as his dark-as-chocolate voice melted over her like hot fudge on a sundae. They were alone in the room. No one except the delivery boy who'd brought her lunch and stayed for all of thirty seconds had entered her office for the past four hours. Besides her desk, credenza, and computer station, her office had only one closet with space for a few coats and some supplies, and an adjacent half bath—no room for cameras, hidden screens, or projectors to lurk out of sight.

Something inside her head told her it was time to find out what was really going on. "Who are you? And this time, I'd like the truth."

Looking perplexed, the man held his hands out at his sides. "I have already told you, Master. I am Abban ben-Abdullah. I am yours to command."

Maddie stood and marched to stand in front of him, wedging herself between his body and the desk. Raising a finger, she poked at his rock-hard chest. Smooth flesh gave way to muscle, and he folded his arms. "I am real, I assure you."

"Right." Maddie gritted her teeth. "And I'm Little Bo Peep."

She walked around to his back and caught herself admiring the same nicely packaged view as before. Furious she could even begin to approve of the charlatan, she stomped around to face him again, an angry frown on her face. "You say you're mine to command, right? That means you'll do whatever I say?"

He nodded. "Within reason."

"I knew there'd be a catch. 'Within reason' means whatever you've brought along to make magic with, right? Say, pulling a rabbit from the bottle or a river of scarves?"

He raised his deep blue eyes over her shoulder to her desk and took in her half-eaten tuna sandwich. "It means I can grant you what I understand. Perhaps you are still hungry. I could make you a plate of ripe pomegranates, succulent figs, or the sweetest of dates. If you are thirsty, some honeyed goat's milk or cooling wine. If you wanted jewels, I could give you pearls as big as pigeons' eggs or diamonds the size of stars from the sky."

Her hands on her hips, Maddie nodded. "Uh-huh. Ooo-kay. Show me."

"Show you? Which?"

"All of it, and the sooner the better. Come on. Hurry up." Impatiently, she began tapping her square-toed shoe, daring him to implement his bragging. "I want it all."

The man stepped back and folded his arms. "Very well." A second flew by, then a few more. Lowering his arms, he clapped his hands once.

Staring smugly, Maddie put her hands on his chest and began pushing him toward the door. "Out, out, out, you idiot. And don't let the door hit you on the way!"

"You do not like them?" he asked. Looking disappointed, he inclined his head toward the desk at her back.

She whirled on her heels, ready for another trick. Instead she was blinded by the flash of light glinting off her desk top. Jewels of all colors and sizes, pearls and sapphires and stones she didn't even recognize, were piled high on her blotter alongside an immense platter of fresh fruit and assorted golden goblets.

For the first time in her life, Maddie was at a loss for words. When she found she couldn't speak, she did something she'd never done before. She fainted dead away.

Four

Prince Abban ben-Abdullah stared down at the woman lying in a crumpled heap at his feet. A huge sigh lifted his shoulders as he gazed at his newest master. Perhaps he *should* have let her toss his bottle back into the ocean. But his first taste of freedom in over a thousand years had been too tempting to throw away. Knowing his choices were few, he took odds on the fact the woman knew little about her rights as a master and squatted, picking her up in his arms.

As he juggled her weight, his hand brushed against her breast. It was a pity her unattractive attire did nothing to enhance what he knew lurked under her dark, bulky clothing. Why did she dress as if she were in mourning?

He walked to the oddly shaped chair behind the table and gently set her down. Stepping back, he appraised the room, worried he might not get the chance to do so again. Wondrous things he had never before seen called out to him: a box with winged figures flying across its front sat to the side of her chair, lights without flame glowed brightly overhead while another light shining from a stick decorated her table; a small black box with numbers and little bumps on it . . .

. . . made a jarring noise. He started, pulling his hand back. When the clamor stopped, he picked up the strangely shaped top and held it to his ear. At the sound of a droning buzz, he shrugged and set the object back in its holder.

He walked to the large square hole in the wall which let in outside light and placed his palms on the cool, clear panel. *Glass*. He remembered glass from his last taste of freedom, over a thousand years ago. He had thought it a miracle then, when only the wealthiest could afford something so fine. He stared at the buildings lining the streets. Now, it seemed, glass was a very common thing.

Lowering his sight, he blinked at the crowds below. Like insects scurrying at his feet, hundreds of people and odd-looking carts were rushing to and fro. He'd known he was in a strange time when the bottle maneuvered itself into her suitcase and he'd felt himself transported skyward, but this was magnificent, more than he had ever dreamed.

He heard a soft moan and turned back to gaze at the woman in the chair. He had the worst of all luck. First to be the object of Ashmedai's wrath in atonement for his father's greed; then to have no one rub the bottle for so long a time he thought he would never be released. And now this—slave to a woman. He truly was cursed above all men.

The woman moved from side to side, rustling the spiky tufts of hair that sat straight up on her head. He couldn't help but wonder what type of female would cut her tresses as short as a man's. Her hair was a beautiful shade of gold, vividly alive, with all the colors of a sunset shining through it. Was she ashamed because it would not grow, or was she doing penance for some serious sin?

He stepped closer to the table and gazed over the pile of jewels he had produced. Had their sight caused her to faint with joy, or had he displeased her so greatly she'd lost all control? Because she was a woman, he suspected the former, but one could never know for certain what went on in a woman's pea-sized brain. Perhaps, if she proved kind, he would ask her himself.

The woman's eyelids fluttered open, and she stared at him through amber eyes. For a scant second, he found himself unable to move, captured in their compelling, honeyed warmth. Her eyes were wondrous. Large and lushly framed by dark lashes and russet brows, they sat over a strong, straight nose and wide, expressive mouth. He could almost taste her lips pressing softly against his while he touched her again.

He fisted his hands at his sides and glanced furtively about the room. It was not proper for a slave to have such brazen thoughts about his master. If caught by Ashmedai, he could be beaten or staked alive over an anthill.

In an attempt to banish his disrespectful imaginings, he moved closer to the table and bowed from the waist. "I trust I have pleased you, Master?"

The woman ran a hand over her face and eyes, peering at him from between splayed fingers. "What happened to me?"

He cleared his throat, praying to Allah she wouldn't punish him for her collapse. "I believe you fainted, Master."

She muttered something unintelligible under her breath. "That's ridiculous. I never faint. And how did I get over here?"

Knowing he had done the unforgivable and touched her person without permission, he bowed again. "Forgive me, Master, but I carried you. I beg of you, do not beat this illegitimate son of a flea unworthy to sit on a donkey's behind."

She closed her fingers and groaned. "That's cute. Original, too." She peered out again. "Are those real?"

"Real?"

"The jewels, the pearls and stuff. Are they real?"

He nodded, still wondering if she was pleased or angry.

Any harem woman worth her salt knew a real jewel from a fake. "Of the finest quality, I assure you. Did I leave out a particular kind of stone you might like?"

The woman ran a hand over the pile of gems, sifting them through her slender fingers like a waterfall. Gnawing at her lower lip, she sighed, then gazed at the platter of fruit. Hesitantly, she reached out and picked up a date, bit into it with perfect white teeth, and chewed slowly. Next, she lifted a golden chalice, sniffed its contents and set it down, then lifted another and did the same.

"You do not like pomegranate juice or honeyed goat's milk?" he asked, fearing he'd produced nothing which pleased her.

She raised her gaze to his, and the heat he felt from those golden eyes flowed over him like a warm desert rain. But the glorious orbs held confusion and unease.

"Afraid I'm not much for alcohol or goat's milk. Maybe some cold spring water?" she asked politely.

He smiled at her request, so simple and innocent. Clapping his hands once, he nodded at the chalice that appeared in front of her. "As you please," he whispered, suddenly aching to see her smile.

She picked up the cup, raised it to her mouth, and drained the contents. Licking at her lips with her small pink tongue, she rewarded him with a hesitant grin. "That was very good."

He released the breath he was unaware he'd been holding. "I live to serve, Master," he murmured, bowing from the waist. His eyes cast downward, he waited. It was not seemly to be forward with one's master, no matter she was female and made devilish work of his senses.

The woman cleared her throat. "Uh . . . you can get up now."

He straightened. "As you wish, Master."

She rolled her eyes and slumped back in the chair.

"Will you please stop calling me that? My name is Maddie."

He held back his scandalous thoughts. It was not proper for a genie to call his master by anything other than *master.* But she was a woman, and it seemed she was, as he had hoped, unversed in proper genie conduct.

She arched one of her russet brows and leaned forward. "You have a problem with that?"

He bowed again, determined to remain as formal as he knew he should, but it was becoming difficult. "As you wish, Maa-dee."

That made her smile for real. "It's Mad-ee. Maddie. Say it again and stop trying to sound like a sheep. You'll get the hang of it," she encouraged, her luscious lips wide.

"Mad-ee," he repeated, testing the word on his tongue. "Maddie."

She stood up and held out her hand across the mound of gems. "Pleased to meet you. And your name is?"

For want of anything better to do, he imitated her actions and held his hand to hers. She grasped it and pumped once, her touch creating sensations inside him he had long forgotten. He took a deep breath to clear his head. "Abban ben-Abdullah."

Her yes wide, she smiled. "Boy, that's a mouthful. How about Ben? May I call you Ben?"

He pulled his hand away and made to bow, but her giggle stopped him.

"Uh-uh, Ben. It's the twenty-first century. No one bows and scrapes anymore, not unless they're kiss ups or servants of a royal from a foreign nation or something. You're not one of those, are you?"

How could he tell her he had been a prince of the royal house of Balthazar III, next to succeed his father as ruler and heir? It had been a thousand lifetimes ago, when he had been young and free and unindentured for his father's sins. *Before Ashmedai appeared.* Now he was a slave, bound to the owner of the bottle for eternity or until . . .

"I am your slave," he reminded her, blotting the past from his mind.

Maddie made her way around the table and walked to his side. "Don't be ridiculous. Lincoln abolished slavery one hundred thirty-some years ago. There is no such thing as a slave."

He looked into her eyes and felt himself drowning. If only he could believe her. But she was woman, treacherous and deceitful and not very considerate. He would play along, but keep his guard up as well. This first taste of freedom in close to ten centuries was too precious to waste. "Then I am here to do your bidding. Will that suffice?"

She cocked her head as if thinking. "My bidding? Sounds interesting." Waving her hand over the desk, she asked, "Can you make all this disappear, too?"

He nodded.

"OK, do it."

"As you wish." Getting back to form, he clapped twice and brought the desk top back to normal.

She blinked and shook her head, then went around the table and pressed her fingers into an instrument with small tabs. Suddenly, the winged squares on the box were gone. She pointed at the bottle. "Would you mind getting back inside of there. while I take us home? I'll let you out again when we get to my place. Until then, I have a lot of thinking to do."

Praying she had more honor than other women he had known, he obeyed immediately. She had, after all, said *take* us *home.*

Clutching her briefcase like a life preserver, Maddie walked from the elevator to her apartment. On the way, she shot a disapproving glare at the garbage chute, won-

dering for the hundredth time how the bottle had found
its way back into her life. She unlocked her door and
quickly rebolted it, deciding it didn't matter. For want of
a better explanation, the bottle belonged to her, and nothing she did seemed to change that.

She set the briefcase on her foyer table, lifted the bottle
out, and carried it with her down the hall and into her bedroom. After carefully positioning it on her dresser, Maddie
rested her hands on her hips and gazed at the bottle for
several long moments. With all the strange things the bottle
had managed to accomplish, she wondered how much the
man inside could see and hear of the outside world.

Feeling a little silly, she opened a dresser drawer and
stuffed the bottle under a sweater, then shut the drawer
tight and changed into jeans and a comfortable, oversized
T-shirt. Gazing at the drawer, she sat back on her bed and
thought again of what had happened over the past forty-
eight hours. Could this all be real?

Concentrating, Maddie tried to remember everything
she had read about magic lamps. Long ago, in her quest
to stay alive, Scheherazade had spun the tale of Aladdin
and his own personal genie. Disney had turned the genie
of the lamp into a manic, bright blue Robin Williams. Ben
didn't resemble either character.

Who was he? How had he gotten into the bottle—
become a genie—in the first place? Did he need to
sleep? Did he get hungry or sick, like a real person?
How had he made the bottle invisible and manipulated
it to follow her? What did he do in there, anyway?

Well, she certainly couldn't find out the answer to any
of those questions by sitting here and staring.

Stiffening her spine, she stood and opened the drawer,
removed the bottle, and took it to her kitchen. If she was
hungry, Ben must be starving, locked away inside of there
for who knew how long. Setting the bottle on her counter,
she opened a drawer, took out her best silver polishing

cloth, and started to scrub. The bottle still had plenty of tarnished spots on it, places that needed sprucing up. If Ben was going to work for her, he deserved a nice home.

In less than two seconds of rubbing, the top popped off and a thin stream of smoke rose in the air. Maddie stepped back to make room, deciding she liked the sweet, aromatic scent of the smoke as it filled her kitchen. One way or another, she was going to figure out how the darned bottle worked. Ben formed quickly and gave her a look of thanks, but he didn't bow as usual.

"Maddie," he said politely. "What is it you wish of me?"

She frowned, wondering the same thing. What *did* she want from him? "Uh . . . not much, for now, though a little friendly conversation might be nice. I have a ton of questions I'd like answered."

Ben's eyes grew wide. "You do not wish more jewels or a pile of gold? A ride through the desert on a flying carpet? Some special food or drink? A coat of finest silk or slippers of softest lamb's skin?"

Bowled over by his generous offers, she gave a little whistle and dropped softly into one of her antique ladder-back chairs. "Is that all you do? Grant wishes, I mean. Can't you just talk to me? Answer a few questions, at least?"

His face held such a look of amazement she began to laugh. "Golly, hasn't anyone just wanted to talk with you before? It's not a crime, you know."

Ben raised a dark brow. "Never."

Maddie's heart wrenched. How final he sounded, and how sad. What was it he'd said to her on the beach? He'd been a prisoner since ten-ninety-nine. How horrible to have been locked inside that tiny space for so long. No one, not even the cruelest of souls, deserved such punishment. She smiled, a bit too brightly. "Well, there's a first time for everything. Sit down and relax. You can answer my questions while I fix us something to eat."

Ben stood stiffly, his gaze scouring the room, almost as if waiting for a hand to reach out and pluck him up or smack him down. Seconds passed before he became comfortable enough to sit across from her at the table.

Maddie ignored his look of terror and walked to the refrigerator. "OK. What'll it be?" She opened the freezer door and stuck her head inside. "Chicken, chicken, or chicken? I have Lean Cuisines, Weight Watchers, and a couple of other brands that don't taste too bad. We'll just pop—"

She backed out and her rear bumped into a hard, unyielding presence. Heat rose as she realized her backside was nestled snugly into his front; she quickly moved. Her gaze settled directly on his mysterious blue eyes, open wide and staring inside the freezer compartment. It came to her then that Ben was like a time traveler, trying to get a handle on a whole new world. How would she feel if she arrived on Mars in the year twenty-ninety-nine?

Hesitantly, he raised a hand to the chill. "What is this box?"

Maddie stepped aside to give him room, took his hand, and set it on a frozen dinner. "It's called a refrigerator. This is the section that freezes things." She opened the lower door. "This is the bigger part. It's meant to keep the food we eat every day cold so it doesn't spoil. It's really not a big deal. They freeze everything nowadays— meat, bodies, even sperm."

He recoiled as if she'd said a dirty word. "Human bodies?"

She blinked. "Yeah. It's called cryogenics and it's very experimental, but someday some genius will make it work."

He wrinkled his forehead. "And sperm?"

Maddie felt the blush rising to her hairline. She'd really have to watch what she said around this guy. "I'll explain it later. Now, about dinner?"

He nodded as if filing away her promise, reached into the freezer, and pulled out a box. Running a finger over the artfully arranged meal pictured on the front, he asked in awe, "There is food in here?"

She pulled out two more boxes. "Yup. And it's not half bad, once you get used to it. I'd treat us to a restaurant, but I don't think you're ready for that just yet. Make yourself comfortable while I nuke a little of everything. One of these won't fill up a big guy like you."

She left him playing with the refrigerator door, opening and closing it like a three year old. After unwrapping the dinners and setting them to cook in the microwave, she walked back to the fridge and held her finger on the little tab that turned out the light. "It's not magic—just science. See?"

"Science?" He stood and pressed the button a few times, smiling down at her. "And truly amazing."

Maddie took his hand and led him to his seat. "Not really. When you see what else has been accomplished in a thousand years, you'll realize that's just the tip of the iceberg."

The microwave beeped and she retrieved their dinners, determined to put him at ease and gather a little information at the same time. Later tonight was soon enough to show him what the world had become. "So, Ben, how long since you've eaten? You do eat inside that bottle, don't you?"

"I do not think so," he answered, eyes downcast.

"You don't think so? Well, what do you do in there if you don't eat?" Maddie brought silverware to the table, then ran the tap and filled two glasses with water. She turned to find him gaping and let her question hang. "It's called indoor plumbing. Brings hot and cold water into every home," she said, setting the glasses on the table.

"There is no longer a need to draw water from a well?"

She placed his dinner, two Healthy Choice double portions, in front of him and sat down with her own food. "Not anymore. Only the most backward places, mostly third world countries, still draw water from an outdoor hole in the ground."

He nodded and picked up his fork, but didn't dig in as she'd expected. Balancing a bite of chicken on her fork, she eyed his plate. "What are you waiting for? Does it smell that bad?"

"You are sure you do not wish me to feed you? Or give you wine or another delicacy? Anything you desire will appear in an . . ."

She shook her head and raised her fork in salute. "Positive. Now try your dinner. I insist."

Slowly, Ben did as she ordered, taking a small bit of rice and vegetables on his fork and placing it into his mouth. Maddie sucked in a breath as he chewed, watching the pleasure build in his handsome tan face. He swallowed and her gaze rested on the strong column of his throat. Glancing lower, she stared at his almost-bare chest. Trevor, the only man she'd ever been with, had a well-formed but slim body. This guy was built like a weight lifter, with washboard abs and rippling muscles. Guiltily, she lowered her eyes and concentrated on her own dinner.

They ate in silence, Maddie watching him finish his double portions almost as fast as she'd eaten her single. "Good?" she asked when he'd downed the last of his water.

"I've never had anything quite like it," he said, wiping his mouth on his napkin. "I had almost forgotten how wonderful food could taste."

He was praising the likes of a *diet* dinner? Maddie couldn't imagine anything more pathetic, unless it was those posters asking for donations for the starving children of Korea or Bangladesh. It took very little of her monthly salary to support a child in each country.

She smiled when he went to the microwave and began

fiddling with the buttons. Ben seemed harmless, and so eager to please her. The least she could do was see to it he was well fed.

Obediently, Ben sat in the place Maddie called her living room. Resting comfortably on a divan, he gave the small black box he held in his hand a curious look. Maddie had called the gadget a remote, but it wasn't. It was right here in his palm. More amazingly, he could point it at a larger box, one that looked very much like the box in her office, only bigger, and the voices and pictures changed.

Ben heard Maddie in the kitchen, drawing water, banging drawers, and rattling all manner of things in the process of what she called "cleaning up." He had offered to clap his hands and take care of the clutter for her, but she had insisted on doing the work herself, as if she felt no shame in being a servant. She was a very unusual woman.

He held out his hand and pressed the button she'd shown him on the remote. The picture on the screen changed from one of a man and woman sitting at a table talking about the weather to men on horseback. The men seemed intent on harming each other with pointed sticks that sparked fire. Clicking again, he found a moving picture filled with brilliant colors. An animal that looked like a rabbit, except it walked on two legs, was being chased by a round little man with a fire stick. "Eh, what's up, Doc?" the rabbit said, making the little man furious.

He clicked once more and stared. The scene had changed to a dry land with rugged mountainous terrain, a land that looked very much like his father's kingdom. Men, some in uniform and some dressed as in his father's time, were running after each other and pointing the same fire sticks he'd seen in the other pictures on the screen.

Entranced, he slid to the edge of the sofa. Thunder sounded as men ran at one another, charging and stabbing with the sticks. Carrying weapons of destruction, they fought like the bitterest of enemies. His country, or one very near it, was at war.

He hardly noticed when Maddie walked in and set a tray on the low table at his knees. "What are you watching?"

"This . . . this battle. My countrymen are killing each other. I do not understand."

She took the remote from his hand and clicked, leaving a blank screen for his perusal. "I'm sorry. I shouldn't have let you see that without an explanation. Where are you from, anyway?"

He stood and paced to the window, staring out onto the millions of lights twinkling in the distance. "People not of my country called it Persia. My father ruled a small principality there, as did his father before, and other ancestors before him for many generations. Do you know of it, my country?"

Concentrating, Maddie sat on the sofa and poured coffee into a mug. "I know of it from my world history classes. But Persia as a country no longer exists. It's been divided into several countries—Iran, Iraq, and Kuwait, to name a few. If you listen to the news reports, the Persian Gulf is a hotbed of money, power, and cruelty. It's been that way for a very long time, Ben. I'm sorry."

"There is no more Persia?" he asked, unable to believe her hesitant explanation.

"Not really."

Ben hadn't felt so desolate since Ashmedai's last visit. His country as he'd known it gone, his brethren at war with one another for years. If he had been ruler, it would not have happened. If he had been left to his own destiny—

"Who are the rulers there now? What are their names?"

He paced back to the sofa, waiting for her answer. Maddie stirred her coffee and sipped, not meeting his eyes, and he knew it could only mean one thing. The truth was too terrible to hear—Ashmedai had taken control. Bracing himself, he sat and accepted the cup she handed him.

"A man called Saddam Hussein is in charge of most of it. The other countries are led by religious zealots and other factions that seem to change from day to day. It's pretty complicated and, to tell you the truth, I haven't paid too much attention. A lot of it has to do with the petroleum."

He gave silent praise to Allah that the current ruler was not the world's most evil jinn and homed in on Maddie's last word. "Petroleum? What is it, this petroleum?"

"A chemical substance more commonly called oil. It's found far underground and has to be pumped from the earth like water. The entire world needs it. Those countries seem to have most of it. I'll try to explain oil later, along with a whole bunch of other things. Now please, taste the coffee."

He sniffed at the cup, then sipped the steaming liquid. "You do not mean to call this coffee?" he asked with a grimace.

Rolling her eyes, Maddie sighed. "Don't tell me you've never had it before. Coffee's been around a long, long time."

He took another sip. Not wanting to hurt her feelings, he gave an encouraging smile. "It is like our coffee, yes, but it is very weak. I like coffee that will put the hair of the camel on my chest."

She giggled. "Weak, huh? Next time I'll make my famous espresso. Trevor used to say it—"

Ben set his cup on the table so hard it clattered. "Who is this Trevor? I have heard you use his name before, but always it brings a sadness to your eyes. I would like to meet this man who has the ability to make you so unhappy."

Maddie lay back on the sofa, gazing out at the room. "Trevor is—was my fiancé. We were going to be married."

The words took him by surprise. Since that first day

on the beach, he had thought of her as *his* master, as someone who would control his destiny. He found it difficult to imagine her answering to another. All his past masters had been men. Everyone knew women were the slaves of their husbands. If Maddie were married to this Trevor, that would make her a slave. And he could never be the genie of a slave . . . or could he?

But she used the past tense, and the man obviously made her miserable, so it sounded as if she were no longer to be his wife. Relieved, he took another drink of the coffee before making a simple statement. "If you wished it, I could kill him for you."

When Maddie gasped, Ben knew instinctively he'd said the wrong thing. Preparing for his punishment, he turned to her and dropped to his knees. "Do not beat me, Master. For you, I would do so and more. It is my duty to make you happy, to please you in all respects."

Maddie's mouth opened wide. "Beat you?" Suddenly, she laughed out loud. "Would you please sit down? You're just like Max. He offered to have a 'friend' take care of Trevor, too. Honestly, don't men know how to settle anything without violence?"

Ben resituated himself on the sofa, his mind focused on all the horrible ways he'd learned to kill a man. Women, he knew, didn't usually appreciate the descriptions. "There need not be violence. You could arrange for me to meet him and I would merely clap my hands. I could send him to the surface of the moon or the inside of a glacier. No one would ever find him again. I assure you, it would be no trouble at all. And it might please you."

Maddie closed her eyes. Finally staring up at him, she shook her head, her eyes amber pools of misery, her voice a whisper. "No, thanks. Trevor married someone else, and I can only wish him well. It was fate he met Felice. Deep in my heart, I think I always knew we weren't suited to one another."

Though her words were convincing, Ben knew her eyes told the real tale. Maddie seemed kind and good-natured, not devious or self-serving as most women. He vowed then and there he would replace her despair with joy, no matter how much of his magic it took. Gamely, he changed the subject. "In my country, marriages were arranged by parents. Did your parents arrange yours with this Trevor?"

Her eyes remained sorrowful as she chewed at her lower lip. "My parents are dead, but they never would have done such a thing. Even today, in your country, a lot of the more rebellious and modern young people run away together without permission, or insist on picking out their own mates. Things have changed, Ben, big time."

"This is the United States of America," he said, raising his hand to his forehead in a mock salute.

She brightened a little. "Where did you learn that?"

Pleased he had made her feel better, he nodded toward the box. "In a picture there in the machine. Men in uniform, all standing in line and telling me so."

"Uh-huh. Well, that machine is called a television, TV for short. I think the first thing we need to do is get you caught up on your history and introduce you to the good old US of A. You have a lot to learn. You'll need clothes and—"

Insulted, he stood and grabbed at his gem-studded vest. "What is wrong with my clothing? These rubies and emeralds are of the highest quality. The leather is of finest goatskin, my trousers of softest silk. Ashmedai assured me I would be dressed in a manner befitting my birth, and he has kept his word."

Maddie wrinkled her brow. "Ashma—who?"

He'd done it now. He had spoken the name of the world's most feared jinn aloud. Nits on the behind of an ass had more sense than he. He stood, waiting for the wrath of Ashmedai to strike him down.

"Ben? Who is Ashma—whoever you said?"

His gaze roamed the room. Ashmedai must be asleep or disciplining some other disobedient slave to not show himself and mete out punishment. And how could she not know of such a powerful and diabolical jinn? He glanced down at Maddie, who was looking up at him as if she really cared. Could she truly be so innocent? "He is someone from my past I cannot speak of. Now, back to my manner of dress. What is it I should wear that would please you?"

She grabbed at a book sitting on the table and flipped through the pages. "All right. Let's try *GQ* for starters. If we don't find anything you like, we'll keep looking. All I know is I can't have you coming with me to meet Max tomorrow dressed like a retro *Mr. Clean.*"

He folded his arms over his chest. "I think you are making a jest with me, no?"

She smiled, and he forgot completely about Ashmedai and his miserable curse. It sounded as if she planned on keeping him out of his bottle and at her side, an almost unheard of honor. He resolved then and there that if Allah could grant him one wish only for the rest of his days, it would be that Maddie remain his master for eternity. For the first time in hundreds of years of enslavement, he was actually having fun.

Lucius Fulbright hated to sweat, hated it more than any other bodily function. Right now, the rivulets of perspiration trickling down his back and sides revolted him almost as much as the man sitting across from him.

The dimly lit room reeked of cigars and despair, as if this were a place prisoners visited to have a final smoke before execution. The thought of an execution made him cringe inside, but he sat straight and waited, refusing to show any hint of weakness.

Making a huge production of lighting the six-inch cigar in his hand, the burly man across the desk inhaled heavily, then blew out a ring of smoke and watched it float lazily into nothingness. "I thought you told us the waiting would be over soon, Fulbright. 'Sooner' better be here in the next few days, or you're a dead man."

Lucius curled his fingers, fisting his hands under his thighs. "My niece is stubborn. She thinks she's going to make it work. I tried to talk her into selling, but she was adamant about giving it one last shot."

The man leaned back and took another puff, filling the air with noxious fumes. "And you mean to tell me you can't convince that old lady, that sister of yours, to vote your way? You disappoint me, Fulbright. And you've dicked us around long enough."

Lucius swallowed past the clogging lump forming in his throat. He'd known the man was crude and ruthless, but he'd never thought his life would be in danger if he wasn't able to carry out his plan. "I need a little more time. I cut Madeline back to fourteen days. I promise you, she'll be ready to sell by then."

The man gazed through the filthy smoke, his slitty eyes drilling like lasers. Suddenly, he waved a hand and stood. "Knowin' how she's pulled off miracles before, I'd say that's definitely too much slack. You better have something up your sleeve, or that neat little bow tie you always wear will be knotted so tight it'll make your eyes pop—if you know what I mean."

Lucius stood as well. "I have a plan. I'll keep you informed, as usual." He didn't bother to hold out a hand and shake on it. He would only want to wipe his palm on his pants leg, a gesture sure to irritate the other man.

He left the office and headed for home. The first thing he would do when he got there would be to swallow a bottle of antacid tablets. Then he would take a long hot shower.

Five

Maddie woke the next morning with her mind in a whirlwind of confusion. After tossing and turning until well past midnight, she had finally fallen into a drug-like sleep in which she'd had strange, disturbing dreams of mysterious men riding horses across a barren desert. Though she knew the dreams were because of Ben, they still made her feel reckless and wild, as if she were poised on the edge of the world and about to plunge into something unbelievably exciting.

But before she'd slept, she had spent time mulling over everything they had discussed after dinner. Most of what Ben had explained had been difficult to accept, but something in the faraway longing in his disconcertingly blue eyes made her want to believe he was telling the truth. He had, after all, been able to produce what she'd asked for yesterday: exotic food and drink and a mound of priceless gems.

Last night, she had watched him carefully while he'd prowled her apartment, seemingly amazed over anything the least bit modern or scientific. His look of awe over inventions as simple as electricity and indoor plumbing had been genuine. When he'd thought she wasn't looking, he had glanced furtively around the room, as if waiting for lightning to strike or someone to jump him. For reasons he refused to reveal, Ben acted as if being out of the bottle was a fate worse than death. Only after a lengthy argument, during which she ordered him to sleep in the guest room, had he obeyed.

The things he had told her made little sense, but they certainly explained his lack of knowledge of the modern world. He had lived in the bottle for centuries. When he was inside, time passed in a kind of suspended animation where Ben wasn't sure if he ate or slept or performed any normal human functions. If he knew where his powers came from, or how he could read and comprehend a language he'd never heard before, he was unwilling to tell her.

Put simply, he was positive of only one thing: if he understood what was ordered of him by his current master, he clapped his hands once to make it happen; twice to undo what he had done.

He'd also told her he had no control over to whom he was enslaved. He'd had a dozen masters over the centuries; his last one had set sail for Egypt in the year 1099. A storm must have wrecked his master's ship and set Ben's bottle afloat somewhere in the Arabian Sea, causing it to drift until it found its way to the Florida Keys. Once Maddie pulled the bottle out of the sand and polished it, she became its owner. Ben was committed to her until she gave the bottle away or she died.

Maddie still couldn't accept her odd luck, or the fact that she held in her hands something so fantastic no one would believe her unless she showed them. And Ben had explained that showing anyone else what he could do was not allowed. He belonged to one master at a time, could follow her orders and perform for only her. If Maddie tried to command him while in the presence of others, he would be powerless.

He had also shared a lot of other bizarre rules, rules that made little sense but, judging by Ben's serious facial expression and body language, were best not ignored.

Maddie could not ask for things for anyone other than herself, but once her wish had been granted, she could give the gifts away freely. Ben could only manage specific physical acts. He was unable to grant her eternal life, cure a fatal illness, or call up anything he did not know the inner workings of, but he could send someone into the heart of a mountain or drop them in the center of a whirling tornado.

If she had asked him yesterday in her office to produce a frozen meal, he could not have done so. This morning he would be able to make dozens of frozen dinners because he now knew what they were.

When she had asked the big question—why he'd been made a genie and imprisoned in the first place—he'd clammed up tight. His mumblings of "forbidden" and "eternal damnation" were so melodramatic she'd almost laughed out loud until she'd seen the very real fear in his soulful eyes. For Ben, the topic of how and why he'd been enslaved was taboo.

Now, facing the morning light, Maddie knew she had to accept his presence. She had to admit she *owned* a genie—a genie she had released from a magical bottle after a thousand years of imprisonment.

She heard the toilet flush and stifled a giggle. After they had leafed through the magazine and picked an outfit for him to wear today—Levis, a soft-washed denim shirt, Nikes, and a leather bomber jacket—Ben had clapped it into being. Then she had escorted him to her guest bedroom and hung the clothes in his closet. It had been a challenge to explain about underwear, then find an ad he could use to create his own. It had been even more difficult to explain why he was expected to wear it.

After that, she'd led him to the bathroom situated between their bedrooms. She had demonstrated the sink and shower, which he'd found more fascinating than the refrigerator light, and then turned to the toilet. Five minutes and ten flushes later, he'd gotten the gist of the potty and, from the sound of it this morning, had remembered how to use it.

Maddie heard the shower run and checked the clock. She was due at the plant in less than an hour, which she now admitted was an impossibility. It would take at least that long for them to dress and eat and get out of the city. She had also promised Ben that sometime today they would go to a library and find books on Middle Eastern history, as well as let him watch the television to bring him up to speed on modern customs and language, though Maddie had her doubts on that idea. Somehow she couldn't imagine the vast wasteland as an educational tool, unless it was tuned to PBS or the Discovery or Learning channels.

The sound of running water ceased, and Maddie's mind wandered to a vision of Ben, just steps away on the other side of her bedroom wall, his impressive physique and sexy good looks wet and glistening from the shower. Ben's commanding presence reminded her of the old movies she'd seen about tall, darkly bronzed sheikhs of the desert. She had always thought men who looked like Ben would be empty-headed or full of themselves. Instead, he seemed completely unaware of his charms, acting polite and kind and inquisitive, more like a ten-year-old Boy Scout on steroids.

Rousing herself from the covers, Maddie shook her head. Ben might be a hunk, but she had more important things to do than daydream over a man who, when he got a look at the rest of the twenty-first-century female population, would certainly not be interested in her.

She knocked softly on the bathroom door. "Ben? You about through in there?"

The door popped open and Maddie skittered backward. Ben stood in front of her in the underwear she'd chosen for him, snug-fitting black briefs and a matching sleeveless undershirt. Her heart gave a little *tah-thump* as the blood in her veins came rushing to her head. She forced her gaze away from his sizable male attributes to his still damp hair and lashes. "Why the long face?" she asked, concentrating on his disgruntled features.

He began to bow, then caught himself and straightened, running a large hand over his square, stubbled jaw. "Forgive my unhappy visage, Mast . . . Maddie, but this is what happens when I am out of my bottle. You have commanded I may not work my magic without your permission, yet you have no straight razor—no sharp instrument I can use to cleanse my face of its beard." He sighed. "May I take care of this?"

Maddie blinked. He was asking her permission to shave? She tried not to giggle. "I know it'll be quicker if you clap your hands, but we have to be careful. No one can find out what . . . who . . . uh, I think it would just be smarter if we stopped the genie stuff altogether unless I say so. Besides, wouldn't it be fun to live like a regular man for a change?"

A look of pain so intense Maddie thought he might cry showed in Ben's eyes. He turned to the mirror and nodded, staring at his reflection for long seconds, his shoulders slumped in defeat. Finally he asked, "Do you have a razor I might borrow?"

Maddie pulled her robe tighter, stepped into the bathroom, and dug into the cupboard under her sink. "Sure. Here's a bag of disposables and here"—she flicked open the medicine cabinet—"is something you can use for lather. Don't worry about the girly smell. It'll go away after a while. OK?"

He took the razors from her hand and smiled at her through the glass. "Thank you."

Maddie's heart skipped a beat—again. "I'll go make us breakfast. When we're done eating, you can watch television while I take my turn in here and get dressed."

She headed to the kitchen, but not before remembering

to call out, "Oh, and, Ben, put on your new clothes *before* you come to breakfast."

So far, thought Maddie as they approached her car, the morning had gone well. She and Ben had shared a breakfast of scrambled eggs, toast, and coffee, with Ben also enjoying three slices of microwaved bacon. After she had explained the workings of a telephone to him, she called Max and left a message to tell him she was running late.

Coaxing Ben inside the elevator had taken a bit of doing, but he'd calmed after she held his hand while they rode it down to the basement garage. She had pressed the "hold" button long enough to give him a few minutes to climb into the ceiling and inspect the elevator shaft, where he had examined the ropes and pulleys thoroughly before finally satisfied no magic was involved.

He walked with her to her car, his head swiveling. "What are all these carts with wheels?" he asked, his keen eyes scanning the garage.

"Cars. Automobiles, actually. They run on gasoline, made from the petroleum I told you last night was so important. Cars are only one of the reasons we need oil. There are hundreds more." She stopped in front of her practical little Volkswagen Jetta and smiled. "Well, what do you think?"

Ben walked around the bright red compact, appraising it as if he were in the market for a used horse—or camel. He patted the roof, squatted down to peer at the tires. "It is . . . nice."

He stood, and his gaze combed the garage. Instantly, he made a beeline for the shiny black Porsche parked three rows away. "But this," he said loudly, "is much nicer."

Maddie skipped to catch up, insulted by his typically masculine attitude. Why was it no matter the century, sleek, souped-up machines appealed to every member of the male population? "Yeah, it's nice. It's also about five times the price of my little honey, and a whole lot noisier. And a gas-guzzler, to boot. Believe me, you don't want one."

He raised a brow. "I don't?"

"No," she firmly replied. "That car is testosterone on wheels. You couldn't afford the gas, let alone the insurance premiums necessary to keep it on the road. Now come on. We have to get going."

Ben gave a wistful sigh and followed her back to the Jetta. After lowering the passenger seat so his head didn't hit the roof, he moved the seat back as far as possible until he was finally settled in. "I would have more room on a camel," he confided aloud, struggling to hook his seat belt as Maddie had instructed.

"Maybe so. But a camel is much slower and you won't find any within a thousand miles of here, unless you visit a zoo. Just sit back and relax. Look around and enjoy the scenery."

The usually heavy city traffic made driving hectic and kept Maddie on her toes, but Ben was so busy staring it didn't matter. He had eyes only for the vast numbers and styles of cars clogging the roads. The trucks, vans, and sport utility vehicles intrigued him, while the eighteen-wheelers knocked him sideways.

"And all of these cars and other vehicles run on gasoline, a by-product of oil, most of which is now found in my country? Amazing," he managed, ogling a zippy neon-blue Viper.

Maddie took the exit leading them over the upper level of the George Washington Bridge and into New Jersey, blending smoothly into the mid-morning traffic. "America has oil, too, but not as much of it. In this country, we're trying to conserve our natural resources. It's called being environmentally correct. Since the Mideast has more oil deposits, they have more control on the prices and the international market. It's one of the things that gives them their power."

"Ah. Power," Ben repeated, as if that explained everything. He looked around at the not-too-clean access roads connecting Routes 80 and 46 and several other thoroughfares. "It is very crowded here. Too many people and too much dirt, I think. Is there any place in your America that is clean? A place where one does not smell the cars or the factories? Where the sky is a crystal blue and the birds sing loudly in the trees?"

Maddie knew he was right about the cleanliness of the roadways and the quality of the air, but didn't feel this was the time to get involved in a long conversation on the perils of modern day pollution. She gave him a sidelong glance, smiling when he whipped his head around to watch a huge flatbed truck towing a mobile home pass by. "There are states, Montana and Wyoming for instance, that are still relatively unpopulated and industry free. We can go there sometime if you want, after we get through my current crisis."

He spun forward in his seat and stared at her. "You are experiencing a crisis? Why did you not say so earlier? I can help. I will clap my hands and make it go away."

Wishing to heaven Ben would stop tormenting her with his unworldly skills, Maddie downshifted into a turn. Caving in to temptation and allowing him to help save Winston Design would be the coward's way out—and it wouldn't help her to find and bring to justice the culprit bent on sabotaging the company. It was bad enough she had to figure out a way to explain Ben.

She ran a hand over her hair and cringed. Her cowlick, the one that looked like a giant weed on a putting green, had sprung to life again. Great. They were about a mile from the plant, she needed a pair of hedge clippers, and she'd just realized she had no believable way to introduce Ben to Max—or to anyone else, for that matter.

"Before I can even think about letting you clap your hands to help, we have to come up with a reasonable explanation for your presence. Got any ideas?"

Ben shrugged. "Could I be a relative? A long-lost cousin, perhaps?"

"Everyone knows my only living relatives are a widowed grandmother and an unmarried, childless uncle. We couldn't fool anybody with that story."

He lowered his eyes as if embarrassed by his thoughts. "Your betrothed or a new lover, then?"

Maddie's breath caught in her chest. She only wished a guy like Ben would fall in love with her. "Well, since I was supposedly gaga over Trevor until three days ago, that might be a little tough for people to swallow. I would have no way of explaining how we met or anything. Besides, men who look like you don't . . . aren't usually . . . ahh, never mind. I'll think of something."

They rounded the final turn into the plant parking lot and pulled into the space marked "Madeline Winston" directly next to the doorway. The mellowed red brick was a welcoming beacon to her, the place her mother, father, and grandparents had carved into a family business with their hard-spent sweat and tears. "We're here," she said, a bit too brightly, reminded of her duty to keep the business alive and running.

Ben undid his seat belt and opened the car door. Standing, he stretched. "This car is a tighter fit than my bottle. I think if we are to continue traveling together, we might need a more spacious vehicle, Maddie. If that is not possible, I could transport us to wherever you need to be."

She slammed her door and locked the car. "No magic, remember? If you're really cramped, I could rent something larger for a while, but that's it."

He smiled, a slow lazy grin which crinkled his outrageous blue eyes. "Perhaps there is more room on your

side of the car. If you let me steer, I might have more
space."

Maddie rested her hands on the Jetta's roof. He was, she
suddenly realized, teasing. She grinned right back. "Just
like a man, always wanting to be in the driver's seat. Well,
guess what, buster? You don't have a license, and without
one you can't drive." She smacked a hand onto her forehead. "Jeez, I'm a dope. You don't have a license or a birth
certificate or a Social Security number or anything. It's
like you don't exist. I'll have to talk to Max about it. You
need ID if you're going to become a real person."

Ben stepped back, looking perplexed. "ID?"

"Identification. Documents and photographs proving
your existence. There's no way around it in the modern
world. You need to prove you *are,* otherwise, you aren't."

He raised his hands, palms up, and ran them down his
front. "But I am here. You and everyone else we meet can
see me."

Maddie made her way to the door and Ben opened it,
letting her in first. "It's hard to explain what I mean, but
trust me, you need ID to be recognized in the world. I'll
talk to Max. He'll know what to do."

She passed the receptionist's station and noted it was
vacant. Paulette, Max's right hand, was probably running
an errand or overseeing the assemblers. She charged up
the stairs, Ben following at her heels. At the landing, she
turned right and followed the hall to Max's office. Maddie
knocked, then let herself in, dismayed to find it empty. "I
guess he's in the plant. I'd better go find him. Can you
sit here and be good? Not touch anything?"

Ben glanced about the room, its shelves and bookcases
piled high with loose papers, manuals, and magazines. Like
a little boy making a promise with crossed fingers, he gave
her a look of supreme innocence. Hands clasped behind
his back, he wandered to Max's desk. "But it is so tempting

to touch and feel. There is so much I want to know. I saw one of these in your office yesterday. What is it?"

Maddie smiled at his look of longing. "It's called a computer. Right now it's running a screen saver called Flying Toasters. We manufacture the parts housed inside that help it run. Until you learn how to work one, don't touch. Understand?"

He nodded, still seemingly entranced. "I will try."

"Try very hard," she admonished, heading out the door to find Max.

Ben watched Maddie leave the room, her back straight as she forged out the door. She had dressed in trousers again, made of a material very much like his own. Denim, she had called the material this morning. Stone-washed denim. It clung to her shapely bottom like the softest velvet, outlining her wonderfully long legs and lush curves.

Ben sighed, wondering why he kept having such sensually charged thoughts about *this* master, when he had never done so before. Then again, all his other masters had been men. Ashmedai had never intimated a female master might be possible.

And he hadn't told Maddie what he'd done last night after she'd left him in the guest bedroom and gone to her own bed. He had probably broken another rule of genie etiquette, one more crime to add to his list: staying outside his prison bottle, calling his master by name, thinking of her in a sexually explicit manner. He was lucky Ashmedai had yet to strike him down with all the rules he had disobeyed.

Last night he had waited a respectable time, then walked to Maddie's door and peered inside, where he'd found her tossing and turning, her long white limbs clearly visible in the moonlight. It had brought an ache to his heart, knowing how much his presence worried and upset

her, so he had clapped soundlessly and watched her settle
into a fairly peaceful slumber. Then he had entered her
living room and turned on the moving picture box—the
TV—and stayed awake until dawn, absorbing all manner
of astounding scenes.

He'd learned about global warming, trips to a planet
called Mars, rock music, and something called the Acad-
emy Awards. He'd watched animals living in the wild
roam countries he had never heard of, and he had sat
through dozens of cartoons, as Maddie had called them—
colorful, animated drawings of strange-looking creatures
that sounded and acted like people.

He had learned much.

He sat at the computer and observed the flying toasters.
Maddie had ordered him not to touch, but she hadn't said
a thing about thinking. He concentrated, and a key on the
board in front of him dipped. Immediately the screen
changed to a written message: Enter your password,
please . . .

What in the sands of time was a password?

He heard voices and the patter of footsteps and snapped
his fingers, bringing the winged toasters back to the
screen. Quickly, he stood and walked to the windows that
looked out onto the parking lot. The door opened and he
turned, wearing his most pleasant smile.

Maddie entered the room first, her eyes wide and worried. The man following her, Ben reasoned, was the al-
mighty Max, the person Maddie seemed to rely on so
heavily. Tamping down a sudden quiver of jealousy, he
strode forward and held out a hand as he had seen men
do on the TV. "You must be Max," he said politely, his
grip firm. "I'm Ben."

The older man, gray-haired but still energetic-looking,
also had a strong grip. Though Max only came up to his
shoulder, Ben sensed he would not cower in front of any
man.

"Ben. Maddie tells me you're her new personal assistant. Says you can be trusted." Max looked him up and down.

Ben stepped back and held his ground, knowing instantly he was being evaluated. "I am unconditionally loyal to my Mas—to Maddie, just as she says."

Max raised one bushy brow. "Uh-huh. Now, tell me, Ben, how was it again that you and Maddie met?"

Ben looked to Maddie, who immediately rushed to his side. "I already told you, Max. Ben just moved into my building. I met him at the . . . the garbage chute. He asked if I knew of any companies looking for help and I said yes—mine. He met me at work yesterday afternoon and I gave him the job. You needn't be so suspicious."

Obviously exasperated, Max folded his arms. "You hired him just like that, after all the hot water we're in? This isn't the same as taking in a stray puppy, Maddie. And it's not like the time you gave men from the homeless shelter work sweeping out the plant and pruning the hedges. Letting a stranger into the company at this particular time isn't a bright move."

Maddie made a little *tsking* sound. "Those men needed a chance, exactly like Ben does. They also needed a little self-esteem. Just because I can't pass anyone wearing a sign that says "will work for food" without giving them a donation doesn't mean I'm stupid. Besides, he has an honest face. Show him your honest face, Ben."

Ben smiled sheepishly, trying to look honorable. He would do anything to impress this Max. Anything to stay with Maddie.

"Hmmph," Max muttered. "I still don't like the idea."

Maddie cleared her throat. "There's just one teensy-weensy problem, but I know you can take care of it. He needs ID."

Max's jaw dropped. "ID? Are you telling me this guy's an illegal alien? Jeez, Maddie, that's all we need—immigration breathing down our necks." He peered up at Ben. "What is he? Some kind of camel-jockey?"

"Max Hefner! You of all people should know better than to use ethnic slurs. Didn't your father land on Ellis Island straight from Latvia? Weren't you teased and taunted about your own ancestry? You should be ashamed."

Max looked embarrassed but indignant. "Yeah, but my people didn't try to start World War Three or bomb the World Trade Center."

"Max!" Maddie shouted.

Ben was impressed by Maddie's quick retorts, though he wasn't quite sure what she was shouting about. Where was Latvia? What was this World Trade Center? And *ethnic slur?* Those certainly didn't sound like good words.

Max ran a hand over the back of his neck. "OK! OK!" He turned to Ben. "Tell me straight out, son. Are you here illegally?"

Ben took his cue from Maddie, who nodded imperceptibly.

"Yes, I am."

"And are you wanted for anything? Any type of terrorist or criminal activity? Tell the truth now."

Ben had no idea what those phrases meant, but he sensed Maddie beside him, willing him to give the proper response. "No, sir."

Max heaved a sigh. He folded his arms and appraised Ben a full minute before coming to a decision. "All right. I got a friend in Jersey City, does fantastic work on fake passports and birth certificates. What does he need?"

Much to Ben's displeasure, Maddie rounded the desk and threw her arms around the older man. "Thanks, Max. I knew we could count on you. He needs the works— passport, Social Security number—"

"And driver's license," Ben chimed in, figuring he had nothing to lose.

Maddie stepped back and raised her gaze to the ceiling. "Oh, all right. Driver's license, too."

"Jersey or New York?" Max asked, shaking his head.

"New York. Use my address on everything. And the sooner the better."

"Yeah, yeah, yeah. Now, what other miracles do you need from me? Want me to snap my fingers and get us out of the real mess goin' on around here?"

Maddie's eyes dimmed. "Oh, Max, if only you could."

Ben opened, then quickly closed his mouth. Something told him Max was not a jinn, so he certainly must be joking. He took in Maddie's teasing smile and grinned as well. "I would like to learn about these." He pointed to the screen and its flying toasters. "I want to know how computers work."

Max raised a brow. "Oh, you do, do you? And your reason for learning about them would be?

Maddie gave a sigh. "As my personal assistant, Ben will need to learn how to manage my correspondence, chart sales, and do quite a bit of graphics. Maybe someone here could take him under their wing for a while, give him a crash course?"

Max scratched his balding head, his brow wrinkled in concentration. "Hmm. Best person I can spare for that would be Paulette. I've been so busy in the plant that she's had a lot of free time on her hands."

"Paulette." Maddie frowned and looked toward Ben. "I guess so, but where is she anyway? Her station was empty when we got here."

At that moment, a crisp knock sounded and the door opened. In walked Paulette Jamison, five feet, three inches of silky, shoulder length blond hair and enormous baby blue eyes, packaged in a body made to stop traffic. Her four-inch heels added height and definition to her naturally curvy legs, emphasizing her tiny waist and well-rounded bottom.

Paulette smiled as she scanned the room, her full, red lips freshly shellacked and shining. "Hi, Max. Maddie."

She did a double take worthy of a Disney character and showed every one of her perfectly capped teeth as she made a beeline for Ben. "Well, hello. I don't believe we've met," she purred. Her tiny hand outstretched, she rounded the desk in Olympic time. "I'm Paulette."

Six

Maddie spent the afternoon working with Max in his private laboratory at the top of the stairs. From the doorway, she could look down into the front foyer, almost on top of the reception area. With practice, she found she got a much better view of the first floor if she ambled along the hall and bent over the railing as she made her way to the ladies' room—which she had done numerous times.

In between, she and Max had worked on various ways for WD to meet its commitments on the delivery of the nonexistent microchips as well as draw up a list of potential candidates who would most benefit from ruining Winston Design. They had also conducted a thorough search of the lab, production rooms, and offices, checking for any signs of industrial espionage, but found no listening devices or hidden equipment of any kind.

To her great dismay, the entire time Maddie had been with Max she'd felt distracted and unable to concentrate. The last time she had made a trip to the rest room, she'd gotten a disheartening aerial view of Paulette and Ben, heads bent close, thighs touching as they sat in front of Paulette's computer terminal.

Though Paulette had been in Maddie's class her first year at college, they'd never hung out together. For a while, Maddie thought the girl might want to cultivate a friend-

ship, but during their sophomore year, Paulette had
dropped out. Three years ago, she had surprised Maddie
by showing up at the company and asking for a job. Impressed with her credentials from an excellent computer
programming school, Maddie had encouraged Max to hire
her.

Since her promotion to Max's assistant, Paulette had
conducted several training courses on some of the more
popular company programs. Over the years, Maddie had
managed to accept her enthusiastic personality and aggressive attitude, realizing the young woman was a born
tease. Men flocked to Paulette like lint to a wool suit.
Paulette had flirted with Trevor, and she flirted with Max.
It was just her way.

Still, every time Maddie heard Ben's deep, chuckling
voice or Paulette's sexy giggles, her heart sank to the pit
of her stomach. She knew she was being possessive,
something she had never been with Trevor. Even though
she'd only known Ben a day, *she* wanted to be the one
who answered his questions and satisfied his curiosity—
she wanted to be the one to make him laugh.

While listening with half an ear as Max went over his
next plan of attack, Maddie had an epiphany. Ben had
told her he could duplicate anything once he understood
how the thing worked. She assumed he meant the components of an object, as well as the object's capabilities.
Could he, once he knew what their chips were made of
and understood what they did, recreate them? Would he
be able to clap his hands and will a pile of working microchips into existence?

"Maddie? Maddie, girl? Have you been listening to a
thing I've said?" Max asked, shaking his head. "Don't
tell me you have to go to the rest room again?"

Maddie started from her daydream. She hadn't heard a
sound from Paulette's work station in over ten minutes,

and the silence was killing her. Whatever Paulette and Ben were doing, it was being done in absolute quiet.

"Sorry," she mumbled. More than a bit embarrassed, she wandered to the office door. "I'm so worried I can't seem to put my mind to anything. What were you saying?"

Max gave her a grin. "Not much, I guess, considering how little you've been paying attention. Have you been to a urologist lately? Maybe you should start drinking cranberry juice instead of coffee. Or we could talk about that young man who's got you so distracted. What do you think?"

Maddie felt the heat rise to her cheeks and tried to act insulted. "Ha-ha, very funny. Like I've told you, Ben is my personal assistant. I need to keep an eye on him to make sure he's being trained properly, that's all. Besides, this forged memo business has me so jumpy I'm having a hard time concentrating."

Max held his hands up in acceptance. "OK, anything you say to keep the peace. But I still have serious reservations about this Ben character. What country is he from, for instance? And did he ever tell you how he came to be in America in the first place?"

Maddie heard the sound of Ben's laughter and gave a sigh of relief. Laughing was good. It was hard to indulge in hanky-panky if one was laughing. She decided it was time she paid a little more attention to Max. "He's here, and that's all I need to know. He looks kind and he seems honest. He also knew absolutely nothing about computers until today. If you ask me, he doesn't sound like the most likely candidate for a techno-spy."

Max scratched at his chin, taking in her practical observation. "All right, let's say he was a computer illiterate when you hired him. What's to stop the enemy from contacting him once they figure he knows what's going on around here? They might make him an offer he can't refuse. Anyone can be bought for the right price, Maddie. You should know that by now."

At the sound of footsteps coming up the stairs, Maddie raced to Max's side. "Shh. He'll hear you. Now give me the name and address of your 'friend' in Jersey City. If Ben and I leave right away, we can be there before rush hour traffic is in full swing. I want to get him legal as soon as possible."

Paulette and Ben sauntered into the room, giggling like children. Ben's swagger and preening smile lit his face as he walked up to Maddie. "Paulette says I have graduated," he announced proudly.

Max tossed Paulette a look of pure skepticism. "Surely he couldn't have absorbed all the information stored in that head of yours in under four hours? He'll need at least another day."

Paulette's confident grin stretched from one pearl-clad ear to the other. "He's telling the truth. I have never seen anyone pick up techno-babble so fast. Ben's got all our systems down cold, including Unix. It's like he has his own little microprocessor for a brain."

Max gave Maddie a disgruntled I-told-you-so frown as he reached over and pulled out the chair at his PC, indicating Ben should have a seat. "That so? Well, let me be the first to congratulate you, son. Why don't you sit down and show us what you've learned? How about getting into the system and pulling up the last three files on our inventory? Get them printed out in triplicate with a graph showing our current rate of inventory decline, as well as a profit and loss sheet for the last quarter. Think you can manage that?"

Ben nodded, sat down, and eagerly began to clack away at the keyboard, oblivious of Maddie's gaping stare.

Max took Maddie's elbow and pulled her into the hall. "Come along, young lady. You, too, Paulette. Get out here. Now."

Paulette, not one to buckle under her boss's fits of temper, spoke first. "Honest to God, Max," she whispered. "The guy's brilliant. In the beginning he didn't even understand the concept of a computer, then bingo"—she snapped her red-lacquered nail—"it was like the sun broke through. He knew what I was going to say almost before I said it."

Max's frown turned fierce. "Paulette, have you been sniffing the correction fluid again? That's just not possible." He winced at the sound of a triumphant "Aha!" from Ben.

Paulette faced Maddie, who'd been trying to spy on Ben through a crack in the door, and made a curious double-edged comment. "Looks like you've finally found yourself a capable man, Maddie. Some girls have all the luck."

Before Maddie could figure out if the assistant's remark was a compliment or not, Paulette turned and headed down the stairs. Max, who'd been watching Ben through the partially opened door, turned to her with both brows raised. "A computer illiterate, huh? You're losing your touch, Maddie. This Ben's a ringer."

Maddie tugged at his sleeve, pulling Max further into a corner of the hall. "Don't be ridiculous. You heard Paulette. He's got a natural aptitude for computers. Some people do, you know. My father had it. So do you," she accused, reminding Max of the "wonder-boy" status with which her grandfather had crowned him years ago.

Max's face reddened. "Aw, Maddie, that was different. Your father and I went to computer school first. And I had a passport. I was a legal U.S. citizen."

"That has nothing to do with it," she muttered, smiling broadly at the sound of another little cheer from Ben. "Now, once Ben finishes the totally bogus tasks you've given him, we'll be on our way. Please call your 'friend' and tell him so."

She strode back into Max's office to find Ben standing

at the printer gathering his reports. Stacking them carefully, he laid them on the desk. "I am finished, Maddie," he announced. "Can we now get my driver's license?"

Maddie gave Max a sidelong glance. "You betcha, Ben. Let's go make you legal."

The Chinese restaurant's overhead lights dimmed suddenly, causing the colorful paper lanterns hanging above each table to cast a romantic glow over the diners. Maddie and Ben had just finished a delicious five-course feast complete with bowls of tangy lemon sherbet, and were ready for the check. Their conversation had run from meeting Max's "friend" in Jersey City and having Ben's picture taken for his passport and driver's license to the use of credit cards in the modern world.

After Ben had received his forged documents, Maddie had taken him to a Coach store located in an upscale shopping mall in Bergen County. She had embarrassed him by purchasing a handsome leather wallet and giving it to him as a gift. An hour ago, they had arrived back in Manhattan and Maddie had brought them to The Golden Lotus, her favorite Chinese restaurant, to celebrate Ben's new status as an American citizen. The wallet now sat on the table next to Ben's plate. In between courses, he would open it and gaze at his identification, reading and rereading all the information on his new life.

"What are these?" asked Ben, holding a crispy fortune cookie up to the pale red light of the overhead lantern.

Maddie smiled, relaxed and happy. For the first time in two years, she was in the company of a man who didn't scrutinize her plate and comment on the amount of calories or fat grams she was consuming. Ben had eaten his dinner with enthusiasm, tasting everything and liking it all. The sherbet had fascinated him, and Maddie had so enjoyed watching him eat it she had given him hers to devour as well.

"It's called a fortune cookie. Break it open and you'll find a message inside." She proceeded to open her own cookie, reading aloud, "Nothing is impossible, if you believe it to be so."

Seemingly amazed, Ben sucked in a breath. "Who is writing these telling proverbs, Maddie? And how do they get them inside?"

Maddie giggled at the sight of Ben's large capable hands holding his fortune as if it were a delicate flower. "They're wrapped inside the cookie before it's baked. And nobody really believes in them. It's just a fun thing to do. What does yours say?"

Ben held his slip of paper under the light. "A strong wind blows the sands of time. Change is in the future." He looked up and smiled. "This fortune cookie is very wise. After so many years, everything I see or do is a change."

Maddie couldn't help but notice the faraway look in his cobalt blue eyes again, mysterious eyes that reflected pain and regret in their heavy-lidded depths. To lighten the mood, she made a teasing observation. "So how do you like your new name? I think Benjamin Able sounds very distinguished."

Ben wrinkled his forehead as if thinking hard. Reaching across the table, he picked up a bit of Maddie's cookie and popped it in his mouth. "The name is acceptable. But had I been in my father's house, I would have consulted a soothsayer on the birth date. Are you sure June twenty-first is a good day on which to be born?"

Maddie didn't quite know how to tell Ben it was also her father's birthday. When Max's friend had asked for a date, it just slipped out. Besides, there were a few other good things about June twenty-first she could mention. "The next king of England has that same birthday, Ben. If it's good enough for Prince William, it should be good enough for you. And it's the first day of summer. We'll celebrate and have a party."

Mrs. Cheng, the bird-like woman who owned the restaurant and had known Maddie for several years, set a small black lacquer tray holding their check on the table. "Maddie, is so good to see you. And with a new fella. Nice . . . velly nice," she said, sizing Ben up through wise brown eyes. "Much betta than you last fella."

Maddie ignored the heat rushing to her hairline. Not one to mince words, Mrs. Cheng loved playing "the modern woman," frequently joining Maddie and Mary Grace for a cup of tea whenever they ate at the restaurant. She was never surprised by any of the older woman's outrageous statements. "Now, Mrs. Cheng, Trevor wasn't so bad. I guess you've heard we're no longer engaged."

Mrs. Cheng grinned. "I lead paypah, Maddie. Sometimes things wolk out best. Besides, you last fella was a velly bad tipper."

The sight of Ben, looking angry and disgruntled at the sound of her ex-fiancé's name, forced Maddie to quickly change the subject. She reached into her wallet, took out her corporate gold card, and laid it on the tray alongside the tab. "While we, on the other hand, are very good tippers. Here you go."

Maddie waited until the woman shuffled off before tackling Ben's disapproval. "I told you it's over between Trevor and me. You're going to have to stop looking like you want to chew nails whenever his name is mentioned."

Ben sighed and picked up his wallet, tucking it into his jacket pocket. "I will try. But it is very difficult to have kind thoughts about someone who has so obviously caused you pain. My job is to please you, Maddie, to make your life full of wonderful things which bring you delight. If it were a thousand years ago, I would have dropped this Trevor into a pit of starving tigers."

"Well, that's just not how it's done these days. The

world is a more . . . civilized place," she stammered. "We don't deal with conflict by using force. At least, those of us who respect our fellow man don't."

"Ah, but then Trevor did not respect you, did he? If he had, he would have come to you first and spoken with you like a *civilized* man before marrying that other woman and hurting you." He laid a warm palm over Maddie's hands, which were busy shredding her napkin into a tattered pile on the table. "I would never hurt you, Maddie."

Mrs. Cheng brought back the charge slip and receipt. Maddie pulled her hands from under his and quickly added a generous tip to the bill. After scribbling her name, she tore off her copy and tucked the card and paperwork back into her billfold.

Uncomfortable with Ben's all too truthful statement, she grabbed at her cup of tea and swirled the pale liquid round and round. When would the hurt go away? When would she be able to think about Trevor's betrayal and not feel as unattractive and useless as a worn-out boot? Right now, she wished she was anywhere but here, where her heart lay open and exposed to Ben's intimate scrutiny. Suddenly, she wanted to be far away from the bustle of the big city and memories of her broken engagement, her company's impending disaster. She wished—

Without warning, the paper lantern hanging above their table began to sway. The lights flickered and Maddie blinked. A cool breeze caressed her cheek and she heard the sound of a bird's soulful call. The fragrance of tangy night air and pungently exotic flowers enveloped her and she raised her gaze to find Ben smiling strangely. Ready to stand and leave the table, Maddie felt her stomach roll when she and Ben rose as one into an eerie, inky blackness. She looked down at the ground, now far below them, and reached out, her hands clutching at nothing but the warm, scented air.

As if in a dream, they were flying, riding high into the

vast night sky. Maddie gasped, her fingers curling around the edges of a small rug. Ben was taking her on a magic carpet ride!

He turned his back to her and grasped the fringe decorating the front of the carpet, steering it like a wagon. "Hold on to my back, Maddie. Hold on and look around you."

Terrified, she wriggled further up the carpet and looped her legs over Ben's from behind. Too shocked to say a word, she wrapped her arms around his rock-hard middle and hung on tight.

Ben's stomach muscles rippled as he chuckled at her distress. "There is nothing to be afraid of, Maddie. I would never let anything harm you," he promised, guiding the rug into a sweeping dip and curve.

Through a wispy cover of clouds, Maddie peered down onto a vast expanse of sand and space. She could barely make out what she assumed were palm trees dotting the desert scenery and clusters of tents around brightly burning campfires. "Where are we?" she shouted over the wind whistling through her hair.

Ben dipped lower, his heady laughter filling the air. "Persia," he called out. "My people were once nomads. This is the place of my birth."

Maddie's stomach churned as the carpet rushed to meet the ground and she clutched harder, her fingers wound into a tight painful knot. Ben sounded like a little boy, as proud of his homeland as she was of Gram's house on the Keys. The carpet took another giant dip and he boomed out his delight, throwing her stomach into a tailspin.

"If you don't slow this thing down, I'm going to be sick all over the back of your new jacket," she warned, snapping her eyes closed.

Suddenly, the carpet rose. Higher and higher, faster and faster it climbed, back through the clouds and into a black-as-pitch sky studded with diamonds. No, with stars. Slowing, they began to coast like a sailboat on the water, riding gentle waves of air. The ride became peaceful, the night an unbelievable cocoon of warmth and comfort as it surged around them and lulled them into serenity.

Maddie softened her grip, loosely linking her fingers around Ben's firm abdomen. Nestled against his back, she felt closer to him than she had to any other human being for a very long while. Well-being filled her as she leaned her head against the soft leather of his bomber jacket. Something about the way he had promised never to let anything hurt her tugged at her heart.

Closing her eyes, Maddie let the cares of her life fade away as she opened her senses to the sounds and smells around her. Ben's back, so hard yet so yielding, felt like a pillow she could rest on forever.

Snuggling closer to his backside, she fell into the first peaceful slumber she'd had in days.

Ben steered the carpet for hours, flying high, then low over the country of his birth. Throughout the ride he peered into the darkness, trying to recognize landmarks, familiar places he could remember from his youth. Instead, something malevolent about the land raised the hairs on the back of his neck. The monuments and great cities he expected to find were piles of rubble or ruined buildings with sandbag bunkers hiding large guns and cannons atop their roofs.

Ben knew their little carpet was invisible and safe from any danger, but the feeling of death and destruction still permeated his senses and made him sad. Could his homeland and the life he had once lived truly be gone?

He felt Maddie's arms relax as the tension left her, and he quickly changed their positions on the carpet. Turning himself around, he let his legs encase her from behind as he grabbed the back end of the carpet. In the blink of an eye their direction reversed and they were flying toward the western sky.

Maddie gave a gentle little snore, snuggling kitten-like into his chest, and he groaned. His reaction to her nearness was disconcerting and decidedly improper. Maddie was his master, not a houri to be toyed with or a woman of the streets. She was caring and warm and generous. She had released him from his prison and taken him into her home, something no other master had ever offered. And she was teaching him many wondrous things while asking nothing in return. He'd never had a master who had wanted nothing.

Strangely, Maddie seemed completely innocent of her handsome looks or the effect her lush body had on a man. The women from his past were well-versed in the wiles of seduction and conquest. They had preened and pranced, anointing their bodies with precious oils or henna rinses for their hair while vying with one another to attract the eye of the sultan or his son. And they were jealous and petty, spitting and clawing like alley cats in a sack over the baubles and trinkets they were given. Selfishly, they thought of no one but themselves.

Ben couldn't keep himself from bending his head and resting it atop Maddie's spiky hair. She smelled of gardenias and spring rain, a heady combination that entranced him. Ashmedai should have struck him down by now for his scandalous thoughts as well as his brazen actions. Where was the powerful jinn, that he would let such insolence go unpunished?

Ben thought back to the first days of his imprisonment so many years ago. If his father had not been dishonorable and broken his word to Ashmedai, he would never have been placed in such a horrible predicament. Ashmedai had humiliated his father by forcing the great sultan's son and heir to toady to a most heinous enemy, the braying caliph Almad-Fahdir. Though it was his father's fault Ben had been made a genie, it had almost killed him—if a genie could be killed—to know how much pain his enslavement had caused his father.

Almad-Fahdir had been forced to give Ben to his second master, a royal visier, after losing the bottle in a frivolous game of chance. The merchant had then given the bottle to a sultan of the highest order, who later traded it to an Egyptian merchant. By that time, Ben's father was dead, along with his sister, who had been taken captive. Ashmedai had stolen Amyri and had his revenge after all.

Ben settled his arms more closely under Maddie's generous breasts and felt himself grow as hard as a saber. He hadn't known the feeling of a woman in his arms, the touch of soft, yielding lips or a gentle hand, for a very long while. He told himself his reaction to Maddie was simply physical. She had been kind, treating him like a human being—a real man—for the first time in many years. It had been so long since his body had known a woman it had no choice but to respond.

How could someone like Trevor, that flea on the behind of an ass, have wronged her so? Hadn't he felt Maddie's gaze flowing over him like sweet, warm honey? Hadn't he touched her wondrous breasts or flaring hips and reached heaven? Didn't he know the generosity of Maddie's heart or the beauty of her soul? Obviously, this Trevor was a fool.

Ben steered the carpet over the Atlantic, heading into the night. New York City was his home now, and Maddie his master. Her word was law, no matter if he agreed or not. He had used his magic to take her away tonight because he had sensed her weariness, her sorrow for things he was just beginning to comprehend. In her heart, she had begged for a bit of rescue. After her fear subsided, she had seemed thrilled with the ride and hadn't admonished him for taking her away without her permission. He had pleased her.

But Maddie had said she was having a crisis, and he wondered what kind. Surely not the midlife crisis he had heard about on the TV. She was much too young for that.

He could only assume her worry was for her company, Winston Design. She and Max had seemed distracted today, whispering and talking in secret as they quietly inspected all corners of the plant. They had exchanged telling glances and raised brows over small comments that sounded mundane and pithy. Yes, it could only be the company.

Through a canopy of stars, the lights of Manhattan rose up to meet them. Ben swooped low, coasting to the top of the building that had become his new home. After a gentle clap, Maddie was in his arms and he was carrying her down the hall of their apartment and into her bedroom. He planned to lay her on the covers when she surprised him and opened her eyes.

"Are we home?" she murmured sleepily.

Ben's heart turned as he gazed into her dark-lashed golden eyes. Against his aroused body's wishes, he set her on her feet. "Yes, Mas . . . Maddie. We are home."

She smiled as she stared up at him and gave a little yawn. "That was very nice, but you shouldn't have done it. I thought I told you *no magic*. Aren't you supposed to obey me in all things?"

He almost raised a hand to touch her and thought better of it. If he touched her now, he might not be able to stop. "But you were wishing to get away from the city, away from the problems with your company and all your troubles. I only gave you what you wished for, Maddie, for just a short while."

She gave a little smile. "Oh, so that's how it is. You can read minds, too?"

He nodded, not sure he should tell her how special their relationship was becoming. "Only when there is a connection—a strong bond between genie and master—can the genie grant his master's heart's desire with a thought. We have it, I think, this unusual bond. Does it bother you that such a thing exists between us?"

Maddie sat on the edge of the bed and lay back, curling into her side, too exhausted to comprehend what he was saying. "I guess not, but I don't want to be hurt again, Ben. Please don't make me love you."

She gave a little moan of contentment and his heart, the one he had sworn never to listen to again after his imprisonment, began to thaw. He sighed and leaned over Maddie on the bed, letting one hand rest lightly on her soft-as-silk cheek.

Why would he harm her after she had been so good to him? How could she not want love? And how could she stop *him* from loving her? Damn Trevor for being an idiot and hurting her so. Damn all men for not seeing what a treasure they could have in Maddie Winston.

And damn Ashmedai for robbing him of the life of a normal man.

Seven

Maddie heard a buzzing noise from far away, like the sound of an angry bee trapped inside a glass jar. Dazed, she rolled over and checked her alarm. She'd overslept again, darn it. Who would be ringing her bell at eight on a weekday morning?

Swinging her legs over the edge of the mattress, she glanced down at her wrinkled clothes. Why in the world was she still wearing yesterday's jeans and sweater? She rubbed the sleep from her eyes as the previous night's events crept in through the fog.

Dinner at The Golden Lotus—with Ben. Racing like the wind, through the air and over Persia—with Ben. Coming home and being put to bed—by Ben . . .

Oh, lord. Had she really flown over Persia on a magic carpet? And afterward, had she let Ben calm her and put her to bed like a child? Maddie held her head in her hands. Had she spoken to him about love?

Shrill and persistent, the doorbell buzzed again, reminding her she had a visitor. Well, whoever was at her door at this ungodly hour would just have to wait long enough for her to pull herself together. She went to the bathroom and struggled out of her dirty clothes, then wrapped herself in a bathrobe, brushed her teeth, and washed her face.

Suddenly, she remembered Ben, asleep in the other room, and stumbled down the hall to the front door. She peered through the peep hole and found Trevor Edwards III, in all his manicured glory, glaring from the other side.

"Madeline? Madeline, I know you're in there. Open up and let me in."

Maddie's heart turned as she took in his golden-boy good looks and impeccable dress. She had sworn never to lay eyes on him again looking anything but her best, yet here she was in considerably less than passable condition. He'd take one look at her and thank his lucky stars a thousand times he'd married the petite and perfect Felice.

Running a hand over her rumpled hair, she smoothed down the cowlicks, straightened her robe and, taking a deep breath, undid the chain and locks. "Trevor," she said, opening the door to his fulminating glare. "What a surprise. Good morning."

With a greeting that sounded more like a grunt, Trevor barged past her and down the hall. Maddie's mind raced as she tried to get a handle on what could have made him so angry. He stopped in her living room and began to pace, running a hand over his tanned-to-perfection features.

"Don't be flip, Madeline. You know why I'm here."

"I do? I mean, I do not. What's gotten into you?"

"Why have you changed your telephone number? Afraid I'd find out what you did and call to read you the riot act? Or did you think Felice and I would be in Europe and we'd never see the latest copy of *Talk of the Town?*" He pulled the gossip rag out from under his jacket and smacked it down so hard it rattled the crystal dish filled with potpourri sitting in the middle of the coffee table.

Maddie furrowed her brow. She hadn't returned any of Greta's calls, so whatever he'd read couldn't possibly have anything to do with her—could it? Stubbornly, she refused to pick up the disgusting tabloid. Instead, she walked calmly into the kitchen, calling over her shoulder, "I'm making coffee, Trevor. If you can sit down and talk rationally, you're welcome to join me."

She filled the pot with water, poured it in the reservoir, and set the carafe in place. Always finicky about her coffee, she took out fresh, whole beans and measured them into the grinder, adding an extra spoonful for the stronger brew Ben liked.

Oh, my gosh! Ben! If Ben heard Trevor ranting, he would come out fighting, ready to turn him into a . . . a . . . cockroach or something.

Trevor walked into the kitchen behind her and pulled out a chair. The staccato of his drumming fingers, so impatient and superior-sounding on the table top, was as irritating as the ringing of her doorbell had been, gosh darn it.

Unbidden, a picture of Trevor's perfectly-coiffed head attached to the slimy little body of a cockroach appeared in her brain. Maddie choked back a smile. She turned to sit primly across from him at the table and held out her hand, determined not to laugh. "While we wait for the coffee to brew, let me have a look at what's got you so upset."

Trevor opened the paper to a well-creased page and slapped it in her hand. "This is what I'm talking about. Read the second paragraph of Greta Miller's column."

Maddie held the paper up and cleared her throat, ignoring the little ripple of foreboding racing through her mind. Whatever Greta the Gossipmonger had to say could not be good.

What little bird is flying fancy free, obviously unwounded by T.E. III's traitorous ways? WD's resilient company head must have known something was in the wind all along to have found a new love so quickly. Who was the darkly mysterious hunk she shared dinner with at The Golden Lotus last night, anyway? Could it be that F.L. actually did M.W. a favor when she stole the unfaithful playboy away? Only time will tell, but this columnist has three words of advice for the brave M.W.: You go, girl!

Maddie felt herself flush crimson. Greta had actually complimented her, calling her resilient, turning the little blurb into a cheer for the underdog. But why would she have done such a thing?

Who had seen her and Ben at the restaurant last night? Mrs. Cheng's establishment wasn't the in place for celebrity watching or table-hopping. It had to have been someone who was on her side and knew Felice had stolen Trevor from her. Maddie wanted to chuckle out loud at the furious look on Trevor's face, but knew it would not be appreciated.

"Trevor, believe me, I don't know a thing about this," she said truthfully. "I didn't even see anyone suspicious lurking in the restaurant last night."

Trevor narrowed his watery blue eyes. "Then you admit you were there with a man. For someone who kept telling me she didn't date much and led me on such a merry chase, it didn't take you long to replace me, did it, Madeline?"

Maddie's stomach quivered as all her insecurities came rushing to the surface. Trevor's barbs always went right to the heart of the matter. She squared her shoulders and set the paper down, looking him straight in the eye. "The man is a business acquaintance, Trevor. My personal assistant and nothing more. And may I remind you, it's no longer any of your concern whether I'm dating or not."

Before Trevor could formulate a nasty response, the doorbell buzzed again. Maddie stood quickly. Though perturbed her apartment had suddenly become Grand Central Station, it was still a relief to escape his unpleasant attitude. "Oops, there's the bell again. And me without my party clothes," she said with a sardonic little smile. "Please excuse me."

Maddie headed up the hall at a trot, grateful all the racket had yet to wake Ben. A loose cannon was exactly what she didn't need at this hour of the morning. She opened the door to face a flustered Mary Grace Mortenson, who was dressed in a short knit skirt and tight-fitting pink sweater.

"Golly, Maddie, I'm sorry it's so early, but you blew me off for lunch Monday, and I was busy yesterday. I tried calling here, but the phone company says you now have an unlisted number. How could you do that and not tell me?" Mary Grace complained, pushing her way inside.

Maddie closed the door and sagged against it. In all the business with Ben and the company, she had completely forgotten about her very loyal and caring best friend. "Lord, Mary Grace, I meant to call, but things have been so . . . so . . . why are you here, anyway?" she whispered, hoping to avoid a confrontation between Mary Grace and Trevor. And Ben and Trevor. And Ben and Mary Grace.

Oh, boy!

As quietly as possible, Maddie led her into the living room. At five-foot-five, with lustrous curling brown hair and bright green eyes, Mary Grace was a knockout. Maddie had never understood why the wealthy, with-it young woman from Manhattan had chosen her as a friend almost from their first days at school, but she had. Mary Grace had tried to steer her away from Trevor, but Maddie had been so starry-eyed with the idea that a man like Trevor Edwards could be interested in a woman like her, she hadn't listened. She would never toss Mary Grace's advice away again.

"What was so important it couldn't wait, Mary Grace? Trevor's here and I don't have time to—"

As soon as Maddie saw the look on Mary Grace's flushed face, she had an inkling of what had happened.

"What have you done?" she hissed, trying to keep her voice low.

Mary Grace sat on the sofa with a little plop and crossed a shapely leg, swinging her high-heel-clad foot. "I take it you've already seen Greta Miller's column?"

Hands on hips, Maddie nodded her head. Mary Grace had the decency to look guilty. "Mother and I had a late dinner last night at The Golden Lotus."

"You talked with Mrs. Cheng, didn't you?"

"Don't get in a snit. Mrs. Cheng naturally assumed I knew about your new fella. She started going on about how wonderful he was, and I just couldn't help myself. I called *Talk of the Town*. Lo and behold, Greta Miller was sitting at her desk like she'd been waiting for my call. I made excuses for why you hadn't returned her messages, told her you were a great fan of her work, and dropped a few hints. She must have stopped the presses to get my information added to her column so fast."

Before Maddie could answer, Trevor sauntered in, gripping a coffee cup in his white-knuckled hand. He gave Mary Grace a killing leer. "So it was you. I might have figured. Well, thanks to you, Felice has locked herself in the bathroom and won't come out. I hope you're both satisfied."

"Listen, Trevor—" Mary Grace began.

"Now, Trevor—" Maddie said at the same time.

"Good morning," came a deep voice from the living room doorway.

Mary Grace sat up straight and uncrossed her legs, her green eyes wide. "He-ell-oh-oh-oh," she said loudly, turning the simple two-syllable word into five.

Trevor spun on one foot, sloshing coffee down the front of his camel-hair blazer. Swiping at the liquid, he ran his unpleasant gaze over a barefoot, bare-chested Ben, who was dressed in jeans with the top snap unbuttoned.

Maddie began to sputter like a boiling tea kettle.

"Trevor, Ben. Ben, Mary Grace. Mary Grace, Trevor, this is Ben, my new assistant. He . . . I . . ." She ran a hand over her hair and swore the wayward spike had grown six inches since yesterday. "Oh, hell," she muttered, bracing for the worst.

Ben smiled, his teeth sparkling like a Crest toothpaste ad. Grasping Trevor's free hand, he pumped it like a piston. "How do you do? It's a pleasure to meet the man who let Maddie get away. I owe you quite a debt."

Mary Grace hooted loudly over Trevor's stuttering growl.

"Yes, well—" Pulling his hand from Ben's, Trevor ignored Mary Grace's laughter and gave Maddie a chilly glare. "Since when, Madeline, do your 'assistants' spend the night?"

"Since you tossed her over, you toad," Mary Grace managed through tears of laughter. "Trevor, you are such a boob."

Maddie groaned. She hated to admit it, but Mary Grace's greeting was right on the money. Ben looked sleep-sexy and thoroughly masculine. Sidling over to Ben, she whispered, "Go put on a shirt, would you please? And don't come out until I call you."

Ben raised a brow in amusement. Glancing over Maddie's shoulder, he smiled innocently at Mary Grace, and she jumped to her feet. "I could help, if you'd like. I happen to have excellent taste in clothes. Why, before Maddie met me she dressed like a total frump. Personally, I think you look great just the way you're dressed right now, but society dictates—"

Maddie grabbed her chatty friend by the elbow and dragged her down the hallway. "Out, out, out, Princess Foot in Mouth. I think you've done enough damage for one day. I will call you later and tell you the whole story. I promise."

She slammed the door on Mary Grace's grinning face

and raced back to her living room to find Trevor, alone and furious, pacing at the windows.

"This is great, Madeline. Just perfect. You couldn't wait three days before finding someone to replace me, could you?"

Maddie straightened to her full height. "Where's Ben, Trevor?"

"Where's Ben, Trevor," he mimicked. "Probably in your bedroom examining your bankbook. What other reason would a guy who looks like that have for sleeping with you?"

Too stunned by his hurtful statement to respond, Maddie watched as he slammed the mug on her coffee table and marched out the door.

Ben's hands clenched his bottle in a death grip. So that was Trevor, the man who had hurt Maddie. It had taken all of his self-control to not turn the idiot into a steaming pile of camel dung there on the living room carpet, but he had held his temper, as he'd promised. As soon as Maddie had escorted her lively little friend down the hall, he'd left the room, knowing if he spent any time alone with Trevor Edwards, he wouldn't be able to control his actions.

He heard the hurtful things Trevor shouted at Maddie, then the slamming of a door. The crust of ice around his heart melted a little more. From the sound of it, Trevor had thrown the worst of all insults. He had implied Maddie could only attract a man with her money. And Trevor had insulted him, as well, implying he was a paid companion!

Hah! If only he had known this Trevor centuries ago, he could have shown him who would attract more women. When he'd lived in his father's house there had been dozens—no, hundreds—of women throwing themselves at his feet. Women in the harem had fought for the right to initiate him in the art of pleasure and seduction. From the time he'd turned sixteen, every sultan and sheikh's daughter within caravan distance had been presented before him as a gift. He couldn't remember how many contracts of matrimony he had been offered and refused.

His father had complained over and over that as his son and heir Ben needed to choose a mate, a first wife who would give him strong sons and daughters, but he hadn't been enamored with any of them. All the women placed before him had been physically beautiful, many more so than Maddie, but not one had captured his heart. Unable to make a decision, he had waited until well past the usual age for a man to marry.

Then Ashmedai had come along and demanded Amyri's hand and hell had been unleashed on Ben's family. Ashmedai had turned him into a genie to pay for his father's deception. In the end, Amyri had been sold as a concubine, his father had died, and his family had lost its kingdom. Ashmedai had won.

Ben sighed, not wanting to remember the pain, the regret and misery he had suffered. He heard Maddie's soft footsteps in the bath, her quiet weeping, then the shower running. He turned his thoughts to what she had just endured. She had been embarrassed by his presence in her home this morning, ordering him to leave the room and dress, and he had done so.

Though it was becoming more difficult, he needed to remember to obey her in all things. Instead of doing her bidding, he had an overwhelming urge to protect her from the Trevors of the world, from herself and her silly notions of what a failure she thought she was. He didn't want to be her genie or her slave. He wanted to be her man.

He picked up the magazine on his dresser and thumbed through it until he found a handsome sweater of finest black cashmere. He had no coins or plastic cards to purchase his garments and he was not about to let Maddie continue to pay for his personal apparel. She had allowed him to conjure his clothing into existence yesterday. Surely he could do so today.

He clapped his hands once, then smiled at his reflection in the mirror and the fit of the sweater, letting the soft wool caress his body. Closing his eyes, he imagined Maddie doing the same to him with her long, gentle fingers. He heard the water turn off and quickly donned his shoes and socks. Maddie had made coffee. He would surprise her and make breakfast—without using magic.

"I have a license, Maddie. Why is it I cannot drive?" Ben questioned, standing at the door of her Jetta an hour later.

Maddie shook her head. "Try for a little patience. You're not ready to do certain things alone yet, though I'll admit breakfast was delicious. You did a great job. And that sweater is very . . . nice."

Never good at giving or accepting simple compliments, Maddie's cheeks warmed, but her minor discomfort was worth it when she saw Ben break out in a boyish grin.

"It was the least I could do to repay you for your kindness."

Maddie raised a brow. "Repay me for my kindness? Right. You were just pitying me for Trevor's nasty reaction to that gossip blurb. When I get my hands on Mary Grace, I'm going to kill her."

She opened her door and slid behind the wheel. Noting the shocked look in Ben's eyes, she realized he thought the worst of her remark. "Relax. That was a figure of speech, kind of like 'dying of embarrassment' or 'dressed to kill.' Mary Grace is my dearest friend in the world, and I would never hurt her."

Ben breathed a sigh of relief as he took his seat in the car. "I am happy to hear you say that, but what about Trevor? Do you still consider him a friend?"

Maddie started the engine and backed slowly out of her parking space, noticing the way Ben ogled the steering wheel and imitated her shifting action with his hands. Maybe this weekend she would take him to the company parking lot and let him drive the car around for a while. What could go wrong?

"Yes, he is. Friends sometimes say things to one another that they don't mean, Ben. I'm sure once Trevor realizes what he said, he'll come to his senses. His new wife was very upset with what she read in the papers. Being pictured as a man stealer isn't very easy for any woman to accept."

Ben adjusted his seat belt and leaned back, taking in the bustling Manhattan traffic. "And is it easy for you to hear you can only attract a man if he is paid for? Somehow I think not."

She sighed and headed uptown toward the entrance ramp to the George Washington Bridge. The idea Ben was becoming so perceptive he could sometimes read her mind or see into her heart and dissect her personal life was very disconcerting. "Trevor would never say that to anyone else. He was overcome with anger, that's all. Now let's move on to a more pleasant topic. What did you think of Mary Grace?"

Ben's eyes crinkled. "She is an interesting female, very independent, I think. How long have you known her?"

"Almost ten years. We went to school together. We weren't roommates, but we had the same class schedule. For some reason, Mary Grace decided to be my friend, though I never would have gravitated to her on my own."

"And why was that?" he asked, scanning the river below as the little car made its way through traffic.

It was a beautiful sunny day, with sailboats skimming the water like low-flying birds. Maddie checked her rearview mirror, put on her turn signal, and smoothly changed lanes, determined to set Ben a good example. "She was a high school cheerleader and a debutante—attended a real coming out ball and everything. The boys flocked to her at orientation, while I stood in awe. She didn't show a bit of interest in any of them. Instead of sitting with her adoring fans in the Student Union, she came and sat down next to me. A few months later, I asked her why, and she said I looked like I had potential. I never could figure out what she meant by that remark, but we've been friends ever since."

Ben turned in his seat, and she felt his heated gaze scour over her. "What were you like as a child, Maddie? When you said you were not like Mary Grace, what did you mean?"

She cruised through the mid-morning traffic, wondering how she could explain herself to a man who had spent the first part of his life with gorgeous harem girls and women who had nothing else to do except to look beautiful. How could she explain that she'd grown up gawky and plain, always being compared to her outgoing and attractive mother? Would he understand the feeling of guilt that coursed through her whenever she remembered her parents had been killed on the way to her college graduation?

Could he see how the company's failings were equal to failing them both?

"I was an only child, with no sisters or brothers or cousins to play with. My dad and grandparents were wrapped up in the company business, so I spent a lot of time with my mom. She was a social butterfly, a wonderful hostess. People used to call her the perfect woman."

Ben cleared his throat. "Perfect? There is no such thing, Maddie. In my day, the perfect woman would have been chained to a bed and have no voice."

She gasped.

He boomed out a laugh. "Now, Maddie—"

"Don't you 'now Maddie' me. That is a terrible, chauvinistic thing to say, you . . . you . . ." Suddenly, she realized he was teasing and she broke out in giggles. "All right, so you're joking. At least you'd better be. Talk like that could get you in a lot of trouble in this century."

"I realize that. Women's liberation, the N.O.W.—I have heard of it all. Your TV is a wondrous thing."

"And when have you had the time to watch television?"

He took such a long time adjusting his seat and seat belt before he answered Maddie feared he might have done something illegal or worse. "Ben? What haven't you told me?"

He cleared his throat, stumbling over the words. "At night, I am . . . restless. It seems I do not need much sleep. When it is late and I am lone . . . alone, I find myself wandering your apartment, so I turn on the television. Do you know one can buy a machine that slices, dices, juices, and seals the food in a plastic bag all at once, making it perfect for freezing? It will save you much money if you purchase such a device, or I could clap my hands and—"

Maddie took the final turn before the plant entrance and glanced his way. "Whatever you do, don't call into one of those shows and place an order with my credit card, understand? And no magic, either—except maybe what you did last night. Got that?"

His eyes grew bright. "Then it did not offend you, what I did? You enjoyed the ride on the carpet, seeing my country? It made you feel—less despondent, perhaps?"

Maddie thought for a second. The ride had been magic, pure and simple. Clean fresh air, exotic sights and smells, and a feeling of freedom she hadn't experienced in a long while rushed from the recesses of her mind and wrapped themselves around her. Though she could only remember her impressions of the ride, she knew instinctively Ben had been more than just the driver of the carpet. He had given her the memories, the feelings she needed to put her mind at ease and make her secure. Vaguely, she recalled his hard strong arms around her, holding her and keeping her safe, carrying her to her bed. . . .

Warmed by the recollection, she was about to tell him how much she appreciated his care. Unfortunately, the two police cars, red and blue lights flashing, which decorated Winston Design's parking lot momentarily distracted her.

Eight

Maddie jumped from the car and slammed the door in one frantic motion. Bolting into the foyer, she skittered in her tracks when she saw the keypad for their security system wide open, its wires and inner workings hanging askew. She gave a cursory glance at Paulette's vacant reception area and flew up the stairs, not waiting to see if Ben had followed.

At the top of the stairs, a uniformed patrolman stood guard over a man who was dusting the top of the railing for fingerprints. The patrolman held up a hand, halting her run. " 'Scuse me, miss, but this area is off limits. I can't allow you any further without clearance."

Maddie caught her breath as she peered over the officer's shoulder. "I'm Madeline Winston, one of the owners of the company." She felt Ben's presence behind her and tossed her head backward. "This is my personal assistant, Benjamin Able. What's happened? Where are Max Hefner and Paulette Jamison?"

Max entered the hall from his office, along with Paulette, another patrolman, and a tall man who looked like he had spent the night in his drab brown suit. "It's all right, officer," Max called out, walking swiftly toward her with the others at his heels. "Miss Winston is a principal in the company. Let her through."

"Max!" Maddie pushed past the first officer. "What's going on? Are you OK?"

Max nodded, his brown eyes weary. "I'm fine, but we have a new wrinkle in the works. When I arrived this morning, I found the front doors open and the security system out of whack. There were no other cars in the lot, so I went inside and called the police, then did a quick inspection of the building. I went directly to the assembly rooms and walked to the back where we keep the finished chips—"

Maddie's stomach plummeted. "What are you trying to say?"

He sighed, his shoulders slumping as he gave the rumpled man beside him a quick glance. "They're gone, Maddie. Our first run of replacement chips is gone. And whoever took them put two of the etching machines out of commission and contaminated the silicon."

Before she could phrase a response, the man in the suit cleared his throat and made a halfhearted effort at straightening his tie. "I'm Lieutenant Fox, Miss Winston. Can you come into Mr. Hefner's office to answer some questions?"

"I'll see how the guys in the plant are doing, if that's all right with you?" Paulette gave Maddie a commiserating smile. "Please feel free to call on me if you need any help, Lieutenant."

The detective nodded, then led the way into Max's office. Maddie, too stunned to ask further questions, followed. Despite the condition of his clothing, Lieutenant Fox immediately took control, his voice firm as he wrote in a small spiral notebook. "Miss Winston, Mr. Hefner has told us that besides Phil Dunlap and Miss Jamison, only he, yourself, and your uncle have keys to the building and the alarm codes. Is that correct?"

"Yes, sir," Maddie responded in a daze.

"He also told me there was a recent development, a forged memo that caused your company a serious time delay. Because of the memo, you stopped production and were now attempting to catch up. Is this also correct?"

Maddie grabbed her upper arms and rubbed hard. A little voice in her head told her she should have suspected more bad luck. After all, it was the only kind she'd experienced since she'd taken over the helm of Winston Design. She looked to Max, who nodded encouragement. "It is."

"I see. And have you any idea who might want Winston Design to fail at bringing its orders in on time?"

She paced to the windows and looked out onto the parking lot and the few cars it held. The company was small, always had been. Besides Max, Paulette, and Phil, there were only about twelve employees, including a day custodian, working at the plant in New Jersey. The corporate offices in Manhattan employed a full-time receptionist, a girl Friday, a part-time sales assistant, and a small cadre of accountants.

But each person was like family to her. Most of the assemblers had been hired by her father ten years before. Phil Dunlap had started with her grandfather when they were manufacturing electronic components over fifteen years ago. She knew all the employees' birthdays and the names of their spouses and children. She even knew who had kids in college or who was expecting a baby or grandchild.

They were her responsibility now. Without Winston Design—without the successfully completed contracts—they would be in the unemployment lines, something her father and grandfather would never have allowed to happen.

Unsure of who had leaked WD's problem to Butler & Maggio, Maddie decided to hold off telling them of Dominic Maggio's threatening phone call. "It could be any of a number of competitors, Lieutenant, even someone to whom we supply our product. We've had several buyout offers in the past year and managed to turn them all away."

Lieutenant Fox again scribbled in his notebook. "Well, until we have something concrete to go on, we have to look at this in the worst possible light—breaking and entering, burglary, and malicious damage of private property, to begin with. It will take my men another hour or so to fingerprint all your people here and take their statements. I have a few more questions for you and Mr. Hefner, if you don't mind."

He stepped back and stared up at Ben, who'd stuck like glue to Maddie the entire time. "Who is this gentleman, Miss Winston?"

Ignoring Max's pensive frown, Maddie moved protectively closer to Ben. "This is my personal assistant, Benjamin Able."

Ben held out his hand; the detective hesitated a hair too long before giving it a perfunctory shake. "Mr. Able. Might I see some identification?"

Maddie folded her arms and glared at Max. "Lieutenant, is that necessary? I can personally vouch for Mr. Able."

Ben, eager to produce his ID for the first time, proudly pulled out his wallet and handed Detective Fox his driver's license. "I also have a passport and Social Security card," he added.

Maddie held her breath while the lieutenant scanned the license, studied Ben for a second, then handed the ID back. "And where did you go last night after you left here with Miss Winston?"

Maddie gave a frustrated sigh. Max was waiting expectantly for Ben's answer, as was Detective Fox. He had obviously filled the detective in on his suspicions about Ben. At least he'd had the decency to not reveal Ben's suspected illegal status.

"I spent the evening with Miss Winston," Ben matter-of-factly replied.

"The entire evening?" came Fox's quick retort.

Maddie nodded her head imperceptibly and Ben said simply, "Yes, sir."

"Maddie," blurted Max, a look of astonishment in his eyes, "please don't tell me the man's living in your apartment."

"I can explain—"

Detective Fox had the decency to look embarrassed. "I'm just doing my job, Miss. Mr. Hefner led me to believe Mr. Able was a fairly new acquaintance. Are you sure he can be trusted?"

Her cheeks burning, Maddie looked Fox square in the eye. "I'm sure, Lieutenant. Now, let's discuss what you need to know to help you with the investigation."

Two more hours passed before Detective Fox finished his questioning, gathered his men, and left Winston Design. He had taken down Lucius Fulbright's address and phone number in the city and told Max and Maddie he would call on the man later in the day. He also advised them to hire security guards for twenty-four-hour surveillance. Both felt it would be like locking the barn door after the horse had been stolen, but they agreed.

"I've got this friend in Ft. Lee," confided Max, pacing behind his desk. "Runs a real professional organization. He'll have a man out here in an hour, no problem. I'll take care of it, Maddie girl."

Maddie smiled through a shimmer of tears. She wanted to be angry with Max over his treatment of Ben, but knew he was as upset as she was about what had happened. "I know you will, but I can't help thinking it's too late. How many chips did we lose?"

Max picked up a sheet of paper from his desk. After a

second, he ran a hand over his chin and sighed. "Ten thousand. It will be next to impossible to catch up now, Maddie. You know that, don't you?"

Ten thousand microchips. Twenty percent of the amount needed to fulfill their contracts. Worth about half a million dollars on the open market, the chips would have fit easily inside a large briefcase or gym bag.

Her gaze was drawn to Ben, who stood at the window as he listened to Max. What did he think about all this? Did he have any magical perceptions, any insightful wisdom on how to go about handling this current disaster?

"How long will it take to get us back in production mode?" she asked.

Max sat down in his worn desk chair and leaned back, tapping his chin with steepled fingers. "Forty-eight, maybe seventy-two hours. I might be able to locate the machinery I need by the end of today and have it couriered over; same with the silicon. But the machines are damned expensive. We'll have to put in an insurance claim and wait for payment. Meantime, I'll have Phil put the maintenance crew on alert and have them do as much as they can without the proper equipment."

"Can we rent more machines?"

Max raised a bushy brow. "We might be able to fit one more inside the assembly room, but that means we'll need extra men to maintain it. I'd have to check it out. You want us to run twenty-four-seven on this?"

Maddie nodded. "I don't see how else we can make it, do you? Even if the cost breaks us, we have a reputation to uphold. I have a small stock portfolio and a trust fund I can liquidate to carry us through. We have to do something."

"I can't let you do that. You sank enough of your own money into the company last year," Max reminded her. "There must be another way."

Ben turned to them, his ocean blue eyes insightful.

Maddie hadn't asked, but he'd felt her thinking there was another way, if he was taught what he needed to know. "Maddie, didn't you want Max to show me your chip today and explain to me how it worked?"

Before she could give Ben a grateful smile, Max huffed out an indignant protest. "I don't think that's such a good idea. I really don't have the time, what with all the ordering I'll need to do."

"Paulette is perfectly capable of making the calls. You just have to set them up."

"Now, Maddie."

"Please, Max. Show Ben the chip and make him understand how it works—for me?"

Max gave a grumbled curse, and she *tsked*. "Now, now. It'll take forty-eight hours to get us back up and running, right? At least you'll have something to do while we're waiting. Come on, be a sport."

Maddie waited while Max struggled with his conscience. She knew he was only doing his job. He had made a promise to her grandfather before William Winston had died five years ago, giving his word he would look after Sylvia and Maddie like family, as well as guide the company to the best of his ability. She was asking a lot from Max, and she knew it.

Max took his time answering. He ran a hand through his unruly hair as he sized Ben up with a baleful glare. Finally, he seemed to come to a decision. "Ben, could you leave Maddie and me alone for a while?"

Ben kept his eyes on Maddie while he answered. "I will look for Paulette. I have some questions from yesterday, some things that are not yet clear about computers and a few of the programs. You will find me at her desk when you need me."

Maddie waited while Max followed Ben to the door and closed it firmly. She could tell by the determined look on his face what was on his mind.

"Maddie, I know you feel betrayed by Trevor. I know the sneaky bastard hurt you. But do you really think it's wise to become involved so quickly with a virtual stranger? This Ben isn't even an American citizen, for gosh sake. He could be working for the enemy, playing on your vulnerability to get close to the situation. What do you really know about him?"

She wanted to tell Max the truth so badly her insides hurt, but she couldn't betray Ben. And even if she told Max how she and Ben had *really* found one another, there was no chance he would believe her. Heck, Maddie wouldn't believe *herself* if she didn't know it to be true.

No, the best solution was to let everyone go on believing she'd met Ben by chance and trusted him for no reason other than gut instinct. The one thing that didn't sit well was the fact that Max thought she and Ben were sleeping together.

"I know you think I'm crazy bringing Ben into the business like this, giving him a job and showing him our company's inner workings, and maybe I am a little nuts. I'll admit Trevor hurt me. Worse, he took away what little self-esteem I'd managed to build up over the past several years. But Daddy and Grandpa Will trusted me enough to leave the running of Winston Design in my hands. I'm aware that up until now I haven't done such a brilliant job, but I promise you, I'm going to find out who's behind all the dirty tricks and get us back on our feet again."

Max rubbed a hand over his balding head, thoroughly mussing the meager amount of hair he had left. "I know you want to, Maddie, but good intentions aren't always enough. And I still don't know why you seem so keen on this Ben character. I guess he's handsome enough. You women seem to go for those dark, mysterious types, but I never thought physical beauty was something you put much stock in."

Maddie walked to Max and gave him a hug, as much

for herself as for the older man. "I've decided to simply trust my feelings where Ben is concerned, Max, and it has nothing to do with his looks. I can tell you one thing: We are not sleeping together. I did take him in, but he's using the guest bedroom. Our arrangement is strictly professional, and it's going to stay that way. I have no intention of becoming personally involved with him. It's just that something inside me says he's basically a good person. Can we leave it at that for a while?"

Max gave her a reluctant smile. "If you're so sure of him, I can try. Just promise me one thing. After what Trevor did to you, please don't rebound into the arms of another creep bent on taking advantage of your generosity or good nature. Listen to your head before your heart. Think you can do that?"

She sighed and walked to the phone at the corner of his cluttered desk. If only Max knew how different Ben really was, he'd never even hint at their having any kind of relationship. But Max didn't know—could never know—the truth about Ben. He just needed to trust Ben enough to explain the microchip production process to him. She and Ben could take care of the rest.

"I promise. Now I'll phone Gram to tell her what happened. She needs to be informed before Uncle Lucius gets a visit from Detective Fox and has the chance to call and upset her. Think you can find Ben and start instructing him on our product while I set Sylvia straight?"

Max gave her a wink. "All right, I'll do it. But you tell Sylvia for me everything will be fine. We may be down, but we're not out—not by a long shot. And certainly not if I have anything to say about it."

Ben walked slowly up the stairs, still processing all he had learned from Max in the last three hours. Computers were truly amazing inventions, their concept alone mind-boggling. He remembered how elated the overseer of his father's counting house had been when he'd learned the use of an abacus for his tallies, bragging of his newfound prowess with numbers and thanking the caravan leader who had brought the wonderful invention to his attention. If the man had seen an adding machine or a computer, he would have been so overjoyed he might have wept.

Of course, no one in his father's house would have believed such a thing could exist, even if they had seen it with their own eyes. Looking back on what his tutors had taught him, Ben now realized he had lived in a limited world where most people had more imagination than vision. Compared to the world of today, at least in the United States of America, they had been barbarians.

He heard the tinkle of Maddie's laughter and stopped on the landing. She sounded so happy, even after what had occurred this morning, that he hated to interrupt her. He knew it was wrong to listen at the door, but he wanted to enjoy for just a bit longer the carefree sound of her voice.

"God, Mary Grace, you are bad. I'm telling you, Ben and I are just friends. Why won't you believe me?"

Ben heard his name and waited, intrigued two women would find him interesting enough to discuss.

"All right, you can come over for dinner tonight. I'll let you talk to him yourself. How's that?"

Maddie sounded hesitant, though he knew Mary Grace was her best friend. Was she ashamed of him again, as she had been this morning when he'd met the scurrilous Trevor?

"Mary Grace, I do not want a makeover. Keep that waxer and those cosmetics you like to trowel on your face away from me, you hear? I do not want to experiment tonight."

Maddie giggled like a child at whatever Mary Grace said in return, causing Ben to smile as well. For all her efficiency and business sense, it was good to know Maddie could be as silly as most women when they gossiped together.

"I know you've been waiting ten years to get near me with a tube of lipstick. Just forget it." Maddie huffed.

Seconds passed, then Maddie gave an exasperated sigh. "Lordy, you are persistent. OK, OK, OK. Just promise me you won't go overboard. And if I don't like the way I look, the deal's off. Dinner's at seven, so be on time."

Maddie hung up the phone, and Ben peeked around the corner. She had returned to Max's computer and was concentrating on a colorful chart displayed on the screen. She had slipped back quickly into her businesswoman persona, firmly erecting around her the wall of professionalism she was so proud of.

He had sensed this morning, during the police interview, that Maddie felt there was something unacceptable about his staying in her apartment, but he hadn't been able to discern why. In many of the movies he'd watched on the television, men and women of this century cohabitated. Couples who were engaged to be married lived together first and thought it an agreeable arrangement. Most colleges had coed dorms. Some gyms and fitness centers shared steam rooms and saunas, as well. The only place it was still unacceptable for men and women to commingle seemed to be the rest rooms of the world. And that, too, would probably change in the near future.

Why, then, did Maddie find it so embarrassing to have the police and Max think they were living together?

Ben sauntered into the room as if he had just arrived. "Maddie. I am through for the day. Max says he has taught me all he knows. Now it is up to me to absorb and retain. How does that sound to you?"

Her expression cheerful, Maddie turned to greet him, and he silently thanked Mary Grace for keeping her from becoming saddened over the break-in and robbery.

She grinned up at him. "It sounds like he was describing a roll of paper towels. If you've absorbed and retained, how does he propose we extract the information? By wringing your neck?"

He lifted a hand and rubbed his nape in mock pain. "I do not think so. When the time comes, I will be able to output the data by myself." Hoping that he'd read her thoughts correctly, he asked, "Have you a plan for using what I have learned?"

Maddie leaned back in the desk chair, studying the chart on the computer screen. "It would be so easy to have you clap your hands and create fifty thousand microchips. There's just one tiny problem—how do we explain them to Max? He keeps a daily count on production, as do Phil and Paulette. They know down to the last diode how many chips were produced in each run. We have to think of some way to infiltrate the chips into the count without it looking like anything unusual happened."

Ben's mind began to spin. His youth had been full of the supernatural. Soothsayers and magicians abounded in stories and folklore, even everyday life. The people of his time chalked up many of the unpredictable things that occurred to any number of superstitious or unnatural causes. When Ashmedai had appeared in his life, he'd known for certain another world existed outside of the one in which normal people lived. With all the wonders of the twenty-first century, had people lost whimsy? The desire to believe in a higher power?

"Couldn't we just let it happen, Maddie? Make the chips appear and let Max simply not understand how production could have doubled? Would it really be such an unusual thing?"

Maddie tapped the desk blotter with a pen, her brow furrowed. "With Max, there is no such thing as unexplainable. He would work and fuss and worry himself into the grave trying to find a reason for how those chips magically appeared. Max is a true man of science. It would be heartless to give him a puzzle he couldn't possibly hope to solve."

Ben walked to her side of the desk and sat on the edge, folding his arms across his chest. The world had changed greatly since his imprisonment, it seemed. "In my time, many men of science called themselves wizards, yet their belief in things unworldly was as strong as an uneducated peasant's. Besides studying the stars or inventing new theories on bizarre phenomena, they spent their entire lives trying to turn various metals into gold or concoct potions that would harden into precious gems. It did not bother them when they could not find the answers. They simply continued to try. And when something supernatural occurred, it caused a stir, but it was accepted."

Maddie gave an indelicate snort. "And in your time they still thought the sun revolved around the earth and chants and spells cured deadly diseases. They were wrong, Ben. Today, no man of science would accept those foolish notions. Very little of what goes on in the world nowadays is taken at face value. People have become skeptical of everything, no matter how insignificant."

"Ah, but what about God, Maddie? Surely they believe in God. And He can create many miracles, can He not?"

Maddie's amber eyes turned cool and distant. She seemed to search her soul before she spoke. "The matter of God's existence is still up for discussion. Too many bad things happen to good people for them to believe a kind and forgiving supreme being is out there watching over us. Today's scientists can talk for hours against the idea of God, Ben. Don't get me started."

He raised a brow, surprised by her statement. Maddie, the most puzzling woman he'd ever met, did not believe in God? This could not be. "How, then, would you explain *me,* Maddie? I have tried for centuries to come up with a reason for why I am imprisoned. I must have done something evil in a past life to have angered Him so. God wanted me punished for the sins of my . . . my sins, and my penance is to live out my days in the bottle, doing the bidding of others. It is the only reasonable answer, I think."

Maddie's face had hardened into a frown. "So why can't you explain it to me? Why can't you tell me how you came to be in the bottle? You couldn't have simply awakened one morning and found yourself inside it. What did you do to so anger your God that He put you in there?"

Ben realized in his zeal to convert Maddie to his way of thinking, he had revealed much more than he should have about his situation. Ashmedai had not been a god, but a devil sent to torment his family. He had been warned that to speak aloud the truth about the jinn was grounds for eternal damnation, and eternal damnation would take him away from Maddie forever—a fate, he suddenly decided, much worse than death.

He hung his head in contrition, hoping she would feel sorry for him and not order him to tell. If she did, he would have to comply. She was his master, after all. "Please, Mas . . . Maddie, do not make me say the words aloud. It is too painful and will cause me great sorrow."

She *tsked* at his miserable expression, and Ben knew he had won a reprieve.

"Oh, all right," she said, "can the sad-sack routine. I won't make you tell if you don't want to. It's time to go home. I promised Mary Grace she could come over for dinner, so we need to stop at the store for supplies. After she leaves, we'll put on our thinking caps and figure out a way to get those chips into the daily count without arousing suspicion. OK?"

"You will take me to one of your marketplaces? I have been wondering what the inside of those bazaars would be like. Thank you, Maddie. You are very good to me."

She stood and gave him a bright smile, her honeyed

eyes again bathing him in their warmth. "Lord, Ben, you are a trip. Come on, let's get going."

Lucius Fulbright drummed his fingers on his immaculate desk blotter, a smile more like a leer marring his patrician face. He had just finished a very heavy interview with a Lieutenant Fox from Englewood Heights, New Jersey, and the experience had left him elated. He didn't like accounting for his whereabouts any more than the next man, but his alibi for last night had been carefully documented in order to keep suspicion from him.

The detective had, of course, believed every word. Why wouldn't he? Lucius had made sure he'd been noticed last night when he'd arrived home from the office. He'd stopped and had a friendly chat with the doorman, informing him that his BMW was badly in need of a tune-up and almost undriveable. Then he'd made a point of calling the super in his building at eleven to complain about the noise the tenants in the apartment above were making. To all with whom he had spoken, he had given the impression of a man with plans for nothing more than staying inside and going to bed.

No one had seen him slip down to the basement to let himself out the back door and into the alley. From there, it had been simple enough to walk to the auto rental office a few blocks away and pick up a car. He had returned three hours later and entered the apartment building the same way he had left. The microchips were stashed in an ordinary suitcase in the farthest corner of his closet. Unless someone produced a search warrant, there they would stay until he had time to destroy them, or find a way to use them to his advantage.

The phone rang and Lucius jumped, startled from his daydream. When he saw that the call had come in on his private line, he became instantly alert. "Fulbright here."

"How ya doing, Fulbright? Taking care of business, I hope?" came the guttural voice on the other end of the line.

Lucius sucked in a disbelieving breath. How could the mere sound of the man's harsh voice bring the scent of stale cigars and expensive whiskey seeping through the line? "Things are running quite smoothly at the moment. You might read about it in tomorrow's papers, if you look carefully," he said as he exhaled.

The man on the phone gave a derisive chuckle. "Fuck reading about your little midnight escapade in the *Daily News,* Fulbright. I never believe anything I read in newspapers. I have the preliminary police report on my desk as we speak."

Lucius bit back a gasp. Lieutenant Fox had just left his office and was probably hitting momentous rush hour traffic. How could the report, even in its earliest stages, have already reached another's desk?

"You there, Fulbright?" demanded the voice.

"Yes. I hope you're pleased with the results."

"Yeah, yeah, we'll see. That bossy niece of yours is a little too resourceful for my taste. Should of married that hoity-toity rich kid, stayed home, and had babies, if you ask me. And you'd better keep an eye on the old guy, too. You caught the ball on the fifty-yard line. Now run with it. Understand?"

Lucius wiped a sweaty palm on his trousers, stammering, "Of course we will—I will. You can count on it."

"That's what I like to hear, Fulbright, a man who's in control. I'll check in later."

The line went dead and Lucius took a deep breath, shuddering at the thought of what might happen if he failed to score a touchdown.

Nine

"I don't believe you." Mary Grace tapped her fingers against her folded forearms as she braced herself against Maddie's overflowing kitchen counter. "This is a secured building. No guy who looks like Ben would be allowed to lurk in the hallways asking strangers for a job. Why is it I get the feeling there's a whole lot more to this story than what you're telling me?"

Maddie swiped at a wayward spike of hair, sighing at Mary Grace's logic. She'd known she was in trouble the second she started babbling her lame explanation about how she'd met Ben. When she argued with Mary Grace, Maddie knew she had about as much chance of winning as a Chihuahua tossed into the ring with a pit bull. Mary Grace was as tenacious as she was clever, and Maddie had never been a worthy opponent. She'd always been too open to fool her best friend for long.

Instead of answering directly, she bent at the waist and continued loading dirty dishes into the dishwasher while Mary Grace rambled aloud a few moments longer.

"He seems clever, but naive at the same time, if you know what I mean," Mary Grace said with the authority of a woman who had dated, dissected, and discarded hundreds of men. "A very lethal combination. And when he looks at you with those Caribbean blue eyes—good Lord, how do you resist?"

Maddie stacked silverware and arranged plates in the racks, resigned to letting Mary Grace's observations run their course. If she were lucky, the woman would exhaust herself and fall asleep standing up before she demanded answers Maddie wasn't able to give.

"Maddie. Maddie, are you listening to me? Tell me again what Ben said when you first met?"

Your wish is my command? Yeah, right.

Maddie stood up and gave her best deer-caught-in-the-headlights look, the memory of her first meeting with Ben still vividly etched in her mind. The explanation of how they had found one another sounded flimsy and unbelievable—and she had *been* there. No way would Mary Grace buy the incredible story, even if it *was* the truth.

"He asked if I knew of any companies in Manhattan looking for office help. What's so strange about that?"

As if disgusted at being forced to explain the theory of relativity to a three year old, Mary Grace snorted loudly. "Because it's not the usual hallway pick-up line, kiddo. And Ben doesn't look the type to try something so stupid." She raised a penciled brow. "OK, I'll let the way you met slide for now. Just explain how he talked you into hiring him."

Maddie flipped the switch on her disposal, watching as bits of their dinner—lettuce and tomato salad, asparagus, and pasta covered in a creamy Parmesan pesto sauce—swirled down the drain. She cringed when the din of the disposal didn't deter Mary Grace from further probing.

"Better yet, what made you decide to take him into your home? If there's nothing sexual going on, why is he here?" Mary Grace shouted over the racket.

Maddie rubbed at the bridge of her nose, hoping to forestall the headache she felt positive was waiting to explode behind her eyes. Pit bull or no, she had to put an

end to Mary Grace's nosy tirade. "I'm paying him," she
said aloud, remembering Trevor's nasty insinuation from
earlier this morning. If he thought it was believable,
maybe Mary Grace would, too.

Silence, blessed silence for a full ten seconds, gave
Maddie the time to gather her wits. Her outrageous an-
nouncement had taken the wind out of her friend's bil-
lowing sails and allowed Maddie time to finish concocting
a story.

"You're what?" came the flat-as-a-pancake question.

"I said 'I'm paying him,' " Maddie repeated, waiting
for the ridiculous words to sink in. "You were right about
the job story. I didn't find Ben in the building. I found
him on the beach in Key West. Actually, the idea was
Sylvia's. She put the bug in my ear that Trevor needed a
dose of his own medicine. I decided I wasn't going to
take what he did to me lying down, so I found someone
to make him jealous. All the better if I want people to
think I was the one who tossed him over for a guy like
Ben, don't you think? And Ben's so good looking he even
has you drooling. He made Trevor furious this morning—
exactly the reaction I'd hoped for."

Mary Grace shook her head, a look of admiration suddenly shining in her bright green eyes. "I knew you had
potential, but—wow, even I, in all my scheming glory,
wouldn't have had the balls to try that one. So what's it
been like? What's *he* like?"

Maddie took a bag of coffee beans from the freezer
and carried it to the grinder, her head spinning. Instead
of laying Mary Grace's questions to rest, the story had
only lighted a new fire under her relentless friend. She
measured the beans and let the noise of the grinder buy
her a few more seconds. How could she ever describe
what Ben was really like?

He's a time-traveling genie from hundreds of years ago.

He lives in a bottle and he takes me on magic carpet rides through the desert. He makes me feel special.

Maddie filled the carafe and poured the water into the coffeemaker. Acting as if she hadn't heard Mary Grace's last question, she took down mugs and arranged them on a wicker tray alongside a pitcher of milk, bowl of sugar, and plate of chocolate-chip-studded cannolis she'd purchased at the Italian bakery they'd shopped in earlier.

"Maad-ee," Mary Grace persisted. "You're avoiding my question."

Her hands on her hips, Maddie turned. "It's a business arrangement, plain and simple. When Ben told me he was an out-of-work actor and a part-time body builder, I laid out the proposition and he said yes. He's promised to keep me company, act attentive, and, if necessary, carry out the duties of a bodyguard. I told you about the robbery at the plant. Now I have live-in protection, at least for a short while."

Maddie picked up the tray and headed for the living room, but not before Mary Grace laid a hand on her shoulder. "OK. At least that story is one level more plausible than the first fairy tale you tried to slip by me. And, sadly enough, I believe it when you say the arrangement is strictly business."

"What do you mean, 'sadly enough'?" Maddie hissed, knowing Ben was only a few feet away.

Mary Grace smiled through curvy lips. "Because I have a gut feeling Benjamin Able is the kind of man who could take a woman to the stars and back again before she knew what hit her. It's about time you had someone so invigorating in your life, Maddie Winston. I just hope you're smart enough to realize it."

Hours later, Maddie found herself staring in amazement at a face she barely recognized. Exhausted from fielding

Mary Grace's endless questions, she had finally managed to escort her friend out the front door with only a minor promise of lunch sometime over the weekend. Though it was close to midnight, she couldn't help but be drawn back to the place where she and Mary Grace had spent most of the night—the bathroom.

Still in shock, Maddie stared at the lightly freckled face she saw in the mirror. Her eyes, the ones she'd always thought of as small and muddy brown, stared back sherry-colored and sparkling through dark, curling lashes. The brows above them were thinner and slightly arched, giving her eyes a wide open and innocent look. A soft apricot blush suffused her cheeks, while a toffee-hued stain softened her lips, contouring her mouth into an attractive wash of color.

The total effect made her whole face more—dare she say the word?—*pretty.*

The new look had Maddie reeling. Her mother had been a beautiful woman, with hair like a blazing sunset and eyes the color of molten copper. Catherine Winston hadn't worn cosmetics and Maddie's father had always remarked she didn't need to. Because he thought his wife beautiful without the fancy over-the-counter products with which most women felt it necessary to adorn themselves, he had frowned on Maddie's doing the same.

Maddie had gone through high school honoring his wishes, a plain-Jane who concentrated instead on the things she felt would make him proud. She'd been captain of the debate team, a math club officer, and a National Honor Society member by her junior year. By the time she'd been accepted to Harvard, her weight outmatched her IQ by about forty points and she wore the "nerd" label like a banner. All of Mary Grace's cajoling hadn't been able to convince her to use cosmetics—until tonight.

Maybe it had been Trevor's cruel and taunting words, intimating she couldn't get a man without her family's money. Maybe it had been the thought that even dear, sweet Max sounded as if he'd never believe a man who looked like Ben would want someone like her. And maybe it had been her own insecurities rising to the surface and crying out to set her free, but whatever had made her change her mind, Maddie was happy she had.

She felt like a whole new person. Would anyone notice the new and improved Maddie? Would Ben like the way her eyes took over her face and said "look at me"? Would Paulette snicker while Max grilled her on why she had felt the need to enhance herself physically? Would her Uncle Lucius tell her she was embarrassing him and the company by trying to look like someone she was not—the ever-perfect Catherine?

Hesitantly, she slipped out of the bathroom and down the hall. The sound of Ben's laughter rang out and she smiled. He had been the ideal male dinner companion, attentive to her, polite to Mary Grace, and appropriately innocent whenever Mary Grace asked him one of her very pointed and probing questions. He had teased, charmed, and flirted his way through the evening, causing her and Mary Grace to giggle like a pair of lovesick teenagers, something they hadn't done with a man since college.

Come to think of it, she couldn't remember the last time either of them had acted like lovesick teenagers. She had never found the nerve to flirt, even with Mary Grace by her side to give her courage, and Mary Grace rarely giggled. She purred or taunted or chuckled huskily, but not once had Maddie ever heard her giggle as she had tonight.

Ben had woven a spell of calm and relaxation over them, making them feel and act like young, carefree girls without a problem in the world.

Engrossed in a nature film, Ben took no notice when Maddie slipped into the living room, picked up the wicker tray, and carried the remains of their dessert into the kitchen. After starting the dishwasher, she made ready to march back into the room and discuss the microchip problem, only to find Ben propped against the doorjamb, eying her intently. Startled, she jumped.

He gave her a lethal grin. "Sorry. I didn't mean to frighten you."

Heat crept into her cheeks and she grew annoyed with herself. She was a grown woman, the head of a company, living alone in New York City. She'd graduated with honors from a prestigious university, negotiated contracts for millions of dollars, and made executive decisions every day. Yet this man, a man she still had a hard time admitting came from a magic bottle, had the ability to make her twitter and stumble like a little girl.

"You didn't. Frighten me, I mean. I was just coming to see you. We need to address that small problem about the chips and I thought now might be a good time."

Ben fixed his laser blue eyes on hers and pushed away from the door. "Did you know the African elephant mates for life, Maddie? As soon as the males and females mature into adulthood, they find a partner. If that partner dies they mourn as if they were human, living out their days alone until they, too, pass away. Isn't that a sad state of being?"

She clutched at the back of a kitchen chair, not sure she was ready to discuss mating of any kind with Benjamin Able. His smile, his eyes, his formidable presence enveloped her.

She sat down with a thud. "Yes, that's quite . . . sad. But right now we have a more pressing problem. Have you come up with a way we can slip the microchips into our current production line?"

Ben pulled out a chair and faced her across the table, his eyes crinkling at the corners. "I liked your friend Mary Grace. When will she eat with us again?"

"Oh, Mary Grace usually finds a way to see me once

or twice a week. I get so absorbed in the company, nego-
tiating contracts or working with Max, that sometimes
she's my only link to the outside world."

He raised a brow. "And what do you do when you are
together? You hid away in your bedroom for hours tonight.
It was all I could do to not follow, but I sensed the two
of you wanted to be alone. Was I right?"

Maddie fussed with her hair, patting at the spiky mass
as she blurted out an answer. "We had things to do. Girl
things."

Ben's gaze ran over her face and she stopped fussing,
suddenly self-conscious.

"You look different, Maddie."

She huffed out a breath, positive she looked like a two-
dollar hooker. "Is it too much?"

He narrowed his gaze. "Too much?"

"You know." She brushed her cheeks with her fingers.
"This stuff on my face and eyes. I look stupid, right? I
knew it! Mary Grace and her bright ideas. I'll—"

Without warning, Ben reached out and ran a finger over
her cheek. She sat motionless as his fingertip slid to her
lips, softly tracing their outline.

"I don't usually wear this stuff," she muttered, unable
to pull away from his seeking touch.

Ben nodded. "I noticed, and no, it is not too much. The
women of the harem used kohl or colored berries to enhance their beauty much more dramatically than what you
have done. It is very . . . attractive. But I thought you
beautiful before—without it."

Beautiful? Maddie's heart gave a little *tah-thump*. How
could one word and the simple touch of a man's finger
distress her so? She felt as if she had run a marathon,
climbed a mountain, or taken another magic carpet ride.
Numb with feeling, she struggled to ask a question.
"What did the women of your harem look like?"

He smiled and drew his hand away. "Most were young

and lovely. The sultan's four allowed wives were older, of course. It was my father's harem and I a mere visitor. I never took much notice until I began to grow to manhood."

"What about your mother? Wasn't she jealous of the other women?"

Ben's eyes filled with sadness. "My mother was a captive from a faraway land. She was sophisticated and beautiful, with blue eyes and yellow hair. She died when I was seven. My father waited to take his other women to bed until she had been dead one year—a most unusual thing for a sultan."

Maddie picked up a napkin from the holder and began to shred in earnest. "But you would have been sultan someday, right? Then the women would have been yours. Isn't that so?"

He leaned back in his chair, a line of concentration rising between his black brows. Maddie realized she was again asking questions he didn't want to answer, but Ben was so secretive about his past life, about anything personal, she just had to know. His eyes darkened to midnight and she waited, refusing to let him put her off a second time.

"If I had become sultan, the women would have been my responsibility, yes, but I would not have used them. Because they'd belonged to my father, I would have seen them happy—perhaps given them their freedom or set them up in favorable marriages with merchants once I was in charge. As sultan, I would have had the right to pick my own harem."

The idea sounded so outrageous Maddie wanted to scream. To her, a harem signified the forced imprisonment and sexual slavery of innocent women—women who had been sold or stolen away from their families and had lost their individual rights. A totally distasteful thought.

Angry that Ben would partake of such a despicable act,

she asked through clenched teeth, "And these women you would have chosen, what would they have been like?"

Ben sat straighter in his chair. Unaware of her distress, he seemed almost eager to explain some of the customs of his past. "All would have been virgins, though well-trained in the art of pleasing a man. In my religion, a man could have up to four wives, provided he could keep all of them equally housed and fed and satisfied in bed. If he could afford it, he was also allowed to own an infinite number of concubines. It was the law."

Maddie folded her arms. *Well-trained virgins.* She'd have been out of the running before the game even started. And to think that, instead of getting an education, young girls would be taught the art of seduction, merely to please a man. Intent on letting him know her true feelings on the matter, she glared. "Well, it was a stupid law. A law that demoralized women and turned them into objects instead of human beings. It's morally wrong to own people, Ben."

His face filled with confusion. "The women were well cared for, Maddie. They wanted for nothing. Have you ever been in a harem? Do you know what goes on inside them?"

"Of course not." She sputtered, then took a deep breath. "And I don't think I—"

Smiling broadly, Ben winked one bright blue eye and clapped his hands. Suddenly, the sharp, tangy scent of oranges mixed with the perfume of some exotic flower and permeated Maddie's senses. The air in the kitchen swirled into a mist of soft, pale color as strange and seductive music sounded in the night.

Maddie looked down and found she was no longer seated in a hard-backed kitchen chair, but reclining on a low, tufted sofa. The realization that Ben lay behind her, his formidable body curled intimately against hers, filled her with little currents of electricity and heightened her awareness of the scene playing out around her.

"Watch, Maddie, and learn," Ben whispered, his deep voice tickling the back of her ear.

Maddie opened her eyes to the unfamiliar sights and sounds, taking in a living picture she imagined might have come straight from one of Scheherazade's mythical tales of wonder. It was broad daylight, and they were in an enormous marble-floored room filled with a variety of potted plants and towering trees. The room's dramatically painted and domed ceiling arched upward some thirty feet, several of its huge sections open to let in the sun and fresh air along with the aromas of frangipani, jasmine, and dry desert air.

Women of all shapes and sizes filled the room, many reclining on sofas while they ate from golden trays or drank from jewel-encrusted goblets. Some were dressed in sheer silks and colorful satins decorated with pearls or other precious gems and sat in clusters, giggling and whispering or playing games. A few swam naked in a pool of pale green water set in the center of the white marble floor. All seemed content and happy with their luxurious way of life.

"Where are we?" she managed to mutter, afraid to take her eyes off of the women and their surroundings.

"A harem," Ben said with a chuckle. "Do you like what you see?"

Before Maddie could answer, the double doors at the far end of the room were flung open. The women grew silent. Several stood, intent on getting a better view of the doorway.

The sound of tinkling bells and clanging cymbals filled the air, along with the pulsing beat of tambourines and the soft strumming of strings. A group of children, led by two huge black men wearing turbans, raced into the room juggling balls and tossing hoops, followed by a dozen musicians playing various instruments.

The women of the harem applauded loudly as the musicians paraded inside and circled the bathing pool. They wore jackets and pants in brightly beaded materials of red and yellow, along with tassel-trimmed hats. One of the men playing a tambourine had a small monkey sitting on his shoulder, dressed in identical clothing and carrying its own set of tiny cymbals.

Except for the eunuchs, all of the men wore blindfolds, but Maddie could tell the impediments didn't dampen their enthusiasm for the task at hand. "Why are their eyes covered?" she asked, sitting upright to take in the scene.

"It is forbidden for any man except the sultan, his immediate family, or the imperial eunuchs to view the women of the harem. If any of the musicians were to behold them, their eyes would be put out."

Maddie cringed and turned to face him. "That's a bit harsh, don't you think?"

Ben shrugged, a strange gleam in his eyes. "The musicians are aware of the custom and willing to abide by it. It is considered a great honor to play before the sultan's family."

A melody, alluring and seductive, wove itself through the crowd, and the women began to dance to the haunting music. Some glided in pairs, while many swayed alone to the tune. The little monkey hopped from his perch and pranced among the women while the young jugglers clustered about the pool and waited, watching the bejeweled ladies lose themselves in the mysterious strains that filled the air around them.

Maddie fought the urge to close her eyes and lay back on the sofa, but found she had little resistance to the enthralling music. She could feel Ben's breath, soft and tingly, caressing the back of her neck. The scent of sandalwood, a heady fragrance she always noticed when

he was present, enveloped her. Almost against her will
she relaxed against the planes of his hard-muscled chest
and thighs. His large hand, warm and comforting, rested
gently on her upper arm, rubbing in small, concentric circles of heat.

Worries over the plant and the humiliation of Trevor's
rejection fled from her mind as Maddie lost herself in the
evocative and exciting trappings of a long-ago land. Her
senses succumbed to an exotic paradise the modern world
had forgotten as she let Ben show her a different kind of
life, a world filled with secrets and hidden intrigue, with
hot nights and even hotter bodies surrendering to the beat
of an ageless rhythm.

Minutes passed as Maddie breathed in the strange
scents and sounds. Her heart skipped at Ben's nearness.
The thought that he might touch her in other, more intimate places set her pulse racing. If she turned her head,
his lips would be just inches from her own, waiting for
the brush of her mouth to bring them together. But could
she, dare she do such a brazen thing? What if Ben laughed
at her or, worse, rebuffed her advances with pity in his
knowing eyes?

Fighting the temptation to turn, she heard the music
slow to a whisper, then speed up to a rousing circus-like
tune. The jugglers began their performance, tumbling and
twirling with their hoops and balls as the women broke
from their dancing to clap along with the music. When
the jugglers finished, the band played a lively march and
bowed low, backing out of the room, the dancing children
following.

After moans of disappointment, the women went back
to gossiping and eating. Maddie, cut adrift and embarrassed, sat up and placed a small, fringed pillow on her lap,
hoping to distance herself from Ben and his imposing body.
"Now what?" she asked, nervously chewing her lower lip.

Ben swung his legs around to sit beside her. "The day

will pass exactly as the one before and the one after. The women are free to talk or sleep or paint with watercolors, even take a walk in the walled garden if they wish. To-night, the sultan will call one of them to his sleeping chamber and she will go willingly. If she is blessed, she will become heavy with child. If she births a son, she may be raised to the title of *haschi sultana*. She will enjoy many of the rights and privileges afforded a wife and live in luxury for the rest of her days."

Maddie unraveled the fringe from the pillow and wound it around her index finger, illogically angry over some-thing she knew had happened thousands of years ago. 'You mean she'll be a prisoner for the rest of her days, don't you? Doomed to live behind these walls and never stroll the bazaar or inhale a breath of freedom."

"The women did not complain, Maddie. They accepted it as their lot in life."

"Kind of like your living in the bottle?" she snapped, unable to suppress the cruel remark. Seconds of heavy silence passed. What had made her say such a terrible thing? Ashamed of her tart tongue, she gave him a side-ways glance.

Ben's eyes glittered in reaction, but he made no com-ment.

"I'm sorry," Maddie whispered. "That was unkind of me."

After a few seconds of uncomfortable silence, Ben laid a hand across her own, and her heart gave a little lurch. "I know it seems strange to you, Maddie, but I cannot make excuses for the traditions of my people. I have learned from watching your television and listening to you, Paulette, and Mary Grace that the women of this time want more from life. I understand the world I once knew no longer exists, and I accept that the women of today have the same rights as men."

Maddie sighed. Of course, Ben was right. The important thing was that he grow comfortable living in the twenty-first century. Little by little, when he was ready for it, she was going to give him his freedom. Now just didn't seem the right time to tell him so.

"Sorry. I didn't mean to get on my soap box. I guess it's the one thing I've always held on to—the fact that a woman could be or do anything she wanted. To see it like this, as it was hundreds of years ago, just makes me so angry I want to—" She shrugged her shoulders in resignation. "Could we go home now? I'm really tired, and we have a ton of work at the plant tomorrow."

Maddie's eyes, so large and luminous, touched Ben's soul. He had brought her here to show her things she didn't understand, hoping it would help her to see inside of him and know him for the man he had once been. After living with Maddie in her time, he knew he could never go back to his own, but somehow it had become important to let her see into his past and glimpse what he had experienced growing up.

He stood over her and looked around the room. This harem was not his father's, but a close replica of what he remembered from his youth. He had once dreamed of owning a harem of his own, of siring many children and living out his life as a wise and compassionate leader. Ashmedai had changed all that with one snap of his evil fingers.

The room had emptied and they were alone. Night had fallen and darkness surrounded them. Again, he wondered if Ashmedai still existed. He had done things, thought many thoughts the jinn had once told him were forbidden, yet nothing untoward had happened. He still had his powers, he was still enslaved to Maddie, and he was still alive and well, Allah be praised. Could the passage of time somehow have weakened the powerful sorcerer? Dared he hope the creature had done a deed so evil it had cast him to the dark side forever? Was there a way to creep out from Ashmedai's spell and fly free again?

Ben only knew of one sure way to escape his bottle. His current master had to release him of his—or, in this case, her—own free will. The seven simple words, "I release you, genie of the bottle," would allow him to be a man in charge of his own destiny again.

How he longed for that day. But, sadly, he knew it would never come. He had been forbidden to say the words out loud or influence his masters in any way, and he had never known a master with so generous or giving a heart who would say the sentence of his own volition. Even Maddie, with her kind spirit, had just reminded him of his eternal imprisonment.

He looked down at Maddie and smiled, then took her hands in his and pulled her to her feet. "Of course. I can whisk us back to New York with the clap of my hands, or we can again ride the stars on a magic carpet. What is it to be, my Maddie? The choice is yours."

Maddie gave a small yawn. Like a trusting child, she closed her eyes and swayed against him, letting her breasts brush across his chest. His manhood sprang to life with a vengeance. Pulling her close, he caught her before her exhausted body hit the cool marble tiles.

In the blink of an eye they were flying through the night and its blanket of stars, heading west toward the skyline of Manhattan . . . and home.

Ten

The next morning, while riding the elevator to street level, Maddie explained the concept of taxis to Ben. After last night, she decided it was time to teach him some basic big city survival skills. When she told Ben he was a free man and they parted company, it would be a comfort to know he could get around in the world without using magic.

They would be spending today in WD's corporate offices, working on proposals and checking in with Max. In the excitement of the past week, Maddie had almost forgotten about the meeting with a potential new client she had scheduled for this morning. Apex Inc., one of the industry's leading manufacturers of mid-range systems, was coming in to discuss the possibility of a very large order.

Preoccupied with the thought of impressing the executives of such a huge company, Maddie was amazed to see Ben march to the curb, raise his hand, and give a commanding wave. She smiled as he carried out the flagging arm movement as efficiently as any born-and-bred New Yorker, exactly as she had described.

And he looked more than handsome this morning. Obviously, he'd been studying the fashion magazine she'd given him that first night. Dressed in tan chinos and a navy blazer over a white linen shirt, he resembled an up-

and-coming businessman on his way to an office job. He looked like a man in control.

Maddie glanced down at her own drab burgundy suit, white blouse, and clunky shoes. The practical, no-nonsense outfit resembled something a college professor would wear to a lecture. She sighed. It would take more than new makeup techniques to turn this sow's ear into a silk purse. Maybe she really did need to find the time to let Mary Grace take her to one of the upscale boutiques she frequented and help with her wardrobe. Feeling like a frump next to Ben was not a pleasant experience.

A racing cab careened from the far lane and pulled to a stop in front of them. Ben held the door open for her, his face full of pride. "Nice job," Maddie praised as she slid inside.

After last night's less-than-gracious comment, she had promised herself she would be encouraging and positive with him from now on. She would think twice before she let another nasty remark slip from her lips. Ben had done nothing to deserve her wrath. It wasn't his fault her life had fallen apart.

He had been awake and dressed when she'd entered the kitchen at seven. He had surprised her with a simple breakfast of toast, jam, fresh fruit, coffee, and juice—all things he had learned to make on his own without magic. And now, even after her nasty comment of last night, he was being solicitous and caring.

Ben climbed into the other side of the cab, his gaze thoughtful. "You look very serious this morning, Maddie. I sensed at breakfast something was weighing on your mind. Please say you are not angry with me for the little trip we took last night."

Maddie hadn't forgotten about their midnight visit to the harem or their return trip on the magic carpet. She was simply uncertain of her reaction to them. Never had she felt more alive or free than when she was with Ben on those exhilarating excursions. The hours she'd spent lying close to him while in the harem would be permanently etched in her memory long after he left her to make his own life.

She was just coming to realize how much Ben and his gentle consideration meant to her. Once they figured a way to recreate the microchips and slip them past Max, she was going to give Ben his freedom, no matter his feelings about staying on as her genie, but how much of her heart would go with him?

Unsure of how to resolve her dilemma, she challenged his probing gaze with a different thought. "What if something went wrong, Ben? If you got hurt or found yourself in trouble, we might be stranded forever in that other world. It's a very scary thought, you know."

Ben barked out a laugh. "You doubt my powers, Maddie? Let me assure you that in all these centuries, not once have I failed in granting a wish. There is no need to worry. No, I sense it is something else that saddens you this morning."

She set her briefcase on her lap. The realization that even Mary Grace and Gram weren't this perceptive of her inner feelings was unsettling. She and Ben were beginning to communicate like a devoted couple, two people who planned to marry and make a life together, something she knew they could never do.

"I'm concerned about this presentation. We've never had a customer with the potential for such a large order before. And Apex is expanding into the laptop market. Max says I need to *wow* them, convince them we have an exciting and innovative product capable of launching them into the forefront of the industry. He just needs a few more weeks of development time. If I can get them to agree to come back for a second look, he'll be able to attend our next meeting with a big surprise."

"You have much faith in Max, I think. He is like a father to you."

Maddie smiled in earnest. "He's my godfather, my adopted uncle, and, except for Mary Grace, the dearest friend I have in the world. After Gram, Max holds the next biggest place in my heart."

"And your Uncle Lucius, Maddie? What space does he occupy?" Ben asked bluntly. "You do not speak of him often."

She fiddled with the catch on her briefcase, stalling for time. How did she explain Lucius Fulbright without making Ben want to turn him into a squid? "Uncle Lucius is Gram's only sibling. He's a lot younger than she is, a little spoiled and full of himself. He means well, I guess, but he just doesn't give most people a warm, fuzzy feeling. He had a thing for my mother when they were younger, but she chose my dad instead. I can never get anyone to talk about it. I'd rather you met Uncle Lucius and formed your own opinion."

The cab driver, a small, wrinkled-looking raisin of a man, took that moment to glance in the rearview mirror and give a toothy grin, greeting them in a distinctly foreign tongue. Looking shocked, Ben stumbled out a reply. The cabbie choked out a laugh, and Maddie realized he and Ben were speaking the same language—or at least trying to. Ben's accent sounded stilted, but the cabbie persisted, asking questions and encouraging Ben to answer as best he could.

She settled back against her door and watched the unfettered joy in Ben's eyes when he realized he had found a fellow countryman, even if the man was from this century. Though the cabbie looked old enough to be Ben's grandfather, the two chatted amicably for the remainder of the ride. By the time they reached their destination and Maddie paid the fare, the driver had handed Ben a business card.

Ben raised his hand in farewell as the cab shot down the street, and Maddie had to ask, "Did that guy give you his name and number? You two sounded like old friends."

Ben held the card up for her inspection, but she couldn't read the exotic-looking words. "It is the address of a shop that carries artwork and crafts from my homeland. I thought we might visit sometime and browse. Hajisani said we would both find many things of interest there."

He took back the card, pulled out his wallet, and tucked it inside. "I would be honored if you would come with me to this place, Maddie. I might be able to find out much about my country if we visited together."

Remembering the disturbing thoughts Max had voiced when he'd first met Ben, Maddie had a difficult time hiding her concern. Surely the store would be an innocent ethnic meeting ground, not a den of subversive terrorist activities. "Uh . . . sure. We can go there as soon as we straighten out WD's mess and get the company back on track. You don't mind putting it off for a while, do you?" she asked, hoping her misgivings weren't apparent in her voice.

"I understand, Maddie," Ben replied, his eyes taking in the busy sidewalk filled with city dwellers rushing to work. Her vague answer didn't seem to bother him. Like a kid in a candy store, he walked swiftly to a storefront and gazed intently at the display in the window.

She strolled to Ben's side, curious to see what had caught his eye. Hands pressed to the glass, he was staring at a mound of brilliant stones, obviously fake, made to look like a waterfall of precious gems tumbling from a pretend river. She smiled at what she thought would be his childlike enthusiasm. "Pretty, isn't it?"

Ben surprised her by raising a disdainful brow. "It is a ruse to trick the public. These people should be arrested and their hands cut off in the town square for perpetrating such a blatant act of thievery."

Maddie swallowed. "Cut off their hands? Ben, we do not do that sort of thing in this country, remember? Besides, how did you know they were fake?"

His eyes grew bright, his frown softening. "I am an expert on the appraisal of precious gems. In my day, Father had me authenticate all of his jewels. Were it real, this paltry display would not match a tenth of his store in the royal treasury. Why do your people approve of such trickery?"

Impressed by his knowledge of first-quality merchandise, Maddie smiled at him. "It's called advertising. No one walking by would believe all these gems were real. It's just an interesting display meant to catch the eye and encourage people to visit their establishment. Here, look at this window," she said, tugging him down a store.

The window belonged to a travel agency. Displayed behind the glass were a variety of miniature scenes from different countries around the world. The central focus was the earth, surrounded by Mars, Venus, and various other planets. "See, here's a mock-up of our solar system. This display makes the traveler think of going to out-of-this-world places, but everyone knows they can't buy a trip to a planet. The premise makes the customers curious and lures them inside so the travel agent has a chance to tell them about all the places they really can go."

Ben gazed at her through eyes filled with suspicion. "And everyone knows this to be a sham?"

"Yes, everyone knows. And everyone does it. Just like on television when you watch commercials and . . ." Assuming Ben would follow, Maddie had continued talking as she set out for the Winston Design offices just a half block up the street. When she turned to enter the building, she found she was alone and babbling to herself. Scanning the sidewalk, she saw him a block in the opposite direction, staring into another store window.

"Jeez," she muttered, "I'm going to have to put him on a leash if I expect to get anything done today."

Maddie reached Ben's side and her gaze drifted to the window with which he seemed so fascinated. The store, *Risky Business,* was one she had passed many times.

Catering to the modern businesswoman, it featured suits and dresses that, while tailored and elegant, were daring in color and style. She had always wanted to go inside but had never found the time.

Ben was eyeing a deep purple silk suit with a fitted jacket and pencil-slim skirt trimmed in black braid. A pair of black, open-toed pumps and a small black clutch completed the snappy outfit.

The suit was form-fitting and smart, exactly the kind of thing Maddie had often wished she could wear. But with her full-sized figure and ordinary looks, she'd never had the nerve to try. "Some outfit, huh?" she said with longing.

Ben stared at her through their reflection in the window. "This would look wonderful on you, Maddie. The color would be very complimentary to your hair and complexion."

"Oh, really?" she bristled, suddenly thinking he sounded just like Trevor had when he'd talked her into her stringent diet nearly one year ago. "No, thanks. We have to get to work." She folded her arms and waited, impatiently tapping the toe of one chunky-heeled shoe. After several seconds, Ben turned and followed her down the sidewalk and into the building.

They rode the elevator in silence, Ben smiling at her with a crooked grin. Maddie, busy fuming at the thought that he was trying to tell her what to do, ignored him and marched through the double doors of her company's suite of offices with a grim set to her lips. Stopping at the reception area, she held out her hand. "Messages, Letitia. And is my uncle in?"

Letitia let loose with a little whistle, her chocolate brown eyes wide with approval. "Girl, what's got into you? You look fantastic."

Maddie gave a tsk. "Really, Letitia, it's only a little makeup. I finally gave in last night and let Mary Grace near me with her waxer and trunk load of cosmetics. From the grin on your face, I gather I didn't do a very good job of recreating the look this morning. Is it too much?"

Letitia sat back in her desk chair and ran her gaze down to Maddie's toes and back up again. "The makeup's good, but that outfit is to die for. You look like a million bucks."

"What are you talking about?" Glancing up, Maddie caught a glimpse of herself in the mirrored tiles over Letitia's desk.

Carefully, she set her briefcase down, then lowered her gaze to her feet. There, peeking out through sheer black hose, were her toes, nestled into a pair of open-toed black pumps. She stuck out a leg and got a good look at her calf and knee, then the start of a slim purple skirt. Raising her head, she stared past the receptionist, back to her reflection in the mirrored squares.

The vision staring back made Maddie gasp. The jacket's wide lapels tapered over her bust, the piping outlining a sweetheart neckline that bared a hint of cleavage. The suit's darted waist nipped at her middle, giving her a real waistline as it flared out slightly at the hips. The skirt just skimmed the top of her knees, showing off shapely legs and trim ankles encased in sexy leather pumps.

Could she be the woman in the mirror?

"What's the matter? Can't take a compliment?" Letitia teased, her face wreathed in a smile. "No offense, but those new clients must really be important to have dragged you out of the fashion graveyard you've been buried in for the past five years."

Dazed, Maddie looked back in the mirror and met Ben's grinning face. Her hands on her hips, she cocked her head. He shrugged innocently. Not sure how to handle this latest predicament, she realized Letitia was staring. "Thank you for your candid comments. Now, is my uncle in?"

Letitia gave a snort. "Lord, yes. And fit to be tied. Claims you haven't answered his calls at the plant and you didn't have the courtesy of giving him your new home number."

Maddie realized she was scowling and smiled down at the woman. Letitia had never been shy about her feelings for Lucius Fulbright, and she had always been one of Maddie's staunchest supporters. "You know what, Letitia? Even *I* don't have my new number. The phone company said I'd get it through the mail. Try to reach them for me and see if they'll release it to you."

The secretary's curious gaze wandered to a spot over Maddie's left shoulder. Imagining what might be going through the older woman's mind at this moment, Maddie stepped aside and made the introduction as if it were an afterthought. "Letitia Moore, Benjamin Able. Ben is my new personal assistant. Please pass all my calls through to him."

"Hm-hmm-hmm, when you make changes, you really do go all the way," Letitia muttered, her eyes wide. "I didn't realize you were looking for a male assistant. If I'd known this was the kind of guy you wanted, I would have suggested my son a long time ago."

As far as Maddie knew, Rufus Moore was still a male model gaining some small acclaim on the fashion runway circuits in Milan, Paris, and Rome. "I'm sure Rufus would have jumped at the chance to make thirty-five thousand a year instead of the quarter million he pulled down last year. Don't let Ben's looks fool you. He's a real hard worker, aren't you, Ben?"

She turned to find Ben returning Letitia's naughty grin. "Maddie is correct, Ms. Moore. And I find it hard to believe a woman of your youth and beauty has a son old enough to be earning a living on his own."

Letitia gave an honest-to-gosh giggle and Maddie sighed. With this latest little trick, Ben was turning into Trevor before her very eyes. More angry at his outrageous flirting than his new suit magic, she hoisted her briefcase.

"When the Apex people get here, show them into the main conference room and buzz me immediately. We'll need a fresh coffee setup, and order some of those little pastries from the corner deli."

She headed down the hall. "Come along, Mr. Able. We have work to do."

Ben stopped at the cluttered desk just outside Maddie's office door. "Is this now my place in the company?" he asked, hoping to keep Maddie off a topic he knew she was determined to discuss.

"The desk belongs to my assistant, so I guess this is where you need to be in order to keep everyone from gossiping. But before you get settled, I think we should talk." She opened the door to her office and marched inside. "In private."

Ben followed. Well aware of the lecture Maddie was preparing, he made ready to argue his point. When he'd seen the look of longing in her eyes as she gazed into the store window, he hadn't been able to stop himself. He'd known instantly the suit would look perfect on her. He had merely taken the decision out of her hands and given her something she truly desired. He'd only been doing his job. But from the look in her amber eyes, he could tell she was not pleased.

Strangely, he wasn't concerned that he had overstepped his boundaries as her genie. It was becoming apparent Ashmedai had forgotten about him. He would enjoy this freedom for as long as it lasted. Making Maddie happy, seeing her eyes light up with pleasure, brought him more joy than anything else had in the past thousand years.

He watched her swaying backside with admiration. The new suit showed off her feminine curves and long, shapely legs much better than the drab clothes she usually wore. Although she still didn't realize it, Maddie was a desirable woman. And she made him feel more of a man than any female he had ever known.

Maddie set her briefcase on her desk and took a seat. Ben couldn't help but smile when he saw her flutter her hands over her skirt, pulling it to her knees as she scooted primly to the edge of her chair. Looking down at her from across the desk, he had an enticing view of her breasts gently swelling above the daintily scooped neckline.

"Please sit down," she said sternly, gazing up at him.

Ben pulled a chair closer to her desk and sat. He watched as she patted at her hair, her hand trailing down her collar and onto the black piping outlining her jacket. How perfect a single jewel—an emerald, or perhaps an amethyst—would look gracing her delicate skin. He grinned as her hand grazed the heart-shaped purple stone surrounded by diamonds that suddenly hung from a golden chain about her neck.

Maddie fingered the pendant and her eyes grew wide. "Stop that," she said from behind tight lips. "Stop all of it right now. Do you hear me?"

He could only smile in return. "Do you not like the suit, Maddie? It is very attractive on you. Much better than the other you were wearing."

She raised her eyes. "I know it is. It's just that I . . . what if someone had seen what you did? I thought you weren't supposed to do magic in front of others. How would we have explained it?"

He shrugged, thinking of the most reasonable explanation he could give. "Lately, I have sensed that some of the rules can be broken, but I have no proof of it being so. No one saw, because these things happen more quickly than the human eye can discern. Besides, I did it when we were alone in the elevator. Even you did not feel the difference. I would not jeopardize my position with you," he said with sincerity. "I want only to please you."

She gave an exasperated sigh. "I know you do, but that's no excuse."

"You do not like the suit?"

"Yes, I like it. I can't believe it makes me look so—so—"

"Slender? Sophisticated? Sexy?"

Her face flushed a becoming pink. "Yes. No! I mean—" She stared down at the amethyst in her hand. "I can't possibly own something as expensive as this. It must have cost a fortune. Besides, it's too showy, too . . . too much."

He smiled at her naivete. "Maddie, all women deserve jewels. And the more beautiful the woman, the more lovely the jewels should be. You could wear a diamond the size of a pigeon's egg and it would not be too much."

A knock sounded at the door and they both turned. Lucius Fulbright charged into the room and straight to Maddie's desk without giving Ben a second glance. "Madeline, please explain why I haven't as yet received your new home telephone number. For that matter, why did you change it in the first place? Are you ready for the presentation this morning? Have you checked the conference room?"

Maddie stood and tugged at her suit jacket. "Uncle Lucius, I have everything under control. Please calm down."

Clearing his throat, Ben rose as well. Lucius turned and immediately pulled to his full height of five-foot-eight. "I'm sorry. I didn't realize you were in a meeting with someone."

Maddie folded her arms. "It's not exactly a meeting. Lucius Fulbright, Benjamin Able. Ben is my new assistant, Uncle Lucius."

Ben raised his hand, wishing he held a wasp in his palm. Perhaps a taste of the insect's venomous bite would make up for the stinging words Lucius Fulbright threw so carelessly at his niece.

It was a long second before Lucius took Ben's hand in

his and gave it a quick shake. First he stared at Ben's chest, then his shoulders, and finally his face. "Mr. Able." He looked to Maddie. "Madeline, may I have a word with you in private?"

Maddie nodded. "Of course. Ben and I were just finishing up. Ben, you will try to remember everything we discussed this morning, won't you?" she asked with a little warning.

"I'll keep your words in the forefront of my mind, Ms. Winston. It was a pleasure meeting you, Mr. Fulbright," he said as he turned and left the room.

Maddie watched her uncle walk back and forth in front of her desk. She knew him well enough to recognize the frustrated sigh he reserved especially for her. On more than one occasion, a vein in his left temple had throbbed so hard she thought it might burst. Instead of prodding him into an argument as she usually did, she waited patiently, giving him time to calm down.

Lucius stopped his frantic pacing and began to tap a bony finger on the edge of her desk. "Madeline, have you gone completely off the deep end? I demand you explain yourself," he said on a hiss of breath.

She checked her watch. The Apex executives were due in less than ten minutes, and she needed her uncle at her side to provide a united front. For some reason she had yet to comprehend, Lucius Fulbright had the ability to convince clients of the company's solvency and sterling reputation, a trait Maddie badly needed to make this morning's meeting a success.

"I'm not sure exactly to what you're referring, Uncle. And I don't think this is the time to explain it, do you? The Apex people will be here any minute and we need to discuss our strategy."

He stopped tapping and gave her a disapproving glare.

"Who is that man? Where did you find him? I don't remember your conducting any interviews," he said in a tone of authority.

She picked up a stack of colorful drawings and began sorting them on the desk top. "It's a long story. I believe Benjamin is the kind of person I've been looking for, but to be on the safe side, he's on trial for the next four weeks. If, at the end of that time, I'm not satisfied, I'll let him go. Now, these are the new diagrams Max made of our latest—"

"He looks suspicious. Have you checked his references?"

Maddie raised a brow. "I didn't get any references. I went with my gut instinct on this one."

"Hah!" The vein in his temple began to throb frantically. "He probably read about your breakup with Trevor and wants to take the man's place. I'll bet he's already tallied your assets and spent them."

Maddie resisted the urge to lose her temper and toss her uncle out on his self-important rear end. She'd expected the worst from him, but hearing his cruel chastisements out loud still hurt. "Enough, Uncle Lucius. This morning's meeting is crucial to—"

The new look he threw at her told Maddie her uncle had already found a fresh wound to probe. She sat with a little plop, hoping to distract his gaze.

"What *are* you wearing, Madeline?" Fish-like, his eyes bulged from behind his horn-rimmed glasses.

She sat straighter. "A new suit. Do you like it?"

Lucius took a step backward. "Who do you think you are? Your mother? That's the kind of thing Catherine would have worn."

It was? Suddenly, Maddie felt empowered. "Well, it's nice to know I've finally developed the same excellent taste in clothing as my mother, don't you think? Now, about this meeting—"

Obviously surprised at her reaction to his comments, Lucius took a ninety-degree turn to the left. "It should be canceled."

"Excuse me?"

"How can you represent us as a viable company when we haven't been able to fulfill our latest contracts? I say we cut our losses and send them to another supplier, then call Butler & Maggio and accept their last buyout offer."

Shocked by his negative attitude, as well as the erratic way his mind was darting from topic to topic, Maddie grew furious. "That's exactly what I don't need to hear before this meeting, Uncle Lucius. You gave me fourteen days, and during that time I intend to conduct business as usual as well as try to drum up future contracts. Now, if you're through, I suggest you go to your office and prepare. I'll meet you in the conference room in ten minutes—sooner if Letitia buzzes."

As if knowing he'd lost this small skirmish, Lucius feigned contrition. "Now, Madeline, I'm sorry if I upset you. It's just that you surprised me with a new assistant and your . . . ah . . . manner of dress. We can talk about this later; when you're more yourself. You're right. The meeting comes first."

He backed toward the door. "I'll be in my office until I hear from Letitia."

Maddie waited until the door closed before she let the tears fall. She blinked, knowing the watery drops would probably cause her eyes to redden and swell—not a good idea for a woman who had an important meeting at any moment. Her phone rang and she sniffed. "Maddie Winston," she said into the receiver.

"They're here," came Letitia's cheery voice. "Three men in navy and white pinstripes and wingtips all waiting in the main conference room."

"Thanks, Letitia. Buzz my uncle, then offer the gentlemen coffee and pastries, please. I'll be in shortly."

Determinedly, she headed for the powder room to freshen her hair and makeup. She would show Lucius Fulbright he was wrong.

Eleven

Ben sat at his tidy desk, staring at the figures on his PC screen with a self-satisfied grin. Finally, he was getting the hang of this personal assistant position and becoming useful to Maddie. The job would give him the opportunity to keep a close eye on her and protect her from harm, while at the same time teach him more about computers and the inner workings of the modern world.

Their meeting with the Apex Inc. executives had, he thought, gone quite well that morning. Maddie had allowed him to observe the proceedings, even though Lucius Fulbright had objected strongly to his presence. She'd asked him to take notes and he'd done his best, scribbling on a steno pad like the secretaries he'd seen on a few late night TV shows. Right now, he was deciphering his scrawl into a legible report which needed to be on Maddie's, Max's, and Fulbright's desks first thing Monday morning.

Unfortunately, this job did not give him the right to do the one thing his fingers had itched to try since nine o'clock—throttle Lucius Fulbright until he screamed for mercy and promised to show Maddie the respect she deserved.

If Lucius were left to him, the man would be in the desert right now, buried to his neck in a sand dune—or, better yet, shoveling camel offal in the streets of Baghdad. But such a righteous thing was not to be. The man was Maddie's only living male relation. Ben knew no matter how cruelly Lucius treated her, Maddie would not be pleased if her uncle was harmed.

He finished the final paragraph on the meeting's wrap-up and sent the report to his printer, gratified to find he remembered how to use the simple word-processing program Paulette had explained to him days ago. While waiting for the printer to do its job, he sat back in his chair and contemplated the morning's events.

Maddie had gained control of the meeting instantly, even when the Apex executives had acted as if Lucius were in charge. Lucius, of course, had taken umbrage at Maddie's command of the room and immediately began to chip away at her credibility. The third time Lucius had interrupted Maddie to disagree with a point in her proposal had been his last.

Smiling broadly, Ben relived the moment Lucius had begun to cough, slowly at first, in little fits and starts, then in earnest, choking as he drank glass after glass of water. Of course, anyone who drank that much water needed to relieve himself—many times. Perhaps his urgency to visit the rest room had been more frantic than necessary, but could Ben help it if the man had a bladder the size of a dried fig?

In doing his part to embarrass Lucius, Ben had allowed Maddie ample time to show the three executives she was intelligent, organized, and in control. They had left the building with the promise of a return appointment while Lucius had been on his eleventh—or was it his twelfth?—trip to the bathroom. All in all, a positive point in Maddie's favor.

If Maddie remained innocent of his minor interference, Ben would chalk up the day as nearly perfect.

He collected the finished reports from his printer, righted the pages and paper clipped them at the corners.

After inserting each report in a folder, he walked to Letitia's desk and handed her two. "Please see to it Max has this report by Monday, Letitia. And this one is for Lucius Fulbright."

"I'll take care of it. By the way, it's all over the office Mr. Fulbright had some kind of fit this morning during the meeting. You were there. What happened?" She smiled smugly. "As far as I'm concerned, it couldn't have happened to a nicer guy."

Ben shook his head. "It seems Mr. Fulbright has the thirst of a racehorse and the kidneys of a gnat—a very sorry combination."

Letitia giggled and Ben walked away grinning, positive he had an ally in his quest to protect Maddie. He arrived back at his desk to find his intercom light blinking. He picked up the phone and buzzed Maddie's line.

"Yes, Maddie?" he asked politely.

"Can you come in here for a second? I need to speak with you," came her terse response.

With a tiny ripple of unease, Ben entered Maddie's office. Still looking efficient and cool in the eye-catching purple suit, she was reading from a folder while absently fingering the diamond-studded amethyst heart hanging around her neck. When she realized he had entered the room, she raised her gaze and quickly dropped the pendant.

Smiling, Ben handed her the report. "I have given copies of this to Letitia. She will relay them to Max and your uncle. It is a pity Mr. Fulbright found it necessary to leave early today, is it not?"

Maddie shifted in her seat, her voice firm. "Hmm. A real pity. I don't suppose you'd have any idea what caused him to start coughing like a tuberculosis victim this morning?"

Ben tried for his most innocent facial expression. "Why do you think I would know, Maddie? It looked to me as if he simply had the beginnings of a chest ailment. It was best he went home to rest, I think."

Maddie raised her russet brows questioningly and tapped a finger on her desk blotter. "Oh, you think so, do you? Well, let me tell you this, Benjamin Able. If I find out you were the one responsible I'll . . . I'll . . ."

"Thank me? Fall at my feet in gratitude?" He leaned forward onto her desk, meeting her disapproving glare. Golden flecks began to dance in her eyes and he grinned at the start of her smile. "I like to see you happy, Maddie. Your uncle does not. It was a simple choice."

Maddie's eyes softened to the warm honey color he loved. If he leaned just a bit further, their mouths would touch, an idea he hated to admit had been simmering in the back of his mind since he had first appeared in front of her on the beach.

An improper idea upon which he had no right to act.

He came to his senses when he saw Maddie lower her gaze and lick at her lips, her fingers a tangled knot on the blotter. He had no business desiring her, and she knew it. She was always in control, always the one to keep a clear head, he realized, standing upright. Thankfully, Maddie did not want him in the same way he desired her.

Staring down, he made a stab at changing the path upon which his errant mind had wandered. "Why does your uncle find the need to discredit you so important, Maddie? You are the president of the company."

Maddie sighed, her hand again fondling the amethyst necklace. "That's the problem, I guess. I have the position Uncle Lucius thinks should be his. It came as quite a blow to his ego when I was given complete control of Winston Design in my father's will. Once Grandpa Will died, Lucius thought he would automatically take over the spot, but with Gram and Max's forty percent of the votes added to my thirty, it wasn't possible. Ever since, he's been impossible to work with."

Ben gave a snort. "From what I witnessed in the meeting, impossible is an understatement. You must admit, things went much more smoothly when Lucius occupied himself in the rest room. By the end of the morning, you had the Apex men eating from the sole of your foot."

Maddie's pert nose wrinkled in confusion. "Sole of my—Ben, I think you mean 'palm of my hand,' " she said, and giggled.

He grinned at his ability to make her laugh. "Sole, palm, what is the difference? They were enthralled."

Maddie blushed, a delicious shade of apricot that set his heart to racing. She looked feminine and vulnerable, flushing over a simple compliment as though it were a new and precious gift.

"It's true, Maddie. Those men couldn't take their eyes off of you. It made me quite . . . jealous."

Her amber eyes grew wide. She looked almost shocked. "I . . . um . . ." Glancing at her watch, she gave a little gasp. "Golly, look at the time. It's five-thirty. We should get out of here, or I'll owe you overtime."

"Owe me?" he asked, puzzled by her words. "It is I who owe you. You released me from my prison and gave me my first taste of freedom in hundreds of years. I can never repay you for what you have done."

Pushing away from her desk, Maddie stood. "Nonsense. You're doing an honest day's work, for which you'll receive an honest day's pay. First thing Monday I'm calling payroll with your vitals. We cut checks on the first and fifteenth of the month around here."

Pay? He would be receiving coin for taking care of Maddie? He would have money of his own to buy her things—to purchase his own clothing, perhaps a car.

Overwhelmed by the thought he might be able to take care of Maddie like a normal man, provide for her and begin a new life, sent a wave of heat straight to his iced-over heart. He smiled as Maddie opened her briefcase and stuffed the report inside, his self-esteem growing by the minute. No master had ever offered him anything in return for his talents. No master had shown even the tiniest spark of gratitude.

And now he had Maddie.

Maddie loaded the dishwasher while Ben sat at the kitchen table drinking a final cup of espresso. They had shared a dinner of lime-basted grilled chicken breast, steamed broccoli with fresh ginger, tossed green salad, and then dessert, slices of pound cake covered in fresh strawberries. Ben had helped by setting the table and washing the salad fixings, chores Maddie knew Trevor wouldn't have been caught dead attempting.

The heat radiating from Ben's presence sent little jolts of current rushing through her body, warming her while making her feel strangely vulnerable. She could sense his heavy-lidded gaze caressing her as he took in her every move.

Maddie fought the urge to turn and smile at him. A smile would only encourage his gratitude, making it more difficult when she gave him his freedom. If she ignored her feelings for him, maybe it wouldn't hurt so much when Ben left her, as it had with her parents and Trevor.

The entire scenario of acting normal and cozy with a man in her kitchen made her heart ache. She had dreamed of experiencing life with someone exactly like this since she'd been a little girl. Her grandparents had shared the duties and joys of marriage as well as the hardships. Her parents, too, had laughed and toiled side by side from as far back as she could remember. Just a month ago, she had envisioned this very scene, but the man sitting at the table had been Trevor.

She had enough common sense to know she and Trevor were never meant to be together. Trevor hadn't cared very much for her attempts at gourmet cooking, preferring the prestige of dining in the most popular restaurants, where he could be seen by other wealthy New Yorkers. He had never wanted to stay home with her and cuddle or talk about his day of visiting customers and presenting them with the merits of Winston Design's excellent products.

And when they'd had sex, Trevor had never spent the night. He always went back to his own apartment soon after they'd completed the act, telling her he didn't want to chance ruining her reputation.

Thinking back, Maddie remembered how empty she'd always felt afterward, lying there and wondering if making love was supposed to leave a person feeling so disjointed and cold. Was she supposed to feel so alone?

Lost in thought, she didn't realize Ben had come up behind her until she was enveloped in the subtle aroma of sandalwood mixed with his own unique scent.

Ben reached around her and set his espresso cup and saucer neatly in the dishwasher, lingering at her back. "Is there anything I can do to help?" he whispered, his voice a raspy tingle in her ear.

She knew if she turned around she would be close enough to be held in his arms, close enough to rest her head on his broad chest and pretend for just a few moments she was with a man who loved her. Close enough to feel safe and warm and cared for, as she had always dreamed.

Maddie picked up her dish towel and scrubbed at a nonexistent spot on the counter. Ben's shirt front grazed her back, and her nipples hardened into aching points of desire. Pushing into the cabinets, she tried to hide her wanton reaction to his nearness. "I don't think so. I'm just about through here. I thought we might take time to talk about the computer chips. You haven't told me if you've come up with an idea for slipping them into the production line yet. Have you?"

Ben took a step backward, and she let out the breath

she hadn't realized she'd been holding. Still, he made no move to step further away. "I have a way. But it would be better if I showed you rather than told you. The actions necessary are . . . unexplainable."

"Do they require magic?" she muttered, sliding slowly toward the sink. She sensed his body gliding along behind hers and suppressed a little quiver.

"Only a small amount—so small as to be insignificant. I promise you, I will be very discreet."

Maddie fisted her hands on the counter, resisting the urge to turn and rest them on his chest. She knew her palms would tremble from the warmth of his body, the beating of his heart. Ben would feel perfect under her hands. Absolutely perfect.

She felt his hard, hot chest brush against her and caught her breath. Never before had his touch been so intimate. The walls of the kitchen closed in around her, and she found herself scrambling for a coherent thought. "That's . . . um . . . good. Very good. We wouldn't want Max or Phil or Uncle Lucius to be suspicious of anything, would we?"

"Maddie, why are you avoiding looking at me?" Ben asked, his words almost a groan.

"Avoiding you? That's so silly. I look at you. I always look at you." Turning, she skittered from between him and the counter to safer territory. Ducking behind a kitchen chair, she faced him, staring directly into his eyes.

Ben leaned back against the counter and folded his arms, his gaze raking down, then back up her jeans and oversized T-shirt. "I have been thinking, Maddie. When this crisis with your company is over, what will you next wish from me? What part will I play in your life?"

I'll want you to hold me, Ben . . . and make love to me. I'll want you to love me.

Maddie bit at her lower lip to keep from blurting out the ridiculous words. Ben pinned her with his laser-like gaze, and for a split second she feared he could hear what her heart had whispered. "I already told you, I have no need for what you've been offering—jewels, clothing, exotic food and drink. I have everything I want in this world."

He nodded imperceptibly, his voice dry of emotion. "Then if you no longer have need of me, will you send me back to my bottle?"

Of course, she told herself logically, that's why he's so concerned, why his presence feels so overwhelming tonight. And who could blame him? No one would want to be ordered to live inside a cold dark cave for all eternity. But how could Ben think she would be so cruel?

She straightened her shoulders and gave him her best glare. "Is that what you think? That after all this time, after all we've shared, I would be so unkind as to banish you to the bottle again? Do you truly think so little of me?"

He continued to stare as he matter-of-factly stated his point. "It is the law, Maddie. And you have allowed me—us—to live outside of that law for a very long while. Through the centuries, I have come to accept the laws. Perhaps it is time you did, too."

Maddie gripped the top of the chair tight as she corralled her growing anger. "Well, whoever said they were good laws? Not me. Laws were made to punish the guilty, not imprison the innocent. Besides, this is the twenty-first century. As far as I'm concerned, you never have to go back inside your bottle again—unless you want to, of course. You'll be free to do whatever you choose. Is that clear?"

A kind of serenity seemed to wash over Ben's features when she spoke her promise. His rigid shoulders relaxed and a gentle smile lit his eyes. "It's clear. And again, I thank you from the bottom of my worthless heart. If it pleases you, after this current crisis is finished, I would like to continue with my job as your assistant. The law says I am still your slave."

She nodded, too shocked to say another word. After a few empty seconds, Ben murmured a soft "good night" and left the room. Maddie pulled out a chair and sat down with a thump, unable to do anything more than hold her head in her hands. Of course Ben wanted to stay with her, work with her. He thought he would still be her slave. And he was grateful for all her kindnesses, for her ability to give him a useful occupation and a place in society. But could she continue to work beside him day after day, knowing she loved him?

Maddie squeezed her eyes shut against the pain shooting through her heart, but she couldn't deny it any longer. She was in love with Benjamin Able—a man who was a spirit, yet not a spirit. A hopelessly spellbound magician with the ability to grant her heart's every desire.

And as long as Ben the slave continued to look upon her as his master, as long as he continued to feel such undying gratitude, he would never be able to see past his duty—his damnable law—and be free to love her as she longed to be loved.

And he could never grant her the one gift she desired above all others—the gift of himself.

Ben tossed and turned on his double bed. Though it was much more comfortable and real than the resting place he had laid upon for the past thousand years, tonight it felt like a bed of nails jabbing him into reality. He had to accept the fact that Maddie didn't want him in the same way he wanted her.

Of course, she was correct in her feelings. Master and slave could never be more, could never have a relationship or share a life, could never love one another freely, without guilt or shame.

The constraints of the law would always be with them, always hovering like some huge mythical beast of prey.

Even if Ashmedai had disappeared or died, his evil spirit would win.

He looked to the streetlight slipping into the room, casting its glow over his dresser and the bottle sitting on top. The rubies and emeralds winked back at him, mocking him in the night.

We are the guardians. the keepers of your soul. As long as we are in your life, you will never be free. No master will ever let you go.

He knew Maddie was different. She might not ever love him, but she didn't want him to be a prisoner. She wanted him to have his freedom, a worthy profession, even money of his own with which to purchase the things he desired. Maddie was willing to give him all the trappings of freedom.

Sadly he realized he would never have the one thing it suddenly seemed so important to own: Maddie's heart.

"Slower. Slower, Ben. Now pull straight down. Ease up a little with your right foot. Press down with the left. That's it. Good. Good. Now up and over. Depress the clutch. Turn . . . turn . . ."

Maddie bounced with delight on the seat next to Ben. They had been driving back and forth through the nearly empty Winston Design parking lot for the past half hour, and it seemed Ben had finally gotten the hang of a stick shift. Her little Jetta was buzzing around as if it were running laps in the Indy 500, flying in wider and wider circles.

"Pull over. Depress the clutch and put it in neutral. Set the brake, just like that. Now, turn the key toward you."

The engine stilled and Ben gave a wide grin, settling back against the driver's seat. His blue eyes bright, he looked as if he had just scaled a mountain or won a gold medal in the Olympics. "I have done it, Maddie. I have mastered a mechanical beast. That was thrilling."

Maddie nodded. "I know it feels great *today,* but just wait until you're stuck in rush hour traffic someday soon and the temperature outside is a hundred and one. Not to burst your bubble, but I don't think your enchantment with driving will be quite the same. Still, you did a good job." She looked at her watch. "I'm starving. How about a celebration lunch?"

Ben grabbed at the key. "Just tell me where and we'll be there in a second. I will drive us wherever we need to go."

Maddie quickly covered his hand with her own. "Not so fast. Driving in a parking lot is one thing. Being on the road with another thousand cars going sixty miles an hour is totally different. We should switch places."

Wounded, he gave her a pleading look. "But I have mastered the automobile, Maddie. Surely the road is not more difficult? Perhaps if we only went a little way down the highway—and in a straight line. No turns or jug ears to stop us . . ."

"Jug ears? Oh, you mean jug handles." She giggled, thinking of the pesky right-to-go-left turns needed to cross over most major intersections in New Jersey. "Well, there *is* a diner straight down Route 46. We just have to get out of the lot and follow the road, then make a right onto the highway."

She thought hard, rolling her eyes when Ben cleared his throat impatiently. "Oh, OK. But go slow. And look all ways before you merge into traffic. And if you kill the engine, put on the flashers and coast onto the shoulder. I'd hate to be rear-ended and—"

Maddie almost bit her tongue as Ben slid the gearshift into first and jerked them out of the lot. But he quickly regained the tricky rhythm of shifting gears, and soon they were motoring more smoothly down the road.

The Galaxy Diner, its neon sign of small red and blue stars and planets winking in the sunlight, loomed ahead. The diner's boxy construction and huge plate glass windows were typical of the many other roadside restaurants that dotted the highways of several east coast states. With so many families needing to run their errands on the weekend, Saturday morning traffic was always heavy. Huge semis and delivery trucks sped along at a faster pace than many cars, and the aggressive Jersey drivers took it all in their stride, honking and weaving between lanes like professional race car drivers.

Acting responsibly, Ben put on his right blinker, preparing to turn into the diner parking lot. Just as he began to slow down, Maddie saw the semi barreling from the lanes of westbound traffic across the grassy center divider of the highway. A day care minivan, filled to capacity and traveling in the far lane on their side of the road, noticed the truck at the same time and swerved directly into their path, nudging the car in front of Ben and Maddie onto the shoulder of the highway.

Horns blared. In slow, motion, Maddie watched as the semi kept coming. Ben hit the brakes, but the minivan's driver seemed to be in a panic, the little bus jerking and veering in front of them as if driving on a patch of ice.

Maddie could see the semi's driver slumped over the wheel and realized he was asleep or drunk—or worse. She clutched at Ben's arm and let out a scream as the truck made a beeline for the minivan. Squeezing her eyes shut, Maddie could only wait for the sound of crunching metal and grating steel.

Seconds passed as silence surrounded them. Cautiously, Maddie opened one eye then the other. The first thing she saw was the semi, only a foot from the Jetta's front bumper. Blocking all three lanes of traffic on their side of the highway, the semi had stopped just inches in front of them. She glanced to her left and found two other cars, the drivers looking dazed, so close they almost touched the truck. Turning right, she saw people pouring from the diner and running toward the accident.

Maddie looked toward Ben and found his face grim, his hands clasping the wheel in a death grip. "You OK?" she asked in a small, squeaky voice.

He barely nodded. "Fine. But I think I have finally developed a few gray hairs and possibly aged a hundred years at last."

Maddie let out a breath. "I know how you feel. Let's go see if anyone needs help."

She hopped from the car and ran around the truck. Where, she wondered, had the minivan gone? And how had it managed to escape being hit by the truck?

On the other side of the semi, two men were helping the driver of the truck climb out. Crumpled over, the man was clutching his chest in obvious pain. She looked a little further and found the minivan angled precariously into a curbed flower bed at the side of the diner.

Several people were standing with the children from the day care van, helping them to sit on the grassy space in front of the diner or holding them close and calming them down. A few of the children were in tears; others seemed fine. All were uninjured. The van's driver appeared the most shell-shocked.

"Honest to God, I felt it," the woman was saying at the top of her voice. "I felt that truck hit us. But on the moment of impact, it was as if we were driving through a wall of cotton. Mercy, it was a miracle!" She began to cry in earnest. "A true God's miracle."

"I saw it, too," chimed a bystander. "We were looking out the diner window and, plain as day, that truck hit that little bus. I winced and, just like that"—the man snapped his fingers—"the bus was sitting here, and the semi landed there. I can't believe what happened."

Maddie stood still. Sirens sounded in the distance and

she breathed a sigh of relief. After a minute of confusion, several police cars found their way across the median and began setting up a roadblock, diverting the blocked cars. An ambulance crawled slowly across the highway's grassy strip, heading straight for the semi and the hovering policemen who were searching for witnesses.

Everyone watched as the ambulance attendants hoisted the driver of the semi onto a gurney. Finally, a harried-looking officer approached her. "Ma'am, did you come from the diner or were you in one of the involved vehicles?" he asked politely.

Maddie nodded, her speech stilted. The woman's words about driving through a wall of cotton rang in her ears. "A Jetta. On the other side of the semi."

"Are you injured? Do you need medical attention?"

She shook her head. "I'm fine, officer. We weren't hit."

"Were you driving?" The patrolman took her elbow and steered her around the semi and back to her car.

"Ben . . . my friend was at the wheel." Maddie looked around, hoping to pinpoint Ben in the crowd.

The officer stopped at the front of her car. "I'll need to speak with your friend and get a statement."

Maddie nodded again, still trying to make sense of what she'd seen and heard. She gazed at her car and squinted at the sunlight bouncing off the windshield. Blinking, she ran to the driver's side and wrenched open the door. The car was empty.

Ben was gone.

Twelve

Maddie scanned the milling crowd, positive she would spot Ben wandering somewhere nearby. After several minutes of holding the policeman in check while she stared over his shoulder and searched diligently, she realized Ben was nowhere in the immediate vicinity. Putting on her blankest face, she took a stab at temporary amnesia. The officer escorting her looked skeptical, so instead she dropped into the driver's seat and began to sob.

Concerned he might try to give Ben a ticket for leaving the scene of an accident, it had taken all her powers of persuasion to convince the policeman she'd been overwrought and not thinking straight when she'd mentioned her friend's name. She had just left Ben at the plant and, dazed and confused, had mispoken. In the end, Maddie had given her account of the near tragedy and accepted responsibility for being the driver of her car.

It had taken hours for the rescue workers to move the semi and clear the clogged roads. The Galaxy had provided everyone involved in the cleanup with coffee, tea, and sandwiches, so she did have a bite of lunch. And the more she listened to people giving identical accounts of the accident, the surer she was Ben had a hand in the outcome.

The semi had hit the minivan. The children and driver,

who should have been killed or at least seriously injured, had survived. A miracle had occurred.

Maddie wracked her brain, attempting to explain his disappearance. After Ben had prevented the accident, one of two things must have happened: either Ben had found a passing cab willing to take him to the city, or he had deliberately disobeyed her no magic rule and clapped himself back to New York. But why? Neither option made any sense.

On the ride home, she rehearsed a speech about ethical conduct and responsibility, certain Ben would be waiting for her at the apartment. He needed to know that having his freedom did not give him the right to disappear merely because something near tragic had happened. Responsible drivers never abandoned the scene of an accident for any reason.

She parked her car in the garage and rode the elevator to her floor, resolving to stay calm. After hanging her jacket and purse in the front closet, she called out Ben's name as she walked quickly into her empty kitchen. She raced through the dining room and into the living room, crossed the hall and knocked sharply on his closed bedroom door. When she received no answer, she opened the door and peered inside. The bed was made, but there was no sign of Ben.

A bolt of fear rippled through her as she went into the room. She checked his closet and found the few items of clothing he'd worn the past week hanging neatly. Torn between panic and fury, she tried calling again, but his name came out in a squeak.

Quickly, she flew through the connecting bath and into her room, resigned it would be empty. Heartsick, she plopped on the edge of the bed and stared. Where had he gone? Had he left her after all his promises and caring words?

The phone rang and she jumped. Letitia had received

her new number from the phone company that afternoon and given it to Ben, who had called Max, Mary Grace, and Uncle Lucius and left the number on their answering machines. It could only be one of them phoning her.

"Hello," she whispered into the receiver.

"Hi, kiddo," came Mary Grace's cheery voice. "Are we on for brunch tomorrow morning? And will it be just the two of us, or will I get to sit and drool over Ben the entire meal?"

Maddie sighed into the phone. "I'm not sure, Mary Grace," she said softly. "I . . . Ben's . . . I've lost him."

"What do you mean *lost* him? How can you lose something . . . someone that big? Where did he go?"

Maddie sniffed and grabbed for a tissue from her nightstand. "I don't know. I was teaching him how to drive, and he did so well I let him take us to a diner for lunch. On the way, we kind of had an accident. I got out of the Jetta to see if I could help and when I returned to the car he was . . . gone." She gave a little hiccup and blew her nose hard.

"What do you mean *kind of* had an accident? Were you hurt? Was Ben?"

Maddie realized she should have been more cautious in her explanation. "I'm fine. I thought we were both fine. Ben just sort of disappeared."

"Well," Mary Grace began practically, "he probably got out to help and just lost you in the crowd or something. Did you stay around to look?"

Maddie gave a frustrated sigh. "Of course I did. I looked for hours. I hung around so long the police wanted to call someone to come and drive me home. They thought I'd had a concussion and forgot where I lived. It got so embarrassing I finally had to leave. Without Ben."

"Ooo-kay. So he left. Maybe *he* had the concussion. Maybe Ben was taken to the hospital or wandered away and got on a bus or something. He could be headed for

Pittsburgh as we speak. Have you filed a missing persons report?"

Maddie stifled a groan. She could only imagine the furor filing a report about Ben would cause.

Well, Officer, I'm looking for my genie. That's right, straight from the magic bottle, but he's disappeared. No, sir, I haven't been drinking.

"I hadn't thought of the concussion part, but don't you have to wait forty-eight hours before the police will consider someone missing? Didn't I hear that on one of those TV shows once?"

It was Mary Grace's turn to sigh. "Yeah, I think you're right. You could call the hospitals yourself, though. He had ID, right? I'd try a few in the North Jersey area before I gave up the hunt."

Thinking it was a long shot, but certainly a possibility, Maddie agreed. "How about if I start making some calls? You stop by Mrs. Cheng's and pick up dinner and come over to help. I really don't want to be alone tonight, Mary Grace. I'd like some company."

The line was strangely silent for several seconds. "OK. Just let me tie up a few loose ends and—"

"Oh, gosh, Mary Grace. You have a date, don't you? I'm so sorry. Just forget about my whining."

"Now, don't you worry. He's only a corporate attorney, single *and* straight, pulling down two hundred thousand a year. Men like that are a dime a dozen in this town," she said wryly. "It'll just take me a minute to blow him off. I'll be over in an hour."

Maddie smiled through a shimmer of tears. "Thanks. You really are the best friend."

By nine o'clock Maddie and Mary Grace had put a healthy dent in three containers of Chinese food and polished off two cartons of Ben and Jerry's Mocha Heath Toffee Crunch. They had called all the hospitals in northern New Jersey and several of the local police stations as well.

They hadn't found a trace of Ben.

Resting her head in her hands, Maddie stared down at the table and the empty ice cream containers. Had she really eaten an entire pint by herself? She hadn't even been that desperate after Trevor had dumped her. In disgust, she pushed the carton to the middle of the table. "You might as well go home," she said sadly, standing to escort Mary Grace to the door. "There's not much more we can do tonight."

Mary Grace put a hand on her shoulder and squeezed. "I guess not. If you want, I could spend the night in the guest room. I don't mind, you know." She walked into the hallway. "Unless Ben is really sleeping in there? It might be a rush if he came home at two A.M. and found me in his bed."

Maddie snapped up her head. "How many times do I have to tell you? Ben and I are not sleeping together. And that comment wasn't very funny."

"Take it easy. You know I make it a rule never to poach in friends' territories. I just thought maybe by now you'd come to your senses and found the nerve to seduce him or something."

Maddie sat back in her chair. "Ben doesn't . . . I don't . . . it's like I keep telling you, Ben doesn't think of me in that way. Even if I . . ." Her voice trailed off as she realized to what she had almost confessed.

Mary Grace smiled a little too knowingly. "I see the way he looks at you, Maddie. I think he'd be interested if you showed a little curiosity yourself. How are things going at the office? He *is* working for you, isn't he?"

Maddie stood. "Yep. And he's doing a good job. Yesterday, he took a corporate meeting in stride and helped control Uncle Lucius. He even took minutes and transcribed them into a coherent, readable report. Not bad for a guy I found in a bot—on a beach."

Mary Grace hoisted her bag over her shoulder and headed up the hall with Maddie at her heels. "You know what this situation reminds me of? What was the name of that old movie with Rosalind Russell and Cary Grant? *Her Man Friday?* Seems to me—"

She passed the doorway to Ben's room, did a double take, and walked in. Going directly to the closet, she peeked inside. "Travels light doesn't he? Hardly anything in here."

Maddie raced to the closet and shut the door. Mary Grace's scattered observations were making her head swim. Ready to lecture, she whirled in time to find her friend opening one of the dresser drawers. She ran over and stilled Mary Grace's hand. "Hey, nosy, this is Ben's room."

"I know. I just thought maybe we'd find a clue to where he'd gone. What's this?" She lifted Ben's bottle from the dresser and held it to the light. "I never noticed this in here before."

Maddie resisted the urge to whisk the bottle away and fisted her hands at her sides. "It's Ben's. He told me it was a . . . family heirloom. His father's. Put it down."

"Hmm. Think these stones are real? They look real. Can you imagine how much this thing is worth if those are genuine emeralds and rubies? Wow."

Maddie finally grasped the bottle and gave it a tug, but not before Mary Grace managed to pull hard on the stopper. "Is that thing stuck or what?" she muttered.

"I wouldn't know," Maddie said primly, hugging the bottle to her chest. "I don't snoop into things that aren't my concern."

"And that's why you lead such a boring life," Mary Grace replied perceptively. "I guess you don't need me anymore tonight. Maybe I'll page that lawyer and see if he wants to meet for a drink or something. You go to bed at nine, but for me the night is just beginning."

She waggled her eyebrows and Maddie tried for a positive smile. "I am tired. And worried. Lord, Mary Grace, what if something serious has happened to him? He could be lying in an alley—or worse."

Mary Grace walked to the front door. "I'll bet the accident just confused him and he lost track of the time. In typical male response, he's sitting in some bar drinking beer and watching a baseball game. He'll probably come stumbling home at dawn, all innocent, to explain where he's been. I'll call tomorrow and we'll have a good laugh over it, you'll see."

Maddie, still clutching the bottle to her chest, followed Mary Grace to the front door. "Well, maybe." She chewed at her lower lip. "Thanks for everything. The dinner and moral support, I mean. Have fun tonight."

"Don't I always?" Mary Grace countered, heading out the door.

Maddie walked slowly to Ben's room and sat on the bed, the bottle firmly in her hands. What else could she do? Where else could she look? Hunching her shoulders, she rested her chin on the bottle top. After a second she blinked. Was the bottle growing warmer? And did she feel a vibration, small but insistent, coming from its insides?

A ray of hope flickered. How could she have been so dumb as to ignore the obvious? Ben had been frightened by the accident. If he had panicked, it made perfect sense he would head for the only place he'd known for centuries—his bottle. Quickly, she picked up the corner of her shirt and began to rub, positive it was the only answer.

After several seconds the stopper popped off and she set the bottle on the floor. Gray smoke began to rise and form. In a wink, Ben stood before her, dressed exactly as he'd been that morning.

Maddie's mouth opened and closed, but she couldn't

seem to form the words. "You . . . where . . . what . . . ?"
she dithered, feeling ten kinds of stupid for not looking
in the bottle in the first place.

Ben made a little formal bow. "Maddie."

"For pete's sake, stop that. And tell me what happened.
How did you get from the accident back into there?" She
pointed at the bottle resting on the floor.

Ben wrinkled his brow. "I do not know," he said, sounding as perplexed as she did. "I remember sitting in the
car, then your getting out and slamming the door. The
next thing I knew I was inside the bottle." He gave a small
shudder of disgust. "The thought you might not figure
out where I was became frightening, Maddie. And it was
the strangest thing—I felt it when you came into the room,
and I knew when Mary Grace held the bottle. I could also
tell when you took it from her. It was a very odd feeling."

It was all Maddie could do to keep from jumping up
and hugging him. "Well, put the stopper back on and hide
it in the closet or something, will you? The thing's giving
me the willies."

Ben stared at the bottle resting near his feet. "I don't
think I can do that, Maddie."

"Why not?" she demanded.

Ben gave a shrug. "I'm not sure. The bottle has powers,
I think. After all, it nourished and protected me those hundreds of years I was adrift at sea. I knew and felt very
little that entire time, but somehow the bottle had the intelligence to keep me alive. It must contain much of the
jinn's magic."

"The who's what?" she asked, recognizing the foreign
word but not sure what it meant.

Ben reached down, picked up the bottle and placed it
back in the center of the dresser. Carefully, he took his
wallet from his jacket pocket and opened it, setting the
business card the cab driver had given him next to the
bottle. "Never mind. It is of no importance."

Frowning, Maddie crossed her arms. He was avoiding her questions again, and she didn't like it one bit. "Ben, this jinn, is he the one who imprisoned you? Is he the reason you've been in the bottle all these centuries?"

He stepped back from the dresser and headed out the door, calling over his shoulder. "I am starving, Maddie. Is there anything in the refrigerator to eat?"

Maddie stood, refusing to let him ignore her. This latest scare had convinced her it was time she knew more about Ben's past. Damn it, she wanted—no—she would *demand* answers. She arrived in the kitchen in time to see him nuking one of the containers of leftovers.

"Ben? Don't run away from me. Why can't you answer my questions?"

He made a big production out of selecting a fork. The microwave dinged and he took out the carton and dug into the container. "This is different, but very good. It is shrimp, is it not? I don't think I have ever eaten shrimp before."

"Then how did you know what it was?" she asked, not forgetting how clever he could be at distracting her.

"Television. A documentary on ocean farming in Louisiana versus the same in Japan. It was very interesting. Did you know that the industry is huge? Multimillions of dollars—"

"Ben, stop it. Come sit down and talk with me. Please."

He sighed, but did as she asked. Maddie brought two glasses of iced tea, something he'd told her he liked, to the table. Sitting across from him, she squeezed her lemon wedge and waited while Ben methodically emptied each of the cartons.

Finally finished, he set the fork and last container on the table. "What is it you wish to know, Maddie?" he asked, looking her in the eye.

"I want to know if a jinn was responsible for imprisoning you in the bottle."

"Yes."

Waiting for more details, Maddie raised a brow. Ben sipped at his tea, his features unreadable. "That's it? Just yes? You aren't going to tell me his name or what happened?"

Ben closed his eyes. "I cannot."

"Who says?" Maddie demanded.

"It is part of my curse. The jinn"—he whispered the word—"forbade me to mention his name aloud or tell how I got inside the bottle. I have obeyed his orders all these years."

She gave an indelicate snort. "And you think he's still alive? Look around you, Ben. It's a new century. And you already know my position on God and the devil. They don't exist."

"You are wrong, but that is neither here nor there. I am forbidden to say his name to anyone."

She took a drink of her tea, determined to help him with his fears. "I distinctly remember you muttering a strange name when I first brought you to the house. And you've lived outside your bottle for over a week now, right? You say both those things are forbidden, yet nothing bad's happened, has it?"

Ben raised his hands in protest. "What about today? After I blinked the front of the semi into a harmless puff of vapor, the bottle brought me back of its own accord. Why did that happen? You were able to rescue me, to release me, but if I broke the rules again, it might not be so easy the next time."

Maddie's brow wrinkled in confusion. "But you said *I* was your master. My wishes must be honored first and foremost. Isn't that correct?"

Ben nodded, his face pensive.

"So if I order you to tell me, then it should be all right, shouldn't it?"

He gazed at her across the table. "Logically, yes. If I do your bidding, I cannot be punished."

Maddie smiled. "OK. I order you to tell me how you got trapped inside the bottle. Right now."

"It is not a pleasant story, Maddie."

She reached across the table and laid her hand over his. "I didn't think it would be. But I'd still like to hear."

Ben took a breath, as if debating her command. After a full minute his shoulders slumped and Maddie knew she had finally won a battle. "It was the twentieth year of my father's reign as sultan. He was a wealthy and powerful man, beloved by his people. I was his oldest child, heir to his kingdom and brother to a half-sister named Amyri by my father's second wife."

Maddie grinned at the way he said his sister's name. They had obviously been very close. She gave his hand an encouraging pat, and in return Ben smiled wistfully.

"Amyri was beautiful, not only on the outside, but inside as well. She had a kind and generous spirit and a gentle heart. You remind me of her at times. You and she would have liked each other," he said with a sigh of sadness.

"I bet we would have. What happened to her?"

"Amyri had just turned sixteen. She had received many proposals of marriage. Wisely, my father was weighing them all, hoping to make the most advantageous match for his kingdom, when it all began."

Maddie resisted the urge to spout her views on the subject of arranged marriages. In his own way, Ben was telling her Amyri had been used as a political pawn, something she refused to approve of. But she also tried to remember that whatever had taken place had happened more than a thousand years ago. There was nothing to be done about it now.

"On the day before my father was to make his final decision on who would win Amyri, he received a visit from a man claiming to be a great prince from a faraway land. The man looked young and healthy. He brought with him many chests of gold and jewels to barter for Amyri's hand. He impressed my father greatly, but there was something about the man I did not trust. I told my father of my fears and he agreed, confiding he was planning to refuse the man. But my father was greedy. And his greed brought about our family's ruin."

Ben stopped to take another drink of tea and Maddie thought back to her own family. From the sound of it, Ben had lost everyone he loved in one fell swoop, just like she had. She waited while he set his glass on the table.

"My father turned the man down but, unbeknownst to me, connived to keep the chests of jewels and coins. On the morning of his rejection, the suitor surmised what was about to happen and began to scream his rage. In doing so, his true face was revealed. He was old, ugly, and gnarled, unfit to wed Amyri, and he had known it. He had changed himself into a young prince so he would be pleasing to the eye and my father would approve. He, too, was a cheat.

"In his rantings, the evil one admitted he was a jinn, one of the demons created by the devil. I challenged him to a duel and he laughed. Then he cursed me, condemning me to the bottle forever. After proclaiming my punishment, he spirited Amyri away. I was given to my father's greatest enemy to be his slave. The jinn forced Amyri to be his concubine. She died in childbirth some months later and my father died shortly after, alone and ashamed of the evil he had brought upon his children."

Ben stared down into his lap with his eyes closed, as if telling the tale had worn him down. Maddie looked about the room and felt nothing amiss, no demons lurking or apparitions peeking from behind the toaster. She imagined what it would be like to reveal such a horrific story after so many years of fear and gave Ben's hand another squeeze. "I'm so sorry. It must have been terrible for you, finding out what had happened and not being able to prevent it."

Ben raised his gaze to hers and Maddie saw a shimmer of pain reflecting from his eyes. She stood, but not as quickly as he did. Before she could reach Ben's side, he had left the kitchen, walked to his room, and closed the door.

She knocked softly. "Ben? Please let me in. I have a few more questions and I . . . I need you."

She was surprised when the door opened with a little *whoosh* of air. Ben's eyes were brighter, but he still looked defeated and beaten. "You *need* me, Maddie? How may I serve you?"

OK, so she'd lied. Maybe revealing what she was going to do for him later would cheer him up. "Not in that way. How many times do I have to tell you your magic isn't what's important to me? Except, of course, for my company. And once that's straightened out I don't ever intend on using it again. You'll be free to be your own person, Ben, live your own life however you see fit."

He blinked owlishly, and she smiled. "You didn't really think I would keep you a slave, did you? Have a little faith."

But instead of smiling at the news, he seemed more upset. "You said you needed me, Maddie."

She stepped back at his abrupt tone. "I only meant I needed to ask you a few more questions, if that's OK? And I'll try to make them less . . . painful."

His gaze narrow, Ben opened the door wider and let her in. Maddie walked to the dresser and glanced at his bottle. "You think that somehow the jinn's magic is still inside the bottle, controlling you and keeping you in line?"

He folded his arms and stared at the bottle with her. "Small things, your purple suit or riding on a magic carpet, are unimportant when weighed against the lives of others. You, as my master, did not command I save the minivan, Maddie. I did it of my own volition. In the eyes of the jinn, I am a slave and have no rights. It was not my choice to prevent an accident. I tampered with fate and was punished for it."

"So you worked your magic to save the people in the van, and the bottle brought you back here as a warning? Is that what you think?"

Ben shrugged and walked to the bed. Sitting down, he rested his hands on his thighs. "It is the only logical answer to how I ended up in the bottle."

"Yet it has allowed you to do little things—things I don't always ask for, but you think I need or want?"

He gave a small smile. "But in your heart, you did wish for those things. I heard the longing in your voice when you gazed at the purple suit. That night at The Golden Lotus, you asked in your heart to be taken somewhere to forget about your cares. In a way, I did grant your requests."

She gave a hopeful sigh. "Maybe its powers are dwindling, breaking down after so many years. What would happen if I commanded you to send the bottle to the bottom of a live volcano or the deepest part of the ocean?"

Ben rubbed the bridge of his nose, his brows raised in a furrow of confusion. "I don't know. And please do not ask it of me. What if I were imprisoned forever for attempting to destroy the bottle? Then what?"

Maddie hadn't thought about that possibility. But she saw where Ben was coming from and recognized his concern. The bottle was unpredictable, a ticking time bomb at best. Playing with its rules might take Ben away forever, something she did not want to have happen. "So you think we should go on as we have been, because the bottle doesn't seem to mind if you're walking about at my command?"

He nodded. "It's for the best, I think." He rose and stood in front of her. "I am tired. May I go to sleep now?"

She dragged both hands through her hair. It had been a long day for both of them. Hesitantly, she stepped closer and wrapped her arms around his middle. Squeezing tight, she opened her heart and tried to show him how much she cared. "Sure. I'm going to call Mary Grace to let her know you've returned, then go to sleep, too."

Stepping back, she gazed into his dark, shining eyes. "Thank you for explaining what happened all those years ago. I know how much it hurts to dredge up old memories. I promise I won't ask anything so painful ever again."

Ben had lied when he'd told Maddie he was tired. In all his years inside the bottle, he couldn't remember ever being so aware of what was happening around him. He'd known the instant Maddie had set foot in the apartment, calling his name as she walked through the empty rooms. He was growing so sensitive to her he could even read most of her thoughts. And tonight, while she was looking for him and telling Mary Grace what had happened, he'd been torn in two by what he had sensed coming from her heart.

Maddie loved him.

Her reticence at getting close to him was not because he was distasteful to her, or because he was her slave. She was holding herself from her emotions because she thought she wasn't good enough for him, and she was fearful he might mock her if he knew the truth. Trevor had fanned the flames of her inadequacy and made her afraid to love.

So Maddie had shown how much she loved him in the only way she could. She had told him he would be a free man after he helped her save Winston Design. He would be free to go his own way in the world—without her.

But he had found out an ugly truth today. The bottle controlled his destiny. Unless it was out of their lives forever, he and Maddie could have no peace together. In reality, he had no idea what might happen if he admitted out loud his love for her or she for him. The bottle might suck them up and keep them both prisoners for all eternity, something he refused to risk. As much as he liked the idea of spending forever with her, Maddie did not deserve such a cruel fate.

To save her, to at least have her as a part of his life, he needed to hold her at arm's length and continue to do her bidding. It was the only way to keep her safe.

Besides, in order for Maddie to set him free, the seven words had to be spoken exactly as written. There was no way she could ever know those words on her own. And he was forbidden to tell them to her.

Thirteen

Maddie woke to the tantalizing aromas of cooked bacon and fresh coffee. Still unused to someone going to trouble for her, she lay with her eyes closed while the comforting smells seeped into her senses. After a few minutes, reality crept in, reminding her she had to get up and dress. With a little groan, she rolled over and checked her bedside clock. It was almost ten, well past her usual Sunday wake-up time.

She sniffed the air, dismayed by the guilt niggling in the back of her brain. Ben had listened carefully yesterday when she'd explained how to make bacon in the microwave; this morning he had fixed her breakfast. He had performed another little kindness in her life she didn't deserve.

Last night, she had poked and prodded where she didn't belong. She had hurt him by stirring up memories he wanted forgotten. To appease her childish curiosity, she'd broken the promise she'd made to herself and had inadvertently been cruel.

Maddie remembered she had called Max from the accident site to find out if Ben had walked back to the plant from the diner. Though Max hadn't sounded concerned when she informed him Ben had disappeared, he was a humanitarian at heart. If he knew the truth about Ben,

knew how much Ben wanted to help Winston Design, he
would have been as worried as she was for his safety. And
deep down inside, she really wanted the two most important men in her life to be friends.

Maddie dialed the plant number. Expecting Max to answer, she was taken by surprise. "Paulette? What are you
doing there on a Sunday?" she asked at the sound of the
secretary's voice.

"Maddie. It's you," Paulette sputtered, sounding perturbed at being bothered on a Sunday morning—and the
fact that Maddie was questioning her right to be there.
"Just a little overtime. Max asked if I could make a few
calls and do some paperwork, so I said OK. He also told
me Ben had gone missing yesterday. You find him yet?"

Maddie fought the urge to be jealous of Paulette's concern. She and Ben had gotten along from the start. It was
only logical the woman might worry. "He surfaced and
he's fine. Tell Max for me, would you? By the way, do
you think Ben and I need to come in today?"

"I don't think that's necessary. The new assemblers are
busy, Max is supervising, and Phil has the day off. Oh,
by the way, Mr. Fulbright called to check on things. I
assured him we were on schedule, but I don't think he
believed me. He just kept grumbling about what it was
costing us to run twenty-four-seven. If you ask me, that
man needs to get drunk or get laid. The sooner the better."

Maddie was mildly surprised at Paulette's crude assessment of her uncle, since the girl usually acted as if Lucius
Fulbright was invisible. Still, Maddie couldn't help but
laugh at the idea Paulette presented. "And where," she
began, giggling, "would he find a woman worthy enough
to have sex with? I always got the impression Uncle Lucius disapproved of the female gender."

"Ain't that the truth? Still, he needs something in his
life to take his mind off this company."

Maddie silently agreed, but didn't think she should gossip further about her uncle with an employee. "Guess I'll see you on Monday, Paulette."

"Maddie, can I ask you a question?"

"Of course," Maddie answered, eager to help. Though she'd gone to school with Paulette and encouraged Max to promote her, the young woman had never shown any interest in cultivating a friendship.

"What about Ben? I mean, is he married or anything? Personnel doesn't have him on file, and I was wondering if you had his home number."

Maddie swallowed. She should have figured it would be about Ben. It was only logical an attractive woman like Paulette would be interested in such a hunky guy. If he was going to work in the real world, she would have to get used to women coming on to him and trying to date him. Maddie closed her eyes and said in her most innocent voice, "I think you should ask Ben that question yourself. I'm not privy to his personal life."

Silence hung in the air for a second too long before Paulette finally responded. "That's funny. I heard a rumor that the two of you were . . . very close."

Maddie had known that when she told people Ben was staying in her apartment there would be speculation over the arrangement, but she hadn't thought anyone—besides Mary Grace, of course—would have the nerve to discuss it out loud. If Paulette was commenting on her and Ben, she could only imagine what Letitia and the rest of the staff had to say.

"He's my assistant and nothing more, Paulette. And office gossip is so tacky."

She heard the girl sigh. "Isn't it, though? Bye, Maddie. You and Ben have a nice day."

The line went dead and Maddie stared into the receiver, realizing she would have to make another stab at setting the record straight with everyone about her relationship with Ben. It just wasn't the kind of topic she found easy to address.

She knocked on the bathroom door to be sure the room was empty, then went in and showered. After dressing in jeans and a T-shirt, she opened the drapes to a beautiful, sunny day.

Her hands on her hips, Maddie thought about Paulette and her assurance that everything was running smoothly at the plant. Maybe she could make it up to Ben for being so pushy last night. Maybe they both deserved a little break.

She grabbed a roomy straw tote from her closet, stuffed an old bathing suit, cover-up, sunblock, and several beach towels inside, and set the bag at her door. It was the weekend before the Memorial Day holiday, a little early for the sun worshipers to be out full force, so traffic would be light. Ben had never been to the Jersey shore. He didn't know what he'd been missing.

Gulls shrieking overhead pierced the quiet drone of the surf. Hot sun warmed the still cool May air, beating down a promise of the torrid summer to come. Maddie lay still, letting the salty ocean breeze wash over her as gently as a lover's touch. With her eyes closed behind her oversized sunglasses, she reached out a hand and sifted fine grains of sand through her fingers in a slow little fall. It wasn't Key West, but if she tried hard, she could pretend she was with Gram at Winston's Walk, far away from all the cares in her life. Safe from the world.

Drops of water, as cold as pebbles of ice, pelted her body and she opened one eye. Ben, resembling a Greek god from some ancient painting, stood over her. Shaking the water from his sleek black hair like a friendly puppy, he smiled, showing brilliant white teeth in his tanned face. Wisely, he had chosen a loose-fitting, plain red bathing

suit from the fashion magazine instead of one of the nar-
cissistic little spandex types. She couldn't help but notice
how much better Ben filled it than the model in the ad.

"Are you having fun?" Maddie asked out loud, attempting to look perturbed.

Ben grinned in return. "This is wonderful, Maddie. Except for Key West, I can't remember when I last spent
time on a beach. In my country, water such as this was a
great luxury."

"I imagine so." Sitting up, she adjusted her glasses.
"We're lucky. It's too early in the season for jellyfish. The
cleanup crews have worked hard, so there's not a lot of
debris."

Ben sat on the towel beside her and gazed at the ocean,
returning the eager waves of two big-haired girls wearing
string bikinis over very little of their tanned, model-perfect
bodies. "Everyone is so friendly here, Maddie. Jennifer
and Linda invited me to dinner. When I told them we were
together, they said you could come along as well."

Pulling her cover-up a little tighter, Maddie scanned
the shore. Jennifer and Linda had joined two other young
women in equally scanty suits. Four pairs of eyes were
now trained in their direction; Maddie could see the drool
from where she sat.

"I just bet they wanted me along," she mumbled, wag-
gling her fingers at the staring quartet. In seconds the
girls stopped gawking and got down to the serious business of tanning.

She glanced at Ben. "Do you *want* to have dinner with
them?"

He lay back on his towel, hands behind his head, and
gazed at her through inky-dark lashes. "Only if you do.
It is of no importance."

What a guy, she thought, suppressing a sigh. With a
small grimace of envy, she reinspected the long-haired,
sunbathing girls. Thoughtfully, she ran her hands over her

head. Her cowlick had settled down to a manageable
bump and the rest of her hair had begun to curl softly.
Maybe she would let it grow back into the unruly mass
it had always been. Mary Grace had big ideas about spiral
perms and defrizzers, swearing she could turn Maddie's
tresses into hair fit for a goddess. Suddenly, it didn't sound
like such a lame idea. At the sound of Ben's voice, she
started from her goddess-hair dreams.

"Maddie, why have you not been in the water? I thought
you liked the ocean."

She felt the beginnings of a blush and searched her tote
for the sunblock. Maybe if she ignored him, Ben would
get the hint and let the topic drop.

"Maddie? You are doing exactly what you so often ac-
cuse me of. It was a simple question," he persisted.

She pulled out the bottle and opened the top, then
squirted a goodly amount of lotion in her hands and began
to slather her legs with the greasy stuff. "Uh . . . I burn.
And when I don't burn, I freckle—ugly things, big as
dimes sometimes. They make me look like a Dalmatian,"
she muttered. Rubbing harder, she hoped the silly answer
would shut him up.

"But I thought that was the reason one used sunblock.
To keep from burning or looking like a . . . spotted dog,"
he replied, all too logically.

Maddie stopped her frantic scrubbing long enough to
spare him a sideward glance. The smile on Ben's face ran
from ear to ear. Disgruntled, she flipped the bottle back
into the straw bag resting on the sand between their towels.
"Yeah, well, it doesn't always work, smart guy."

She busied herself by folding an extra towel into a pillow, jumping at his next impertinent query. "Why are you
ashamed of your body, Maddie?"

Her hands stilled and she took a breath. "Where did
you get such a ridiculous idea? I'm not ashamed of anything."

Maddie thought she heard Ben *tsk*, but he said nothing. Instead, he sat up and reached into her bag for the discarded sunblock. Setting it on her towel, he scooted over and knelt behind her. A second later, the cotton cover-up slid off her shoulders. From the corner of her eye, she saw Ben pick up the bottle, remove the cap, and squeeze a bit of the cream into his palms, rubbing them together to warm the lotion.

Maddie sat as if carved in stone. She knew what Ben was going to do—thought seriously about stopping him—but the words wouldn't come. Against her better judgment, she sat and waited for his touch.

It began at the top of her spine; faintly at first, his fingers radiated outward in powerful yet caressing strokes. His strong, gentle hands kneaded her shoulders and upper arms; his thumbs probed deep as they moved in small tight circles across her now burning skin. Unbearably, his hands glided over her backbone and down to the dip in the curve of her bathing suit.

Is it my imagination, or has this suit shrunk since the last time I wore it? Are Ben's hands really touching the base of my spine?

His palms slid slowly upward, over her shoulders and onto her collar bone, then lower, toward the top of her suit. The heat of his hands burned her too-sensitive skin, creating a flurry of warmth in her belly unlike anything Maddie had ever felt before. A tingle of anticipation shot through her when Ben's fingers dipped further, barely brushing the swell of her breasts.

"Are you cold, Maddie?" Ben's voice tickled her ear.

Maddie looked down at the smattering of goose bumps dotting her arms. Somehow, her cover-up had dropped onto the sand. The ocean breeze caused it to flutter as fast as her beating heart. She took a deep breath.

"Certainly not. It must be ninety out," she managed, determined to enjoy the touch of his hands. Today was supposed to be a day of play, a day to toss caution out the window—something she hadn't done in months.

Ben's palms worked the muscles of her neck, relaxing her into a languid puddle of pleasure. "You are tense, Maddie. And I do not see any of those gigantic freckles you complain about. Your skin is as creamy white as the finest of pearls. I think you are tugging at my arm."

She moaned, too limp to laugh at his inept statement. "Pulling your leg? Maybe just a little. But I never seem to tan like the Jennifers and Lindas of the world, either. I've always been totally unfashionable."

Ben stopped his ministrations, but still knelt close to her back. "In my time, women with skin such as yours were envied, as were women with full breasts and flaring hips. They were marked as good breeders who would bear strong sons and daughters. Women who had bodies like yours showed them off to their best advantage, many wearing diaphanous blouses of finest silk, some no clothing at all from the waist up."

Yikes! Maddie fumbled for her cover-up, but came away empty-handed. She sat up straight and pulled her arms to her chest. "Hey, let's not get any ideas. This isn't a nude beach, you know."

Ben's laughter rumbled against the nape of her neck. "I am well aware of your new millennium morals. It is permissible for a man and woman to live together openly without the benefit of marriage. Condoms are sold everywhere, including grade school restrooms. The modern woman keeps them in her nightstand and handbag. Yet most human beings hide their bodies as if they have something of which to be ashamed. For all your forward attitudes, some things are still backward, I think."

Maddie smiled at his logic. He was right on many points. She *did* wear the plain black suit because she was ashamed of her body. Trevor had convinced her she was too top-heavy and rounded to look attractive, yet Ben kept complimenting her. Two points of view from two completely different men. And whose words meant more to her? Ben's or Trevor's?

Suddenly brave, Maddie stood and turned. Ben gazed up at her, and the look of stark approval in his ocean blue eyes gave her newfound courage. "I think it's time I tried the water. How about you?"

Ben ran his sparkling gaze up and down her body, his appreciation for her clear. "I enjoy looking at you, Maddie. The sight of you makes me glad I'm a man."

All her life Maddie had been given boring, impersonal praise for her intelligence and practicality. No one—no man, at least—had ever told her he simply enjoyed looking at her. Ben's compliment, the nicest she had ever received, registered deep in her woman's heart. As if guarding a treasure, she tucked his words inside where she could keep them near at all times.

"Race you to the water," she called over her shoulder, running into the surf with a gleeful smile.

And Ben sprinted after her, wishing their days could always be as satisfying and happy as this one.

Maddie gave Ben a sideways glance as she maneuvered her car into the busy Route 46 traffic. When they left the garage that morning he had buckled his seat belt immediately and was now sitting a bit straighter than usual. Though his head continued to swivel at the passing cars, it was obvious the memory of their near-accident still bothered him.

After Saturday's scare, Maddie was relieved Ben hadn't asked to drive to the shore or to the plant this morning. Accidents such as the one they'd almost been involved in didn't happen often, but another tragedy was always possible. She didn't know whether the thought of a crash or the idea of being banished to the bottle was his worst fear, but at least the experience had given Ben a healthy respect for automobiles.

She stared at the storm clouds gathering in the west, a stark contrast from the beautiful sunny day they had enjoyed yesterday. After a final swim at sunset, she and Ben had driven to a quaint little seafood shack located at the end of a weather-beaten pier. They had shared a delicious dinner of steamed lobster and shrimp while watching the last of the sailboats dock beneath them.

By the time they arrived home it was near eleven, and both were too tired to do much talking. She'd gone to bed and slept like a stone until her alarm rang at six. When she'd entered the kitchen, Ben had already prepared his usual morning fare. They had read the paper together, making comfortable small talk over some of the articles on the front page.

A story about an altercation between Iran and Iraq had Ben agitated, but she hadn't the expertise on world affairs to answer his probing questions, so she suggested he watch CNN that night to further educate himself on the situation in the Middle East.

Right now, both were so wrapped up in their own private thoughts that conversation was at a minimum. Maddie swung the Jetta into the company parking lot, angled into her designated space, and turned the key. She and Ben climbed out of the car and entered the building in silence. He had yet to inform her of his plans to get the extra microchips into the daily count, and she was beginning to worry.

Did he really have a plan, or was he still thinking?

Paulette, sitting at her desk and engaged in a heated phone conversation, took the time to wave and then bent to her tablet and continued scribbling. Politely, Ben let Maddie go first up the stairs, following her into Max's office. Once inside, Maddie closed the door and turned to him.

"So are you finally going to tell me about your plan?"

Ben smiled. "I was wondering why you took so long to ask. We could have talked about it on the ride, but I had the feeling you were thinking of other things."

Maddie rested her back against the door. "Funny, it looked to me like you were the one with the secret thoughts."

Appraising her starkly through darkened eyes, he said with a mischievous little grin, "I spent the ride remembering the way you looked in your bathing suit yesterday. I thought about it all night long."

Maddie felt the flush to her hairline. Looking away, she cleared her throat. "That's not funny. Now, please tell me you have a plan."

His smile widened as he put a finger to his lips. "We must be quiet if we are to keep this from Max. Where would he be right now? In his laboratory, perhaps?"

Maddie nodded. "He's been working on some big hush-hush project for the past year, until our latest problem pulled him off track. Knowing things in the assembly room are running smoothly, he's probably back to tinkering. Should we check?"

Ben folded his arms and walked to her side. "Let's go to the lab together. If he is occupied, good. If not, I will think of something to keep him busy."

They made their way down the hall, stopping at Max's laboratory door. A small GENIUS AT WORK—DO NOT DISTURB sign painted with a caricature of a frustrated Albert Einstein hung on the knob. Maddie had given the plaque to Max as a Christmas gift just last year. Everyone in the company knew he was hard at work when they saw the sign on the door.

"We're safe for the time being," she whispered.

Ben pulled at his chin. Almost imperceptibly, he passed his hand over the knob, then gave her a little smile.

"What did you just do?" Maddie hissed, taking his fore-arm and giving a tug.

Ben shrugged. "Just a precaution. Nothing more," he confided as he followed her down the hall. "We may now go to the assembly room."

Maddie frowned, wondering what he had done to the door. If Max became suspicious, he would be as relentless as a bloodhound dogging a scent. Still, Ben seemed con-fident he'd taken care of the problem.

"I hope you know what you're doing," she muttered, leading the way down the stairs. Ben gave a small chuckle, which she chose to ignore. Maybe it was better she didn't know what he was up to.

The trip to the assembly room began with a stop in the clearinghouse. Visitors were required to set aside their extraneous clothing—jackets, shoes, and the like—then walk through another door which lead to a sterile area where they changed into sanitized, lint-free gowns, hair nets, and paper booties. When finished, they climbed a flight of stairs to an observation deck and watched the process from above. The workers and maintenance crew also used the clearinghouse and sterile area, but they changed into one-piece white uniforms that looked like space suits, complete with independent air hoses and fil-ters, before going to the assembly room.

Maddie and Ben took the stairs and, being the only visitors, stood in the center of the walkway. From there, they had a perfect view of the massive room, the etching machines and doping units, as well as the drawing tables holding schematics of the specialized chips. Sheets of sili-con, some less than three-hundredths of an inch thick, were stacked up waiting to be stamped and etched.

The thrumming of a huge filtering system, which kept any particles of dust and foreign matter that might be floating in the air moving in a downward motion, filled the air. When the particles reached the tiny holes in the floor, they would be filtered out while the clean air recirculated. The process made it easy for Maddie and Ben to speak to one another and not be overheard by the workers.

"Well," she said in his ear, "now what?"

Ben's gaze searched the room. "Do you see the clock on the far wall?" he asked.

Maddie raised her eyes to the round utilitarian wall clock and nodded. Ben clapped his hands once, and she gasped. The clock's second hand began to slow until its movement was barely noticeable. Confused, it took her a few seconds to figure out what had happened.

Had Ben actually slowed down time?

She took a little breath, unwilling to accept the idea. Looking at him with her mouth agape, she started to stutter, "What . . . how . . . are you doing that?"

"Watch," he replied. Pointing down at the workers, Ben's index finger drew a few quick little circles in the air.

Like a scene out of a cartoon, the operators and maintenance crew began to move in double, then triple time as they raced through the aisles, running the machines. If the sight of them looking like alien robots souped up on caffeine hadn't been so amazing, Maddie would have laughed out loud at the crazy scene.

Minutes passed as the air from the filtering system rushed by her ears. Her head began to throb. She heard a dull ringing as, finally, the reality of the situation struck.

Ben *could* manipulate time.

She turned away from the racing assemblers to stare at him. Smiling broadly, he was gazing at her like a child waiting for his reward. Unsure how to react, she frowned with frustration. "And how will this explain the extra chips? There's still only so many hours in a day."

His smile faded. "Ah, but I have done one other tiny, inconsequential little thing, Maddie."

She raised a brow, almost afraid to ask. "How tiny?"

"So small as to be insignificant," he assured her.

Maddie stared back down at the workers and the first thought that came to mind was ants on speed. "Explain insignificant."

Ben placed a hand on her shoulder. "I have fixed it so they will remember nothing. To them, today will be a normal day, perhaps a little more tiring than usual. The crew will be proud of the fact the machines completed double the number of microchips, and Max and Paulette and Mr. Dunlap will think nothing of it."

Maddie gave a little gasp. "You went into their heads? You have the ability to control time *and* the human mind? Ben, how could you?"

He stepped back, his look of confusion genuine. "It will not hurt them, Maddie. And I've only done such a thing when it has been absolutely necessary. You did ask me to come up with a plan. It was the only thing that seemed sensible."

Maddie had a hard time arguing against what she knew he felt was a perfectly logical solution. But she hadn't meant for him to manipulate other human beings, only the situation. Something in her conscience, some little part of her ethical inner self, had the feeling the scene before her was very very wrong. But how could she explain it to Ben?

"You're telling me you've done this before?"

He nodded. "A time or two. Only when my master wished it."

She glanced quickly around the walkway. "Where are Paulette and Phil? What's happening to them and the other people in the building that aren't in this room?"

He gave her a sheepish smile. "A few minutes ago they became very tired. I would imagine they are all napping. They will probably sleep until the end of the day and wake feeling completely refreshed."

She straightened. "I see. And what will they think happened here today?"

Ben shrugged his broad shoulders. "They will be impressed that the machines made such wonderful progress. It will not concern Max that they doubled production. He will be pleased, I can assure you."

Maddie still didn't like the idea that Ben could control minds. And she couldn't even address the thought of his being able to manipulate time. "I see. And what about the second and third shifts? Will you do the same to them?"

He took a step back, his tone commanding. "I will need to stay the night to take care of the others. I plan on bringing things to a more normal pace an hour before this crew leaves, so their day ends gradually and their actions have time to return to normal. If I handle each shift in the same manner, no one will be the wiser and there should be enough microchips to fill both orders by the end of the week."

Maddie laid a hand on her heart. That meant Winston Design would fulfill its contracts—and save its reputation, as well. Exactly what she had been hoping for.

Just what her father would have wanted.

But she couldn't help wonder if James Winston would have wanted the problem solved in a not-quite-ethical manner. Did it really matter how Winston Design succeeded?

And when it did, what would happen between her and Ben?

Fourteen

Ben gazed down at Maddie, asleep on her cot in Max's office. Admiring her in the predawn silence, as he had done the past four mornings, gave him the greatest of pleasure. In a short while Max, Paulette, and the day crew would arrive, breaking the spell darkness cast over the plant; for now he was content to simply stare.

It had been a week of exhausting effort, but they were close to reaching their goal. If all went as planned, today would be the day they filled the quota for Winston Design's orders. And only he and Maddie would know what they had done.

Maddie had left the building for a few hours on that first morning, when she had driven back to the city and packed a bag with clothing and personal care items for herself, as well as a small overnight bag for him. Since then, they had lived together at the plant, eating catered meals from a local diner, showering in the small bath off the employees' break room, and sleeping on cots. During the day Maddie used Max's office as her own, setting up sales meetings and figuring proposals for the coming month while faxing her uncle of their progress. While she worked, Ben observed proceedings from the assembly room platform or walked the floor on inspection tours, keeping a close watch on the workers.

Over the past four days, he had found the business of controlling time and men's thoughts nerve-racking. Unsure of the ramifications of his handiwork, he'd had Maddie dismiss the security guard so he himself could closely monitor every move made by the assemblers. He didn't know how much interference in the passage of time or the inner workings of the human mind was allowed through his powers, and he feared what might happen if he slipped up.

Much to Ben's relief, after that first day he hadn't needed to touch Max's mind. Once the older man realized production was on the rise, Max had squirreled himself away in his laboratory in order to continue his top secret project. He acted pleased that Ben and Maddie were handling things and didn't seem to mind they were living in the plant, either. It looked like Max was beginning to approve of Ben's consuming interest in the company—and in Maddie.

Ben knelt beside the cot and lightly brushed his hand over the fringe of bangs at Maddie's brow. Even in sleep, her forehead wrinkled in a worried frown. She had been so pensive this past week, never questioning him outright about the morality of his acts, but he knew her doubts were simmering right below the surface. Still, as long as Maddie forbid him to make the chips magically appear, he had come up with no other logical way to infiltrate thousands of them into the company's daily output.

Today was Friday, the last day of work for the extra assemblers. By next week, he expected everything in the company to be back to normal. Monday was a holiday called Memorial Day. The microchips would be packaged over the weekend and couriered to Comdisc and Butler & Maggio first thing Tuesday morning, sure to arrive by the contracted due dates.

But what would happen then, when Maddie no longer had need of him?

He walked to the coffeemaker Maddie had installed in the office and poured a steaming cup, adding a drop of cream just the way she liked. Carrying the coffee to the cot, he squatted and held the aromatic brew under her nose. Maddie sniffed and he smiled, thinking how wonderful she looked first thing in the morning. The sight of her, all relaxed and sleep-tousled, brought a tightening of desire to his groin.

She opened one honey-colored eye and gazed up at him. "Hmm. That smells heavenly. You're spoiling me, Mr. Able."

Ben stood, still holding the cup. "It's the last day we need to spend here, Maddie. After tonight, things will be as they were."

Maddie sat up and swung her legs around. Pulling at her sleep shirt, she scooted to the edge of the cot. "Thank goodness. I don't mind doing my work here, but I really am happier in my office in the city. And poor Letitia, having to field all those messages and transfer the calls. I'm sure she'll be relieved to have us back, too."

She rose and ran a hand through her softly curling hair, then accepted the coffee cup from Ben and took a healthy swallow. "Mmm. Perfect, as usual. How long have you been up?"

Ben had told Maddie that, in order to be close to the production department, he was sleeping on a cot on the overhead walkway. In truth, he had stayed awake the entire four nights, monitoring each shift change or time fluctuation while he worried about staying on schedule. In between, he had found himself wandering to Max's office, where he sometimes simply sat on the sofa and stared at Maddie as she slept. He knew she would be angry if she found out he hadn't closed his eyes once all week.

"I took my shower a short while ago," he said, not really telling a lie. "Why don't you take your turn while I call for some breakfast?"

Maddie drained the coffee cup and set it down. Stretching, she walked to her suitcase propped in a corner of the sofa and began digging for clean clothes. "OK. Just order me a plain bagel with a little cream cheese. And maybe a fresh fruit cup or a banana. What about you?"

Ben picked up the phone and dialed the number for the diner. "I'll have the same. If you go slow, it should be here just about the time you're finished."

Maddie carried her clothes to the door. "Yes, sir. See you in a few minutes."

After placing the food order, Ben powered up Max's PC and honed in on the production statistics. Scrolling to the end totals, he nodded in approval. If today's output was up to par, they would have reason to celebrate. He sent a request to the printer for a paper report and waited, listening to the sounds of the plant beginning its daily grind: cars turning into the parking lot, the chatter of employees as they left or entered the building, Paulette's voice calling out a greeting . . . and footsteps—determined footsteps—pounding up the stairs.

The door to Max's office swung open with a rush, the air undulating with an almost palpable wave of annoyance. Ben looked up calmly, guessing correctly who he would see.

"Where is Madeline?" Lucius Fulbright demanded, casting an imperious glance around the cluttered room.

Ben stood. Why was it that Lucius Fulbright always called Maddie by her formal name? Why did he never refer to her as his niece? "Good morning, Mr. Fulbright. What brings you to the plant at such an early hour?"

Lucius stretched upward as if willing himself taller. "I received a fax from Madeline stating things were . . . progressing, and decided to come see for myself." He ran his gaze to Maddie's disheveled cot. "Have you finally moved out of her apartment, or has Max actually taken to living here?" he asked with a disdainful sniff.

Ben reined in the urge to turn Lucius into a wart-encrusted toad. "The cot is Maddie's. We . . . she has been sleeping here this week, overseeing production."

"I see," murmured Lucius, taking a step nearer the desk. "Then the reports she sent were accurate? We'll make our contract dates?"

"Wonderful, isn't it?" Ben observed. "Maddie took it upon herself to inspire the workers and they actually doubled production. She's quite an incredible woman, wouldn't you say?"

Lucius glared over the top of his spectacles, his gaze resting on the cot for a long second. "She's amazing, all right. Tell me something, Able. Are you and she involved?"

Ben walked to the front of the desk, rested his backside against the edge and folded his arms across his chest. It was difficult, but he managed to keep his voice steady. "My cot is in the production room, Mr. Fulbright. As to any involvement, perhaps you should ask your niece yourself."

"Ask me what?" Maddie chirped from the doorway. Smiling broadly, she lifted two paper sacks in the air. "Met the delivery boy coming up the stairs and intercepted our breakfast. Uncle Lucius, if we'd known you were coming we would have baked a cake," she quipped. "We have a lot to celebrate."

Lucius's lips curled into an almost feral grin. "So I heard. Congratulations, Madeline. I didn't think you had it in you."

Maddie set the bags on the desk, seemingly unconcerned by his nasty comment. "I didn't do it alone, Uncle. The workers kicked themselves into overdrive, and Ben proved invaluable."

She gave Ben a grateful look, then began to rifle through the sacks. "I'd have to say it was a team effort."

Lucius stepped smartly around the desk, picked up the

report from the printer, and gazed at it without comment. "And where was Max while all this was going on?" he asked, dropping the paper on the blotter.

Maddie handed Ben his bagel and cup of fresh fruit. "Here you go," she said, ignoring her uncle's pointed question.

"Thank you," Ben replied, noting Lucius Fulbright's *tsk* of disapproval.

"Madeline, I asked you where Max has been. Surely he doesn't condone the idea of your setting up housekeeping in his office."

Maddie unwrapped her own bagel and pulled it apart, spreading the cream cheese evenly over the chewy bread with a little plastic knife. "It was only for the week. Besides, Max has been so wrapped up in some new project he hardly noticed. He trusts me, Uncle Lucius. Something I wish you would do every once in a while."

Lucius glared. Sitting on the edge of the sofa, he began to straighten the pleats in his slacks. "I'll trust you, Madeline, when you give me reason to, and not before."

Ben marveled at Maddie's patience. Her eyes grew dim and she bit her lower lip, but she didn't blurt out a rude comment or burst into tears. Or toss Lucius Fulbright out of the office, something he was tempted to do himself. Instead, she took a deep breath, seeming to gather her thoughts.

"I can understand your feelings, but I wish you would find a way to file them in the past. I know I haven't done enough with the company to warrant your complete trust, but even you have to agree that the holdup in production and theft of the microchips wasn't my fault. And I've done everything in my power to rectify the situation. I intend to keep a much closer eye on things in the future, too. With Max's newest invention, Winston Design will be—"

"Max is an old fool. It's time he retired," snapped Lucius, coming to his feet.

Ben watched in fascination as a vein in Lucius Fulbright's temple began to throb. Clearly furious, Maddie clenched her fists around her coffee mug, and he gave a small grin. Her amber eyes had turned to flame. At last, Lucius had said something to truly anger her.

"Max Hefner may be a senior citizen, but he's still a genius in his field, capable of breakthrough ideas. Right now he's working on something he says will revolutionize the computer industry as we know it. With our current contracts almost settled, I will encourage him to concentrate his efforts toward that goal. I expect you to cooperate fully and give him your support as well. Now if you'll excuse us, Ben and I have a ton of work to do."

Lucius began to pace, his color rising to an indescribable shade of crimson. "I demand to see the microchips, Madeline. I want to speak with Dunlap regarding quality control. If those chips were etched in a slipshod manner— if quality was sacrificed for quantity—it will reflect badly on the company and myself. And I want to speak with Max. Is he in his laboratory?"

Maddie glanced at Ben and he shrugged his shoulders. "I would not know, Mr. Fulbright, but you are welcome to see for yourself."

Lucius spun on his heels. "I didn't ask you, Able. You're the new man in the company, so I would advise you to speak only when spoken to. Is that understood?"

"Uncle Lucius!" Maddie shouted, but it was too late. Lucius Fulbright had already marched from the room.

As if on cue, the phone rang. Ben picked it up and passed it to Maddie. It was growing late. The longer it took to get Fulbright out of the plant and on his way, the longer it would take for him to set the wheels in motion for finishing the remainder of the chips. The last person he wanted within a mile of the plant at a time like this was Maddie's nosy, manipulative uncle. He left her to han-

dle the call and walked into the hall to see what he could
do about escorting the man from the building.

Ben closed the door on his way out. From the determined look on his face and the set of his broad shoulders,
Maddie knew he was furious with her uncle and his childish tirade. Lucius's visit had her thoroughly rattled, too,
but if they didn't carry on business as usual, the man
would be even more disagreeable.

She only hoped Ben could hold his temper long enough
to allow Lucius to leave without incident. Giving Lucius
another coughing fit or bladder problem would only make
him more suspicious than he already was. Definitely not
a good idea.

She turned her attention to the call and muttered into
the phone, "Winston Design."

"Miss Winston, this is Detective Fox."

Maddie sat upright in the desk chair. It had been nearly
a week since she had spoken with the detective, and she
was eager to hear his report. "Yes, Lieutenant. What can
I do for you?"

"Afraid I don't have anything new to report, Ms. Winston. Your burglary is still under investigation. But I'd like
to tie up a few loose ends today. Letitia Moore told me
you'd been at the plant all week. Would it be possible for
my men to do a routine search of your apartment and New
York offices today, as well as fingerprint and speak to
your employees there?"

Maddie hesitated. She'd never been involved in a police
investigation before and wasn't quite sure of proper pro-
cedure, but she had nothing to hide. "Is that necessary,
Detective? We've already told you all we know."

The detective cleared his throat, as if grasping for the
correct answer to her question. "Ms. Winston, I think it's
possible one of your employees was nursing a grudge

against the company or was paid by a competitor to steal those microchips. We need prints on everyone if you want us to rule out that possibility. And it would help if you'd call the superintendent of your apartment building and give him word of our arrival."

"Well, I . . . suppose so, but I've always had complete faith in our employees. I can't believe any of them would—"

"If you insist, I can get a warrant, but it would be better if we had everyone's cooperation," the detective stated flatly. "It would cover all our bases."

Maddie felt immediately guilty. She wanted the culprits found and arrested almost as much as she wanted their current contracts met, and she certainly didn't want the lieutenant to go to the trouble of obtaining a court order. Besides, wouldn't someone who resisted having their fingerprints taken be a possible suspect? "Of course, Lieutenant. And if anyone complains, tell them you have my blessing. I'll be here all day if you need to reach me."

She hung up the phone, then called the super of her building and left a message on his answering machine requesting he cooperate fully with Detective Fox when he arrived. After that, she called Letitia and warned her of the policeman's impending visit, asking that she, too, show the man every courtesy and encourage their employees to do the same.

Maddie finished her second cup of coffee and picked at her fruit, telling herself the stolen microchips really didn't matter. Their biggest worry would be over by the end of the day. Winston Design was going to meet its contracts, keep the good will of its customers, and, most importantly, retain its reputation. Her father and grandfather would have approved.

And she owed it all to Ben. Her genie from the bottle.

Standing, she wandered to the windows in time to see her uncle's formidable black BMW race from the parking lot. She sighed. Her relationship with the man was one of the great sorrows of her life. Growing up, she'd heard her parents tease one another about the crush Lucius had on her mother, but she'd never really taken the quips to heart. If her uncle *had* been in love with Catherine Jessup, Maddie had never seen any sign of it interfering in her parents' marriage.

In fact, her mother had always treated her bachelor uncle-in-law with the utmost kindness and respect, including him in all their family get-togethers and holiday parties. Her mother had been the person who'd tolerated Lucius the most.

Unfortunately, ever since she could remember, Lucius had always looked at *her* with disdain. Maddie had never understood why he didn't treat her as a normal great-uncle might, but she had learned to live with his disapproval. Once he'd learned Maddie had inherited control of the company, his dislike of her had become a well-known fact. Her main goal, to have a pleasant working relationship with the man, now seemed to be slipping further and further from her grasp.

Maddie heard solid footsteps and turned. Ben, his handsome face chipped in a frown, walked in and headed straight for the coffeepot. After pouring a cup, he whirled to face her.

"That man is a menace. In my day, he would have been whipped in public for his insolent remarks. My father would not have tolerated such a one as he."

Maddie suppressed a smile at his outrageous statement. Ben had picked up modern ideas and speech patterns quickly, but every so often he slipped into his "old Ben" persona and made her laugh. "My father wouldn't have tolerated it, either, but I don't think he would have had my uncle whipped in Times Square. Personally, I think a good case of the hives would keep Lucius busy scratching another itch."

Ben raised a brow, his blue eyes bright. "Hives? Raised welts that cover his entire body? Even his most private—"

Maddie gasped. "Don't you dare! I was only making a joke."

Clearly deflated, Ben shrugged his shoulders. "Like the tiny grain of sand inside an oyster's shell, Maddie, your jest has the possibility of developing into a valuable pearl. I think the idea has great merit."

Maddie shook her head, holding back the impulse to let Ben have his fun. "Just keep those ideas of great merit to yourself for a while. Now, have you managed to get the day shift settled?"

"The assemblers are racing through their duties. Paulette and Phil are napping peacefully, and Max is hard at work in his laboratory. He would not even open the door to Lucius. It made your uncle quite furious. He left the building without a word, though I feared he might burst a blood vessel in the process. It will be good to have this matter resolved so the company can get back to normal, I think."

She nodded. "I have another meeting set up with Apex for the middle of June. Max guaranteed he'd have his latest invention ready by then. I thought maybe you'd like to help with the figures and graphics. If you promise not to get stage fright, I might even let you do the projections."

Ben's dark brows raised questioningly. "You would trust me, Maddie, to be a real part of the company?"

Maddie shuffled through all the things she wished she could say, holding the most reckless close inside. After this week, living with Ben so intimately and sharing such a big part of her life, trusting him with her company was the least of her worries. "Don't you realize how many times you've proven yourself this week? If you want it, you have a job with Winston Design for the rest of your life."

She reached into a stack of envelopes and pulled out the

one with Ben's name on it. "This is for you. Two weeks salary at thirty-five thousand dollars a year. I realize it isn't much with the taxes and all, but after six months you'll get a review and a raise. If you work hard, you can—"

Maddie caught her breath, watching as Ben walked from the coffeemaker to stand at her side. He took the envelope from her hand and tucked it inside his pants pocket without even opening it. "Thank you. It is more than I ever expected."

They gazed at one another for long seconds and she felt her pulse accelerate. The pungent scents of sandalwood and wild desert wind enveloped her as his presence penetrated her senses. She had come to rely so much on his strength and advice. And Ben's daily observations always made her smile. How she wanted to lean into him and let her cares fade away.

Tentatively, as if reading her mind, Ben set his palms on her shoulders and gently pulled her close. "I would like nothing better than to spend the rest of my life at Winston Design, Maddie mine," he said softly, pressing her head against his shoulder. "Soon, you will be able to pick up the pieces of your life. I will see to it you find the happiness you deserve."

Maddie felt Ben's heart beating fast under her ear. She wished she could see into his mind to find the hidden meaning in his words. Was he staying because she had just paid him, or because he wanted to be with her? Did *he* want to be the happiness he thought she deserved?

Time passed in utter silence. Reluctantly, she stepped away, her gaze focused on the middle button of his denim shirt. "I think you'd better get back to the assembly room. I have to arrange the courier pickup and call Comdisc and Butler & Maggio to let them know the orders will arrive ahead of schedule."

Growing bold, she looked up into Ben's eyes, then leaned forward and placed a fleeting kiss of gratitude on his beard-darkened cheek. "Thank you. I . . . we couldn't have done it without you."

Without warning, Ben turned his head, his lips grazing hers. Maddie opened her eyes wide in surprise, not quite believing the riot of sensations the simple touch of his mouth created. Before she could step away, Ben placed a hand on either side of her neck, drawing her near. His dark blue eyes burned with a strange inner light so hot she swore it scorched her soul.

"Your gratitude, Maddie, is not necessary, for I am still your slave. Your fondest desires, the wishes of your heart, are mine to obey."

Maddie, still reeling from the touch of his lips, could only stare at Ben's warm, hard mouth. Pressing closer, he slanted his head and kissed her fully, his lips firm against hers.

Maddie whimpered under the kiss, a little cry of urgency bubbling up from deep inside. When Ben ran his palms to the nape of her neck, she found her hands sliding from his wrists to his forearms and shoulders to clutch at his shirt front. As he deepened the kiss, she opened her lips, letting his breath capture her own.

Slowly, Ben wrapped his arms around her back. She trembled when one of his large capable hands cupped her bottom and brought her hips hard against the zipper of his jeans. Thrilled by their sudden intimacy, she let her fingers creep into his hair, aching to feel him melt against her. Moving her mouth under his, she felt his tongue fill her with the taste of elemental male desire. She arched her hips and found the proof of his masculinity throbbing against her. Maddie's heart swelled with anticipation.

Ben wanted her as a man wanted a woman.

Shocked by the revelation, she dragged her mouth out from under his and took a gulp of air. Resting her forehead on his chin, she struggled to find the words, desperate to explain her own feelings.

Slowly, she raised her gaze. Ben's face looked carved in granite. Maddie staggered when his eyes narrowed suspiciously, he released her and stepped back.

"I am sorry, Master, for what I just did. Please, do not speak of my shame. I promise it will not happen again."

Dropping his hands to his sides, Ben walked quickly from the room.

Maddie took another look at the clock on the far wall, noting it was seven minutes past five. After Ben's hasty departure, the day had dragged by like an eternity. She had expected to hear a rousing cheer or some special form of celebration when the final chip was finished and wondered what, if anything, had gone wrong.

She'd spent most of her day conferring with art and advertising in the New York office. After speaking with the vice president of Comdisc, she'd made several attempts to locate Dominic Maggio. Secretly grateful she hadn't reached the surly man, she left word with his secretary that their order was being sent on schedule. She only hoped that, after all the warnings of a probable delay, the two companies were pleased they would be receiving the orders as per their contracts.

In between all the calls and proposals, she'd tried to make some sense of what had happened with Ben. Confused, she lay back against the worn leather of the desk chair and closed her eyes. Placing two fingers against her lips, she relived the feel of his mouth, the taste of his tongue as it sparred with her own. Why had he been so angry, so impossibly short-tempered after their kiss? What had she done to make him grow cold?

Maddie tried to remember what it had been like to kiss Trevor, but she couldn't call it to mind. Ben and his demanding touch had erased completely the memory of her ex-fiancé and his lovemaking. He had imprinted her body with the feel of his probing hands and hungry mouth, engulfing her with a longing she had never experienced with any other man.

And he had called her "master," then walked away from her in shame.

Maddie stood, went to the doorway and peered down the hall. Max's laboratory door, absent of its Albert Einstein plaque, was still closed. She heard a little cheer from the first floor and smiled. It sounded as if the last microchip was finally complete. Voices and footsteps floated up the stairwell and she waited, hoping Ben, Phil, and the entire crew would gather in the office with her for a little celebration.

The lab door swung open and Max raced into the hall, his weathered face wrinkled with a smile. Maddie skittered out of the way as he charged into the room. "They've done it, Maddie girl! Ben just called to let me know. Everyone's on their way up, so get back inside and act surprised."

Voices from the stairway grew louder and she braced herself for the sight of the assemblers and Paulette and Phil. And Ben. Always Ben.

Twelve people marched joyously into the office. All talking at once, they congratulated one another on a job well done, boasting to Maddie about how they planned to relax over the holiday weekend. Paulette opened the box she was carrying and began passing out plastic champagne flutes. Phil Dunlap, usually stone-faced and silent, energetically pumped Maddie's hand.

"We did it, Maddie. And thanks to your assistant, we'll probably do it again. Ben really knows how to keep the line moving," Phil said, giving her an impetuous hug.

Maddie smiled at Phil's on-the-mark observation. If he only knew what Ben was capable of. "Ah, where is Ben?" she asked, scanning the room.

The sound of Ben's booming voice swept through the

cheerful throng. "I'm right here—with the champagne. Everyone ready?"

Ben took the huge bottle he was holding and deftly popped the cork. Champagne fizzed, splashing over the carpet and the ecstatic workers as they hurried to catch the sparkling liquid in their glasses. Maddie held up her flute and Ben made his way through the crowd to fill her glass, then Max's.

Eyeing the dusty bottle and ancient label, Maddie raised a wary brow. "And where, exactly, did you find this champagne, Mr. Able?" she whispered, well aware that the vintage and brand marked the bottle as almost priceless.

Ben gave a wry grin, refusing to be intimidated. "I do not think the Rothschilds will miss this one insignificant bottle, Maddie," he muttered. "After all, they had hundreds more just like it lying about gathering dust in their vault."

Maddie bit at her lower lip. Ben reminded her of a little boy who had washed his mother's car with her very best silk blouse. How could she chastise him for *borrowing* a thousand-dollar bottle of champagne when he had done so much for her company? Raising her glass, she winked. "For this one time only, Mr. Able, you're probably right."

Max proposed a toast and everyone sipped at their glasses. Maddie waited for silence, wanting to announce the extra day's paid holiday she intended to add to the long Memorial Day weekend. Before she formed the words, a hard knock startled them all into silence. The crowd turned to find Detective Fox and two patrolmen standing at attention in the doorway. Curious, the workers stepped aside as the policemen filed into the room.

"Detective," Maddie said, holding up her glass, "please join us in celebrating our victory. We reached our quota today."

Looking as disheveled as usual, Lieutenant Fox nodded gravely, his eyes directed at Ben. "Congratulations, Ms. Winston. Now, I have some news for you."

With deliberate movements, he took the champagne bottle from Ben's hand. The entire room gasped as one when a patrolman snapped handcuffs on Ben's wrists.

"Benjamin Able, you're under arrest for burglary, breaking and entering, and theft of private property. You have the right to remain silent. You have the right . . ."

Fifteen

Her arms crossed, Maddie paced in a tight circle of annoyance as she watched the thin, dark-haired man sitting at the table in the middle of the visitor's room. Robert Perlman, the lawyer Max had hired to assist with Ben's release, was shuffling through his worn briefcase like a homeless man inspecting a dumpster. As if searching for the perfect tasty morsel, he squinted determinedly through thick, wire-rimmed spectacles as he picked up and discarded file after file.

Having long ago lost her temper with him and the entire Englewood Heights police department, Maddie halted in her steps and gave an exasperated sigh. Until last night, she hadn't realized Detective Fox was the lone investigative officer of the town's small police force. She'd found out he was expected to handle any and all crimes. The city administrators still adhered to the belief that their tiny town of upscale homes and pristine lawns was the pinnacle of suburban living. It had become apparent that, aside from the occasional drunken driver or peeping Tom, the police here were unequipped to tackle serious felons, one of which they considered Ben.

Unfortunately, this country bumpkin attitude toward crime caused the wheels of justice to roll at a snail's pace—much too slowly for someone like Maddie, who was used to the hustle and bustle of New York City.

Sensing her pacing had failed to attract the attorney's attention, she tried for sarcasm. "Mr. Perlman, what is taking them so long to find Ben? Surely he can't be lost in this one-cell penal colony. And what are you looking for?" she managed through unsmiling lips.

Acting as if Maddie didn't exist, he continued digging through his briefcase. Her tapping foot echoed loudly until, almost as an afterthought, the lawyer finally looked up. "It's the Saturday morning of a holiday weekend, Ms. Winston. Everyone's out of town. Like I told Max, it's going to take some time to find a judge willing to come down and set bail for your friend. You have to be patient."

Maddie leaned against the wooden chair on her side of the table. Clutching at its squared back, she glared at the blinking attorney. "I *have been* patient, Mr. Perlman. I was patient last night when I followed Detective Fox and my handcuffed assistant here. I was patient while I waited for Ben to be booked for a crime he didn't commit. I was patient when I had to wait three hours at the front desk for you to return my call. I ran out of patience when I spent the night at the plant in a tangle of nerves because no one could find a judge willing to set bail. My patience quota is all used up. I want to see Mr. Able—now."

Robert Perlman swallowed so hard his Adam's apple danced a little jig. Staring up at Maddie, a good seven inches taller than his own five-foot-two, he seemed to be digesting her demand. Looking down suddenly, he gave a grin as if he'd just found gold bullion in a trash can. "Ah, here it is. This will only take a minute."

He jumped from the table and raced to the doorway. Maddie almost groaned when the door swung inward, smacking the lawyer hard on his oversized nose. The burly police officer who had opened the door quickly whipped out a clean white handkerchief and offered it like a flag of truce. "Jeez, Perlman, take it easy, would you? And step back. I'm bringing the prisoner in."

Mr. Perlman, hankie pressed tightly to the middle of his face, waved the mysterious file in surrender. "Dood, dood. Let 'im sit wit' Ms. Winston until I we-tuwn," he mumbled, running from the room.

Maddie stood at attention, her gaze on the door. After a little sidestep from the officer, Ben stumbled in. Looking tired and a bit on the shabby side, he gave her a lopsided grin.

"Good morning, Maddie. Have you come to take me home?"

The policeman waited in the open doorway, holding on to Ben's arm. "Miss? Have you been searched?"

Hands out at her sides, Maddie focused on Ben. "You bet, officer. Had to leave my bag at the front desk, along with my Uzi, zip gun, and switchblade."

The patrolman nodded, his lack of humor clear. "No offense, miss. Just doing my job. I'll leave you two alone for a while. Perlman should be back soon."

Realizing the man meant no insult, Maddie gave a small but contrite smile of apology and waited until he backed out of the room and closed the door. Ben, still in yesterday's clothes, a two-day growth of beard on his impossibly handsome face, walked around the table.

Enraged at the thought of him being treated like a common criminal, Maddie swiped angrily at a wayward tear. "Are you OK? Did they feed you? Did you get any sleep? Did they interrogate you or—"

Ben stepped near, just close enough for Maddie to see the glint of humor in his navy-dark eyes. "Torture me? Pull out my fingernails with pliers or force me to eat maggots? Sorry, Maddie, none of the above."

She thumped a finger into his hard-as-rock chest. "Benjamin Able, that's not amusing! I spent the entire night worrying, and you have the nerve to laugh? I didn't sleep a wink!"

Ben grabbed her fingers and held them tight. "Yes, they fed me. From a fast-food restaurant this morning. I'm not sure where dinner came from last night. It didn't matter, since I was not in the mood to eat. I'm fine now. Just a little tired."

Maddie gasped as she took a good look at his wrists. "And you're still handcuffed. How dare they? Well, don't you worry. Mr. Perlman will have you out of here as soon as he can find a judge who'll set bail."

Ben let go of her hands. "Sit, Maddie, and tell me everything you know."

Reluctantly, Maddie obeyed, waiting until he took a chair on the opposite side of the table. In honesty, she knew very little about the case except for what she'd been told by his lawyer. "Yesterday morning, the police received an anonymous phone call from someone who suggested Detective Fox search my apartment, and your room in particular, if he wanted to find the microchips. I haven't been allowed to listen to the tape, but he confirmed the voice sounded more like a woman's than a man's. I realize now that's why Fox seemed so strained when he called and asked if they could check out my place.

"According to Mr. Perlman, the evidence is circumstantial," she confided. "They acted on a tip and found the stolen microchips in a gym bag in your closet, but that's all. Mr. Perlman says they didn't find your prints on the bag or anywhere on the contents. He thinks he'll be able to get the charges dismissed completely if he manages to find a sensible judge."

Ben nodded, seemingly unconcerned over his predicament or the idea of a setup. "It stands to reason whoever made the call is in on the theft, doesn't it?"

Maddie nodded. "But I can't think of a woman who

might gain anything if we lose our contracts. It doesn't make sense."

Ben ran a hand over his stubbled chin. "I've been thinking, Maddie. Whoever stole the microchips is frightened. Somehow they found out Winston Design was going to fulfill its contracts, and they needed to make more trouble. I was the newest employee, a stranger from nowhere. It was only logical they pick on me as the sheep-scope."

Maddie allowed herself the luxury of a smile. Ben's use of slang and his command of the American language had been improving steadily, but this little slip was a good one. Pausing, she fought to keep her grin in check. "I think the word you're looking for is scapegoat. And, yes, now that you mention it, the thought did cross my mind."

He smiled triumphantly. "Then the file I read last night was correct. They found nothing incrimina—"

This time, Maddie's brows shot to her hairline. "What do you mean the 'file you read'? Weren't you locked up last night? And don't tell me they let you examine the evidence they have against you."

Ben had the decency to look embarrassed. "It was only for a short while, sometime around three. I was bored and the station was so quiet. It was a simple matter to snap my fingers and move the file from Lieutenant Fox's desk to my cell. Believe me, it was so small a thing as to be insignificant."

After glancing around the room for a camera or some kind of hidden surveillance equipment, she hissed, "Are you crazy? If they found out you did such a thing they'd—"

"What?" Ben lifted his shoulders and gave a little smirk. "Put me in jail and throw away the key?"

Maddie crossed her arms and blew a breath through pursed lips. "This is not a joking matter. You and I know you're innocent, but I can tell by the look in Max's eyes he's still debating. And we both know what Uncle Lucius will have to say. As long as Max and Lucius have doubts,

Detective Fox will continue to pin the blame on you. Worse, if the police think they have the right suspect, they'll stop looking for anyone else. That means whoever really stole the chips will get away."

Frowning, Ben folded his hands on the desk and steepled his fingers. "Maddie, let's stop and think for a minute. Who knew I was living in your apartment?"

"Mary Grace, Max. Maybe Letitia. Paulette suspects we're more than business acquaintances, too. And Trevor, if anything I said the morning of his visit penetrated his overblown brain," she answered quickly.

Ben's frown grew grim. "There's another person, Maddie. Someone I think we should seriously consider."

"Uncle Lucius?" Maddie wrinkled her brow. "Oh, Ben, not Uncle Lucius. He's family. I know he doesn't like me, but why would he try to ruin the company?"

Ben shrugged his shoulders. "Think about it, Maddie. Does Lucius need money? Does he have any vices? If you can't meet your contracts, you will lose sales and won't be able to meet your own expenses. WD's reputation will be ruined. A buyout will be the only answer."

Not wanting to believe Ben might be right about her uncle, she came to Lucius's defense. "Uncle Lucius has always been paid a generous salary. From what I can tell, he doesn't have any expensive habits. He doesn't date, and I've never seen him with a woman, so who would he have recruited to make that call? Besides, my father and grandfather knew his work ethic was in the right place, even when he acted like a supercilious prig. They always thought he was as proud of the company as the rest of us."

Ben met her hopeful gaze like a man who was used to facing reality head on. "He could have paid a stranger off the street to make that phone call. And what about his sense of honor? Didn't you tell me that when you were given control of the company, Lucius Fulbright's pride took a beating? Pride is a dreadful sin, Maddie. It has led many a good man upon the road to destruction."

Maddie laid her fingers to her temples, hoping to relieve the dull throbbing that had begun there last night. Obviously, Ben was capable of seeing things more clearly where her uncle was concerned. "It *was* a terrible blow. After the reading of my father's will, he wouldn't talk to my grandparents or me for months."

"At this point, I don't think we have anywhere else to look, Maddie. When I get out of here—"

The door opened and Robert Perlman rushed in. Though his nose had puffed up to three times its normal size and his shirt front and tie carried rusty stains, he seemed downright cheerful. "I've managed to find someone who's willing to come and hear Ben's case, Ms. Winston. If I'm successful, he'll be released on bond. I may even get the charges dismissed. Now, let's put our heads together and form a line of defense. We have one hour before we have to meet with Judge Pierce."

Ben stood across the cluttered desk and looked down into Max Hefner's wary brown eyes. Robert Perlman had managed to convince Judge Pierce, who'd been an hour shy of teeing off on the golf course, to conduct a quick arraignment. Though the judge refused to dismiss the charges, he did agree to release Ben on bail. He had been a free man for the past two hours, but only after Maddie had put up a goodly chunk of her trust fund.

"It only makes sense, Max," Ben intoned, determined to win the older man to his side. "Someone has to stand guard over the chips until they're picked up on Tuesday, and we're the most likely candidates for the job. Maddie and I have already lived here four days."

Max raised his bushy brows up to his nonexistent hairline. "And just where is Maddie now? Why did she leave you to argue your case with me instead of doing it herself? I thought she liked our verbal sparring."

Ben hid a smile, noting Max sounded more like a petulant little boy than a respected scientist. Still, the man was right. Maddie had left him to plead with Max all too quickly. She was up to something, and he had a suspicion as to what it might be. "She's gone back to the city to pick up fresh clothes and a few other necessities. She told me it was my job to convince you we're right about this. Personally, I think she's throwing us together to force us to be friends, or at least learn to respect one another."

As if in agreement, Max sat back in his chair. "Hmm. That could be. Maddie never did like confrontation. Always wanted things to run smoothly or she became upset. Used to hate it when her dad would argue with Lucius over company policy or some other trivial, half-assed point Lucius thought was relevant.

"And she needs approval, my Maddie does. She always felt overshadowed by her mother's beauty and her father's brains. For some reason, James never gave out praise any more than a teaspoonful at a time. Definitely not conducive to his daughter's self-confidence. After Trevor, well . . ."

Ben pulled up a chair, eager to hear more about Maddie and her past. It sounded as though Max knew her better than anyone and was willing to share his observations. Perhaps he and Max could be friends, after all. Knowing the man would agree, he blurted out his opinion of Trevor Edwards. "It boils my gizzard to think how much that flea-bitten jackass hurt her."

Max blinked, then said gruffly, "Sounds like you've met the little turd."

Ben leaned forward and set his clenched fists on the front of Max's desk. "Once, but it was one time too many. He came to Maddie's apartment, tried to boss her around, then made her cry. It was all I could do not to smash his face in."

"I know the feeling," muttered Max, staring shrewdly. "But enough about Maddie's past. Let's you and I just lay our cards on the table and admit we know where we stand with one another. If you're out to hurt Maddie in any way, either by messing with her heart or this company, I promise you with every breath in my body I'll get you for it, Able. Do I make myself understood?"

Ben, holding Max's intense gaze with one of his own, waited half a second before answering. "I would lay down my life for Maddie Winston, Mr. Hefner. You have my word on it."

A full minute passed while Max digested Ben's promise. Finally, he relaxed his posture and settled his face into a weary frown. "All right, now that we've gotten that out of the way, I guess I should tell you I don't think you stole those chips. Maddie swears you were with her the night they went missing, and I believe her. You've worked like a dog this past week to help us meet the deadline, and I've seen how careful you've been with Maddie's feelings. Your actions have been honorable and aboveboard."

Ben raised his lips a fraction. "Thank you."

Max nodded, as if the subject was closed. "Now that I've had my say, I'd like your opinion. You've had time to evaluate who's working for us. Who do you think planted those microchips in your closet? Who do you think wants us buried?"

Ben stretched back and crossed his legs at the ankles, taking his time to answer. At this moment, Max reminded him of his father before Ashmedai had torn their family apart. In the beginning, he had wanted Max's approval for Maddie's sake. After today's little talk, he decided he would like the man's respect, as well. "I have an idea, but you might not agree."

"Try me, son. You might be surprised at what I've been thinking."

"Lucius Fulbright." Ben frowned. "I think it all stems from him and his cursed pride, plus his intense and irrational dislike of Maddie."

Max jabbed his desk blotter with a pointed finger. "As far as I'm concerned, you're right on the money. My nose can smell a dirty setup a mile away, and Lucius has been stinking since the reading of James's will. Now, how do we convince Maddie and that inept bungler Fox?"

Surprised, Ben grinned. He had expected an argument from Max; at the very least, a few sentences of doubt. Suddenly, the idea of having an ally in Max Hefner left him humbled. "I don't think Lucius is acting on his own. A man with that much pride needs to be stroked. Since no one around here seems to be doing it, Lucius must be getting his praise from another source—maybe the woman he talked into calling the police or one of the companies Winston Design supplies. Which of those companies has made an offer to purchase WD in the past year?"

Max bent and opened a side drawer. After shuffling through his files, he pulled out three folders and passed them across to Ben. "Powerchip, Datadisc, and Butler & Maggio. They're all midsize companies looking to save money by manufacturing their own components. Tom Allen, the Powerchip president, is a friend. He took it on the chin when we turned down his generous offer last fall, but he still buys from us. I can call and feel him out myself. Datadisc was bought out by Apex Inc. earlier this year. Didn't Maddie and Lucius meet with them a week ago?"

Ben nodded, clutching at the files. "They did. Maddie allowed me to attend the meeting. It gave me the opportunity to observe Lucius myself. It was apparent the men from Apex thought he was in charge until Maddie managed to wrest control. Lucius was so furious he worked himself into a fit and had to leave the meeting," Ben lied, remembering the true source of Lucius's problems. "I don't think he has too much credibility with them right now."

Max ran a hand through his balding head, a glint of amusement flashing in his eyes. "Letitia called me afterward and told me there'd been some kind of problem. We both had a good laugh over it."

Ben grinned. "Letitia Moore is a devoted employee and completely loyal to Maddie. She might be able to give us a fresh viewpoint on the problem."

"All right," said Max, nodding in agreement. "You've convinced me. First thing Tuesday morning, I'll stop by and see Letitia. I have Tom Allen's home number, so I can call him and ask a few questions. Then I'll call Apex. Looks like that leaves Butler & Maggio for you. Can you handle them?"

Ben tossed the Datadisc and Powerchip folders back on Max's desk, then thumbed through the Butler & Maggio file. Raising his gaze, he sat upright. "It will be my pleasure."

Lucius had been left to sit and stew in the dim, smoke-scented room for over an hour. Though he'd reached his tolerance level long ago, he knew instinctively not to get up and walk out. He had angered Dominic Maggio enough to see he was on shaky ground. Worse still, he knew the man thought it was fourth down with ten yards to go.

He detested this dark-paneled room with its overdone wall hangings and outlandish leather furniture. The smell of expensive liquor and ten-dollar cigars clung to his hair and clothes after each visit, making him feel the need to stop at the dry cleaners and drop off the suit he was wearing. His heart lurched when the door to the stuffy office finally opened.

"I thought for a while there you had it handled, Fulbright," came Maggio's deep, growling voice. "But it looks like you fumbled the ball at the goal line. Needless to say, I'm very disappointed. I'd like to know what you intend to do about this fuckup."

The dark gravelly voice mixed with the foul-smelling air, causing Lucius's precariously rolling stomach to lurch. How . . . why had he ever let himself get involved with such an uncouth, detestable person? In truth, it was all James Winston's fault. If James had backed off in his pursuit of Catherine Jessup, he wouldn't be in this position right now. All he had ever wanted was Catherine. But she had turned from him the instant she had met James, had married him and had his child. Now, thanks to James, she was dead.

And he had been forced to live with James's final insult: being an underling to the child James had made with *his* beloved Catherine.

Dominic Maggio took his time walking from the door to the desk chair. He sat and waited, staring at Lucius until Lucius felt the sweat pooling against his back and groin.

"What are you doin', Fulbright? Contemplating your dick? I asked you a question."

Lucius swallowed back a nasty retort, well aware it would not be appreciated. He needed to come through this debacle in one piece or all his plans for revenge would be wasted. "There's time. We can plant more evidence. If need be, I can still—"

Dominic Maggio held up a meaty palm and squinted through the smoky haze. The library door opened and Lucius gaped at the woman who entered the room. Small, voluptuous, and blond, she ambled to Dominic Maggio's side and intimately raked her perfectly manicured hand through his hair, then gave a little pout. "Don't listen to him, Dom. He's had his chances. Let me be the one to bring down frumpy Maddie and her lover boy."

Lucius frowned. Until tonight, he hadn't known which

employee at Winston Design had been planted by Maggio, though he knew there was at least one spy in the New Jersey building. This woman had come as a surprise.

The man took another puff of his six-inch cigar while intimately patting the blond's trim hip. "Nothin' gets me hotter than a bloodthirsty woman, Fulbright. That's why I like this little lady so much. Why don't you tell old Lucius here about our own plan, honey? Give him one more chance to make good on his promise before I call in the boys to take over the job."

Lucius cringed when she pulled her full lips into a feral smile. He'd always thought himself an excellent judge of character, but he had missed his guess on Paulette Jamison. The hard-as-steel glare in her eyes looked more deadly than a man's. Still, he had committed to the ruination of James Winston's dream, He would not back off now.

Paulette walked around and hoisted her rounded bottom onto the edge of the huge desk to sit directly in front of him. With a sly grin, she slowly crossed her shapely legs and rubbed a high-heel-shod foot up and down his calf. "I always thought you and I should get better acquainted, Mr. Fulbright. I think you'd find we have quite a bit in common."

Paulette had done the ultimate to erase the fashion faux pas of panty lines: she wore no underwear. Lucius got a full-blown glimpse of her charms peeking out at him from the tops of her silky, thigh-high stockings. Refusing to stare, he closed his eyes. "And just what kind of grudge do you have against my company?"

With a husky chuckle, she tapped a red-lacquered nail against her pointed little chin. "It's not Winston Design I despise, Mr. Fulbright. It's your goody-two-shoes, always-land-feet-first niece I want to get even with."

Lucius's eyes popped open. Madeline usually got along well with everyone. Until lately, she'd even been tolerant of him. "And what has Madeline ever done to you?"

The blond rested her hands at her hips and clutched the edge of the desk until her knuckles whitened. "Rich, frumpy women have always irritated me. I rather like the idea of ruining a girl who's achieved everything she wanted in life, while someone like me has had to scrounge for the crumbs. I can run that company just as well as Maddie Winston and do it with style and class. And Dominic"—she tossed her head at the man behind the desk—"has promised to give me my chance."

Sixteen

Torn between anger and relief, Maddie made her way back to the factory. She'd picked up clean clothes for herself, along with a new men's fashion magazine for Ben, hoping he would clap himself another outfit or two. After checking her apartment to make sure the police hadn't disturbed anything, she'd headed to her uncle's. Unfortunately, Lucius Fulbright had not been home.

She hadn't said anything to Ben, but her plan had been to confront her uncle and question him about Dominic Maggio. Until now, it hadn't really bothered her that her uncle had been the sole recipient of Butler & Maggio's buyout offers. She accepted the fact that businessmen tended to stick together; Lucius had become friends with many of those in charge of the companies with whom WD did business. She hoped Lucius could give her a logical explanation so she could dispel Ben's negative theory about him.

But, more than making her angry, the thought that her uncle might be the one behind all the ills of the company hurt her deep inside.

Navigating through the holiday traffic, she thought back to other problems they'd encountered over the past five years. When she'd first become president, several of their past clients refused, for no apparent reason, to sign new contracts with Winston Design. Maddie had been young, not quite twenty-two, and hadn't had the courage to insist they tell her why they felt the need to withdraw their support. She remembered the CEO of one of the companies as being especially tight with her uncle. When she had asked Lucius why the man had pulled his contracts, his response had been curt: *Think about it, Maddie. Would you trust your business to an untried woman fresh out of college? My friends have too much intelligence to buy from a company with you as its leader.*

Had her uncle encouraged those companies to defect to another supplier?

And the erroneous quotes in the press, the ones that sounded as if she were making promises WD couldn't begin to deliver? Maddie had thought that somehow she'd mispoken, that in her enthusiasm to sell their technology she'd overstated the truth, but in at least two cases she didn't remember her quotes as being exactly what the media reported. Her uncle had set up, monitored, and closed those press conferences.

The biggest near-disaster had been the financial fiasco she'd managed to divert only last year. She'd checked and triple checked the figures with Max and Paulette, then drawn up a fair contract with a reputable company. At time of payment, the check they received had been for half the amount she'd remembered from the agreement. When she'd reread the contract, the figures were fifty percent less than the amount she was positive had been quoted. She could never understand how the figures on the agreement had changed. Afterward, she'd made up the difference from her own trust fund, upsetting her grandmother and Max with her self-sacrifice.

That company had been Butler & Maggio.

But who had stolen the chips and planted them in Ben's closet? When she'd checked the closet after the traffic accident, it had been empty, so whoever had sneaked into the apartment had done so sometime this week, after they'd found out she and Ben were living at the plant. And who was the mysterious woman who had alerted the police?

As she approached the WD factory, she imagined Ben and Max together in Max's office comparing notes and discussing the strategy needed for the company's next move. Her fondest desire was that they at least learn to tolerate one another. She was counting on Max to understand why Ben was insisting they be allowed to spend the weekend at the plant to guard the microchips.

She could justify her reasons for wanting to stay with Ben: Winston Design was her company. She needed to be there in case of a problem. Ben was too new of an employee to be left on his own. She'd stayed at the plant five nights already. Three more didn't really matter.

Maddie considered it lucky her desire to be near Ben coincided with her need to save the company, and hoped she would never have to make a choice between the two. Her grandfather and father had worked too hard for too many years for her to let Winston Design fall to ruin. And she had finally found the man with whom she wanted to share it and the rest of her life.

She pulled into the empty parking lot and drove to the far side of the building, angling her Volkswagen on the grass behind a row of trees. She and Ben had already discussed the possibility the thief might return over the weekend to steal their finished orders. They had agreed the element of surprise could work in their favor if the culprit thought he had a clear path to the chips.

Maddie killed the engine and set the brake, gathering her thoughts before she faced Ben. Dusk had fallen, and the graying light seemed as bleak as her history with her uncle. For the past few years, she'd convinced herself she didn't believe in God. She certainly didn't believe in the jinns and wizards Ben kept talking about. She really didn't

believe in anything anymore, for no God would have taken
her parents from her, then sent her a man to love who
could so easily leave her for another woman. No God
would let her father's company fall apart.

But *something* had sent her Ben. He'd come into her
life when she was feeling down and almost out. He had
shocked her and made her smile. Then he had made her
feel cared for and loved. Maybe she'd been too hasty in
tossing her dreams aside. Because if Ben was sent from
heaven, if he was a dream, she didn't want to wake up.

She would be taking a big chance if she confessed her
love to him, but she was tired of being timid and holding
back her feelings. She'd done whatever Trevor had asked,
and it had gotten her nowhere. It was time she took a
stand and thought of herself, her wants and needs, first.

But when she gave Ben his freedom, as she knew she
must, would he want to stay with her? Would he feel the
same?

She opened the car door, lifted out her suitcase, and
carried it to the front of the building and up the steps.
Max's car was gone. Ben was probably inside waiting for
her. Resolutely, she unlocked the front door, punched in
the alarm code, and entered the building, then relocked
the door and reset the alarm.

Before she could turn, footsteps echoed in the stillness
of the deserted factory. She held her breath, releasing it
only after she saw Ben striding toward her from the stairway. Even in the dim light of the closed-up building, he
looked impossibly handsome and in control. In the few
weeks they'd been together, he had adapted easily to modern practices and fashions, confidently slipping into the
role of an intelligent businessman as if wearing a well-
worn shoe.

He stopped in front of her and reached for her suitcase
with a cocky grin. "What took you so long? Max left an

hour ago. I finally convinced him we could be trusted not to burn the building down."

Maddie followed him up the stairs, chattering aimlessly, hoping to smother the achy feeling that always settled in her heart whenever she thought about losing Ben. "I had to make a few stops. Traffic was impossible. You know how it is. What did you say to Max to get him to agree?"

Instead of answering her question, Ben led her into Max's office and stood aside. Maddie stopped in her footsteps as she entered the room, almost in shock. The cluttered office had been turned into a scene from some exotic fairy tale.

Fragrant bouquets of colorful flowers sat on every surface, including a small table set in the middle of the room and decorated with snowy white linen and glittering crystal. Clusters of aromatic candles burned on the desk, tables, and bookshelves. A haunting melody, one she vaguely remembered from her visit to the harem, played softly in the background. Over the fragrance of the flowers and burning tapers, the air was filled with a delicious and tempting scent.

She glanced at her uncomfortable cot and saw it had been replaced by a large canopied bed, freshly made up with ivory-colored satin sheets and silky tasseled hangings.

Maddie raised her gaze to Ben's and saw the expectant, almost bashful look on his face. "What's all this?" she managed, daring to believe the message his eyes telegraphed.

Through the dim candlelight Maddie thought she saw Ben blush. He turned and set her suitcase on the sofa. "I know the cot has been difficult to sleep on. I thought that, for the long weekend, you might be more comfortable in a real bed. I hope you don't mind."

"Mind?" she stammered, surprised she could suck

enough air into her lungs to get the simple word out. "No, I . . . it's all so lovely. And what's that wonderful smell?"

Ben strode to a smaller side table and raised the golden lid of a chafing dish. "A delicacy I thought you might enjoy. Roasted haunch of spring lamb, herbed vegetables, and warm flat bread. And for dessert, candied dates and figs."

"And champagne?" Maddie asked in awe, spying the wine stand and the huge bottle it held.

Raising a dark brow, Ben smiled. "Yes, and don't ask where it came from."

She giggled, making a mental note to send the Rothschilds' vineyards a large, anonymous money order.

Ben stepped closer, his gaze searching as he stared deep into her eyes.

Afraid to acknowledge what she thought she recognized in his soulful expression, Maddie raised her head, her heart tripping madly in her chest.

Ben knew he was taking a big chance by arranging the office in such a seductive manner, but he didn't care. He was out of jail. Max trusted him.

And he was in love with Maddie.

He had ruminated over the last fact for days, weighing the possibilities of such an idea, but after watching Maddie work so hard to have him released from prison, he knew it for certain. He considered himself the luckiest of men. To have a woman like Maddie Winston, so courageous and intelligent and honorable, fighting for him was a rare and wonderful thing he would treasure forever. Or at least for as long as Ashmedai, if he still existed, allowed it.

Lately, he'd had more doubts about the evil jinn. He had done so many things he'd once been told were forbidden. Ashmedai had not appeared to condemn him or order him flogged, nor had he been cast to eternal damnation. His only adversary seemed to be the bottle, which watched his every move and sat in judgment of his actions.

And the bottle, Ben had decided, was a very single-minded warden. When this mess with the stolen chips was over, he vowed to put all his energies into finding a way to rid himself of the cursed thing forever.

Tonight, if Maddie asked him to make love with her, he would. He was almost positive there would be no repercussions from the act. Maddie had commanded him to do other things he'd been sure were wrong and nothing terrible had happened. Their lovemaking would be the same.

He saw the worry in her topaz-hued eyes and recognized the tumult of emotion sweeping through her. That same tumult also raged in him. Doubt. Fear. Longing. Love. They all collided, crashing into his heart like a wave to the shore.

Maddie laid a hand to her throat, where her pulse beat as rapidly as the wings of a hummingbird. She closed her eyes and took a breath, then turned to him with a small smile on her lips. "It's beautiful, Ben. Like something from a dream. How did you know what to do to make it so perfect?"

He stepped near and took her free hand, placing it on his heart. "I am a genie with close ties to his master. I read your innermost desires and made them manifest. They are my desires, too. If my fulfillment of them was wrong, I think the bottle would have sucked me up again. There is still that possibility, you see. The damned thing might let me go so far, but no farther. We would have to let the night proceed and take our chances. Are you willing to do that with me, Maddie Winston? Are you willing to take the chance of making love with this cursed and unworthy man?"

Maddie pulled in a breath, squeezing his hand tight. "Oh, Ben. You might be cursed, but you're not unworthy."

One by one, he kissed the backs of her fingers. She sighed and he turned her hand over, biting at her palm.

Her hand fluttered like a netted butterfly as she tried to pull away. "I . . . uh . . . could we eat, first? The supper you've conjured up smells wonderful, and I'm starved. Besides, I need some time to get used to this idea. I've never been seduced before."

Ben quirked up a corner of his mouth. "That is sad for all the men who have passed through your life, Madeline Winston, but very good for me. I will be the first."

Maddie closed her eyes and finally wrested her hand from his. She looked as if she would burst into tears at any moment. "That's not exactly true, Ben," she murmured. "I've had sex before. With Trevor."

Ben nodded and took a step closer. Enfolding her in his arms, he placed his lips to her forehead. "I already guessed that you'd had sex before. And I figured it had been with the mangy dog known as Trevor. But I will be the first with whom you shall *make love,* Maddie. And if Allah allows it, I shall be the last."

Ben pulled his head back and found a smile, so pure and lovely he thought he might weep, brightening Maddie's face, and knew he had voiced his feelings correctly. But he didn't want to ruin the precious moment by rushing through every soft kiss and tender touch. They had time to make this, their first night of passion, one to remember.

And still, he admitted to himself, Maddie had to wish it. She had to say the words.

He tucked his arm around her waist and led her to the table. "You are hungry, so we will eat. Sit and I will serve you, not as a slave, but as one who is about to become your lover."

Ben grinned at her look of embarrassment and pulled out a tufted chair, giving her time to accept his bold statement. More and more, he wondered what kind of man her ex-fiancé was that such simple words of love seemed so foreign to her.

He lifted the napkin from her plate, snapped it open and placed it on her lap. Then he uncorked the bottle of chilled champagne, catching the first fizzy splashes in her glass. After handing her the crystal flute, he tapped his own against it. "I propose a toast, Maddie. May this night be the first of many between us for the rest of our lives."

She gazed up at him, sipping at her wine when he did the same. Ben set his drink down and walked to the warmer, a golden brazier with a small pile of embers glowing red underneath. After lifting the lid, he filled first Maddie's plate, then his own, brought their food to the table, and set the plates down. He took his seat and opened his own napkin, placing it across his lap.

He thought of all the women he'd known when he'd existed as a true man, remembered some of their sly smiles and devious games of seduction. His father had always warned him of women and their wiles, reminding him daily that soon after he took a first wife, he would need to take several more. In this way, his father had lectured, no one woman would have complete control of his heart. No one woman could mean so much that losing her would be the end of his world.

But Ben knew better. Loving Maddie did mark the end of his world—his world of loneliness and uncertainty, his world of imprisonment and fear. Maddie was a new beginning. Whether or not she tried to set him free, he was hers to command for the rest of their lives together.

They ate in silence. He picked a few of the more delicate morsels from his plate and fed them to her. After a bit, Maddie giggled and got into the spirit of the game, feeding him in the same manner. When they'd eaten enough of the main course, Ben cleared their plates and served honeyed figs and sugared dates. Picking up a fig

in his fingers, he lifted it to Maddie's lips and she bit it
in half, licking a golden droplet of honey from her lips
with a stroke of her tongue.

Ben ached inside, wishing she would lavish herself as
freely on a part of his own body. He popped the rest of
the fig in his mouth and chewed slowly. As if able to read
his mind, Maddie's face turned a delicious shade of apricot. Wanting her to taste him on her lips, he raised his
glass to her mouth and let her sip from the place where
he had drunk. Then he set his mouth against the exact
spot on the rim that had met with Maddie's.

He stood and held his hand to her. Maddie grasped it
and stepped to his side. Carefully, as if she were the greatest
treasure he possessed, Ben held her face between his palms.
Slowly he bent and touched his tongue to her lips, licking
a bit of honey from the corner of her generous mouth.

Maddie moaned, a little sigh of wonder and desire,
sending a fiery jolt to his groin. She raised her hands and
rested them at his throat, her thumbs grazing the cords of
his neck. Then she pressed her lips to his pulse and bit
gently, a tender sting of love.

"I want you, Maddie," he whispered. "But in order for
us to continue safely, you must also want me. And you
must say the words out loud, in the form of a wish."

Maddie gazed up at him, her eyes golden in the candle
flame. For a few terrifying seconds, he thought she might
refuse. Then she took a breath, her wide smile telling him
how much she cared, how much she loved him. "I wish
you to make love with me, my genie of the bottle. Please
do as I desire."

And Ben answered in the only way he could. "Your
wish is my command."

When Ben picked her up in his muscle-corded arms,
Maddie felt as if she were being swept away by a tidal

wave. The look in his eyes, so fierce and possessive, set
her heart to racing. As if she weighed no more than a
feather, he carried her to the bed and set her on her knees
on the satin sheets.

"I should like to see you as God made you, Maddie.
May I?"

She faced him and nodded, too embarrassed to do more.

He reached toward her and lifted the hem of her shirt,
pulling it over her head and tossing it into the darkness.
She felt her nipples harden and crossed her arms over her
chest, remembering that Trevor had never seemed to enjoy
her full figure, had never acted as if her body truly enticed
him.

Gently, Ben uncrossed her wrists and unsnapped the
front closure of her bra, helping the garment to slide from
her shoulders. Boldly, he traced a pale blue vein that
crossed her milky-white skin, letting his finger rest on a
jutting nipple. His finger circled the pebbled disc and she
felt the burning touch to her womb.

"Why do you cover yourself? Your body is beautiful,
ripely rounded and tempting, like a bowl of fruit to a starving man." Ben palmed both her breasts, plucking at their
hardened tips until she swayed against him. As if in slow
motion, he lowered his head and took a throbbing peak
into his mouth. Maddie held him, quivering as he suckled
first one, then the other aching bud.

His hands moved in a downward motion, unsnapping
her jeans and pulling at the zipper until he had worked
the pants to her knees. She lay back and let him remove
her sneakers, then her jeans and panties.

She sat up, resting her bottom on her heels as she grew
comfortable with her nudity. "I want to see you, too," she
whispered, more an entreaty than a command.

He smiled, a look of stark male satisfaction gracing his
passion-filled face. Quickly, he gave a small clap of his

hands. In a movement too rapid to acknowledge, he stood before her in all his masculine glory.

Like a fish out of water, Maddie took a little gasp of air, inhaling the scent of sandalwood and male essence. She'd seen Ben in swim trunks at the beach, but she'd been so busy worrying about her own figure that she'd been too embarrassed to pay full attention to his. Here, in the glow of the candlelight, she admitted she had never seen a man so wonderfully formed.

His chest, all carved muscle and sinew, was smooth and hairless, lightly bronzed like the statue of some pagan god. His abs were rippled, his waist lean as it tapered to slender hips and a nest of dark curls.

And jutting from the curls, like a warrior's sword, was his penis, arrow straight and fully aroused.

Hesitantly, she reached out and touched him. Incredibly, he grew larger in her hand.

"Maddie, you are driving me to the insane asylum," he murmured, resting his hands on her shoulders.

Empowered by his words and the knowledge of what her touch did to him, she nipped at his chin. "I think the proper phrasing is, 'Maddie, you're driving me crazy.' "

He leaned close and whispered against her lips, "Crazy, insane, mad with the wanting of you. The words don't matter, as long as you feel the same."

He nibbled at her mouth, ran his tongue over her teeth, sucked the air from her lungs with one inhalation of his breath. Then, like a man unafraid of drowning, he fell on her and pulled her into the warm, pulsing ocean of his desire.

And Maddie let him taste and tease her at will. Hot kisses became fervid. Gliding touches turned desperate. And when she was mad with wanting, wet with the feel of his hand cupping her, his fingers seeking and finding her most intimate core, she shuddered and opened to him fully, ready to welcome him.

Without warning, the candles flickered as a rush of cool air rippled through the room. Maddie stiffened. Ben knelt up between her thighs and stilled, his eyes wide and waiting. She glanced toward the office door and saw it standing open. How could they have forgotten to lock the door!

"Maybe it's Max," she whispered, kneeling beside him.

Ben shook his head, silencing her with a look. In a flash, he clapped his hands. Standing fully clothed at the side of the bed, he whispered, "It's not Max. Get dressed, Maddie. And stay here. For Allah's sake, don't leave this room."

Ben slipped through the office door and headed down the stairs. At the bottom, he could see the keypad to the alarm system blinking red, a sure sign that someone who knew the code had unarmed the alarm and entered the building.

He rounded Paulette's desk and followed the corridor to the production room, knowing instinctively the intruder was headed for the storage area where the finished microchips were packaged and waiting for shipment.

Tamping down his fears, he crouched low at the first door leading into the room. Though Maddie wasn't here to command his powers, Ben knew she would want him to do whatever necessary to protect the chips. But if he wasn't supposed to interfere, he could be whisked back inside his bottle, leaving Maddie alone to face the intruder.

Dare he hold his powers at bay and face the infidel as a man?

Resolutely, he crouched low. He *was* a man, by Allah. Loving Maddie had made him more so in the last three weeks than he had been before his imprisonment. He needed no magic to overtake a cowardly thief bent on destroying his woman and her company.

His hands fisted, he went swiftly past the work area,

ready for battle. Still crouched, he placed a palm on the swinging door that led to shipping and receiving and pushed inward. He focused his eyes and peered into the darkness.

A faint flutter caused him to turn into the room toward the right. He sensed another's presence and made ready to face the intruder. Before he could stand fully upright, something crashed into his skull.

Falling to his knees, he shook his head, trying to clear it of the pain. He staggered under a second blow, more vicious than the first, and crumpled to the floor in a heap.

Maddie watched Ben slip silently through the office door. She tugged on her panties and bra and quickly finished dressing. Several minutes passed while she paced, knotting a napkin from the table in her hands.

Finally she could stand it no longer. She inched to the door and checked the pitch dark hallway. Silence greeted her, but she knew someone was out there. Someone who wanted to hurt Ben—and steal the microchips.

She tiptoed down the stairs, past Paulette's desk, and into the entry hall of the assembly room. Squatting, she pushed open the door and blinked in the darkness, trying to focus.

The sound of a grunt, then something hitting the floor, startled her. Maddie shot through the door and into the main assembly room, trying to pinpoint the location of the noise. She heard another thump and headed in the direction of shipping, where the microchips were stored.

"Ben?" she said with a little hiss of breath when she reached the swinging doors. "Ben, where are you?"

Silence, then a whisper of something . . . a dragging sound.

Maddie pushed into the door and scanned the darkness. A large shape lay tumbled on the floor a few feet to her right and she crawled closer, biting at her lower lip. With a little groan, she laid a palm on Ben's shoulder and bent close, grateful to hear his steady breathing.

Her hand wandered to his nape where she felt something wet and sticky on her fingers. Blood? Someone had hit him and knocked him out. They had hurt her genie!

Maddie's spine prickled when she heard a shuffling noise. Before she could stand and defend herself, a steely object rammed hard into her neck.

A woman's voice, one she thought she recognized, burned in her ear. "Stand up, Madeline. And do exactly as you're told, or your friend will be killed."

Seventeen

Maddie woke with a pounding headache. Already cold to her marrow, she shivered at the frigid dampness seeping through her thin shirt. Pulling at her arms, she was shocked to find them tied behind her back, her shoulders aching from the pressure of a pitted concrete floor. She sniffed and caught the rancid scent of rotting wood and seawater mixed with something more familiar—the stink of a cigar.

Her eyes opened slowly to a murky gray light that told her it was sometime before dawn. Dizzy with pain, she squinted and raised her gaze, scanning her prison. The walls surrounding her soared upward two stories. Stacked all around were wooden crates and large cardboard boxes. Scattered fluorescent lights burned in the high ceiling, shedding little illumination on the huge warehouse-like room. In one corner of the far wall stood a forklift. Opposite the forklift was a metal stairway, which led to a kind of half-floor with an iron landing. Running along the landing were two rooms with large plate glass windows. A light shone from one of the windows, casting an eerie glow onto the metal grating of the stairs.

She rose to her knees and struggled to a shaky stand. Her head felt as though it had been hit with a hammer; her hands tingled numbly. She took a few staggering steps to the nearest crate and slumped against it, landing in a heap on the lid. Frustrated, she tugged again at her ropes, but the scratchy hemp held tight. Glancing down, she stared at the top of the crate, stamped with black letters that made up foreign-looking words. She thought the letters were from the Cyrillic alphabet, but she wasn't sure.

Woefully, she closed her eyes and took a breath to clear her fuddled head. The pain had receded to a dull thumping, but she would need a couple of aspirins to make the ache more bearable. Slowly, a dim recollection of the previous night surfaced.

Ben! She had found him lying in a pool of blood. If her head was pounding, his must feel broken in two.

Knowing the kidnappers had the foresight to separate them, she stiffened her spine and stood, ready to do a more thorough search of the warehouse. Loud voices and the sound of people arguing came from overhead, and she recalled the last thing she'd heard at the plant. She'd thought at the time that she recognized a woman's voice biting out a harsh threat against Ben. When she'd tried to stand, she'd been conked on the head. She could remember nothing after that.

Suddenly, the voices grew quiet. A door opened on the landing and a short, hefty bulldog of a man smoking a cigar walked out of the office, followed by her Uncle Lucius. From this distance, it was hard to tell which was the more dangerous—the bulldog, looking mad enough to eat raw hamburger, or her Uncle Lucius, holding his nose in the air as if he smelled something stale. Neither man looked at her as they made their way down the steps.

When they reached the bottom, the heavyset man turned and pulled the huge stogie from his set lips. "Hurry up, Paulette. Time's money, God damnit."

Anger overrode Maddie's fear. The man's gruff voice brought back the memory of several threatening phone calls. And she'd been right about the voice she'd heard just before she'd been knocked on the head, too. It was obvious now who had placed the memo on Max's desk and called Detective Fox to search her apartment.

Dominic Maggio was out to ruin the company—with Paulette Jamison and Uncle Lucius by his side.

Paulette, wearing trim black slacks and a vibrant green silk jacket, glided down the stairs on spiky, three-inch heels. She planted a delicate kiss on Dominic Maggio's jowly cheek and took his arm.

Maddie squared her shoulders as the trio approached, refusing to let them think they had the upper hand. Paulette had probably committed dozens of other crimes against Winston Design that had yet to come to light. To think she'd felt sorry for the girl and talked Max into hiring her only made the anger more painful.

Determined to stay focused, she ignored Paulette and Dominic. Instead, she stared at her uncle, who was regarding her as if she were a bug trapped in a jar. "How could you, Uncle Lucius?" she demanded. "I knew you were unhappy with me, but to do this to the company, to deliberately ruin what my family worked so hard to build—"

Lucius sneered, contempt darkening his eyes to the color of thunderclouds. "It's always about you, isn't it, Madeline? You're so much like your father it's pathetic. It was always James's ideas, his innovations that went into effect first, before anyone else's."

Maddie would not back down. "It was *his* company, Uncle Lucius, his and Grandpa Will's. They hired you because you had a degree in business and because Grandma Sylvia wanted it. You were given a share in Winston Design because they trusted you, and now you've betrayed them."

"They treated me like a poor relation, all of them. I never got the respect or the salary I deserved."

"Is that what this is all about? You wanted money? All you had to do was ask, Uncle Lucius, and I would have seen to it—"

Lucius puffed out his chest to answer, but Paulette shoved him aside before he got the words out. Clearly bored with the family squabble, she shouldered her way closer. "How does it feel, Maddie, to be bound and helpless? You haven't changed a bit from our college days, have you? Well, this is one time your money can't help."

Maddie widened her eyes and bit back a snappy retort. She gave Dominic a cursory look, acting as if his nasty leer meant nothing, then shifted her gaze back to Paulette. "Whatever did I do to you, Paulette, except encourage Max to hire you as his assistant? What have I done to deserve your hatred?"

Paulette's brittle laugh echoed against the concrete walls. "You really don't know, do you? That's Maddie, all right, always living in her own little world." She stepped closer, her blue eyes mean. "For starters, you had money. I had to drop out of school, while you and Mary Grace and the rest of your friends pledged sororities and lived large on campus. I even dated Trevor that first year. He wanted me . . . until he saw you and Mary Grace together one day.

"I had a part-time job in the administration office. He had me pull your file. Then he researched your family's pedigree and business credentials. After he found out who you were, he dropped me like a rock. Trevor knew you were too plain and shy to attract any other guy, so he played it cool until you trusted him. I have to admit, you led him a long, frustrating chase. I almost thought he'd lost out, but you finally agreed to date him."

Furious, Maddie stood, struggling to get her arms free so she could slap the girl. Realizing her machinations were an amusement for her jailers, she gathered her composure, sat down, and took a breath. "Paulette, your perception of me is completely wrong. It took all my courage just to hang on to Mary Grace's coattails in college. Trevor dumped me, too, remember? And I gave you a job when you came looking for one."

"Oh, you threw me a crumb or two. But I saw the way you looked at me, that disgusting smile of pity. Well, now it's my turn to get a taste of the good life."

"All right. Enough," Dominic Maggio blustered, pushing between the two women like a charging rhino. "I've heard just about all I can swallow from the both of you. Fulbright, you got that shiny black Beamer of yours all gassed up?"

Lucius glanced at Maddie, then back to Maggio. "I think so. Why?"

"Because later tonight, Ms. Winston and her assistant are going to take a little ride, that's why."

Maddie suddenly realized she'd yet to see Ben. What had happened to him? She glanced around the warehouse, but knew she wouldn't find him anywhere. If Ben were here, he would have taken care of this mess.

Time. I need more time.

"I'm not going anywhere with you, Mr. Maggio. But I'd like to know why you're so intent on acquiring Winston Design. What did my father do to offend you?"

Dominic growled. Chomping on his cigar, he leaned into Maddie's face, giving her a good view of his tobacco-stained teeth. "It was simple logistics, little girl. The eastern block market has opened up, big time. They need our technology, but none of their distributors have the cash to buy outright. We help ourselves to your chips, and we can lower prices enough for the mass markets in loser nations like Russia, Albania, Bulgaria, to afford us."

"But they can market their own hardware and—"

"Don't you listen to the news, Ms. Winston? American goods bring big bucks on their black market. We're makin' double the amount on these machines we would in the states. Course, it doesn't hurt to borrow a little from a few of our other competitors, either. So far, you're the only one smart enough to catch us in the act. Once you're out of the picture, your grandma will be too miserable to care. Lucius here will have to sell the company just to get rid of the bad memories. Then we get your patents and go to town. We do it all on our own."

He jabbed roughly at Maddie's shoulder, jarring her backward onto the crate. "Have I answered all your questions, Ms. Busybody?"

Maddie's headache still pounded in her brain like a kettledrum, but she wasn't about to give up to this disgusting man. And she needed to locate Ben. "Where's my assistant?"

Paulette peered down at her, ignoring the question. "It's time you found out what it's like to be on the losing team, Maddie. I hope you're ready for it."

Maddie still had no idea why she'd become the target of Paulette's irrational hatred, but it didn't matter. Nothing she could say or do was going to sway the girl from her current goal. And besides, finding Ben was more important than useless arguing.

"Where is he, Paulette? What have you done with Ben?"

Max steered his car slowly around the Winston Design building and parked in the rear. Climbing out, he searched in all directions until he finally spotted Maddie's little red compact angled on the grass, hidden behind a small clump of trees. He smiled, seeing she'd done as he had hoped and kept her presence at the factory a secret.

After checking the back doors and finding them secured, Max walked to the front of the building and let himself in, noting the main doors were locked and the alarm system armed. He walked up the stairs to his office, hoping to find Maddie and Ben going about the company's business. Halfway up, something made him stop and rethink the idea.

The last thing he wanted was to find Maddie and Ben

in a compromising situation, even in innocence. Maddie would be embarrassed, but *he* would be mortified. Max coughed loudly, calling out, "Maddie! Maddie, I let myself in," as he went up the steps.

The door to his office stood open, so Max walked in, stopping short when he saw the condition of the room. Burned down candles graced every available surface. Flowers bloomed from vases sitting about the desk, shelves, and on the table set with plates and crystal situated in the center of the room. A large four-poster bed, made up with satin sheets and luxurious hangings sat sideways and suspiciously rumpled in the far corner of the room.

Max placed his hands on his hips and walked to the braziers set on a serving cart next to his desk. Lifting the lids, he poked at the meat and vegetables congealed in the pans. A plate of dates and figs lay next to the pans and he helped himself, popping a date whole into his mouth. Chewing, he shook his head.

All he'd been worried about was finding Maddie and Ben in an embrace—at worst, entwined and fully clothed—asleep on the cot. This was a scene for serious seduction if ever he saw one. And he was damned sure Maddie had nothing to do with it. The room looked like something out of the scenes he'd read about in books on harems. Ben, that goat-humping, camel-stealing so-and-so was the one who'd orchestrated this little party. He'd bet his life on it. The man had set out to seduce Maddie, sure as the sun shone in August. Damn him, send his soul to hell and—

Giving the room another sweeping glance, he sighed. Even after the room was cleared, would he ever be able to get the picture of Maddie and Ben together on that bed out of his mind? The guy had nerve, all right.

He checked his watch and found it was only eight. Even though he was thankful he hadn't caught Ben and Maddie doing anything embarrassing, he couldn't help but wonder what had happened to the lovebirds. Where would they be this early on a Sunday morning? Maddie's car was here, so unless they'd decided to go for a walk along Route 46, they had to be somewhere in the building.

He smoothed down his ruffled feathers and reminded himself he was not Maddie's father. The girl was a young woman approaching thirty, free to do what she wanted. He'd warned her enough times about Ben to know he'd done his duty as her godfather. If she wanted to throw herself away on Benjamin Able, that was her business.

Realizing what he had just decided, Max kicked himself. Less than twenty-four hours ago, he and Ben had chatted in this very room and come to a truce. He'd warned Ben about trifling with Maddie or the company, and Ben had sworn his fidelity and devotion to both. With that declaration, he had believed Ben to be an honorable man. Why should his feelings change just because he suspected Ben had spent the night with Maddie? The young man had never said he wasn't interested in the girl. He'd even promised he would lay down his life for her if such a thing became necessary.

Maddie was a warm, giving human being who had overcome her mother's stunning looks and her father's overly high expectations to become a decent businesswoman. Since she'd let her hair grow and started wearing a bit of makeup, her true beauty had come to the fore rather nicely, just as he'd suspected it would. Maddie was a late bloomer, but the flower of her beauty would last all the longer for it. Maybe instead of being angry with Ben, he should commend the man on his good taste.

Max shook his head as he imagined a possibility. Could Ben and Maddie be in love?

Still, he needed to know where the couple had disappeared to. He walked out the door and down the stairs, heading for the assembly room.

The first thing he noticed was the eerie quiet of the

building. Over the humming of the air conditioning system, the halls echoed dully, as if the building was deserted. The closer he got to the assembly room, the more he worried. If Maddie and Ben were in there, they weren't talking. Surely Maddie would have enough decorum and common sense not to have sex in those rooms.

Max plowed through the prep room and into the main plant with a determined stride, telling himself he would not jump at Maddie like a jailer. He would speak with her calmly about his concerns. Once in the assembly area, he could see everything was in order, but that didn't stop the hairs on the back of his neck from standing suddenly on end. He continued into shipping and receiving, thinking how the whole business was growing more curious by the second.

Pushing through the doors to shipping, he stopped in his tracks. The room was orderly, but the wall they'd stacked the boxes of microchips against was empty. Max scanned the room with narrowed eyes, trying to find some clue as to what had happened to the chips. His gaze swept to the floor and his heart gave a startled *thump*. There, on the linoleum tiles, were rusty brown spatters he was sure he'd never seen before.

Walking over, he squatted and rubbed at the spots. Most were dried, but the largest stain still looked damp. He stuck a finger in the thick liquid and held the finger to his nose, smelling, then tasting the substance. He held back a gag as he stood and walked to the wall phone.

Dialing quickly, he thought about all the possible scenarios he'd just contrived about Maddie and Ben. Not one of them had been this bad.

"This is Max Hefner over at Winston Design," he said after his call had been answered. "I want to report a theft—and a probable kidnapping."

* * *

Ben woke to pitch darkness and knew immediately he wasn't in his bottle. He struggled past the pain in the back of his head to tug at the rope binding his hands and feet, growling when the scratchy restraints cut into him. The rag tied over his mouth pressed against his tongue and teeth and made him retch.

He rolled to his back and bumped his knees against the top of the prison, frustrated to find himself securely closed in. Rolling to his side, he opened his senses and held his breath, reaching beyond the confining space to the outside. Unfortunately, he heard nothing that could enlighten him on his surroundings.

Concentrating, he thought he recognized the smell of a by-product of the petroleum Maddie had lectured him on the first night they'd been together. Gasoline? Gasoline meant automobiles. Could he be tied up in the trunk of a car? If so, the car probably belonged to the thief.

Try as he might, Ben could remember nothing after he'd been whacked on the head. Whoever had done this had hit him twice, the sniveling coward. Worse, if they'd had the nerve to hurt him, what might they have done to Maddie?

Thinking positive thoughts, he prayed Allah had been kind and given Maddie the good sense to stay in the office, as he had commanded. Maybe the thieves had taken the chips and kidnapped just him.

But that was doubtful. Maddie was no coward. If he hadn't returned last night after a reasonable amount of time, she would have gone looking. And the thief or thieves would have found her. Where was Maddie?

Inflamed, he jerked on his ropes until he remembered another law of the bottle: Genies imprisoned by man could not free themselves unless commanded to do so by their masters.

Centering himself, he homed in on the silence, hoping to reach Maddie with his heart. Sadly, he found no answering wave of thought. If she were near, she had to be unconscious or she would have connected with him in some small, reassuring way.

He heard a noise through the trunk, muffled at first, then more clear. The sound of several people arguing stopped nearby. He lifted his legs and slammed his feet into the ceiling of the trunk, bouncing on his back to rock the automobile. Perhaps the people were passersby who would hear the noise and call for help.

Something hit the top of the trunk with a bang and he stilled, waiting. Keys rattled and a scraping sound gave him hope. Someone was setting him free.

The trunk lid opened about four inches. Blinding sunlight speared his eyes, causing him to blink back tears. He heard a harsh voice and a muffled curse, then saw the barrel of a shiny black gun poke its way into the trunk and stop a hairbreadth from his face.

"Lie quietly, Mr. Able, or I'll be obliged to shut you up permanently, understand? And if we shut you up, we're going to do the same to your girlfriend. You got that?"

The gun jerked back and the lid slammed closed, throwing him again into darkness. Furious, Ben pulled at the ropes. Damn the bottle and damn its stupid rules! He was going to make someone pay if anything happened to Maddie.

Eighteen

Maddie scanned the dimly lighted warehouse, her nerves the consistency of shredded wheat. In between useless struggles to free herself, she had worried about Ben or dozed fitfully most of the day. She could tell by the way the sun played off the high windows it would soon be night, and their fate would be sealed with the darkness.

Determined to attract the attention of her captors, she shouted, "Hey, how about a little water and a potty break!"

All she received in answer was the faint echo of her own voice and a scuttling noise. Unfortunately, the noise sounded too much like the one she'd heard earlier in the day, when she'd spied several huge rats scurrying between the rows of boxes and crates.

Annoyed, she twisted her head and wiped the sweat beading her upper lip onto her shoulder. Where, she wondered, were the thugs Dominic Maggio had sent to watch her?

Sometime in the middle of the day two stone-faced hulks of muscle wearing expensive suits and carrying guns had untied her ankles and wrists, then given her five minutes to take care of business. Afterward, they'd dragged her back to her corner without saying a word and ordered her to eat. She recalled swallowing just enough of the rubbery burger and cold fries to stave off hunger and keep up her strength.

She really didn't need to use the bathroom. She just wanted another chance to ask the hulks a few pointed questions. She wanted to get the show up and running. She wanted to see Ben.

Stretching to ease her aches, Maddie slid her legs straight out in front of her and took another heated look at her ankles, which were wrapped tightly in several rounds of rope. She gave a tug out of spite, knowing full well the hemp wouldn't tear, and returned her attention to her burning wrists. Though she'd lost feeling in her hands long ago, she could tell her wrists were rubbed raw. Still, she kept up the wrenching arm movement, hoping to weaken the bindings in any small way she could.

It had been hours since she'd seen Dominic Maggio or Paulette. Or her uncle, the traitorous swine. A half smile passed her lips when she formed the words, thinking she sounded just like Ben. Only Ben would have spouted a whole lot more colorful and descriptive words. And Ben would have already taken care of her uncle and the rest of the hulks, Paulette included, sending all of them to the farthest interior of a glacier or the bottom of a live volcano.

Maddie stopped her struggles and breathed deep, willing her mind and body to still. Ben kept telling her they were connected somehow, by a strong master-genie bond. Concentrating, as she'd done several times earlier in the day, she reached out to him, trying to find his spirit waiting to link with hers. Seconds passed before she knew it to be hopeless. If he was near, he didn't respond.

Maddie heard a door slam in the distance. "Hey, I'm suffering here. I need to go to the bathroom," she called again.

Instead of an answer, she heard the sound of an engine, then a whining noise. Rolling away from the wall, she struggled to her knees to get a better view of the warehouse. One of the hulks had started the forklift and was now driving it her way.

Maddie sat back and rested her bottom on her heels, watching as he maneuvered the lift under a crate, then raised it in the air. Someone had opened one of the huge bay doors to the warehouse and she could see the back of a truck, its rear door swaying free. Deftly, the hulk steered the crate-laden forklift out the door and into the truck.

The process continued for so long Maddie's knees grew sore. Finally, she propelled herself back to the wall and propped against it to wait. She wasn't sure how much time had passed, but the sky grew dim before the loading stopped and the bay door closed. Again she was thrust into near darkness, left alone to contemplate her capture.

She'd had plenty of time to figure out what would happen next. This was a holiday weekend, so most people were off work. The odors she'd keyed in on when she'd first woke up, musty dank air and rotting wood plus the scurrying rats, told her she was somewhere in a wharf area, maybe a holding station for cargo waiting to be loaded onto oceangoing vessels. If the warehouse was isolated, it was probable the cargo would leave the country without anyone's knowledge.

From there, the crates would be released to other criminals, the computer components delivered to some unlicensed factory in eastern Europe where they would be assembled, then sold to the highest bidders on the black market—a neat little plan she was sure had met with some success in the past.

Maddie stared up and found the small, high windows shrouded in darkness. It had to be close to nine. If they were planning on getting the merchandise out over the holiday, her jailers would be coming for her soon.

She had willed herself to remain calm all day, positive once she and Ben were together he would save them. Now she wondered just how much of a pipe dream she'd been living. Had Ben told her the truth? Would his damnable laws, especially the one about his not being able to do magic in front of others, allow him to perform a rescue?

More importantly, could earthly dangers harm him, as they did normal men? Could Ben be killed? Would he still be alive when—if—she saw him again?

If he came to harm because of her, could she ever live with herself? Without him, would she even want to?

Footsteps and voices interrupted her musing, and Maddie shoved the worries about Ben to the back of her mind. In the end, no matter what happened, she loved him. She would not betray that love.

She straightened, waiting to face her captors. Finally, she thought, something was going to happen.

Dominic Maggio and the hulks appeared from behind a stack of boxes. "Well, Ms. Winston, I hope you've enjoyed your stay at our fine hotel. Sorry we can't accommodate you any longer. It's time for you to leave on that little trip we talked about earlier."

Maddie showed him her best sneer. "Where are we going, Mr. Maggio? And what have you done with my assistant?"

The hulks reached down, grabbed Maddie by her armpits, and hauled her to her feet. Dominic Maggio himself bent over and cut the rope from her ankles with a lethal-looking knife.

"No more questions, Ms. Busybody. Rico, Gene, hang on to her and get her outside."

Half-dragging, half-carrying her, the two men forced Maddie toward a door, then pulled her onto a small landing and into the cool night air. Frantically, she scanned the area, hoping to find a landmark, some familiar sight that could tell her where she was, but the men gave her little time. Hoisting her up, they skimmed her down the steps and straight to the back of a black BMW. Her uncle's car.

"Okay, Fulbright," Maggio called. The trunk lid popped

and he raised it high, giving her the chance to stare into her next prison.

Maddie spied a pile of rumpled rags strewn about the trunk. Her heart lurched when she realized what the damp-looking heap of clothing really was. "Ben!" she screamed, bending into the trunk.

The men pushed her from behind and she landed with a thud, practically on top of Ben. Then the trunk lid slammed, throwing them into darkness.

Maddie licked at her lips, afraid to breathe. Ben had looked so pale in the dim interior light. He was unmoving now, even with her draped on top of him, crushing him. Was it possible he was dead?

She angled her cheek against something scratchy—his beard?—and thought she felt a breath. Scrunching up her legs, she wiggled down and set her ear to what she hoped was his chest. The steady in and out sounds of his breathing coupled with strong heartbeats caused her to give a little sputter of joy. But why hadn't he freed himself?

"Ben! It's me, Maddie. Can you hear me, Ben?"

She thought she felt the pattern of his breathing shift and nuzzled closer. "Ben, please wake up. I need you."

Her cheek felt clammy, and she realized he was drenched in sweat. Those monsters had kept him locked inside an airless trunk for almost twenty-four hours. It was a miracle he hadn't suffocated by now.

Suddenly furious, she began to mutter, "God, oh God, please let him be alive. Ben, can you hear me? I need a wish, Ben. Wake up. I command you to wake up."

Ben sensed a breath of fresh air, a glimmer of light, something heavy smothering him, but he was too weak to acknowledge the sensations. Long ago, he had become light-headed from the lack of oxygen in the trunk. He had needed a drink of water, too, but his wants had not been met.

Right now, he swore he could hear Maddie calling to him as she pressed her sweet body over his. But he knew he was dreaming, preparing his final thoughts before his death. It was comforting to know the last thing he would hear would be the voice of the woman he loved.

"Ben, I command you to wake up and grant me a wish," said Maddie from the darkness.

Opening his cracked lips, he struggled to answer what he thought was a trick of his desperate mind. He strained to gather air, but couldn't force out any words.

"Ben, can you blink or think hard? Can you snap your fingers or tap them together to get my hands untied?"

He smiled. Of course he could do small things like untying her rope with a simple blink. All she had to do was ask. He furrowed his brow and concentrated. Suddenly he felt fingertips on his face, his eyes, his nose. Overwhelmed, he nestled into Maddie's gentle touch.

"Oh, Ben. You *can* hear me. Come on now, wake up."

"Maddie. I can now die happy, knowing you are with me," he muttered, kissing one of her palms.

The car took a bump and threw them up and down, causing Maddie to land hard against his chest. He shook his head, knocking into something that felt suspiciously like a nose.

"Ow! Hey, take it easy," came Maddie's voice again. "Are you awake now? Can I make another wish?"

In a daze, Ben noticed that his breathing was coming easier. His eyes popped open. Trying to focus in the blackness, he imagined her smile, the crinkling of her honeyed eyes. "Maddie? Is it you?"

"It's me. Are you OK? Turn around so I can undo your hands."

He obeyed, maneuvering his arms to one side. After several mangled attempts, his hands were free.

"Air, Ben. I wish for cool air. Can you manage that?"

He rubbed at his wrists, lightly brought his hands together, and the trunk became cool and sweet-smelling. Reaching out, he found Maddie's face and clasped it in his palms. "Maddie mine, is it really you?"

"Yes, it's me. I don't understand, Ben. Why didn't you free yourself and find me?"

He pressed his mouth to her forehead. "More illogical rules, Maddie. There are dozens we have yet to talk about."

She nodded against him and he ran his thumbs over her cheeks, catching the tears that slipped from her eyes. "No crying. We have to get out of here first. Do you understand?"

She sniffed. "You bet I do. Now I command you to clap that entire bunch of goons to the bottom of a live volca—no, wait. The ocean. Drowning is a horrible way to die, isn't it? Send them to the ocean floor or—no, how about the top of Mt. Everest? That's it. I want them naked at the top of Mt. Everest. Especially Uncle Lucius."

Ben grinned and pulled her close, noting the car had slowed. They would be confronting the enemy at any moment. "Maddie, I will send them to the moon if you want it, but think a minute. This is the twenty-first century. You have told me over and over that criminals in this time are dealt with by the law. Sending the infidels away will not get you justice. They need to be prosecuted, Maddie. Taken to jail and punished for their crimes. It is your law."

The car slowed to a crawl and hit another bump. Maddie heaved a sigh. "OK, you're right. I guess I got a little bloodthirsty for a minute there. What did you want to do to them? That public flogging in Times Square sounds pretty good right now. And hives. Uncle Lucius deserves those hives we joked about earlier."

He held back a chuckle and kissed her, a soft sweet melding of lips and breath, drinking in the taste of her trust. "Say the words, Maddie. Tell me I have your permission to do whatever is necessary."

She sipped from his lips like a thirsty flower, then nodded against his chin. "I give you permission, my genie, to do whatever you wish."

It was almost ten o'clock. Max wasn't sure how or why, but here he was again at the Englewood Heights municipal building, sitting in Lieutenant Fox's tidy office. How could a man who always looked as if he'd slept in his clothes work in such a pristine office?

He glanced around the room and wondered if the man ever did any real police work. He knew Lieutenant Fox had a gun. He'd seen it peeking out from under the man's disheveled suit coat on several occasions. But his office looked like it belonged to a friggin' neat freak. The desk was spotless, the floor waxed to a spit shine, and the files tucked out of sight like he'd never worked on a case in his life.

And after he'd spent the last day with the man, Max knew the police were no closer to unraveling the mystery of the missing microchips and Maddie and Ben.

Earlier today, when he'd finished his first meeting with the police, he'd caught a few hours of sleep, ate a quick dinner, then, with a heavy heart, called Sylvia to bring her up to speed on their negative progress. It had pained him to hear her wistful voice as she encouraged him to keep the faith and continue looking for Maddie. Sylvia was the world's eternal optimist, especially where her family was concerned. In all the years Max had been friends with the Winstons, he'd never been able to complain about Lucius in front of her, no matter what the man did. When he'd voiced his suspicions and confessed to Sylvia that Lucius had not returned his or Lieutenant Fox's calls, she refused to even listen.

It would break Sylvia's heart if she lost her only grand-child and found out her younger brother was to blame.

The strange thing was, after he'd hung up from speaking with her, Max had gotten this urge, this compelling need to visit the detective again. Some little niggle inside his head kept telling him he had to get to the docks at Port Elizabeth and bring Lieutenant Fox along.

Max Hefner was a man of science, but he wasn't a fool. He believed in the powers of prayer, premonitions, and angels, and not necessarily in that order. That was why he'd paged Fox and demanded to meet him here at the office. He was going to drag the man to the docks come hell or high water.

The BMW banked to the right, throwing Maddie against Ben and shoving both of them up against the wheel well. Ben *oomphed,* then grabbed at Maddie and kissed her hard. "Trust me, Maddie mine," he whispered just before they felt the car jerk to a halt. "This is what I want you to do."

Within seconds, the trunk lid popped open.

Ben rose to his knees. His hands clasped behind his back, he clutched the ropes as if they were still tied. He saw the muzzle of a gun glint in the lights lining the park-ing lot and gave a warning nudge to Maddie. In the dis-tance, the landing strips of Newark Airport flickered in the darkness, but the sky and highways around them looked deserted.

Three figures pointed guns at the trunk, motioning for them to climb out. One of the larger hulks pulled roughly at Maddie, tugging her to a stand, and Ben felt his muscles tighten with rage.

"Hey, ease up," Maddie spat out, shrugging from his grasp.

The man gave a nasty chuckle. "What's it to ya, girlie?

Where you're goin', a little bruisin' is the least of your worries."

Maddie turned to Dominic Maggio and gave him a fulminating glare. "Where *are* we going?" she demanded.

Maggio puffed on his cigar, filling the air with noxious fumes. "You're gonna take a little ride with your computer chips, Ms. Winston. My friends at the other end of the line will take care of the funeral arrangements when you two arrive. Now get goin'."

The goons each grabbed one of Ben's arms, while Maggio got hold of Maddie. Just before they stepped away, Lucius Winston opened his car door and got out. He kept his eyes on Dominic Maggio when he spoke.

"Is it absolutely necessary to kill them? I mean, couldn't we just . . . send them out alive in the crates? You could order your friends at the other end to take care of them if they managed to survive the trip. Her blood . . . I mean, it wouldn't be on my . . . your hands."

Maddie raised her gaze to her uncle's and struggled free from Maggio's grip. "Oh, no you don't, Uncle Lucius. Don't you dare try to act like you aren't guilty. You wanted to get back at my father, and now you are." She turned to face her captor. "Mr. Maggio, aren't the condemned usually granted a final wish?"

He eyed her suspiciously. "This ain't no firing squad, Ms. Winston. What do you want?"

Lifting her chin, Maddie gave Lucius a challenging glare. "I demand you make my uncle watch my execution. I want to look him in the eye when you shoot me. In fact, I want *him* to pull the trigger."

Lucius made an appalled, flapping sound through his slack lips. His eyes wide, Dominic Maggio whipped the stogie from his mouth. After a half second, he roared with laughter. Nervously, the hulks followed suit.

"Now s-s-see here, Mr. Maggio," Lucius began with a stutter.

The bullish man slammed a meaty hand across her uncle's thin back, and Lucius's horn rims slid to the end of his nose. "She's got spunk, I'll grant you that, Fulbright." He waved his cigar in Maddie's direction. "Sure, why not? Come on along, Fulbright. We have a freighter to meet and load. And you've just been given a new job."

Ben stifled a hearty chuckle. He had instructed Maddie to waste time. He'd thought she might feign weakness or have a fainting spell. The last thing he'd expected was for her to dare her uncle, spitting in his eye and demanding he pull the trigger. His Maddie was some kind of woman.

He had estimated it would take Max and the police just over thirty minutes to get to the docks. He needed another diversion, something small enough to get the men to stumble, perhaps.

They started walking—that is, Ben and Maddie did. Lucius, Dominic Maggio, and his two henchmen landed on the pavement in a tangle of arms and legs.

"What the hell?"

"Hey, my shoelaces are tied together!"

"Mine, too. Shit!"

Ben gave Maddie a shove and tugged off his ropes. Pointing her in the direction of a stack of abandoned crates, he commanded, "Run, Maddie! Take cover!"

Together they raced across the dock, diving around the crates just as bullets started to fly.

"Guns, Ben. We need guns," shouted Maddie over the noise.

Ben threw her what he hoped was a confident grin. "Guns are not exactly my forte, Maddie. I think we should have a little fun first," he said with a wink and a clap of his hands.

The biting volley of gunshots stopped, immediately replaced with pinging sounds. Maddie bent and picked up a small, roundish pebble and held it up for inspection.

"Gum balls?" she said with an exasperated breath. "You changed their bullets to gum balls?"

Ben shrugged, took the blue pellet from her hand, and popped it into his mouth. On the dock, the thugs had just realized something wasn't quite right with their *deadly* weapons. Their language was enough to make a drunken sailor blush. Her hand to her lips, Maddie giggled.

Ben peered around the corner of the crates, but all he could see was Lucius, sitting with his head in his hands at the side of his car. He thought about walking out and confronting all of them when he heard a gasp of breath.

He turned, just as Dominic Maggio grabbed Maddie from behind and pressed a large, silver-bladed knife against her throat. Maddie's eyes glowed like candle flame in the darkness, sending his anger into overdrive. He felt a presence behind him and knew they were surrounded.

"Playtime's over, Able. I don't know what kind of kooky magic tricks you're using, but it's time to get serious."

Ben blinked and the knife turned into a snow-white feather.

Maddie whirled away from her captor, just as Maggio gazed incredulously at what was once his knife. Hauling back an arm, she whacked him in the nose with her fist.

Instinctively, Ben spun around and slammed his palms against the side of each hulk's face, smashing their heads together like overripe melons.

Maggio swiped an open hand at Maddie and caught her on the chin, but she jumped back in time to set him off balance, and he fell to his knees. She stumbled backward and Ben caught her in his arms. "That's some right hook. You OK?"

Maddie nodded, working her jaw. "Yeah. But I think I hurt Maggio more than he hurt me. What's next?"

Ben pinned his gaze on the downed men, watching as they scrambled for their weapons.

"Get up, you idiots," Maggio sputtered, trying to help them to their feet.

Ben didn't like the idea of being unarmed, even against gum balls, and decided to take Maddie's advice. In a blink, he wore an old-fashioned gun belt strapped to his hips and a six-shooter in each hand.

Maddie gaped. "I thought you didn't like guns? And those look like antiques. Do they really work?"

She plugged her fingers in her ears when he shot each one in the air. "They work." Smiling, he spun the pistols on his fingers like an expert and pointed them at Maggio and his thugs. "Drop your guns, Pilgrims," he drawled.

The trio, looking angry and confused, reluctantly obeyed.

"Maddie, please pick up their weapons."

Maddie stepped over and delicately lifted the revolvers, ignoring the men's threatening growls. She then walked to Ben's side, the guns clutched to her chest, and threw him an adoring smile. "My hero." She batted her lashes.

Police sirens sounded in the distance.

Ben puffed up his chest, basking in her admiration. "I think it's time we escort this group back to your uncle's car and wait for the reinforcements to arrive."

He stepped aside, and the three men began to walk grudgingly toward the opposite side of the dock. When Lucius saw them coming, he jumped into his car and started the engine, but it was too late. Police cars from Englewood Heights, as well as several from Elizabeth and Newark, all sped into the lot and squealed to a halt, blocking Lucius's escape route.

Max jumped from his car and ran toward Ben and Maddie. Their guns drawn, the officers alighted from the other squad cars and began to surround them.

Without warning, hell broke loose as a spattering of bullets split the night air. Everyone ducked, trying to pinpoint the origin of the attack.

"Stay where you are." Paulette Jamison had somehow maneuvered herself behind the cadre of police cars and was holding what looked to be a large machine gun in her hands. Waving the weapon in a wide arc, she sent a round of bullets into the pavement at Ben and Maddie's feet.

"Drop your weapons, or I'll take them out."

Ben felt sweat trickle down his back, a clammy reminder of Ashmedai's forbidden laws. Every commandment he had ever been taught raced through his mind. Maddie had already ordered him to do whatever he felt was necessary to save them, but he was fairly certain he had stretched her command to the breaking point. Detaining this crowd didn't come under the normal guidelines of proper genie conduct, even with her OK. He needed to do something *now* to save Maddie, as well as Max and the police.

He lowered his arms to his sides and blinked the six shooters from existence. The officers, busy setting their guns on the ground while still keeping an eye on Paulette, didn't notice. So far, so good.

Maddie leaned against him and Ben felt her heartbeat pounding through his clothes, melding as one with his. He read her thoughts and knew she wasn't frightened. She was relying on him to take care of this latest roadblock. Empowered by the waves of love she sent his way, he reached around and enfolded her in his arms, then took a breath. What was the modern saying he had heard so many times since his release from the bottle?

Rules were made to be broken.

Raising his hands, he clapped them together.

In less than the blink of an eye, Paulette held a banana in her hand.

Dominic Maggio and his thugs were handcuffed and helpless.

And Lucius Fulbright was sitting, bound and gagged, on the roof of his BMW.

Nineteen

Maddie turned to grab at Ben, but her arms clutched swirling air. Confused, she swivelled her head around to search the dock, but failed to find him in the darkness. Funny, she thought she'd felt him right behind her, holding her in a calming, protective embrace. Had she only imagined being enveloped in his arms or seeing him clap his hands?

She spied Lieutenant Fox in the crowd and suppressed a giggle. He and the other officers looked just as puzzled as she felt, though not necessarily for the same reason. In tandem, the group of policemen were scratching their heads and staring from the cluster of handcuffed men to Paulette and her drooping banana.

Maddie sneaked a sideward glance at her uncle and found him still sitting in a heap on the car roof. Every so often, one of the patrolman would stare at Lucius and shake his head, as if dumbfounded.

"Ben," she managed to mutter when Max clutched her to his chest. "Where's Ben, Max? Do you see him?"

Max pulled back to study the milling crowd. It looked like the patrolmen had finally decided they didn't care what had happened, they just needed to round up the criminals. Two men began to handcuff Paulette and her wilted banana, while another half dozen escorted Maggio and his men to squad cars. Detective Fox and one of his own patrolmen began dragging Lucius from the top of his Beamer. Ben was nowhere to be seen.

Max shrugged his shoulders, then planted his arm tightly around Maddie. "I don't know, Maddie girl. He was standing here a second ago. What the hell happened?"

Maddie knew, or thought she knew, exactly where Ben had gone. Somehow, he had managed to break another stupid rule—probably the one about doing his genie stuff in front of others—and annoyed the bottle, getting himself zapped back inside its clutches. In a way, she was almost relieved at the thought. If there was any more shooting, he would be out of danger.

But Lieutenant Fox would want them all taken in for questioning, and Ben was still charged with the theft of the microchips. Part of his criteria for being granted bail was that he remain accessible and not leave the area. She had to get home and call him out of the bottle before someone grew suspicious and made trouble.

She spent the next fifteen minutes being comforted by Max while thinking hard about the best way to concoct her story. Finally, Lieutenant Fox confronted her. "Ms. Winston, I'm sure you and Mr Able have an acceptable explanation for what happened here and at the plant last night."

Maddie swallowed hard. "We do. But, um, Mr. Able—"

Fox glanced around, then turned to her. "Where is your assistant? Surely he knows we'll need to question him. He'll still have to go in front of a judge in order for the charges to be dismissed. There is that matter of the hundred thousand dollars bail you put up, remember?"

Maddie cringed inside. How could she forget? The money was practically all she had left of her trust fund after she had saved the company last year. She hadn't explained to Ben what would happen to the money if he skipped town, because she never thought the situation would arise. Right now, the money was the least of her worries.

What if this time the bottle wouldn't release him? How many chances did Ben have before he was banished from her forever?

"Mr. Able had to—"

"Get back to the plant," Max interjected, casting Maddie a little wink. "I think with all that's happened you ought to cut him and Ms. Winston some slack, Lieutenant. It's close to midnight, and from the looks of it, Ms. Winston and Mr. Able were treated abominably. I think I even heard Lucius mumble something about a death sentence. Surely you can haul Maggio and the rest of them in and sort everything out in the morning. It is a holiday weekend, remember?"

Fox checked his watch. When he glanced up at Maddie, she screwed her face into the most weary look she could muster. Leaning heavily into Max, she crossed her fingers behind her back, hoping the detective wouldn't question her on how Ben had managed to leave the dock so quickly. "I'd like to go home, shower, and make myself presentable, Detective Fox. Ben was locked in the trunk of my uncle's car for twenty-four hours, while I was held hostage in a dank, dirty warehouse for the same length of time. I promise you we'll be there to set things straight tomorrow."

The detective folded his arms and watched as the culprits—a furious Paulette Jamison, a whimpering Lucius Fulbright, and Maggio and his swaggering men—were finally loaded into squad cars.

A patrolman walked up to them and said, "Excuse me, sir, but I radioed my captain and was told we had to bring these perps into the Elizabeth station, since the Port is our jurisdiction. I'm sure we can hold them a day or so without too much of a problem."

Maddie and Max threw one another grateful glances. Lieutenant Fox merely nodded. "Fine. You do that.

We'll all meet at the Broad Street station at, say, ten tomorrow morning?"

Maddie breathed a quiet sigh. "Thank you, Detective Fox. We'll see you then."

Maddie woke at dawn to the mournful beating of rain against her windows. She'd forgotten to close her drapes after she'd stumbled home last night, but the gray light seeping into the room hadn't wakened her. Instead, the dreary drizzle mirrored the feeling in her heart, calling her to consciousness with its hopeless and plaintive sound.

She shoved her bangs from her forehead and ran her hands over her eyes, letting last night's events play in her mind. After leaving the dock, Max had brought her back to the factory, where they had looked for Ben. Max had raised his brows at the condition of his office, but didn't tease Maddie or press her for an explanation about what had taken place. After a thorough search failed to turn up Ben, Max agreed to let Maddie drive home alone.

He'd been puzzled over Ben's disappearance, but she'd had an argument all worked out in her mind. She simply reminded Max of Ben's scare with the traffic accident, and shared with him Ben's secret fear of anyone finding out about his illegal status. She managed to convince Max that, most probably, Ben had gone back to their apartment to wait until the dust settled. Even Max hadn't thought to ask how Ben had caught a cab on a deserted dock at ten o'clock on a holiday weekend.

And Maddie had been so calm and matter-of-fact in her explanation, she'd almost believed the lie herself.

Close to one in the morning, she had arrived home and entered her apartment. She'd prayed on the entire ride that the bottle had imprisoned Ben again and all she needed to do was go to his room and polish the cursed thing. Her world would be set back on its axis as soon as Ben appeared.

She remembered racing up the hall, skidding into his room, and stumbling to the dresser. But the second she'd rounded the corner, she'd known something was desperately wrong.

The bottle was gone.

She recalled running her hand along the dusty dresser top, but all she had found was the business card the cab driver, Hajisani, had given Ben. Slowly, she'd walked to Ben's closet, thinking he might have taken her advice and pushed the bottle into the back and out of sight. But even after crawling in as far as she could, she had found nothing.

Maddie sighed, left the bed, and shuffled to the bathroom. She'd been so exhausted last night, she hadn't even showered. Now she stepped from her filthy clothes and turned the water to near-scalding, then stood still and let the stinging spray rinse away the stink of the warehouse. After minutes of standing in the steamy heat, she reversed the temperature to frigid and tried to wake her mind up to a new day and a fresh perspective.

She dressed in a pair of tailored slacks and a linen blouse and vest, then walked back into Ben's room to be sure she hadn't dreamed the terrible scene from last night. But the dresser and closet were still empty. Ben was still gone.

As if in mourning, Maddie made her way to her kitchen and brewed a cup of tea, knowing her stomach wouldn't tolerate the taste of the coffee she and Ben had shared. She managed to choke down a piece of dry toast and half an apple before shoving the breakfast into the trash. After a few more minutes, she laid her head on the kitchen table and began to cry.

Maddie wasn't sure how much time had passed when the phone rang, but her eyes felt hot and swollen. She picked up the receiver and, when she heard Mary Grace's voice, held back a sob.

"Happy Memorial Day," Mary Grace chirped. "I take it your being home is a good sign? You met the deadline on the chips?" she asked hopefully.

Maddie sniffed away a tear. "Yeah. We met the deadline."

"Well, you don't sound too happy about it. Is something wrong?"

Maddie took a breath, fully aware her best friend couldn't help her out of this predicament. No one could, even if she managed to convince someone her story about Ben was true. "I'm fine. Just exhausted. There was a little . . . problem last night and the police made an arrest. We . . . I didn't get home until late, and I have to go to New Jersey for the paperwork and stuff this morning."

"Jeez, Maddie, who did it? Was it someone you know?"

She cleared her throat, embarrassed and angry that she had to admit someone in her own family would be so callous and mean. "It was Lucius and Paulette—"

"Paulette Jamison? And your uncle?" Mary Grace spit out the names, making it sound almost unbelievable.

"And a competitor Paulette was spying for. It was . . . I don't know, creepy. Did you know she's held a grudge against me all these years? She blames me for her dropping out of school and a whole lot of other things that never panned out in her life. It was bizarre."

Mary Grace made a *tsking* sound. "That little shit. And after you gave her a job and—what about Ben? You haven't said, but I'm assuming he was there. How are things going between the two of you?"

Maddie placed a hand against her mouth to stifle a whimper. She would have to tell Mary Grace, and everyone else involved, some bit of truth along with the lies if she was ever to get past this crisis. "He was with me . . .

now he's . . . uh. . . . oh, Mary Grace, he's disappeared again."

With that, Maddie began to sob.

Mary Grace gave a huge sigh. "Stay there. Don't move a muscle. I'm coming right over."

Exhausted, Maddie gave her best friend a heartfelt hug. "Thanks for coming with me to the police station today. I don't know what I'd have done without you."

Mary Grace stood in the doorway of Maddie's apartment, a look of concern on her usually perky face. "No problem. I'm just happy that whole obnoxious crew is being held until tomorrow. There were so many charges against them, the police captain did the only thing he could. Thank God it's Memorial Day and the courts are closed, or they'd be out on bail right now."

Maddie sniffed at the word "bail" and rested her head on her front door. "Detective Fox was nice, too, even after I told him Ben had disappeared. He says he's going to stall on the arraignment to drop Ben's charges for the rest of the week, but he's positive Ben will have to be in court next Monday. If not, they'll have to issue a warrant for his jumping bail, even if he's innocent. That will make him a fugitive from justice," she said, a little catch in her voice.

Mary Grace smiled wryly. "Yeah, but just think of the exciting headlines: *Madeline Winston and mysterious hunk save Winston Design and capture the bad guys*. It'll certainly spruce up your image as a hard-nosed businesswoman, won't it?"

Maddie tried for a grin. "Some businesswoman I turned out to be. I almost let my father's company be destroyed. I hired a woman who hated me for giving her a job, and I worked overtime at being nice to an uncle who got me kidnapped and almost killed."

"And you found Ben," Mary Grace reminded her. "Don't forget about Ben."

Maddie wiped her eyes with the ratty tissue she'd been knotting in her hand. "How could I forget him, Mary Grace? I love him."

"I already figured that out. And I'm very happy for you. He'll show up, you'll see."

Maddie shook her head. "I don't think so. I mean . . . it's different this time. I'm so afraid he won't be coming back."

Mary Grace eyed her shrewdly. "Now there's a positive attitude. Makes me wonder what you're hiding. Please don't tell me Ben's a terrorist or something equally distasteful. It was bad enough I pegged Paulette wrong. I pride myself on being a better judge of character than that."

Maddie let out a hopeless sigh. "It would almost be better if he were a terrorist. At least I'd know why he left. Not knowing where he's disappeared to is what's killing me."

Mary Grace nodded. "I understand how you're feeling, but I just can't believe Ben would leave you without a good reason. I bet he'll call you or just wander home tomorrow and tell you what happened. I saw the way he looked at you, remember? I'd bet my next pedicure the man is in love with you, too."

Maddie heaved another shuddering sigh and closed her eyes. She couldn't think of a thing to say in answer to Mary Grace's words of consolation.

Mary Grace tossed her a sympathetic little smile. "Why don't you lie down and take a nap? We can meet at Mrs. Cheng's for a late dinner and plan your next move."

"I'm not hungry, Mary Grace. And I don't have the nerve to show my face in public just yet. There were reporters at the jail and people asking too many questions. But I would like to catch up on my sleep. Maybe I'll be able to think more clearly tomorrow. OK if I take a rain check?"

Reluctantly, Mary Grace agreed. After a few more hugs, Maddie shut the door and waited until she heard her friend's footsteps fade. In slow motion, she threw the locks and turned from the door to walk down the hall and into her bedroom. Robot-like, she kicked off her shoes, then slid out of her slacks and blouse and hung them neatly in her closet. After scrubbing off her makeup and brushing her teeth, she put on a sleep shirt and lay back on the bed.

She had begun to doze when the ringing phone had her wide awake. She said a hesitant "Hello," her heart thumping at the idea Ben might be calling her.

"Honey, it's Gram. Are you OK?"

Maddie blinked. In all the flurry of the weekend, she'd forgotten to call Sylvia. One more mistake to add to her list, she thought, sitting upright in the bed.

"Gram. I'm so sorry I haven't called. I guess you've been wondering what—"

"Nonsense, dear. Max has kept me informed of everything, including today's proceedings at the jail. I still can't believe my idiot brother has been so foolish. Would you believe Lucius had the nerve to call and ask me if I would help him find a lawyer? In my opinion, they should throw the book at him."

Maddie smiled at her grandmother's astute and forthright observation. "He's so bitter, Gram. I had no idea Uncle Lucius held such an outrageous grudge against my father. I knew he didn't like me much, but I never thought he would transfer the whole of his hatred of dad onto me."

Sylvia *tsked*. "My little brother was a late-in-life baby our parents spoiled terribly. I should have known something untoward would happen once Catherine chose James over him. I warned him from the beginning that Catherine only had eyes for your father, but he never listened. I thought he'd managed to put it behind him, but I see now I was wrong. I blame myself for moving down here and not taking better care of you, Madeline. I'm so sorry."

Maddie dabbed at her eyes with a fresh tissue from the box on her nightstand. "It isn't your fault, Gram. And don't feel sorry for me. I'll be OK."

"Max spoke very highly of a young man he says helped you through your terrible ordeal. What happened to him, dear? Is he staying with Winston Design?"

Maddie pressed the tissue to her lips and took a deep breath. "I'm not sure. Ben's . . . he's . . . um . . . taking a few days off to get his head straight. If he wants a job, he'll be welcomed back."

"Well, good. Max tells me he's quite a man. Just what the company needs. Just what you need, from the sound of it."

Knowing Max had revealed more than he should, Maddie felt her heart turn. She wasn't certain she could relive the pain of her loss through her grandmother. "He's a business associate, Gram, that's all. I don't need another man messing up my life right now. I can take care of myself."

Sylvia chuckled softly. "I know you can, dear. I remember how much you hate to be pitied. You stay strong and call me if you need me. I'll be here for you. I love you, you know."

Maddie hung up the phone and fell back on the bed, her grandmother's final words ringing in her head: *I remember how much you hate to be pitied.*

Closing her eyes, she let all the feelings she had for Ben tumble over her in a crashing wave of emotion. She was smart enough to know his being a genie was not the reason she loved him. She smiled at the memory of his silly malapropisms, stated, she suspected, more to amuse her than anything else. He was intelligent, with an almost philosophical interest in the modern world and how it had changed over the centuries. He was fair-minded and clever, witty and understanding, and brave enough to lay down his life for her if the need ever arose.

Unbelievably, he was a handsome, compassionate computer wizard who had confessed the thing he enjoyed most in the world was simply looking at her, Madeline Jessup Winston.

He was the man of her dreams and her heart, no matter what time he'd come from or how cursed he'd been. Ben was the one she loved.

And if she truly hated being pitied, then *why* was she pitying herself?

Resolutely, Maddie punched at her pillow and settled in for a good night's sleep. She couldn't wait for the morning to come. If she wanted Ben, she would have to find him, and she had a good idea of where to start.

It was close to ten the next evening when Maddie finally found her way home. She'd spent the morning cabbing from one major Manhattan bookstore to another, then wasted time in the library researching each section she thought might give her information on Middle Eastern folklore, genies and jinns, but to no avail. Not even a scanned reading of *The One Thousand and One Nights* and the stories of Aladdin had helped. There was no book which covered more than a page or two on the origins of genies, and almost nothing on how to make them appear or disappear.

Dejected, she grabbed a glass of iced tea and brought it to her computer. A kindly librarian and several of the bookstore attendants had suggested she go on-line, reminding her the Internet was a wealth of information on every topic under the sun. Perhaps someone on-line would be able to help in her quest.

The door buzzer sounded and she jumped. Instantly she

thought it might be Ben, too bashful or repentant to just zap himself into her living room. She raced to the door and whipped it open, ready to throw herself in his arms, but stopped short when she saw her visitor was Trevor Edwards.

"Hello, Madeline," he said with a hesitant smile. "I hope I'm not disturbing you."

Maddie stepped back, so surprised to see him in a rumpled jacket and wrinkled pants it took her several seconds to answer. "Um, no." She swallowed. "But it's late, Trevor. What do you want?"

Trevor pulled at the frazzled knot in his silk Armani tie. "May I come in?"

Maddie deliberated over several snappy responses, then decided she was simply too tired to spar. With Trevor, it was usually easier to hear him out. She stepped back, and he headed down the hall and into her living room.

Trevor sat stiffly on the sofa, then made an attempt at straightening the pleats in his beige linen slacks. The almost prissy gesture caused Maddie to cringe inside. It was only at that moment she realized how much he reminded her of her Uncle Lucius. Somehow, she'd been saved from making a horrible mistake with her life. Someone had been watching over her.

"Would you like some iced tea or a soft drink?" she asked, taking time to digest this latest discovery.

"No, thank you, Madeline. What I have to say will take only a few minutes."

She sat down and crossed her legs at the ankles, wishing he would spit out his next criticism and leave. As much as his appearance annoyed her, she needed to get onto the computer as soon as possible to begin her research. Settling back against the throw pillows, she said calmly, "Please say whatever you have to say, Trevor, and leave. I have a lot of work to do."

Trevor gave her a small smile. "Still the same Maddie— polite and caring, but all business as usual, aren't you?"

Maddie opened and closed her mouth, trying to figure out if Trevor was giving her a compliment or taunting her feelings of insecurity.

"I came to apologize, Madeline. For everything."

She sat up and squared her shoulders. "Apologize?" she managed, unable to grasp the meaning of the word when it came from his lips.

He ran a hand over his tousled hair, his forehead lined in concentration. "I heard about what you just went through. My father called Max after he read about the police capture in the paper. Max explained a great deal to him and Father called me. I . . . um . . . thought I should come over to see if you were all right. And I wanted to set the record straight."

Maddie, still too dumbstruck to answer, sipped at her tea.

"I know you'll find it hard to believe, but I wanted you to know that, in my own way, I cared for you."

Maddie set her glass on the coffee table and stared as Trevor, oblivious to her shocked reaction, continued to confess.

"I'll admit that in the beginning I was only after your money. It was a dishonorable way to behave, but I had no choice. Father threatened to cut me off if I didn't find something worthwhile to do with my life, and your company . . ."

Grinning, he shook his head. "I must admit, you were the first and only woman to make me work for the pleasure of your company. I guess that irritated me so much I decided to make you pay. It took a while, but once I convinced you to go out with me, I found you were quite a businesswoman, with an amazing head on your shoulders. After I realized that I knew I would never live up to the image of your perfect man—the image of your father. I hope you can forgive me."

Maddie took a deep breath, not sure she trusted his apology. And had she really been comparing him, comparing all men, to the memory of James Winston? "Why the sudden change of heart, Trevor? For the past three years you've done nothing but try to make me over into your idea of the perfect woman. Paulette told me you set your sights on me in college. Right now, you don't sound very much like the cold, calculating man she made you out to be."

"Paulette told you about that, did she? I was afraid she might someday."

"I guess you know she's in jail. If the police have their way, she'll be there for a really long time."

Trevor moved to the edge of the sofa. "I blame myself in part for her hatred of you. I wasn't very nice to her when we broke up. I let Paulette know you had something she could never attain—money and a family pedigree. I treated her as badly as I treated you."

Wondering what could possibly have happened that would cause him to suddenly become so humble—and so honest—she blurted out the first thing that came to mind. "Where's Felice?"

Trevor's face flushed red. "Felice . . . Felice left me shortly after I came to see you that last time. It took me a while to understand why, but when I dug inside myself, I realized I'd been doing the same things to her I had done to you. I asked Felice to change her hairstyle. I started picking out her clothes. I even suggested she find a little more gumption and stand up to her overbearing father." Trevor again tugged at his tie. "She didn't like my suggestions very much."

Maddie stared, wide-eyed. "More gumption? Why?"

"I found myself missing you, Madeline, missing your spirit and your take-charge attitude—especially after I came here and saw you with your new lover."

Maddie bit at her lower lip. "Ben's my assistant, Trevor. Nothing more."

"Then he's a fool, Madeline, just like I was. I know that now."

Maddie rose to her feet, strangely empowered by their honest conversation. "So where is Felice?"

Trevor stood as well, and took a step nearer. "In France." He walked to Maddie's side and reached for her hand. "I guess it's too late for us to start over, isn't it?"

Maddie surprised herself by giggling. "We were never right for one other, Trevor. I think you should catch the next flight to France and try to make up with your wife. From the sound of it, you hurt her deeply. You once said Felice wasn't as strong as I was, but it sounds to me like she has more guts than you've given her credit for. Go to her and tell her you want it to work, and promise her you won't try to make her into something she can never be."

He gave her a sheepish smile. "That's Maddie Winston. Levelheaded and practical—and always kind." He let her hands go. "Do you think she'll take me back?"

"If you're very humble and grovel nicely, she just might. You can make it work, Trevor, if you really want to."

They stood at the door and Maddie gazed fondly at her ex-fiancé. "Good-bye, Trevor. Be happy."

He leaned over and kissed her cheek. "I really was a fool, Madeline. Please tell your Mr. Able I think he's a lucky man."

Maddie closed and locked her door, then laid back against it, secretly smiling at the first compliment Trevor had ever given her. She couldn't believe what had just happened. He had apologized for his boorish treatment of her and then praised the man he thought was in love with her.

But Trevor had also reminded her of her own failings, of being a bit too demanding and rigid in her standards. Did she really expect the men in her life to be exactly like her father?

Immediately, Maddie thought of Ben. He *was* like James Winston in so many ways, but he was also his own person. And Ben had never tried to make her over into something she wasn't. He had loved her—wanted her—for herself alone.

Remembering Trevor's final words, Maddie smiled softly, hoping against all hope she would get the chance to tell Ben what Trevor had said. Quickly, she made her way to her living room and her computer terminal, and logged on to the Internet.

Twenty

Maddie held the limp white business card in her hand, choking back her surprise. This building's address matched the one on the card exactly. This morning, before she'd set out on her quest, she had made a stop in Ben's room. The card the taxi driver had handed him was on the dresser. Remembering how pleased Ben had acted, how happy he was to be speaking in his native tongue, she'd stuck the card in her pocket for good luck. She'd never dreamed it would tie in to the address she'd been given on the Internet, a place that might help her find Ben.

Was it fate or merely a coincidence, she wondered, pulling at the brass door handle and entering the shop.

She squinted past the dust motes dancing in the thin shaft of sunlight that brightened the room. The tiny store was a hole-in-the-wall kind of place she might have enjoyed exploring on a less demanding day. Curious, she walked across the room to inspect an array of artwork hanging on a far wall. Depicting scenes of ancient lifestyles, harem settings, marketplace happenings, or prayer temples, some of the paintings had elaborate frames. Others were small and simply displayed. Though there were no price tags, they all looked expensive.

Turning, she saw a grouping of musical instruments,

flutes, chimes, and dulcimers, sitting alongside a meticulously kept cabinet. The cabinet was overflowing with bracelets, rings, and pendants all decorated with a variety of colorful gemstones. Set around the room were tables or wooden crates filled with brass pots, figurines, and unusual knickknacks.

Next to a counter that ran across the back wall, looming as tall as it was wide and filled to bursting, stood the reason for her visit—a bookcase. As she passed the counter, she spied a small, tarnished brass bell sitting next to a sign written in both English and what she assumed was Arabic, which read "Ring for assistance." She picked up the bell and gave it a shake.

Too impatient to wait for help, Maddie walked to the bookcase and perused the jumbled shelves. Books of all sizes were nestled upright or stacked sideways on top of one another in absolutely no discernable order. Most of the titles were written in a foreign language; on many, the lettering looked worn and unreadable. A few had no binding, just a rubber band holding the yellowed pages together.

Maddie stepped back and folded her arms across her chest, wondering why anyone would want to shop in such a disorganized store. Then she remembered what she'd been told by haji.com last night on the Internet. This was a shop of magical things, run by a special kind of man. When she had typed in, "What kind of man?" Haji had responded simply, "You will see."

She paced to the counter and raised her hand to the bell, prepared to give it another good rattle, but stopped in mid reach. Goose bumps raced up her spine when the glass-beaded curtain rustled, and a soft rush of air fluttered her hair. Within seconds, a man stepped through the curtain and stood before her.

Maddie looked up—way up—and swallowed. The man, almost six-and-a-half-feet tall, was bald as an egg and good-looking as sin. Dressed in tight-fitting jeans and a bright red T-shirt, he wore a small gold hoop in his left earlobe. After her experience with Ben, it wouldn't have surprised her to learn she was meeting the more typical Hollywood version of a genie.

"May I help you?" the man said, his mouth drawn into a rigid smile.

Maddie stared, at a loss as to how she should begin. As if he could read her thoughts, the giant's sharp brown eyes twinkled pure mischief, his lips twitching upward. She realized she was ogling and felt herself blush. "I . . . um . . ."

"Uh-huh. Well, take a look around. If you manage to find your tongue, sing out and I'll be back." With that witty remark, he turned and made for the glass-beaded curtain.

"Wait. Please," Maddie called. "Haji sent me."

The man halted in his steps and turned. "Oh, he did, did he? And what did Haji think I could do for you?"

She tried for a smile. "A book. He said . . . um . . . you have a book."

"How did you meet Haji? Where did you have the chance to speak with him?" he parried, sounding annoyed.

Maddie refused to be intimidated. "On my computer."

The man frowned. "On the Internet? Bones of a one-eyed jackass, I told him not to—what were you doing? Looking for a little fun?"

Maddie straightened. "Fun? Well, I suppose thousands of people think surfing the net is tantamount to a good time. With me, it was strictly business."

The man folded his arms across his impressive chest and looked her over from head to toe. "Business? Then you're a professional? Funny, you don't look it."

Ignoring his perusal, Maddie imitated his stance and glared back. His arrogant actions and piercing eyes reminded her, in a strange sort of way, of Ben. "I am a businesswoman, Mr. . . . um . . . what did you say your name was?"

"I didn't. I'm afraid I can't let you meet Haji. He's indisposed at the moment."

Maddie stiffened. "I didn't come here to *meet* Haji. He just told me this is where I could find a book I've been searching for. I told him I would be down to get it first thing this morning."

He rested his hands on the counter. "A book? And what would the name of this book be?"

Maddie bit at her lower lip, positive he would laugh out loud when she gave him the title. "*The Mugarribun's Rub al Khali.*"

The man's face blanched as he ran a hand over his gleaming head. "Haji was mistaken. That's a title we don't have in stock. You can see yourself out."

He turned toward the curtain and Maddie felt the beginnings of a panic attack. "Wait. I really need that book. Please."

As if he hadn't heard her plea, the man disappeared through the golden beads. Maddie took a huge breath. What a rude boor! How dare he walk away from her? And how did he know this Haji person, anyway?

She needed that book, damn it.

Boldly, Maddie raced around the counter and through the curtain, but the giant had disappeared. She fisted her hands on her hips, refusing to admit defeat. She had spent hours on the Internet last night and hit a hundred dead ends. Finally, at her wit's end, she had put out a plaintive call in one of the more obscure chat rooms, begging for someone to help her find the way to summon a genie. The only one to answer—other than a few smart alecks who told her she didn't need a genie when they could make all her wishes come true—was *haji.com*.

But he hadn't told her about the jerk she would have to get past to purchase the book.

Gathering her courage, Maddie glanced about the back room. Smaller than the main shop, it was just as cluttered and dusty, the walls filled with more art work, the shelves with more books. Boxes of *stuff*—the only word she could think of to describe the assortment of pots, figurines, and bric-a-brac she spied—lined the floor, leaving a narrow ribbon of carpet that led to a door on the far side of the room.

Maddie threaded her way through the boxes, straight to the door, and opened it slowly. The room on the other side was uninhabited. Instead of piles of junk, it contained an old-fashioned breakfront and a huge antique table surrounded by eight dining chairs. She scanned the room quickly, hoping the rude giant wasn't hovering nearby, ready to call the police. Then she saw it.

Sitting on a narrow table covered with a colorfully fringed silk shawl was Ben's bottle.

Maddie gave a small shout of glee and ran to the table. As if in a dream, she reached out and touched the cool dark metal with one finger, almost not believing she had located Ben so easily. She grasped the shiny bottle in two hands and sat on one of the dining chairs. Pulling a tissue from her purse, she set to polishing in earnest.

It only took a few seconds for Maddie to know the bottle did not belong to Ben.

Holding it to her chest, she felt no familiar vibration, heard no answering laughter, saw no smoky apparition of a genie waiting to do her bidding. With a thump, she set the bottle in front of her. She was such an idiot!

Overwhelmed with despair, Maddie lay her head on the table and began to cry as if her heart might break. She didn't care that she was in a strange place with a decidedly rude and unpleasant man. It didn't matter she'd been deceived by another stupid piece of gem-studded silver. All that mattered was Ben, and the feeling that she had lost him for good.

Maddie cried at full volume, sobbing until every tissue in her bag fell to shreds. Unsure how much time had passed, she finally succumbed to hiccups and shudders as she intuited she was no longer alone. Raising her face, she glanced around the room, positive she would find the disapproving giant rejoicing in her misery. Instead, standing a few feet from her chair was a wizened old man, staring at her in such an open and comforting manner she couldn't help but give a watery smile.

"Sorry," she sniffed, patting at her hair. "I don't usually carry on like this. It's just . . . I mean I'm—"

"Are you madwd.com?" the old man asked kindly, ignoring her stuttering explanation.

Maddie blinked. "Wait a second. I know you—don't I?"

The man bowed from the waist, his nut-brown face wreathed in a smile. "I am Haji, computer hacker and taxi driver extraordinaire. And your real name is—"

"Madeline. Maddie, I mean. Maddie Winston." She stood and held out her hand. "You were the man driving the cab a few weeks ago. You gave Ben your"—she reached in her jacket pocket and pulled out the crumpled business card—"this card."

The little man, not much bigger than a jockey, gave a chuckle and shook her hand. "That is correct. Now, sit down and let me serve you. A glass of ice water or some hot tea, perhaps? It looks like you could use a little something to perk you up."

Maddie sat, but shook her head. "I don't think so. The man I met out front—I guess he's the owner of this shop—I don't think he likes me. And he wouldn't be happy to know I was back here without permission, either."

"Nonsense." Haji folded his arms. "First of all, Al and I are partners. I have equal say in what goes on around here. As for his not liking you, well, that's just the impression he gives. He's a very . . . private person, you see."

Maddie let out a sigh. "Oh. Then you can sell me the

book, can't you? The one you mentioned in the chat room last night?"

His gnarled fingers tugging at his pointed chin, Haji frowned. "Oh, dear. Did I give the impression the book was for sale? I'm sorry, but it isn't."

Maddie sat back down with a dejected little plop. "But I thought you said—"

"I said this is the place you could *find* the book, not purchase it, little one."

Feeling the tears well, Maddie fisted a hand over her lips. "I have some money. And I own stock in a company. If that's not enough, I could take out a loan."

"I'm sorry." Haji shook his head sadly. "The book is not for sale at any price. But that doesn't mean you can't read it, copy down what you need, and try it out. I don't think that would be a problem, do you?"

Giddy with relief, Maddie opened her mouth to thank him. At the same moment, Al entered the room.

"Haji. How many times do I have to tell you that book is trouble and we can't use it?"

Maddie watched as Haji turned and stared up at his supposed partner. The little man appeared to be fifty years older and two feet shorter than the surly Al, but that didn't stop him from bravely squaring off against the towering younger man. If the situation weren't so dire, Maddie thought she might be laughing right now.

"See here, Al. Maddie says she needs the book. I found her and I want to help her. It is my right, you know."

Al's chocolate brown eyes barely acknowledged Maddie before settling back on Haji. "You found her surfing the chat rooms, after I implicitly told you not to go there. Don't you remember how much trouble you got into the last time you stumbled into one of those porno hookups?"

Maddie stiffened in the chair. "Porno hookups? Is that where you think we met?"

Al looked to Haji, who was hanging his head like a

penitent little boy. "Don't worry, he's too old to do anything but talk. It's just that about a month ago he met another woman in one of those rooms and gave her our address. She showed up on our doorstep expecting to make a few bucks. It took a whole morning to get rid of her, and the rest of the day to calm this ancient son of a randy camel down."

Maddie felt her color rise. "Well, I'm not a woman looking to make money plying her charms over the Internet. I told you, I'm here for a book." She looked to Haji for confirmation. "Besides, we met before. In a taxi."

Al groaned. "I keep telling you, you need a license, old man. If you insist on scanning the city for compatriots, you're going to be arrested."

Haji raised his wrinkled face and gave a toothy smile. "Fetch *the book,* Al. I feel in my bones we should let her look through it."

Seemingly unconvinced, Al shook his head and walked to the table against the far wall. Raising the scarf, he opened a drawer and took out a small book bound in faded red leather. After he pulled up a chair, he sat and faced Maddie. Holding the book to his chest with two hands he gave her an angry glare.

"First she'll have to tell us why she needs it so badly. And, lady, this had better be good."

Maddie let herself into her apartment shortly before dinner. She had spent the afternoon with two men she was sure belonged in straitjackets—or worse. Still, she had talked herself silly, explaining everything she'd done from the second she'd met Ben on the beach in Florida until her dialogue with Haji on the Internet last night. In between, Haji and Al had asked her every question imaginable and a few that didn't even make sense.

She'd decided shortly after their interrogation began

that Haji was much older than she'd originally suspected, but just how old was hard to tell. She could see by his reaction to her tale he knew immediately who Ashmedai was. Though he never repeated the word aloud, Haji's silver eyes darkened and his body tightened whenever Maddie said the unusual name.

At first, Al hadn't believed she had found Ben on the Key West beach. He'd thought it impossible a bottle from so far away would still be intact, especially after bobbing around the oceans of the world for so long. But Maddie had been adamant enough in her story to convince him she was telling the truth.

And when she told them the part about Ben and his father and sister, a tear came to both men's eyes, surprising her even more. They knew all about the evil jinn, all right, even if they didn't have the guts to say his name out loud.

Thinking back, Maddie had to admit there was only one question upon which both men seemed, unequivocally, to agree. Did Maddie believe Ben was a genie? When she assured them she did, they seemed pleased, almost eager to continue in their search to find the perfect spell to see the two reunited.

In the end, it had been Haji who'd decided she didn't need a spell to call Ben forth. She already *owned* a genie. Her problem wasn't with Ashmedai's evil power. It was the power of the bottle she needed to overcome.

And there was only one way to release Ben from the bottle's clutches. Maddie had to set him free.

"But I've already told Ben he's free," she had argued, reiterating the many conversations she and Ben had shared and the promises she had made to him.

Not only had this pronouncement surprised Haji, it downright amazed Al. "Let me get this straight. You didn't ask your genie for anything personal—jewels or a new car or clothes—and you've already told him you were giving him his freedom?" Al had asked after a few false starts.

Maddie had carefully assured Al Ben was not *her* genie. She did not want to *own* Ben. "I love him," she remembered saying with a little wail. "You can't truly love someone and own them at the same time."

Al had slumped back in the chair with a look of utter shock, but Haji's wizened face had brightened knowingly. After giving Al an I-told-you-so glare, he'd turned back to Maddie and reminded her it was imperative she say the exact words to set Ben free of the bottle. The laws had to be obeyed perfectly in order to work. The bottle was a stickler for the rules.

Both Al and Haji had their own ideas on what else was needed for the chant to be successful. Al had told her she must concentrate, while Haji insisted she had to believe. Together, they decided Maddie had to use a combination of determination and faith to see the words through. To the best of their knowledge, there hadn't been a genie set free in the last five hundred years. In fact, they both told her they didn't think any more existed.

It was their firm belief Maddie had been in possession of the last real genie in the world.

After copying down the words in her day planner just as Haji said them, Maddie promised she would return, hopefully with Ben in tow, in a few days.

Now, filled with happy anticipation, she walked down the hall and into Ben's room. Methodically, she checked the closet and under the bed to be sure the bottle hadn't magically reappeared. Then she went to her kitchen and poured two glasses of iced tea, one for herself and one for Ben, just in case he was thirsty when he returned.

She carried the tea and the paper holding her chant into the living room and set the items on the coffee table. Sitting back on the sofa, she closed her eyes and imagined Ben as she'd seen him that last night, dressed in jeans and a soft black shirt. He'd looked shy and sexy at the same time—and impossibly handsome as he'd led her into Max's office and showed her the room he had prepared.

With a little clutch in her heart, Maddie sadly admitted to herself if the words didn't bring him back, it was the way she would always want to remember him.

Concentrating as Al had told her, she opened the paper and read the words silently. She took a deep breath, thinking how simple they seemed, but Haji had warned her they must be pronounced out loud, precisely as written, with no deviation.

Releasing her breath, Maddie closed her eyes and licked her lips in anticipation. She said a little prayer to the being—the *entity*—who had watched over her and kept her from marrying Trevor. She owed a great deal to whomever had brought Ben to her on the beach.

Then she opened her eyes and spoke the words to the empty room, believing in them with her whole heart and soul.

"I release you, genie of the bottle."

Far away, in a dank cavern in the farthest mountains of Elburz, Ben woke with a start from his sleep of imprisonment. In an instant, the bottle spit him out like an unwanted cherry pit onto the damp, packed earth of the cave. It took him a few seconds to orient his thinking, then a few more to realize he was alone in a strange place.

He thought about a lighted candle, but none appeared.

He snapped his fingers and wished for a glowing lantern, but was kept in darkness.

He clapped his hands, imagining a flashlight, but his palms remained empty.

Then, with an almost joyous abandon, he gave a little shout of triumph. He no longer had his powers. He was an ordinary man.

"Maddie." The sound of her name brought a smile to his lips. Somehow she had done it. She had discovered the seven words and spoken them out loud. She had set him free. All he needed was to make his way back to her and he would be a happy man.

The cave was pitch black, the air inside stale and cool. Ben crawled on his hands and knees, feeling his way along the ground until he came to a wall, then propped himself against it and sat back, breathing heavily.

He had no way to create light. He could only hope the cause of the overpowering darkness was nightfall and things would look brighter in the morning, for without light and without his powers, he was almost helpless.

Ben slept soundly, a deep, dreamless, and peaceful slumber, totally different than what he was used to in the bottle. After a few hours, he woke to find a dim, gray light filling the damp cave. He stood and stretched, ignoring the rumblings of his stomach. Over the last four weeks it had become used to regular meals and drink. If God was merciful, it would be full again soon.

He peered about the cave and saw the light had grown a bit brighter. Raking his gaze across the floor, he took in a wondrous but eerie sight. Dozens of silver bottles, most identical to his own, were strewn haphazardly about. The bottles had no tops, nor were they still decorated with their jewels. Instead they were on their sides or standing upright, abandoned and empty, devoid of beauty.

Ben thought about what he saw and grimaced. For all the years of imprisonment, each bottle had paid its debt. Pulling a small knife from his pocket, he found his bottle and carefully pried the emeralds and rubies free. When he was finished, he held a dozen of each in his hand. His fresh start in the world—his ticket home to Maddie.

He pocketed the precious stones and took another look around, searching for the escape tunnel. Walking to all sides, he finally found the opening and ducked. He followed the scent of fresh air, stopping now and again to read the messages written on the smooth, chalky walls by those who'd come before him. Most were in ancient Arabic, but a few were in French or Hindi, one in Russian, and another in Spanish. Ashmedai, it seemed, had been a devil who'd enjoyed his travel.

Ben smiled as he read each message. Many were grateful to their masters for their release. Some thanked Allah, others cursed Him. But all were hopeful. He felt a sudden gust of fresh air and stared straight ahead. He saw the bright light of day and his heart rejoiced. Finding a clean space on the wall, he took his knife and gouged out a message.

On this day I. Abban ben-Abdullah Benjamin Able, am a free man. I leave here to find my master, the woman of my heart. And I thank the God above for leading me to her.

Smiling broadly, he approached the tunnel exit. Finally, he could smell the sweet desert air, almost taste the freedom waiting for him. He marched toward the morning light and stood tall as the tunnel opened to a larger hole.

Without warning, Ben heard the sound of gunfire and halted his steps. Pressing himself against the wall, he inched his way to the mouth of the cave, fearful of what he would find. Sliding slowly, he craned his neck and peered past the opening. The cave was situated high in the mountains and looked down onto a small valley.

At this moment, the valley was filled with men. Some wore uniforms and rode in iron tanks, a few were on horses. Others looked beaten and ragged as they ran on foot. All had guns raised and firing.

Ben knew, in that instant, he had happened upon something he had seen on the television.

He had stumbled into a war.

Twenty-one

Maddie made sure the coffee was extra strong and hot, the cookies moist and chewy. After adding a small plate of sugared dates to the display, she surveyed her handiwork. The tray looked elegant and inviting, perfect for her guests. Haji and Al had come to see her tonight, even after she'd called and told them there had been no sign of Ben.

She patted at her hair and forced a smile to her lips. Finally, there was no wayward spike floating like a buoy on the ocean. Her hair curled softly around her chin now, into what Mary Grace called a stylish bob. A month to the day had passed since she'd last seen Ben.

Maddie peered into the side of the toaster and checked her makeup. Soft and subtle, it defined her hollowed cheeks and pale face in model-like fashion. In the past four weeks, she'd dropped ten pounds to the worry and sorrow of losing Ben. She'd been forced to shop with Mary Grace for new clothes, her jeans and T-shirts too baggy for even her dowdy taste.

At first, Mary Grace had complimented Maddie on her more svelte look. After their decidedly subdued shopping excursion, she'd scolded. "Please promise me you're not turning anorexic over Ben. He was a terrific guy, but no man's worth that serious a condition."

Maddie had put on her best smile and assured Mary

Grace she wasn't pining away. She simply had too much work at the company and hadn't been eating regular meals. Even though she'd had to forfeit the hundred thousand she'd put up as Ben's bail, Winston Design was thriving. The court had ordered the chips stolen by Lucius Fulbright returned to WD, and Maddie had sold them to another company at the contracted price. Her company had won the Apex contract, then two others. Max was all excited about a new invention and Lucius, Paulette, and Dominic Maggio were in jail awaiting trial on so many charges she couldn't remember them all.

She was back in control of a flourishing company. Her professional life was on the upswing.

Her personal life was down the tubes.

When Haji had insisted she meet with them to see if another chant might be more appropriate at bringing back Ben, Maddie had decided to invite them to her place. She hadn't entertained in ages, and she couldn't muster up the energy to go to their shop. Over the past weeks, when she hadn't been working with Max or thinking of Ben, she'd found herself wondering what kind of men she was dealing with in Haji and Al. Something about them tugged at a memory. Tonight was as good a time as any to get a little sympathy, and maybe a few answers to questions from the intriguing strangers.

She straightened the skirt on her lemon yellow sundress and gave a little sigh. Ben would have loved her in this dress. Sleeveless, with a scooped neck, it showed a hint of her generous bosom before hugging her rib cage and nipping in her waist. The belled skirt flared softly, stopping just above her knees to enhance a goodly amount of leg, as well. Mary Grace had picked it out, so Maddie knew it had to be in the height of fashion.

She called up her most pleasant smile, lifted the tray, and headed for the living room. Al stood at her window, staring out at the sun's orange glow as it faded slowly behind the high-rise across the street. His face held the same stoic expression she remembered from the whatnot shop, much too serious for such a good-looking man. Haji, his forehead wrinkled in concentration, sat on the sofa as he flipped through the *Rub al Khali*. He raised his eyes when she came into the room and grinned, reminding Maddie of the faces she'd seen carved into coconuts on her one visit to the Hawaiian Islands.

"I hope you like the coffee," she said, setting the tray on the table. "I made it just the way . . ."

"Sounds good," remarked Al, his disinterest clear.

Maddie bent to pour the coffee. She handed Haji a cup, then carried one to Al. "I have sugar and cream, but Ben liked it—"

"Black," Al said, finishing the sentence. "Just the way Haji and I take ours."

Maddie raised a brow. "You seem to know an awful lot about my genie. Care to tell me how you've become such an expert?"

Al took a sip of his coffee, his gaze decidedly unfriendly. "Just a good guess. Right, Haji?"

Haji set down his cup and saucer with a little thump. "Lighten up, Al. We've been over it a dozen times. You know how I feel about this situation with Maddie and Ben."

"We don't have the right to interfere."

"Who else, my boy, has a better—"

Maddie spun around to face Haji, her gaze darting between them. "But you're not interfering. I *asked* for your help. Please." She walked to the sofa and sighed plaintively. "If either of you know anything more that will help, you've got to say so."

Al ran a hand over the dark bristle now adorning his head and Maddie wondered what had prompted him to let his hair grow. With a more modern cut, she imagined he would be devastating.

"It's none of our business. Besides, Ashmedai has ordered our compliance. We've been sworn to secrecy."

Haji slammed the book shut and raised it high. "Balls of a camel, he exists no more! Ashmedai is dead, I tell you! They're all dead!"

Al whirled to face him. "And if you're wrong?"

Lowering the book, Haji threw Maddie a smile of resignation. "Then I'll be gone, banished to whatever hell the demon has decreed for me. I'm old, my boy. It's time I had my rest—and you your own life."

Al looked stricken. "If I send you away, the life I'll be condemned to will be unbearable—certainly not worth living. I don't want you to leave."

Maddie sat on the sofa with a plop, feeling like a voyeur in some weird, paranormal play. The two men were talking in riddles to which she could *almost* but not quite voice the answers. Al and Haji—Haji and Al? She took a breath and blurted, "Aladdin?"

"What!" Al growled out.

Maddie blinked with sudden awareness. "It's true, then? You *are* Aladdin?" She turned to Haji. "And you're the genie of his lamp?"

Haji stood quickly and pulled at his pointy chin. He grinned at Al, who looked like his coffee had gone down the wrong pipe, then shrugged, accepting the inevitable. Bending from the waist, he said to Maddie, "Hajisani Barjawan, at your most humble service, little one."

Al set his coffee on a side table, stuffed his hands in his jeans pocket, and began to pace. "Great. She'll tell the whole world. We'll never be safe, Haji. Not after this."

Maddie stiffened her spine. "I beg your pardon, but *this* woman can keep a secret. No one knows about Ben, not even my best friend or Max. I would die before I would reveal him to anyone." She smiled at a grinning Haji. "I would do the same for you."

Father-like, Haji laid a hand on her shoulder. "I know

that, little one, and so does this son of a wayward jackass. We can see you love Ben, and you'd protect him to the death. If we didn't think so, we wouldn't be here now, eager to assist you."

Dabbing at the tear that had found its way to her cheek, Maddie sniffed. "I don't understand any of this. If he's Aladdin and you're his genie, he's as old as you are. How can that be?"

Haji laughed, a little too sadly for Maddie to be reassured. "Magic. A magic I have been trying to escape from lo these many years."

"Don't say that, old man," ordered Al, rushing to his side.

Haji patted Al's forearm and guided him to the sofa, sitting him in the corner opposite Maddie. "It's time, Aladdin. You know it as well as I. This genie's bones are brittle, his heart is frail and weak. I am only alive because of you, and you don't need me anymore. I must ask you once again to let me go."

Al laid his palms over his face. Maddie's heart ached with the pain she imagined he must be feeling. Aladdin's genie was asking permission to die. Gently, she placed a hand on his shoulder. "Haven't you given him his freedom?"

Al swiped wearily at his eyes, then rested his arms on his knees. "Of course I have. Giving Haji his freedom is what started this mess in the first place. When I found Haji, Ashmedai and other spirits roamed the earth freely, creating havoc and tormenting mankind at will. Most men who angered a jinn became imprisoned as a genie without hesitation. Your Ben had what they call a simple curse. Haji's curse, for reasons we don't need to discuss, was more serious. That's why he was hidden in a cave, far beneath the treasure of the forty thieves. No one was ever supposed to find him."

Maddie looked up to Haji. "But Aladdin did. He said

the magic words that opened up the treasure cave and called you from the lamp."

Haji cleared his throat as he shrugged. "Bottle. The word lost something in the translation, it seems. Aladdin was a boy, searching for his fortune. I warned him when he first called me out, but he wouldn't listen. After I granted him his heart's desire, he allowed me to live openly with him in a grand palace. When he grew into manhood, he insisted on giving me my freedom, and I again tried to explain the extent of Ashmedai's wrath. In those days, many knew the chant required to set a genie free. Aladdin spoke the seven words before I could stop him."

Maddie swallowed. "And then what happened?"

"The worst part of the curse took hold. If anyone was foolish enough to dare free me, I was condemned to live forever, along with the master who did the deed."

"But how?" Maddie looked back at Al. "Why?"

Haji gave a brittle bark of laughter. "Who can understand the whims of a devil?"

Al settled back in the sofa and folded his arms. "You might as well tell her the rest, old man."

Haji bowed. "As you wish." He sat between them and rested a gnarled hand on each of their knees. "With my help, Aladdin was able to find the woman of his dreams. After his beloved Zenyeb went to her eternal rest, we sneaked back to the cave and stole *the book,* determined to find a way to break the spell. According to the *Rub al Khali,* the only way we can be safely free of one another is if Al finds true love again. Until then, neither of us will be at peace. If he banishes me without finding another true love, I go to hell and Aladdin lives out his life a lonely mortal, dying a mortal's death."

Maddie sighed, trying hard to come to grips with the incredible story. She thought of all the times Ben had disobeyed the laws and added his observation to the boiling pot. "Ben thinks Ashmedai is dead."

Haji squeezed her knee. "As do I, little one. But Al here, he believes differently."

"And if I'm right, you will burn forever. I can't let that happen to you, old friend. I won't chance it."

"Arghh," Haji mumbled, "but you are stubborn. I am tired, my son. I want to find my rest, and I'm willing to take the risk."

Maddie couldn't stop the tears from filling her eyes. These two men had grown as close as father and son, so close each had been willing to live in misery to protect the other. There had to be something she could do.

Maddie gave a frustrated little *tsk*. "I realize finding true love isn't as simple as it sounds, but after all these years—have you tried? There must have been women you could care for."

Al's poignant laughter filled the room. "Princess Zenyeb was one of a kind, a pearl among women. I have looked, but have never found another to equal her in courage, beauty, or spirit."

Haji gave a little snort. "I have told Aladdin she is out there, the reincarnation of Zenyeb, but he will not hear of it. We came to New York because I had a strong feeling he would find her here—a woman brave enough to fight for her true love, like you."

Maddie's heart turned at the compliment. She wished for a fleeting moment *she* was Aladdin's beloved Zenyeb. If she couldn't find Ben, at least she could have helped these men beat Ashmedai at his devious game. "Look, Al, all you need to do is start searching. Manhattan is a single guy's Mecca. There are thousands of unattached women to choose from. If you put yourself out there, you'd have your pick. Zenyeb would gravitate to you immediately."

Haji grabbed at Maddie's hand. "He has tried, little one.

but has not found success. The heart knows the truth, even if the world does not."

They sat on the sofa for a goodly while, each lost in his own thoughts. The doorbell rang and Maddie jumped. "It's late," she muttered, checking her watch. "Who could this be?"

Al raised a wary brow. "Is it him, Haji? Is it Ben?"

Haji closed his eyes, then shook his head, a strange little smile turning up his grizzled lips. "No. It is a woman."

Maddie excused herself, certain it was Mary Grace. She had called earlier and tried to coax Maddie into going out, but as usual, Maddie had refused.

Haji and Al stood and followed Maddie to the door. She checked the peephole, then turned and laid a finger to her lips. "Here's the story. You two know Ben and you're looking for him, too. But you were just leaving. Got it? Mary Grace is like a pit bull when her curiosity is roused, so don't answer any of her questions. I'll do the talking."

"Maddie, I know you're in there," came Mary Grace's strident tones. "My lawyer friend has a buddy we want you to meet. They're waiting for us in a taxi downstairs. Come on, open up."

Maddie suppressed a smile, then opened the door and stepped aside. "Mary Grace, these gentlemen were just leaving."

Mary Grace, wearing a short, slinky red dress and three-inch-high-heeled black sandals, charged into the foyer. After spotting Al, her blinding smile faded into a little O of surprise. She stared dumbly up at Al and Al, just as blank looking, stared back. Maddie swore she heard bells tinkling and cymbals chiming in the air around them. For the first time since Maddie had met Mary Grace, the girl was speechless.

Maddie looked to Haji, who was already turning to smoke. She blinked when he smiled at her and waggled his fingers. "He will remember nothing, little one, and that is for the best. Allah was kind to send you to us. I am sure you will find Ben very soon."

In less than a half second, Haji was gone. Maddie squinted, but even the tendrils of gray haze had disappeared. Suddenly, as if she'd been in a trance, Mary Grace shook herself awake; Al did the same. Maddie still couldn't believe what had happened.

"Maddie," Mary Grace said with a dreamy sigh, "aren't you going to introduce me to your guest?"

Al, still looking awestruck, held out his hand. "Albert Ladding. I'm an old buddy of Ben's, but Maddie tells me he's out of town."

Mary Grace took his hand. "Mary Grace Mortenson, Maddie's closest friend."

Al smiled a thousand-watt grin. "Did I hear you say you had two bottom-feeders waiting in a cab downstairs?"

Mary Grace nodded sadly, ignoring his irreverent remark. She looked as if her dog had just died. "No—yes—no. I mean . . . yes."

Al took her elbow and steered her to the elevator. "Well, I guess we'll just have to inform them you have other plans, won't we? Good night, Maddie. Maybe we'll see you tomorrow."

They stepped into the elevator together. Mary Grace stuck her head out just far enough to give Maddie a silly lopsided grin. The doors slid closed and Maddie blinked, then laughed out loud. *Who would have thunk it?*

She shut her door and threw the bolts, then wandered to the living room to clear the coffee service. If only God could be so kind and send Ben back to her, her world would be perfect.

The Elburz Mountains had become haven to a band of ragged guerrillas fighting against oppression. Ben had known the second he saw the battle being waged on the valley floor he was destined to help the rebels fight.

The skirmish he'd witnessed ended quickly, with both sides in retreat. At first the guerrillas had been suspicious of him, but Ben managed to do some fancy talking and convince them he was not a spy. After showing them his American passport and driver's license, he even collected a few names of relatives the men wanted him to look up when he got home to Manhattan.

He conferred with the rebel leaders, only to be told there was no expedient way out of the mountains to civilization, let alone a large city that had an airport, American consulate, or other easy access to the free world. Seeing the oppression firsthand, Ben felt obligated to stay and fight alongside these people who could have been his countrymen—at least until he came up with an escape plan.

He learned how to clean and care for an automatic weapon, as well as shoot it accurately. For weeks he slept in a crowded tent or under the stars with not even a blanket for cover, eating meager meals and dodging gunfire. In one skirmish, a bullet grazed his left upper arm, and he wore the makeshift bandage like a medal of honor, reveling in the memory of his old kingdom. After all his years of imprisonment, he was free again to challenge infidels invading his country.

But he missed too many things to want to stay here. He missed Max and his quirky but brilliant ideas. He longed for modern conveniences, computers and the wonderful things they would someday do, the challenges of the twenty-first century.

Most of all, he missed Maddie.

When the warring died to a whimper, he said goodbye to his comrades, one of whom had given him the name of a man in Tehran to be trusted, and hitched a ride on a battered transport truck. It took him four dismal days to descend the mountains, and another two to sneak into Tehran and find the man.

Jamal helped him exchange several of the stones from his bottle for local currency, with which Ben purchased fresh clothing and false identification papers. Jamal also put him in touch with someone who could smuggle him out of Tehran, then into and out of Baghdad.

Now, weary and battle scarred, he was standing inside a pawn shop in Ankara, Turkey. The jewels had served him well, but he had only six left—three rubies and three emeralds. The pawnbroker he'd been haggling with had left him alone to check on his stockpile of gems. If Ben was lucky, he would finagle enough money to buy a plane ticket to Paris. Once there, he could barter a better price for the last of the stones. Then he would call Maddie and give her the time of his arrival. Their reunion would be sweet.

The jeweler returned, rubbing his hands greedily. "I can take the stones off your hands for this amount," he stated grandly, slapping a piece of paper onto the counter.

Ben read the amount and sneered. His jewels were of the finest clarity and color. "This is not acceptable for even one ruby, let alone two of each gem. I suggest you recalculate you numbers, my foolish friend."

The man smiled slyly, revealing brown overlapping teeth. "It is the best I can do."

Ben knew he was being cheated. He had been told by another pawnbroker this man, Turin, was the wealthiest trader in Ankara, but not always the most reputable. Turin, his piggy eyes glowing, thought he had the upper hand.

Quick as a wasp, Ben whipped a stiletto from his pocket and grabbed the man by his shirt front, pricking a droplet of blood from Turin's pouchy chin. "I'm sorry. I must not have heard you correctly. You did say you would double this offer for one stone, did you not?"

Turin licked his thin lips. Ben raised him off the ground and shook him like a rat.

"I *did*. I did say that," Turin stuttered through his rat-tling teeth.

Ben smiled. Things were suddenly looking up.

Maddie bit her tongue as she watched Mary Grace and Al, tucked close to one another, coo like lovebirds on her sofa. Haji had been right. After the genie had disappeared, Al hadn't seemed to remember anything of his past. Mary Grace thought Al was a wealthy importer of Middle East-ern artifacts, and he agreed. To top it all off, Mary Grace and Al were madly in love. She was his Zenyeb reincar-nated. He was the man of her dreams.

Maddie tried her best to share in their happiness. She admired the beautiful diamond Mary Grace wore on her left hand, a five carat, emerald-cut stone that cost as much as Maddie had forfeited when she'd lost Ben's bail money. Al had given it to her two days after they had met at Maddie's front door, and Mary Grace had ac-cepted his marriage proposal immediately. Right now, they were planning their honeymoon, a month-long so-journ in the Greek islands.

She smiled at some nonsensical thing Mary Grace said and stood, no longer able to be around such a loving cou-ple. "Trust me, you two are going to have a wonderful time. I only wish I were going along."

Al grinned back at her, his muscular arm locked posses-sively around Mary Grace's shoulder. "If you promised to get separate accommodations, we wouldn't mind a travel-ing companion. It would help to get your thoughts off of Ben. From what Mary Grace tells me, you need a break."

Mary Grace nodded. "Al's right. You could lie on the beach all day, maybe meet one of those dreamy Greek shipping tycoons. Better yet, a boy-toy. Just what you need to take your mind off that missing slug."

For some reason, Mary Grace had decided Ben was a turncoat. No longer did she commiserate with Maddie and tell her he would return. She downright hated Benjamin Able for hurting her best friend, and no matter what Al or Maddie said, she refused to change her opinion.

Maddie cracked a grim little smile. "Right. Me, the original all-work-no-fun girl, living it up in a strange country with a playboy—on *your* honeymoon, no less. No thanks. I've had my fill of wealthy jerks like Trevor. And sleep with a boy-toy, Mary Grace? Are you nuts? You *have* read about HIV, haven't you?"

Mary Grace had the decency to blush. "I'm sorry, Maddie. I just want to see you smile again, like you used to. I don't think Al even knows you can, do you, honey?"

Al winked at Maddie. "Instead of pestering her, why don't you introduce her to that guy you dumped the night we met? He looked OK—for a lawyer."

Maddie had heard enough. She didn't want to meet another man. She wanted Ben or no one. She just didn't have the heart to fight with Mary Grace about it right now. "That's it. Out, both of you. I have to be at the plant early tomorrow to help Max and the architect with the blueprints for the addition. The construction is taking too long to get started."

Mary Grace sighed, staring up at Al as they headed out the door. "Remember, we have an appointment at the dress shop on Saturday morning, first thing. Then you and I and my sister and mother will do lunch. How does that sound?"

Maddie leaned against the door and rolled her eyes. "Fine, Mary Grace, whatever you want. Just let me get some sleep."

Al kissed her cheek. Mary Grace gave her a hug. "I'll call you. Sleep tight."

Maddie locked her door, then propped herself against it, holding back the tears. Mary Grace and Al were so perfect together, she almost couldn't stand being with them. At first, she'd thought it impossible her best friend was the woman for whom Aladdin searched. But after watching them interact, she'd finally managed to accept the truth. Mary Grace had never found the right man because she'd been waiting for Al. There was a God, and He watched over everyone.

Maddie made her way into the bedroom and undressed, then put on her sleep shirt, removed her makeup, and climbed into bed. She tried to settle back against the covers, but her mind whirled with questions and doubts. Mostly doubts.

Suddenly, an ugly idea invaded her thoughts. What if Ben were alive and free, living somewhere else? What if he'd been using her, coaxing her along while he only pretended to care until she learned the words to set him free? What if he had used her, like Trevor, and, after getting what he wanted, left her for another—*his* own true love?

Frantically, Maddie tried to remember all the parts of Ben she was drawn to—his trusting eyes, his sexy voice, his caring manner. She thought of his silly sense of humor, the sound of his robust laugh, his kisses, and his touch. All the wonderful things that made up Ben.

Would she ever get to enjoy any of those things again or had he betrayed her?

Closing her eyes, Maddie recited the same little chant she'd repeated every night for the past six weeks.

"I release you, genie of the bottle."

Patiently, she waited, praying something mystical would happen. But all she did was lie awake and stare into the night.

Twenty-two

Maddie stood at the office windows, watching the workmen stake off the back parking lot for the factory addition. The temperature, a muggy ninety-five degrees, had her hair curling out of control and her newest suit, a creamy linen three piece with a smart button-down vest, looking as crisp as a used napkin. She and Max had just returned from a successful press conference in their New York City offices, where they had announced Winston Design's latest technological breakthrough.

Max held up the small plastic packet, two by three inches and about half an inch thick, he had introduced to the public this morning. "I don't think there will ever be a good time to tell you, Maddie girl. That's why I'm giving four months' notice. You knew I'd be retiring one day soon. This little beauty is my parting gift to your family and Winston Design."

Maddie turned from the window, letting her gaze pass over the compact, lightweight battery straight to Max Hefner's beaming face. "I can't let you do it, Max. That invention of yours is worth billions on the open market. You could sell it on your own and live like a king. You don't need to give it to us."

Max laid a fatherly hand on her shoulder. "Nonsense. I dummied it up during my time as product development manager for Winston Design. My contract states that anything I invent while working here, be it programs, chip circuitry, or gadgets, belongs to the company. The battery is yours."

He set it on his desk and walked Maddie to the sofa. "I'll be selling everything I own up here and moving to the Keys, if Sylvia will have me. What do you think of that?"

Maddie sniffed back a tear. She'd always known it would come to this someday. She'd just hoped it wouldn't happen quite so soon. Without Max, she would be totally alone. "I think it's wonderful. Does Gram know yet?"

He raised a weathered brow, his face turning ruddy. "No. And I've dropped enough hints to sink a battleship. That woman is deliberately tormenting me. I swear she's going to make me come to her on my hands and knees."

"Every woman wants to be wooed," Maddie explained with a knowing smile. "Sylvia is no different. Just go down there, turn on that Hefner charm, and sweep her off her feet. Believe me, if I know Gram, it'll go better for you that way."

Max rubbed at his balding head. "I had a feeling you'd say something like that. But what about you? Will you be all right when I leave?"

Maddie let her gaze wander back to the windows, forcing the lie from her thinned lips. "I'll be fine, Max. We have six new contracts pending, the plant addition is ready to go so we can begin production on the batteries, and Uncle Lucius is—"

"That's not what I mean, Maddie girl, and you know it. What about Ben? Have you heard from him yet? Has anyone?"

Feeling her face burn, Maddie stood and walked to the desk. Even though they hadn't discussed it much, she knew Max had a good idea of what had *almost* happened in his office the night she and Ben were kidnapped. Over the past weeks, he'd been kind and hadn't pushed her to give him the details of Ben's strange disappearance, but she didn't blame him for needing some kind of explanation. "He hasn't gotten in touch, Max, and the way it looks now I don't think he's ever coming back. Guess I've managed to alienate another man from my life. Some woman I've turned out to be, huh?"

Max sucked in his breath at her harsh words. "Maddie, that's not true. You're a lovely young woman. Any man would be proud to—"

She bit her lower lip to keep the tears at bay. Haji had gone to genie heaven and Al, completely immersed in Mary Grace, remembered nothing of his past, so she had no one to talk to about Ben's amazing story. Despite Haji's barely remembered encouragements, Maddie had drifted back to feeling sorry for herself. "Can the soft stuff, Max. I'm not Sylvia and I'm certainly not my mother. Look at me, dressed up as the perfect corporate image of what today's modern woman is *supposed* to look like, and tell me I'm the kind of woman men fall in love with."

Max shook his head as he marched toward her, and Maddie took a step back. In quick jerky movements, he removed his suit jacket and tie, then rolled up his shirt sleeves. "Good lord, Maddie. Haven't you learned anything from Mary Grace? Don't you ever look at yourself in the mirror, or read what the papers are saying?"

She folded her arms and faced him squarely. "You expect me to believe that crap they've been printing in the papers about how I'm some kind of techno-Mata Hari, using my womanly charms to sniff out an international computer theft ring? Get real. We both know it was Ben who saved the day. Then he left me. Just like Trevor, Ben didn't want me, either."

"That's bullshit, plain and simple. Everyone I know admires you. I've had to warn Jim Allen's oldest son, Richard, to keep his distance for the past six weeks, knowing you were still pining for Ben."

"Richard Allen? He's wanted to date me?" Maddie smiled at the thought that the son of one of their biggest customers was interested in her. Mary Grace had once pronounced Richard an eleven on the babe scale.

"Aha! There's that dynamite smile we all love to see." Max waggled his brows. "You'd be a heartbreaker if you'd been raised a butterfly like Catherine. But you went your father's route, turned out caring and strong. A responsible human being."

"My mother—"

"Was the perfect woman?" Max grabbed her upper arms. "There's no such thing, Maddie. Everyone has faults. Your mother's was to be so wrapped up in her love for your father she forgot to notice her little girl. And James did the same. As wonderful as they were, your parents did you a disservice, letting you think you were an afterthought in their lives. I've never told you this, because I didn't realize how much their indifference had affected you, but on the day of your graduation I spoke to your father. He told me he was so proud of you he was making you a vice president as your graduation present. James and Catherine both realized how special you were; it just took them too long to tell you."

Filled with disbelief, Maddie grabbed a tissue from the commode top and blew, causing Max to roar with laughter.

"That a girl. You're so genuine, so real, a man will always know where he stands with you. Ben knew that. He confessed to me he would lay down his life for you, and I believed him. I don't know where's he disappeared to, but he'll be back. Mark my words."

Maddie turned and gave him a bear hug. Max had said the words she'd waited to hear her whole life; words that touched her deep inside and began to heal the guilt of her parents' deaths. "Thank you. You are the very best godfather I could ever have hoped for, and I believe you when you talk about Mom and Dad. But Ben's a different story.

Did he really love me, Max? That's the question I keep asking myself. I keep hoping he did, and that somehow he'll find his way back. Then I think about all my shortcomings, my impulsiveness, my quick temper and I—if Ben doesn't come back, I don't know what I'll do."

Max smiled. "You're a survivor, Maddie. If Ben didn't love you, he was a fool. If he doesn't come back, you'll go on."

Maddie could only pray Max was right. Though she'd done everything *humanly* possible, she was already prepared for the worst. "The police have an APB out on him, and I've filed a missing persons report. I was thinking about posting a reward."

Max held her close. "You won't need to. You just have to have faith that God is taking care of things in His own way and time. I can handle the work here for a while. Why don't you take a few days off after Mary Grace's wedding and go down to see Sylvia—soften her up for me? When Ben returns I'll make him squirm a little. Then I'll send him down."

Maddie sighed. Mary Grace and Al's wedding was scheduled to take place in five days. By Sunday, she would be exhausted and in need of some time off. The Keys had always been a safe haven for her in the past—and it was there she'd first met Ben.

Wishing with all her heart that Max's words would come true, Maddie knew Winston's Walk was where she needed to be.

Maddie sauntered down the beach, her hands fisted in the pockets of her gauzy swimsuit cover-up. She turned once to wave at Sylvia, who was smiling from the back porch of the B&B, then continued on to her special cluster of palm trees.

She could sense her grandmother's concern reaching

out to her as she picked her way through the sand to her favorite spot and opened her straw tote. Quickly, she pulled out a large towel and positioned it in the shade. Kicking off her sandals, she sat on the towel and fixed her eyes on the gently rolling waves lapping at the shore. Seconds later, the B&B's rear door slammed and she let out a breath of relief. Finally, Sylvia had stopped watching over her like a mother hen and gone inside.

Like water overflowing a dam, memories flooded the barren recesses of Maddie's heart. She'd come to this spot for the past three days, waiting for the pain to lessen, for the feeling of hopelessness to fade, but it hadn't happened. Losing Ben filled her with a grief more sorrowful than the loss of her parents, more terrible than the betrayal of Trevor or her uncle. Losing Ben had filled her with despair.

She'd flown to Miami on Sunday morning. Since then, she'd fallen into depression, doing nothing but sleeping or sitting on the beach and staring out at the ocean all day. She realized she had been foolish to let Max talk her into this little vacation, even though it had been wonderful visiting with her grandmother.

Wisely, Sylvia hadn't pressed her for details or forced an opinion. She'd simply taken Maddie in her arms and let her sob out her misery until Maddie was empty inside. Though she hadn't told Sylvia the truth about Ben and the bottle, Maddie had confessed how much she loved him. Sylvia finally understood that, this time, her granddaughter was mourning for real.

As she cast her gaze on the water, Maddie thought seriously about having one more good cry before she went home to New York, then grew grateful when the tears wouldn't come. It was no surprise, since she'd wasted so many in the last six weeks. Besides, she would be back in Manhattan in three more days. Max wanted her and Sylvia there in time for the celebration. On Tuesday, thirty percent of Winston Design's stock, once owned by Lucius

Fulbright, would go on sale on the New York Stock Exchange.

Maddie remembered how she had visited her uncle in jail and heard his stoic apology. Then the guard had handed her an envelope containing documents which gave her full ownership of Lucius's stock. The gift, Lucius had told her, was the only way he knew to show atonement for his part in the debacle that had occurred. He had cut a deal with the courts in order to save himself, promising to testify against Dominic Maggio and his crime ring in return for a reduced sentence—ten years, with the eligibility for parole in seven.

Paulette hadn't been as smart as Lucius Fulbright. Because she refused to testify against Maggio or even cooperate with the authorities, she was awaiting trial for assisting in Maddie's kidnapping and attempted murder.

Dominic Maggio, considered a high-profile criminal, wasn't scheduled to stand trial until the beginning of next year, after the FBI, CIA, and other government agencies had the chance to thoroughly investigate all of his illegal activities. From the sound of it, he would never see the light of freedom again.

Maddie had finally admitted to herself she really didn't care what happened to Paulette or Maggio. But the thought that it had taken the weight of a prison sentence for her uncle to be kind and treat her like a real niece only added to her heartache.

She caught the glint of sunlight as it bounced off something in the water and pushed the dismal events from her mind. Curious, she peered out over the crystalline blue water and concentrated, her heart beating a frantic tattoo. The object—if something were really out there—failed to surface again, and she let out a sigh. She was being silly, thinking she might find the bottle holding Ben. Miracles happened only once in a person's lifetime. She'd had hers, and she had lost it.

She rubbed her eyes, thinking about the other important thing she had to concentrate on. As of January first, Max was moving to the Keys. He had found a small house to rent a few blocks from town and, if Maddie managed to convince her grandmother, planned on spending his free time helping Sylvia around Winston's Walk. Maddie had no doubt the two would be living together by this time next year, with or without the benefit of marriage.

But Max's retirement also meant she needed to hire a new product development manager. Max had put out feelers to all the big companies and promised they would find the right candidate by the time he left, but Maddie wasn't so sure. It would take a big man, a Colossus, to fill Max Hefner's shoes.

What with the investigation and court proceedings dying down, Maddie had kept herself busy with work or hid behind Mary Grace and Al's happiness. After a while, she'd even managed to stop thinking about Ben for hours at a time. Maybe in another ten years, she wouldn't remember him at all.

She started at the disturbing sounds of children and adults at play. The Carters, a family staying at the bed and breakfast, came marching down the beach parade-style, and Maddie tried to shrink within herself. The children were a happy, chatty group, a ten-year-old girl and her two younger brothers almost too precocious for Maddie to be comfortable with.

Last night, after they had returned from the beach, the eight-year-old boy had whispered a question in her ear: *Are you* the *Maddie Winston? The one who was kidnapped and almost killed?*

When she'd told him yes, he had asked for her autograph, and she had scribbled her signature on a Post-it note, wondering what appeal her name could possibly hold for a little boy.

Later, the sister had confessed her brother was into

computers big time. He wanted to be an inventor and work
for a company with cutting-edge technology, just like
Winston Design. Maddie felt better knowing she wasn't
the freak the little boy had made her out to be. If Max
could wait twenty years, maybe they could hire Jason Carter to take Max's place.

As if sensing her need for solitude, Mrs. Carter gave
an apologetic wave. "Sorry to disturb you. We're just
heading to a restaurant for dinner. We'll circle around on
the way back so you can get your rest." Politely, the parents steered their children further down the beach.

Maddie raised her hand and settled her back against
the rough bark of the palm tree. Gram was going to a
movie with a friend tonight. The Walk's other guests were
driving to Miami for a show and a fancy evening out. She
had the place to herself, could do whatever she wanted to
keep the bad dreams away.

She closed her eyes and dozed fitfully, waking only
when she felt the first prickle of anticipation raise the
hairs on the back of her neck.

Lifting her face to the setting sun, Maddie raised her
hands to shield her gaze against the fading glare. She'd
thought she was alone, with only the cries of the gulls for
company. Without warning, a figure loomed. Tall and
ominous, it blocked out the dim rays, while a halo of pink-
ish light surrounded the man's head.

His arms folded across his chest, the figure reminded
her of an avenging angel.

The breath caught in Maddie's throat, but she refused
to blink when she realized who it was.

Ben stared down at her, his smile hesitant, his gaze
reverent and encompassing.

She swallowed, moving her hands from her forehead to
her throat, fearful she would wake if she spoke. All the
doubts and fears she'd felt for the past months tumbled
inside of her as she looked up at him.

"Maddie. I have come back," Ben said, so softly Maddie could barely hear him over the ocean's roar.

She licked her lips, positive she was still dreaming her usual tormented dream. "I can see that. What happened to you? Where have you been?"

His eyes wary, he shrugged. "Iran, Turkey, Bulgaria, France. Then Kennedy Airport, Manhattan, New Jersey, and Miami. I have been traveling for weeks to find the way back to you, Maddie. I couldn't get to a phone with a decent connection until I arrived in France. When I called your apartment, I reached your machine. No one in the New York office would tell me where you were, but I found Max. It took a lot of fancy talking on my part, but he finally told me you were here."

Maddie closed her eyes, remembering how she hadn't bothered to pick up her calls the past week. Lucius's and Paulette's arraignments had taken place, forcing her to hide from the media. Then there had been Mary Grace's wedding. She hadn't had the strength to speak with curious strangers or the press about what had happened, so she'd ignored her message machine. Who would have thought Ben would try to call from genie land?

Maddie's heart tripped in double time when Ben squatted down and laid a finger on her cheek. "You are pale, Maddie Winston. And you have lost weight."

She nodded. "I haven't been very hungry lately. I don't like cooking for just myself anymore."

Ben finally smiled, his eyes bright. "I will have to fatten you up. The wife of a great sheikh cannot look pale and weak," he murmured, going down on his knees in front of her.

Maddie withheld the questions she was dying to ask. All she heard was the word *wife*. She rose to her knees as well and held her hands to his face. "I was so afraid, Ben. I thought something terrible had happened to you. I thought I would never see you again. Where were you? Where did you go?"

He sighed and kissed her palm, the exhaustion in his eyes clear. "It was a terrible place, Maddie, one you needn't ever know about. I escaped. That is all that is important."

Maddie rested her head against his chin. "Were you hurt? Did you see Ashmedai or anyone from your past?"

He chuckled grimly. "I saw the empty bottles of my fellow prisoners. It gave me the courage to admit that Ashmedai is dead. He will torment me no longer."

She continued to stare, running her fingers over his face, and Ben felt enfolded in the love Maddie held for him. He placed his hands on her waist, noting sadly how much thinner she'd become. Her hair had grown long enough to be bundled on top of her head in a mass of fiery curls. Purplish circles of worry ringed her honey-colored eyes, telling him how frightened she must have been. Careful not to rush her, he held her near, just as he had done in his dreams these past many nights.

Tentatively, he bent and pressed his mouth to hers, sipping the intoxicating taste that was uniquely Maddie. She moaned and he let his palms wander to her shoulders, pulling her close. All he wanted was to find a way to bond her to his side forever.

"Maddie," he murmured, laying his mouth on her forehead. "I am a free man. Thank you for saying the words."

She drew back, her confusion clear. "How did you know?"

Ben ran his thumb down her nose and across her lips, then back up to catch the tear that trickled down her silken cheek. "After the confrontation on the dock, the bottle banished me to a hidden cave. Without the words, I would have been locked inside forever. Your generosity and your love set me free."

Her pale face turned rosy and her chin lifted in challenge. "Who said I loved you, Benjamin Able?"

In a blink, Ben had her flat on the towel, her body pliant nder his. She squirmed and he grinned. *"I* say. Remem-er, I have been privy to the feelings in your heart. I love ou, too, Maddie."

Maddie's blush rose to crimson, her earnest smile im-aling his soul. "But I've released you. You're free to go nd live your own life now."

He raised a brow, content to play silly word games or a little longer. "I don't want to be free if it means ving without you. You are a part of me, just as I am part of you."

She touched his forehead, smoothing it gently.

He nestled his growing arousal into the cradle of her highs, and her eyes turned whiskey dark. "I want you, Maddie, for now and always."

She wrapped her arms around his neck. "Oh, Ben, I've nissed you so. Thank you for coming back to me."

Their kiss, at first sweet and tender, grew to a heated renzy. Maddie clutched at him, pulling his shirt up and ver his head as she ran her hands over his shoulders and ack.

Ben knelt between her thighs and pulled her up. Slowly, e reached out and peeled down her cover-up and the top f her swim suit. Reverently, he cupped her breasts, leased to find a place where she had not lost weight.

He looked into Maddie's face and prayed her smile was ne of acceptance. Hesitantly, he began his confession. You need to know that my powers are gone, Maddie. I'm o longer a genie, but a man. Only an ordinary man who oves you."

She blinked and his heart gave a little start. Did her look f surprise mean she did not want him any longer? She ad yet to voice the words he had traveled thousands of niles to hear. "Tell me, Maddie. Say you want me to stay."

She placed her hands on the snap of his jeans and undid

the waistband, then tugged at the zipper until he felt himself burst free.

"It doesn't matter, Ben. Your powers were never what was important to me. I love you for the man you were and the man you've become. I want to be with you for all eternity."

And finally, after hundreds of years of imprisonment, Abban ben-Abdullah Benjamin Able was a free man.

Epilogue

On January second, three news items appeared in the New York papers. The first, of utmost importance to the technological world, read as follows:

Winston Design, a company much in the news this past summer and a recent member of the New York Stock Exchange, announced today the retirement of Maximilian Hefner, head of its project development sector for the last fifteen years.

Mr. Hefner, the genius behind much of WD's technology in microchip manufacturing and creator of the impressive, lightweight battery now taking the laptop world by storm, will relocate to the Florida Keys.

At the same time Winston Design announced his successor, Benjamin Able. Madeline Jessup Winston, CEO of the up-and-coming company, assured her newest stockholders Winston Design was in the best possible hands. To quote Ms. Winston, "Mr. Able trained under Mr. Hefner, and is more than capable of the same computer wizardry. He is a magician with a microchip.

The second notice, of a lesser importance to the business world, but still noteworthy, appeared on the society

Sylvia Fulbright Winston of Key West is proud to announce the marriage of her granddaughter, Madeline Jessup Winston, to Mr. Benjamin Able. Attendants were Mr. and Mrs. Albert Ladding (Mary Grace Mortenson) of Manhattan. After a small private ceremony at the exclusive Key West, Florida, bed and breakfast known as Winston's Walk, the couple left for a month-long honeymoon in Paris.

The third appeared with even less fanfare in a gossip sheet entitled *Talk of the Town:*

What local businesswoman and much-in-the-news modern day Mata Hari has finally caught the man of her dreams? Can MW, primary owner of her family's microchip manufacturing company and the woman who single-handedly broke up a computer smuggling ring this past spring, be the same woman who was jilted just last April by playboy TE (now living in the south of France with his own little bonbon)? Talk about an exciting life! MW and her true love will be honeymooning in Paris, then returning to Manhattan to jointly run the bride's up-and-coming company. Just like this clairvoyant reporter wrote seven months ago—"You go, girl!"